JACKSON'S JOURNEY

HEATHER PEARSON

For my fellow adventurers and beautifully
ferocious cheerleaders,

Robert, Torben, Maiken and Otto.

Special thanks to Fiona Scott-Barrett (The Exit Facility, 2021).

In grateful memory of Helen Lamb's ways with words
(Three Kinds of Kissing, 2018)

and my mum Jean's love and laughter
(1949-2007)

JACKSON'S JOURNEY

PROLOGUE

Saturday, May the 27th, 2034

'I can't believe you're making me go to family therapy on my birthday, and on a weekend. That's some present, parentals.' Jackson Campbell groaned, then slunk lower on the mini leather couch in the therapist's waiting room. His parents, Roy and Rebecca, stood stiffly flanking a console table on the other side of the room. Above the table, a chunky stretched canvas sported a sizeable black daub of paint in the bottom left corner and what appeared to Jackson to be six drunken black lollipops diagonally opposite. Jackson frowned at it, then rose, stretched and crossed the parquet flooring. He leant over the console and stooped slightly to peer at the splodge. Roy tutted and walked towards the couch, then pivoted sharply on his cherry-brown brogue heel and fixed his wife with a pointed stare. Rebecca mutely shifted her eyes upwards to the chandelier above and noticed its lack of sparkle – old money things often did, she thought, chancing a glance back to Roy.

The door to the therapist's consulting room opened. Dr Shaw gestured for the family to enter and invited them to each choose a seat on the other side of the glass coffee table from his own. Rebecca daintily lowered herself to a two-seater sofa in the middle of two tub chairs, then patted the empty seat at her side and smiled at Roy. Jackson squeezed between his mother's legs and the table, then dropped into the tub chair at her side. Roy sat down next to Rebecca, spreading his arms as wide as he could over the sofa's back and armrest to make sure the doctor knew not only that he was confident and successful, but that he was also very much his own man.

'So, let me make sure we're all on the same page.' The therapist's gaze lingered on Jackson. Jackson rolled his eyes then stared at the window behind Dr Shaw's back. 'Mrs Campbell, Rebecca, if I may, has messaged me with an extremely detailed timeline of events which started approximately one month ago, and appear to have accumulated in a breakdown of family communications. This breakdown brings you all here today and our meeting marks the beginning of an attempt to help family life go more smoothly. Are you both aware of those parameters, er, Roy … and Jackson?'

Roy and Jackson nodded in unison.

Dr Shaw continued, 'To recap, you use the social media app Blurt, Jackson, and the content you post on it is very popular, it seems, particularly with people who are strangers to you?'

'Yeah,' Jackson grinned, 'do you follow me?'

'I do not. But based on this summary, your content has gone viral on several occasions, and you regularly receive sponsorship deals and reimbursement from brands as payment for featuring their products, correct?' Jackson yawned, then nodded. 'The most recent occasion of your blurts going viral was four weeks ago when you livestreamed an argument between yourself and your father during which your father threw most of your belongings out of your bedroom window, then chased you furiously from the house while wielding some sort of antique golf driving club and also threatened to kill you, is that also correct?'

'He was not going to kill him!' Rebecca interjected brightly. 'He would only have shouted at him if he'd caught up with him!'

Dr Shaw frowned very slightly at Rebecca.

'Sorry,' Rebecca brushed a fleck of imaginary dust from the pale cream of her cashmere pantsuit. 'I won't interrupt again. I just hate it when the story ends with the killing bit!'

Dr Shaw looked at Jackson again.

'And throughout this encounter, you were reportedly howling with laughter? Goading your father by throwing various household items at him like missiles? All the while commentating to

2

your many viewers as if you were in a live-action game?'

'Have you not watched it?' Jackson asked, impressed by the level of detail in Dr Shaw's description. 'It's still on Blurt! Blurts don't disappear if they're still being shared. Like, it seems like you'd enjoy it too, yeah?'

The therapist stared at Jackson.

'What?' Jackson looked wounded. 'If you think about it, you could just watch it on your tablet and then tell Mum what to do about it, or something? It's my birthday, see? So I want to … You know? Get back online?'

'Happy birthday,' Dr Shaw said in response. 'How old are you today?'

'Twenty-four!' Jackson grinned, pleased the conversation seemed to be moving to a more exciting topic. Dr Shaw blinked several times, waiting for Jackson to follow up with a younger age. When he realised Jackson hadn't been joking, he silently made a note on the pad on his lap and turned to Roy.

'Mr Campbell – Roy – does your recollection of events align with my summary, which is based on the messages your wife has sent me, and what Jackson has asserted here?'

Roy rolled his tongue around between his teeth and lips. Rebecca watched with disgust. On many occasions she had told Roy that habit made him look as though a small rodent were desperately trying to escape from under his facial skin, yet he would not stop.

'It corroborates,' Roy confirmed. 'Though you've missed out on the *beginning*, the behaviour that started it all. The bit where my son insisted on playing a recording of a radio debate from twenty years ago between myself and Michael Templeton through every speaker in the house's audio system. That's a nice bit of kit incidentally … Bulgarian. They're the world leaders in sound, now.' Roy looked at Dr Shaw, expecting him to be dazzled or deferent. The therapist appeared to be neither.

'Your son played a recording of yourself and Templeton from two decades ago and this upset you,' Dr Shaw replied. 'Continue from there, please.'

Roy shifted his weight a little then drummed his fingers on the arm of the sofa. Rebecca stared at him as if he was the problem. Roy shrugged, then tutted.

'Right,' he said, 'well, the thing is, somehow Jackson had managed to speed up our voices, so we sounded like deranged mice. And then he posted all that on his stupid Blurt account as well.'

'To be clear,' the therapist looked from one Campbell to another, 'are we talking here about *the* Templeton, the pro-Empire commentator from Great British England's Broadcasting Service, head of the Make England Great Again movement?'

'And a *massive* tosser,' Jackson laughed. He twisted a section of hair around his finger then pulled it to his nose and sniffed it as he continued. 'Really massive. It was him who made it all go off, to be honest. He camped outside the house for a week. He was blurting all sorts of shite, saying Dad was holding me and Mum hostage and stuff. I thought it was funny, honestly, but these two …'

'It was *you* who made it all go off!' Roy thundered. Jackson sprang back in fright, but Roy continued, 'I had to hire a bloody PR and a lawyer to get rid of the man! I had to apologise to the neighbours and explain myself at the golf club! *I* had to do all that! Not you! I've never even read a blurt, never mind written one! You and your bloody social media! It's the ultimate poison of humanity! The modern heroin!'

'There he is, that's him all right.' Jackson faked nonchalance as he nodded towards his father, 'Rabid Roy. That's why Templeton called him that way back – Dad lost it on that radio programme and then he lost it again with me that day. He trended as his own hashtag – Hashtag Rabid Roy. It was huge. So many memes. The trolling. Epic, but hardly my fault, is it?'

Roy shot upwards from his chair, his face turning puce. He marched to the window and shoved his fists into his mustard cord pockets. A wood pigeon sitting on the gleaming railing on the other side of the Georgian panes turned, looked at Roy, then flew away with a squawk.

'You see, this is what happens when they talk,' Rebecca sighed deeply. 'But it's true. Templeton and Roy debated on telly and radio throughout the Scottish referendums about how Scotland should be within the union. Men had more say back then, obviously. Clearwater's one of the hypocritical sexists responsible for that being lost. Templeton, as you know, sees England as the boss. The other nations should quietly toe the line and be grateful for getting to bask in London's glow – that's his thinking. My Roy wanted it to be different. He and other Edinburgh businessmen, all highly respected, of course, saw an opportunity for Scotland to be an equal partner with England, and stay in the union. They were on the BBC news almost every night, along with writers and all sorts from Scotland's top class. And despite that Templeton *still* blames Roy and the other Scottish Better Together supporters for not being militant enough. He thinks they're the reason why we now have this so-called "New Scotland".'

Rebecca patted her hair as she spoke. 'But we blame Templeton for being too extreme. So, you see? And now this animosity has flared up again since The Scottish Green's ridiculous landslide victory in '26, the year after the second independence referendum. I think they all thought that when the in-fighting finally buried the SNP's credibility, Scotland would beg Great British England to take us back. But instead, everyone just swung even more to the left – not us, of course. We're not stupid! New Zealand's terrible example was to blame, perhaps.' Rebecca stopped and took a deep breath, 'So, every time there's a slow news week, Templeton baits Jackson, or someone like him, and Jackson thinks it's hilarious to bait his father with that, and the merry-go-round starts again. This feud with Roy and Templeton, it should've been a flash in the pan, but it hasn't, it just keeps simmering. And since Jackson became an influencer, well, that's turned the temperature up to boiling, then burning.'

'Templeton hates anyone under forty. Drain on society and all that,' Jackson added, then checked his wristband. Seventy-nine notifications flashed in front of him, making his heart race. 'Will we be much longer? Birthdays are big for me, content-wise, I need to head soon. Are you going to diagnose us with something, or do we just put a muzzle on Dad and hope for the best?'

'Jackson!' Rebecca scolded. 'No screens!'

'And your political position, Jackson?' Dr Shaw asked.

'My what?' Jackson scrunched his nose up.

'Unionist or pro-New Scotland? What's your position?'

'Oh!' Jackson laughed, 'I don't give a shit about politics. The First Minister's hot. But, like, voting and stuff? Look at the state it's got old folk in. I'm staying well back.' Jackson indicated his parents with a blasé hand gesture.

'*I'm* not a state!' Rebecca coloured deeply. 'I'm wearing vintage Beckham, I'll have you know! I have Blurt too! Don't tar me with the same brush as your father, thank you very much!'

Jackson stuck his tongue out at his mum and crossed his eyes. Rebecca frowned furiously at Jackson. Dr Shaw observed Roy smirk, then watched Rebecca as she turned back to meet his gaze and immediately forced a radiant smile.

'And you, Rebecca?' he asked. 'Your political persuasion?'

Rebecca regarded her nails, then pushed the enormous opal of her eternity ring towards her pinkie so it caught the light better.

'Me?' Rebecca asked. 'Oh, whatever Roy tells me. I choose the holidays and Christmas presents, he chooses the votes. It's how we've always done it.'

Dr Shaw appeared to choke slightly then took a sip of water from the glass on his side table. Once recovered, he looked over his shoulder to where Roy stood. Roy turned and met the therapist's gaze, then sighed and returned to his chair.

'I do have some understanding of the situation now,' Dr Shaw said. 'There's a distinctly dysfunctional triangle of co-dependency between Jackson, Roy and Michael Templeton. In these scenarios, each of the triangle points needs the behaviour of the other points to justify their behaviour. The triangle persists because none of the points – or people – are invested in ending the dynamic, however toxic …'

Jackson tuned out of what the therapist was saying and watched Dr Shaw's face more intently as he talked instead. He imitated the therapist's short nods at the end of each sentence.

'… sometimes the points are far apart and there's less tension,' Shaw continued, 'other times they draw together and tension is fraught. Via Blurt, it could be suggested that Templeton gains access to your intimate family dynamic and parasites onto it, using it to exorcise his pain and frustration about the ever-decreasing agency and isolation of Great British England in an increasingly progressive world. That's his comfort zone. And it appears this dynamic is at least partly responsible for preventing Jackson from growing up – he is cocooned in it and wants to stay a child for as long as possible. Roy's comfort zone is mainly resisting change because of fears of the unknown. He also appears to be very blame-focused. That's a common form of martyrdom and false scarcity-thinking that we can easily locate inside the concept of wealth privilege. He has also blocked all expressions of his creative, vulnerable, unique self in order to be validated by the capitalist values he was raised with.'

Roy looked at the therapist murderously and wondered how much Rebecca had paid to hear the pseudo-mathematical claptrap being spouted at them. Rebecca nodded eagerly, delighted that her name had not been mentioned.

'Yes!' she trilled. 'That's it! It's like he lives with us sometimes – that Templeton! If he sees Jackson trending today, he'll blurt him, you wait and see! He'll blurt back something nasty just to keep poking at Roy. Yes! A Triangle of Dysfunction. My goodness,' Rebecca tapped her chin with a cerise fingernail. 'Yes, I like that. You know, we moved Jackson into a tiny house in the garden after the *incident*. He's allowed back into the kitchen, but that's it so far. So yes, maybe when I ordered that tiny house, I knew instinctively about the triangle and the tension. Don't you think?' Rebecca's eyes brightened, 'I've literally taken them further away from each other, haven't I, and that's going to make things better, isn't it?'

Roy rolled his eyes. Jackson tapped his wristband several times, smiling at what he was reading.

'Jackson lives in your garden now?' Dr Shaw raised an eyebrow.

'Yes,' Rebecca nodded. 'It's very modern to have a tiny house. Very smart. It's blue, Jackson's one. And you don't need planning permission because they come on wheels. Maybe it's something your other clients with family difficulties could do too, I suppose? I don't mind you recommending it to them.'

Dr Shaw made another quick note on his pad.

'But how do we help them fix it, doctor? Jackson and Roy, the rest of their problems, I mean?'

'We fix it by acknowledging the fact that the triangle of dysfunction is, in fact, a rectangle, Rebecca.'

Rebecca leant forward, still hugely invested, but also now confused.

'A rectangle,' she repeated, 'go on.'

'You are the fourth point, Rebecca,' Dr Shaw said. 'You are also invested in the dynamic. You've given up your agency, so you don't have to choose. No choosing between father or son. No choosing between youth or ageing. No choosing whom to vote for. The continuing chaos in the triangle awards you *your* comfort zone – a place of zero responsibility or reality. This provides strong role-modelling to your son. His choices often mirror yours. You and your husband are providing very mixed messages to Jackson about what growing up is. And, centrally, as he's said here himself today, he's "staying well back" from the business of adulthood and, by proxy, self-actualisation.'

Rebecca stared at the therapist. She glanced down at each of her arms to check if one of them was hanging limp, wondering if she was having a stroke.

'*Me?*' she screeched. 'Me? Dysfunctional?'

'Indeed.' Dr Shaw nodded. 'No more or less so than any of the others. And you're each employing enormous amounts of denial and distraction to diminish your sense of your role in this joint endeavour.'

Jackson looked up from his wristband and found his mother's mouth opening and shutting, but making no sound. Roy's upper lip was twitching like a spasming purple slug.

'Who's to blame for this?' Roy spat, 'what nonsensical school of psycho-babble do you belong to? Whom do I complain to?' Roy rose and stormed over to the door to the waiting room and yanked it open.

'What's happened?' Jackson smirked. 'What did I miss? Mum looks like she needs rebooting.'

Dr Shaw stood and walked to his desk towards some recording equipment.

'The session is all on film, Jackson,' the therapist explained. 'But not on Blurt. The footage will be encrypted so it can't be shared online, better for people's privacy that way. I'll message the link to you all tonight and you can watch it at your convenience. I'll also send a diagram showing the co-dependencies I mentioned. Then I'll wait to hear who, if anyone, would like a second session. Sound good?'

'So I can go now, yeah?' Jackson looked excited. Dr Shaw nodded.

'Right, Mum, get up.' Jackson jumped up. 'I need dropping at uni. And I need a bakery on the way. I'm going to film myself handing out cakes. Twenty-four of them. Hurry up!'

Jackson stuck his tongue out at his dad as he passed where Roy stood holding the door open, then bounded through to the stairwell and disappeared. Rebecca stood, silently made her way towards Roy's rigid form, then turned and regarded the therapist.

'Rebecca?' Dr Shaw's finger hovered over the button to stop the recording. 'Was there something else?'

'Yes.' Rebecca forced a smile. 'Your chandelier needs cleaning – the one in the waiting room. There are diamanté decals you can add to them now. To bring out even more sparkle.'

'I see.' Dr Shaw looked unimpressed.

'And Dr Shaw?' Rebecca continued, 'We shall never speak of this again. Any of us. Understood?'

'Perfectly,' Dr Shaw replied. 'Good day.'

I

Sunday, May the 27th, 2035

Jackson sprawled on a ten-foot white leather LazySack beanbag
on the lounge carpet of his parent's luxurious home in Edinburgh's Braid Hills. He thrust one leg upwards and pulled a face
as he adjusted his genitals through his faux leopard-skin onesie.
Jackson had three such onesies he'd practically lived in since he
was eighteen and they were now in various states of near thread-
bare and patchworked repair. He'd cut their feet and cuffs off
when he'd turned twenty-one and discovered he needed a bigger
size, but retailers no longer stocked them.

Rebecca abhorred her son's 'leisure' attire. She'd fantasised
many times about throwing the onesies out, but she knew, when
one's child had a vast colony of clapping seals for followers who
rewarded him with attention every time he blurted, the risks were
high; the ridiculous wrath of Jackson's fans was not a prospect she
relished facing.

Rebecca and Roy sat some distance behind Jackson's Lazy-
Sack in matching white leather recliners. They stared at a television programme of political highlights, filling time until the live
ceremony Jackson had insisted they watch together came on. Roy
sighed loudly as Jackson's leg swayed, returned to the LazySack,
then rose again, followed by his son farting loudly. He winked at

his parents as he fanned the fumes, pushing his dirty blonde bob inside his leopard-eared hood as he did so, then indicated towards some old footage of the First Minister cutting a ribbon on screen.

'Do yous still hate her then?' Jackson asked, but gave no pause for an answer. 'Clearwater, I mean, the sexy FM? I'm shook, to be honest. Are yous *still* not feeling it at all, the magical New Scotland vibes, like? I swear you're made of stone. Come on! You've got to admit, this is, like, kinda almost better than Christmas! And from Scotland!'

Roy glared at Jackson, nostrils flaring as he breathed in.

'Jackson, "yous" is not a word. How many times?' Rebecca sighed, then took a long sip of her gin.

Roy's head swivelled to his wife, eyes bulging while he suppressed the response he wanted to make to his son. Rebecca felt the weight of her husband's expression but refused to meet his eye. She knew only too well that Jackson was getting maximum mileage out of having his twenty-fifth on a day that seemed designed to mock hers and Roy's voting choices with cutting precision. Roy cleared his throat but was interrupted.

'You can't say anything, Dad!' Jackson waggled a long finger in his father's direction. 'You can't say anything crap on my birthday because that would be impolite, mum's new rule, Dad! Don't forget it!'

Roy regarded Jackson. His son looked like an overgrown bit-part for a Steiner School's am-dram improv of *The Lion King*, he thought. Weren't children meant to be nice by twenty-five? Or at the very least *gone*? Roy reflected that he'd made partner and was just one chair away from his father's at the boardroom table at twenty-five. At twenty-six, he'd been pictured with Rebecca in *Edinburgh Life* on their first official date. By his twenty-eighth, he and Rebeca had moved into their first flat in the New Town and taken his parents for a slap-up meal at the club as a thank you for the gift of their home. Yet here, thirty years and several easily won upwardly mobile moves later, a six-and-a-half-foot animal hybrid was breaking wind near his feet, and Scotland had become, in Roy's opinion, an almost Communist state. When the hell had everything gone so wrong?

Jackson began cheering for the remnants of the Scottish National Party when they appeared briefly on screen. Jackson had no idea what they stood for other than they were for Scottish independence and therefore annoyed his parents intensely. The words 'NEVER FORGE OUR NATIONALIST HEROES' flapped in the breeze from a yellow and black banner while Jackson tossed popcorn from a stripy bucket at his face, mainly missing his mouth. Duchy the dachshund leapt from Rebecca's lap and began frantically snaffling over and around Jackson for errant kernels.

'Ha!' Rebecca sniggered. 'They've misspelt "forget"! Typical!'

Jackson frowned as he scrolled blurts, trying to understand what exactly all the fanfare meant for him.

'So Clearwater's giving everyone my age a bit of land and it means no one can ever own, like, massive bits of land in the Highlands again, is that right? Like, I'm definitely getting something, amn't I?' Jackson asked.

'Sounds stupid, so it'll obviously be true,' Roy muttered. 'Really through the bloody looking glass now, aren't we?'

'Do we have to watch this stupid ceremony?' Rebecca asked. 'Come on, Jackson, I don't know why your generation is so hyped up about this. It's pure theatre. Optics. Pathetic. Of course you're not really getting something. Honestly.'

'When my certificate comes, I'm going to get it framed and hang it in the hall,' Jackson declared.

'You most certainly will not.' Roy's upper lip twitched as he spoke.

'But it'll look fricking A next to the photo of Grandma getting her OBE,' Jackson replied.

'Jackson, that's enough!' Rebecca snapped. She'd noticed Roy's fist begin to clench his crystal brandy glass. Jackson's access into the house being extended from the kitchen to include the hall and lounge was a new development and she didn't want it to end in another bout of rabidity.

Rebecca looked to a long glass console table beside the TV where she had arranged her childhood dancing trophies, a photo from her brief stint as a model in her late teens and a mix of awards for Roy's excellence in litigation and golf. She longed to add a photo of Jackson doing something of note to the display, but as each of his birthdays passed, the possibility seemed to grow more remote.

'No, but, like, seriously,' Jackson's brow furrowed, 'when my certificate arrives I could, like, take my tiny house and go and find my land, couldn't I? Bet you'd pay my taxi, Dad?'

Roy sighed as he stared, dead-eyed, through the panoramic windows to the distant outline of Edinburgh Castle.

Satisfied he'd collected all possible morsels for the meantime, Duchy turned a small circle near Jackson's feet and settled down to nap again.

'Don't spoil this, Jackson,' Rebecca chided. 'Don't forget you're here on an understanding of good behaviour. Don't ruin things before we've even had cake on your birthday.' Jackson stuck his tongue out, then mouthed a quick 'sorry'.

Rebecca looked to Roy, hopeful he'd seen the apology but found him still staring out the window, clearly wishing himself elsewhere.

'It's a token, Jackson,' Rebecca continued, 'you won't actually have six square metres of New Scotland, I don't care what that stupid Green government says. I can't believe you're remotely interested in this stunt. Poor taste, Jackson, very poor taste.'

'I've got a piece of the moon from Grandma though – remember? She gave me a certificate when I was five. It's still on my bedroom wall, upstairs.'

'It's not your bedroom wall anymore.' Roy muttered.

'Is that poor taste of Grandma then, Mum? Is that what you're saying? That's not very nice, is it, Dad?' Jackson was warming up again now his dad's attention was returning.

'Don't entertain him, Rebecca,' Roy said. 'And if you're recording, Jackson, I'm telling you, I'll roll that tiny house down the drive and into the Braid Burn so fast you'll wonder if it ever existed right before you declare yourself homeless.'

'Of course Grandma Campbell didn't have poor taste,' Rebecca said. She shuffled nervously in her recliner then placed her drink on an inlaid coaster on the fat armrest. 'She was a very wealthy woman, Jackson. Her taste was classic, cultivated over generations! It's just that these New Scotland certificates don't mean anything, is what I'm saying. They're just tokens, they used the money for the moon ones to clean the ozone layer or something. This nonsense from Clearwater will be a lot of fuss about nothing too, trust me. It's propaganda. Plain and simple.' Rebecca inspected her nails as she spoke, pleased her manicure in a high-gloss teal varnish was holding up perfectly after two days. 'Some hideous walking group of Gore-Texed pensioners in a one-horse village called Tullytartan will resurrect a blackhouse into a museum,' she continued. 'All incredibly boring. Nothing will change – it's all for show, you'll see.'

The credits rolled on the highlights reel and the footage switched to live coverage from Glen Coe where a substantial crowd were gathered, all of them grinning up at the drone camera now sweeping over their heads and EU flags.

Roy and Rebecca groaned.

'I think we should watch something else, hmm?' Rebecca attempted. 'How about the ice-skating? I love their outfits.'

'Nope.' Jackson waved a hand then lolled back on the Lazy-Sack. 'It's my birthday –

we're watching this.'

Roy and Rebecca glanced at each other, then rose quietly while Jackson pumped the volume higher. The couple parted wordlessly in the glare of their grand hallway. Rebecca headed to the kitchen to press twenty-five candles into Jackson's cake while watching QVC. Roy headed in the opposite direction towards his study, hoping he might be able to pick up some sanity via Classic FM, broadcast from what felt like the increasingly distant outpost of Great British England.

Oblivious to his parents' departure, Jackson licked his lips as he watched Gayle Wood, the best-known face of the New Scottish Broadcasting Corporation, launch into animated commentary recapping the meaning of the Unclearances initiative and its proposed extensive programme of land reform. Gleaming white camera drones with purple and green stripes hovered steadily at Wood's sides, while behind her NSBC's thistle branding was repeated on a glossy portable backdrop. Jackson felt a tug of arousal when the presenter stopped talking, the tip of her tongue resting against the back of her top teeth as she touched her earpiece gently, listening.

'First Minister is linking now.' Wood nodded, then the camera panned to a glass podium standing inside what remained of four walls of a blackhouse. Daniella Clearwater's hologram flickered, then burst into light behind the podium. The crowd at Glen

Coe roared, their response completely eclipsing a dreich curtain of weather now passing over their heads. Two other holograms illuminated either side of Daniella. On her left stood a sign-language translator, and to her right, her PA, Bryce Cooper. They bowed before taking a small step back from the First Minister who waved as she waited for the cheering to subside. Jackson was rapt. He loved live telly. He loved holograms. He loved his birthday. A distinct lack of sighing and tutting from behind helped him assume his parents were similarly drawn in. Grinning, he pulled his tablet from under the LazySack and shared several #Unclearance blurts, then looked back up when a hush fell over the crowd.

'It's a joy,' Clearwater began, 'an unbridled joy, to behold New Scotland's beauty, and all of you, here today, to help launch our Unclearance initiative.' The First Minister's cheeks dimpled when she paused and the click of camera lenses was the only noise for a few seconds. 'Today is, as we all know,' Clearwater continued, 'a day of momentous resolution. Today we right another wrong – one of many wrongs in Scotland's history. With all New Scottish land reformed from feudal ownership, this particular wrong is, thankfully, an easy one to right.'

Daniella gave the sign-language translator time to go through the complex motions of the easy righting of a wrong among many other wrongs that needed to be righted before she went on.

'Today, we give back what was wrongly taken. From 1750 through to 1860 – that's 110 years – there were thefts from Scottish people that wildly accelerated a culture of greed, disparity, resentment and scarcity. In some cases, these thefts were carried out with ferociously dehumanising violence. In all cases, the horrific abuse of power by the thief over the victims was chilling.'

A grumbling drifted through the crowd and people blotted tears on their cheeks. Noses were blown then small, answering puffs of admonishment and giggling rose then dissipated.

'Yes.' Daniella's smile was warm. 'Today we reset the counter on who belongs, who is welcome, and who *is* New Scotland. Today we hold to an ongoing intention of re-humanisation. We've taken the lessons learned and added them to a commitment to a different future, a future of care and fairness – not division. A future that structurally cultivates healing, connection, growth and empathy. Today we replace the past pains with giving our young people, descendants of cleared clans or not, their very own symbolic piece of New Scotland. And to everyone, we say today and every day, everyone who wants to be here, belongs here; everyone is welcome. This is New Scotland, and we are all here to improve it. To love it. To share it and live it!'

The crowd roared approval. When the sign language translator finished, Bryce discreetly passed Daniella a hankie. Drumsticks hit taught skins, pulling the crowds' attention to the Highland Pipe Band now marching into place between the remains of two other small ruins. They spaced themselves perfectly into a semi-circle facing their audience then began their heart-swelling opening bars. Adrenaline and emotion rushed through Jackson's chest.

'I think I should go and discover our proper roots!' Jackson said. 'Find out who the Campbells really are.' He pushed himself up on his elbow, beginning the turn on the LazySack's unstable sea of polystyrene beads to face his parents. But as he manoeuvred he realised with a sharp tug of hurt that he was alone, apart from the little dog now lying at his feet. He flopped back and watched as the band finished and Clearwater came back into shot, ready to answer questions from the press. Jackson watched the First Minister's eyes narrow for a nanosecond as Michael Templeton cleared his throat and stepped forward.

'Clear-water.' Templeton pronounced the name as if he was sceptically considering a concept rather than addressing a world leader. Jackson cocked his head and felt his excitement dissipate slightly, then reignite when he saw the First Minister's expression. Her eyes glinted with amusement as she regarded the man and the GBEBS camera drone hovering above him.

'First Minister, if that's even you,' Templeton smirked under his deerstalker. 'Exactly how much New Scottish money have you squandered on this reparation indulgence, would you say? And are your many critics right when they say you're just a virtue-signalling robot who's too scared to turn up anywhere for real? And, lastly, will your anger towards those, like me, who've seen you for exactly what you are, guide you to plot and lead an EU war on Great British England? Is that your real aim, behind all your namby-pamby pretence of democracy? It's more power you want, isn't it? Go on, admit it!'

Daniella's dimples flickered. Was she stifling a laugh, Jackson wondered? He scrolled Blurt and saw a litany of bad feeling directed toward Templeton.

'Firstly, Michael, welcome again to New Scotland to you and the viewers of GBEBS,' Daniella began. 'However, as I know you've been warned before, in New Scotland we don't permit the use of tabloid untruths to replace news. The criticism you cite about me is fabricated, as we all know. As you're also aware, whenever it's viable to appear by hologram my government opt for that rather than travel – to continue fulfilling our climate commitment.'

'Lies!' Templeton snorted, his cheeks scarlet against the lapels of his upturned tweed collar. 'All lies! But of course, we knew that's what you'd say. So, what of the cost of this – this farce? How many genealogists worked on this Unclearance project to identify who allegedly got cleared to make way for sheep? How many historians? Wouldn't that money have been better spent on the failing New Scottish Health Service?'

'The New Scottish Health Service?' Daniella raised an eyebrow. 'The NSHS has waiting lists for all hospital services of no more than ten days, Michael. The NSHS has had approval ratings of nine point seven out of ten for the last four years. If that's "failing", we'll take it, thanks very much, and still get closer to ten!'

Templeton mouthed 'fake news' up to his drone while Jackson blurted a selfie, holding his middle finger up to Templeton's on-screen face.

'And as for money squandered on finding the descendants of our cleared-for-greed ancestors?' Daniella's eyes twinkled. 'Well, that came to seven euros and fourteen cents. About the same as one of GBEBS's drones cost, though I think we got markedly more value for the price. You see, eighty-five per cent of the former UK population completed an ancestry DNA test between 2005 and 2020. There was a real interest in tracing genealogical backgrounds, remember? Anyway, all of the DNA results were databased online, and they've been open source since 2025. New Scotland social technologists simply conducted a metasearch, coding the data to cross-reference with our census records. Is seven euros too much, Michael? That's almost seventeen GBE pounds, by the way, in case you're struggling?'

Jackson positioned himself next to the FM's holographic face on the TV, puckered his lips next to her cheek then blurted it as another selfie before flopping back onto the LazySack, sending Duchy briefly into the air then back down again. Duchy growled, but Jackson shooshed him, fixated on Templeton's mouth opening and closing, fishlike, failing to voice an answer. Clearwater moved on, looking for the next questioner. Jackson frowned as Gayle Wood's earnest face appeared again and she launched into asking something complicated about triangular trade and financial reparations. Duchy stared at Jackson, growled again, then settled himself into a tightly tucked ball.

'Don't sleep,' Jackson nudged Duchy's bum with a toe, 'it's my birthday, you have to keep me company.'

Duchy growled.

'Duchy!' Jackson toed again. 'Play with me!'

Duchy jumped off the LazySack, beginning the long trot to the door.

'Duchy!' Jackson yelled, outraged by the small, wiggling backside spurning him. On TV, Clearwater was still in full flow, replying to Gayle Wood.

'Right. Fuck this.' Jackson settled back for a long Blurt session while waiting for his parents to reappear with his cake. His followers were, after all, company that never left him hanging.

/jacksonmcampbell /blurts/

Hey do U all think I should take my tiny house TAE THE HIGHLANDS to see how sexy my ancestor's bones are? #RabidRoy HATES history so it'd be such a shame if it upsets him. ;-) #JacksonsJourney #birfdayboi #cakeytime #freedom #saltireface #unclearance #unclearancehandbackceremony #NewScotland #TheSexyFM #Presents #GTFTempleton

2

/jacksonmcampbell /blurts/
Ffffffffuuuuuuuuuuuuuuuuuuuuuuuuuuucccccccccccccckkkkkkkkkkkk

Twenty-four hours later and severely hungover after stealing a bottle of his dad's brandy, Jackson sprang upright, smashing his forehead directly into the rear-roof beam of his tiny house. The pain held him, petrified, for three silent seconds before releasing him backwards in a writhing, leopard-skinned scream.

A brief flashback of being thrown out of his parent's house the night before for being antagonistic assailed him as his forehead began pounding, but neither that nor the wallop on the head was the worst of it.

Jackson wondered if he dared open his eyes. Had the blow blinded him forever? Was this how it ended – marooned on the mezzanine deck of his tiny home in his parents' back garden, unable to speed dial for help because he couldn't see the screen of his tablet? Would he die with his face swollen to epic proportions, perhaps strangled by his onesie hood? Or perhaps he'd take a tragic fall, a foot inevitably missing the ladder when he tried to go for help, sending him crashing to the floor, hitting every surface and cabinet in his kitchen-cum-living-room-cum-bathroom-cum-craft space on the way down?

And if he did die, would his parents feel guilty forever? He hoped so.

Jackson's hands groped the mattress for his tablet. At last, his right hand found it. Eyes still shut, Jackson counted to three, ready as he could be to confront blindness. He sprung his lids open, met sight once more, then lay still for a moment, calmed by the day's drizzle on the tiny skylights until he remembered the horror that'd woken him. His stomach lurched.

In his dream, Jackson had been sweaty dancing with a Hula girl who looked a lot like Daniella Clearwater; they'd writhed together in perfect harmony, flower garlands around their necks squashing between them when the mountainous, bald form of Professor Drew McAllister, Jackson's terrifying university overlord, had appeared. Jackson had broken from the dance, checking for exits and found none. He'd looked to the Hula Daniella to ask for help but discovered her newly backed by a Hula Girl Army, swaying rhythmically with arms locked together, their robotic stares a firm refusal to his ideas of fleeing. Dream-Drew had slammed a meaty fist on the nearest tiki table, stopping the swaying abruptly. Raising his hand, Drew's middle finger had pinged up at Jackson.

Horror-struck, Jackson realised Drew's finger emphasised unbridled aggression *and* indicated the clock above the bar, both hands of which pointed at the number twelve. Jackson's scream had broken through the dream and wakened him. The *deadline*. The uni deadline. The deadline for the extension on the other extension deadline. Or, "Last Chunce Saloon", as Jackson recalled Drew naming it.

'You've got two months, Jackson, then that's it, right? You better send that final section of your dissertation to me then, or you've had it. Are you listening, my wee Goldilocks of the East? Jesus! My kids built a jetty for a rubber dinghy in the Ooter Hebrides last summer in a week and you get yer hands held to the nth degree to get a qualification over three years! Get out of here and bloody work, *right*?'

Jackson had been here before – almost.

The first degree he'd tried – law – had been too hard. The second degree – Creative Writing – had been too soft. This third degree – Applied Social Technology – was just right. Or so he'd thought until the final year came. He'd been hit with the double whammy that (a) completing (some) coursework was not enough to achieve a pass and (b) as Jackson was showing signs of not sailing smoothly on the waters of New Scottish education, Professor Drew McAllister had been assigned as his counsellor.

New Scotland's social justice programme 'Every Human Actualising', commonly known as EHA, involved giving every citizen who wanted a university education generous support to achieve their goal. Along with his journal writing and collaborations with other EU universities, Drew's role was to make sure every person on his list earned their degree; and Drew was, so far, the only academic with a 100 per cent positive record.

Some of Drew's days consisted of helping a student shop and cook if they were struggling with basic motivation. Other days he'd go through the finer points of a lecture so his charge could make a confident improvement on an essay. Days with students like Jackson were extraordinary in that Jackson had no tangible barriers to success, so Drew's support of him mainly consisted of verbal arse-kickings.

'Fake problems' was how Drew privately labelled Jackson's issues, but, by God, whatever it took to get a student over the line, Drew was there for it. He'd even visited Jackson's home just after Christmas, scaring the living daylights out of Rebecca, who'd thought Roy's predictions of remaining SNP guerrillas commandeering properties for high-ranking, saltire-wielding chavs had come true. Drew had protested, incredulous when Rebecca had thrown the keys to Roy's Merc at him, begging him to let her leave with dignity once she'd located her escape bag. Clearing his throat and holding up empty palms, Drew had taken two steps back while Rebecca had grasped at the brass umbrella stand by her side for a makeshift weapon.

'Mrs Campbell, please, I'm *not* a guerrilla anything. There are *no* guerrilla fighters. The SNP's just a wee club now, they're barely even a political party anymore, they just get-the-gither and do slide shows of the breakaway and that, they wouldn't harm a flea, honest. And the New Scottish Government is, well, kale-obsessed, aye, but … *peaceful*. I'm from the Uni, Mrs Campbell – I'm a Professor, Jackson's EHA counsellor, yeah? He's not turned up again, so I'm here to see where he is, OK?'

Rebecca had stared unconvinced, lower lip trembling.

Drew cleared his throat, affected his best Edinburgh twang, and tried again.

'Mrs Campbell, is your son home? I'm a Professor of Humanities at the university. I'm Jackson's Every Human Actualising Counsellor – EHA, I'm sure you've heard of it? I'm here to discuss what your son might need to help him complete his degree.'

Rebecca's shoulders had relaxed a little. She'd caught some words and found them vaguely reassuring, if unlikely. Everything was unlikely in New Scotland, she'd thought as the sell-out of Waitrose to Lidl on Morningside Road sprung to mind again.

Rebecca pointed up the gravel driveway to a pastel-blue-painted children's playhouse at the side of a triple garage. Confused, Drew nodded his thanks, gently laid the car keys on the step, backed away then crunched across the gravel.

Jackson had witnessed the scene from inside his tiny house and attempted to hide before Drew got to him. However, in a tiny house, nowhere was big enough for all six and a half feet of him to be concealed.

Pushing the outward opening door to reveal himself in onesie and man bun, Jackson's intestines had churned. A tail-end of red tinsel nailed to the tiny house eaves from the previous year's festivities danced in the wind between himself and Drew. Jackson had watched Drew slowly inspect all sides of the tiny house. He could've run when Drew was around the back by the tiny sewage tank, but didn't, mainly because the long stretch of gravel before him would be excruciating on his bare feet.

'Jackson Campbell,' Drew had started after a long spell of kneading at his temples. 'Jackson, do you live in a shed, son? No … hold on … is this just what sheds look like in the Braids? Are you just out here, potting coriander for the garden, or what? What *is this*, son?'

'Em, it's an, erm … it's a tiny house, sir. I live in a tiny house. My mum ordered this after the Rabid Roy thing – gives my dad a bit of space.' Jackson grinned at a speechless Drew, 'It used to be behind that rhododendron, up there, but I moved it closer to the back door at Christmas. I'm allowed back in the house now, too.'

A flash of hilarity had crossed Drew's face.

'Would you like to come in, sir?'

Drew had looked past Jackson to an apocalyptic scene of chintzy chaos inside the tiny house. Coco Pops boxes stood on the floor while a duvet hung from a bunk in the ceiling. A tiny tabletop played host to a giant bong, a tiny potted Nordmann Fir sprayed with fake snow and an empty bottle of vodka. Behind it, three MacBooks sat on a miniature corner sofa upholstered in blue and white gingham and otherwise strewn in headphones, speakers and a bowl with a spoon encrusted onto a congealed pool of chocolate milk.

'Naw, Jackson. You're all right,' Drew had replied.

Unsure what else to say, Jackson thrust his hands into his tired onesie pockets. Drew had spread his stance, rocking back on his heels, crossing his arms over his bulging chest.

'Right. Jackson, enough pleasantries,' Drew said at last. 'Why the fuck are you not at uni?' Jackson grinned and shrugged, praying inwardly.

'Jackson. I've got all day. I've finished my other work. I'm right on target with everything – everything apart from you. So now I'm here to see why *you're* no getting your arse into my good books and a dissertation into my inbox, see?'

Jackson caught a movement from his mum at the utility room window and had hoped she had the sense to film whatever violence Drew was about to enact. Drew took a deep breath and rolled up his sleeves.

'Jackson, get yer clothes on, son,' he said gruffly. 'You're coming with me. I'm going to get 4,000 words out of you this week if it kills me – or preferably you.'

Jackson had pulled a stick of toothpaste chewing gum from his onesie pocket and shoved it into his mouth, chucking the wrapper over his shoulder into his tiny sink. He pushed his feet into a pair of beach sliders that poked out from under his tiny sofa then followed Drew, terrified, to the Vespa. A small whimper had escaped Jackson's lips as Drew passed a helmet.

'It's all right, son,' Drew mumbled, 'it'll take the weight of the pair of us. I've had it strengthened up, bespoke like. Braced. Get on behind me and hud on tight to the wee bar between us.'

As they'd sped off, Rebecca had raced up the stairs. Arriving at the front balconette, she'd clung to the curtain while watching the pair disappear. She had been in shock: as well as the encounter with the giant freckled man, there was the revelation that perhaps Jackson *did* have a chance of gaining a qualification. Still, she'd never left the driveway security gates open again since.

. . .

The memory of Drew whisking him away raced through Jackson's throbbing head now. His senses were on high alert as he keened to hear the growl and crunch from gargantuan DM boots approaching. Quickly scrolling his messages, Jackson scanned for any that might confirm the deadline date. He had had about twenty notifications overnight alerting him that his blurts about seeking out his ancestral land were going viral, but panic outweighed Jackson's ego as at last he found Drew's last message and read it hastily.

Fuck!

His worst fear was true; the uni deadline *was* today. Midday today, which Jackson had, as usual, slept right through. But, he realised he could *pretend* he thought the deadline was for midnight instead. Ha! Enough time to flee the country, or at least tell his mum to recruit security to stop Drew from getting past the gates again. He rolled onto his stomach, grabbed his iPad and began hurriedly typing a message.

Dear Professor Campbell,

I hope you're fine. I'm not really because I've been working so hard on the last section of my dissertation, but I don't mind because I don't want to let you or New Scotland down and it'll all be worth it, as I've heard other tutors say to their students.

Anyway, I'm just writing to say my dissertation will be in your inbox and with the uni by midnight tonight, which is the deadline. I hope you love it I am really proud of it. I am just doing spell-checking and references now. Also, I am not at home, I'm actually staying with my aunt in Australia. It's almost Christmas here. So sorry if this is getting to you in the middle of the night or something! I've lost track of time but I will be in time for midnight either way!

Thanks!

Jackson Campbell

Jackson pressed send, then, listening to his gut, went straight to his tiny toilet.

3

actual scared for my life no biggie defo gonna have to run to the Highlands to hide from my psycho EHA counsellor!!! PS I'm in Australia if anyone asks :-O :-O #ILeaveItAllToDuchy #Duchyismybaebrother #BrotherDuchy #JacksonsJourney

In the three years he'd been attending his current course at university, Jackson and his classmate Niall Horn had barely exchanged two words outside of occasional group work. Jackson had tried to strike up conversation, mainly to get closer to Niall's hot best friend, Hanna Nowak, but with no success. Hanna and Niall had completely blanked Jackson since a couple of months before when he'd last tried to initiate banter during a lecture by throwing Murray Mints he'd stolen from his dad's car at the back of their heads. A mint had relieved itself of its wrapper mid-flight, bounced off Niall's shaven skull and into Hanna's long blonde ponytail. Hanna had eyed Jackson for an unnervingly long time while Niall untangled the sweet.

And yet here Niall was replying to Jackson's blurt, asking what the drama was. Jackson welcomed the distraction. Things got uncomfortable fast on the tiny house mezzanine where he had a sweat on, and anything was better than lying alone, worrying about Drew turning up to stick the heid on him. The conversation moved into their private messages, and, to Jackson's surprise, Niall admitted he'd missed an extension deadline too. Thumbs going numb, Jackson decided to call Niall on speaker instead, picking his nose and chewing on a bogey while waiting for the twenty-three rings that it took Niall to pick up.

'Hey!' Jackson said when Niall answered silently. 'Listen, Niall, if we're both getting murdered, I reckon we may as well chat before the slaughter, eh?'

'You could've given me some warning, Jackson, like, Jesus, you don't just *phone* folk.'

Jackson picked another bogey and wiped it on the roof beam.

'Sorry, man, couldn't be arsed messaging, had to write a massive message earlier, like, my arms are knackered.'

'Oh,' Niall replied, bemused, 'well, still, you could've asked, yeah?'

'Yeah,' Jackson shrugged, 'sorry, I guess?'

Niall looked up at his clock. He had time to chat.

'So, like, why'd you flunk the deadline?' Niall asked, lying back on his student hall's cabin bed. 'I thought Drew was keeping you on track? I liked your thing … what was it …? Something about tiny houses, wasn't it?'

'Yeah,' Jackson replied, 'just all the social media shit that's out there already, and, like, building one on a trailer light enough to be pulled by one person, a no-engine thing, innit? Fucked my back for, like, a week moving my tiny house in my back garden, so that's where I got the idea.'

Niall visualised Jackson, a modern capitalist nomad, moving his home but somehow never learning to hunt.

'I couldn't get a big bit of it sorted though,' Jackson continued. 'All that shit about new sustainable materials. Drew said I couldn't say the only suitable material was wood because we're tight on wood while all the new council houses get built, and post-growth market, you know? Anyway. I had the rest of the thing down. Plans and everything. Drew used to stand over me and breathe down my neck till I did each stage, but he said I had to do the last bit alone. Man, is that even legal, like? He eats a lot of olives and garlic, too, I'll tell you that for free.'

Niall remembered Drew taking him and Hanna for surprise birthday tapas the year before when he'd discovered Niall had nothing planned with family.

'Drew's cool.' Niall said fondly.

'With you, maybe,' Jackson replied. 'So, like, what was *your* plan, Niall?'

Niall glanced at the clock, remembering he had some dark time to fill, then began.

'Mine was about plastic bottles, Jackson. Remember Clearwater banned them in her swearing-in pledges, and folk got decent money for handing them in for recycling, yeah?'

'Yeah. Totally.' Jackson lied.

'Right, so they collected all the plastic, and they were like, well, what the fuck do we do with it now?'

Jackson listened, still clueless.

'Yeah, totally, what the fuck?'

'Well, I've worked out what to do with it. My project proposes heat recovery from the cryptocurrency servers the SNP landed us with during the breakaway from the UK and uses that heat to melt the bottles down. It'd mean we could stop spending thousands on energy for cooling fans, too—'

'Cryptocurrency?' Jackson interrupted. 'Melting? Slow down! Like, *what*?'

There was a long pause before Niall spoke again.

'Seriously, Jackson, *you know* about cryptocurrency, don't you? Like, how many of the years since partition have you blurted exclusively about your dad and your dog?'

Jackson laughed awkwardly, 'I didn't know we followed each other till tonight.'

'Wow. Jackson, *man*. OK, so for the good of humanity, I'm going to follow Drew's example and explain something in, like, remote hopes it penetrates a part of your brain that knows it needs to understand the world, yeah?'

Jackson flushed as he muttered, 'Cool, cool,' feeling anything but.

'I'll keep this short, so listen,' Niall replied. 'Cryptocurrency's currency like euros and Great British English pounds, US dollars, all that, right? But unlike other currencies, cryptocurrency's *all* in the cloud, OK?'

'OK. Cryptocurrency, cloudy, got it. Next.'

'Good. Right, next important thing. During the breakaway, the SNP had to prove we had fallbacks to the Euro when Westminster said we couldn't have the pound, so they panicked and asked the cryptocurrency folk to be like a back-up to a back-up plan on a Scottish pound. The cryptocurrency folk said yes, but it had to be a two-way street and New Scotland had to host a ton of crypto servers whether they used their currency or not, for like, twenty years.'

Niall stopped to sip water from the glass by his bed.

'Sorry, right, so those servers are a big deal 'cos a heap of currency in the cloud uses a heap of tech, all backed up to the hilt, so that tech needs high energy cooling fans to keep the servers at the right temperature. Cryptos' big fail has been that energy use – like, it's not Green, even though it's a much smaller footprint than capitalist banks, but the right-wing media talk it down easily, and folk believe it 'cos they don't understand the whole picture. Still with me?'

'I think so,' Jackson replied, surprised to find he was. 'So the SNP got a heap of servers to look after, but we ended up with the euro anyway, and it all fucks up our climate footprint?'

'Correct,' Niall confirmed, 'and we had to stick by the deal, so now there's a massive server room out at Faslane, where the old UK weapons cache used to be, and the servers will be there for years yet unless Clearwater can get us out of the deal with the crypto folk.'

'Right …' Jackson kept his eyes shut, concentrating hard.

'The SNP thought they could recover the heat instead of cooling it, then join it up to the district heating system when it was being built, but there's restrictions around linking Faslane to anything domestic, so that didn't work.'

'Shit,' Jackson said, pondering, 'I have heard my dad muttering about some of this stuff, actually. Especially about the SNP. He hates them. Doesn't give a shit about Green stuff, like.'

'Typical,' Niall replied. 'So now the Green government are stuck with these massive servers and fans, pissing heat outside. Clearwater's going spare, it's a huge SNP hangover she's picking up receipts for, so there's major beef about it. Plus, it's just straight-up shit on the environment.'

'Bloody hell,' Jackson mulled it over.

'Well, you know more now, huh?' Niall replied, pleased to have done some enlightening, 'So listen, what I'm thinking is if we take the heat straight out the server rooms, condense it and shoot it through a highly insulated micropipe, we could melt the plastic bottles right there, then mould the plastic straight into sheets, like an old steelworks. See? A construction material to use while wood's running low? And I'd call the sheets, wait for it … *Transpariboard*, 'cos, like – '

'To support trans folk!' Jackson cut in, delighted at being ahead in the conversation for the first time.

Niall tutted. '*Jesus* Jackson. No. Transpariboard because the material is *transparent*. Oh, for fuck's sake. Is this a really shit idea? I knew I hadn't thought this through enough.'

Jackson squeezed his eyes shut, too terrified to say more, surprised to hear the confidence disappear completely from Niall's voice. He waited to hear the line go dead, but instead, Niall's breathing slowed.

'Jackson, name aside for a second, do you *get* it? I mean, like …? Do you think it works? If it doesn't make sense, you know? Tell me? I'm sending you the docs now. Look at page twenty-five. There's a flow chart and some calculations. I don't even know if any of it makes sense anymore. 'sake.'

Jackson clicked on his messages and opened the files from Niall. Page after page of neat, highly structured drawings, charts, calculations and models filled Jackson's screen.

'Niall, mate, wait. I'm looking now. You … you're like, a *genius* or something. Jesus … like. *Shit*. I mean, fuck knows about your numbers, obviously. But this looks seriously impressive. Your plan's good, man. It looks *perfect*. Honest.'

'You think?' There was a shake in Niall's words, 'I mean, don't shit me, yeah?'

'I'm not, man. Like, Professor McAllister always says to me, if I can't make it make sense to a five-year-old, I'm fucked. And, well, my dad reckons I've got a mental age of, like, three, and I'm *feeling* your work from what you've said, man, so … like micropipes, condensing, all that. I mean, if this is what a dissertation's meant to look like, I'm not even close.'

Niall laughed, assuming Jackson was exaggerating.

'Thanks, Jackson, that's nice to hear.'

Jackson released a deep breath, pleased he hadn't fucked up with Niall any further but also mortified with the dawning reality of how little work he'd done compared to his peers.

'Jackson?' Niall's voice was lighter. 'Fuck it, I'm just going to ask, *how* have you managed the years since the partition *not* worrying? Not, like, glued to the news every night? How are you so, well … *oblivious?*'

It was Jackson's turn to be silent. It occurred to Niall that the answer to his question could be denial. Everyone copes in their different ways, he thought. A wave of regret ran through his body, a sadness that began with him not completing his degree and bled into worry about being unkind to Jackson.

'Sorry Jackson, man, that was like, insensitive.'

'Nah. Nah, Niall, man, you're all right. I'm just, like, I just don't really watch news and shit. My dad's legit obsessed with it, so I just tune out, unless it's holograms – they're cool.'

'Relatable,' Niall agreed, 'I'm going into residential mental health recovery tomorrow, near Glasgow, so that's my world, right now.'

'Fuck. I didn't know Niall. Shit. That's heavy, man.'

'I guess it is. It's been a shitty few years. It can only get better now though, right?'

'Totally,' Jackson agreed, feeling massively out of his depth. 'How long will you be in for?'

'Dunno,' Niall replied, 'a few months at least, maybe longer. Six, for a lot of folks, they say. But hey, can I tell you the thing about Transpariboard being transparent, like, if it's not too boring yet?'

Jackson noticed Niall's voice lighten when he talked about his ideas.

'Yeah, go for it.'

'OK, get this, red-dyed plastics neutralise the colouring in green and blue-dyed-plastics, and they *all* react to create a clear plastic with, like, minuscule kind of pixel pieces of colour your eye doesn't pick out. So mental.'

'Really?' Jackson was perplexed. Niall made the world seem so much more interesting than he'd realised.

'Yeah, really. If it worked, Transpariboard could make, like, big windows or panoramic roofs, couldn't it? Like for more indoor farming and shit. Or weatherproofing public seating areas. Like, I dunno, it could be, well, *important*?'

'Fuck. Yeah.' Jackson pushed one of his tiny skylights open with his big toe; the parallel complexity and simplicity of Niall's thinking made him uncomfortably warm and self-conscious; Niall had ticked *all* the boxes, all the sustainability bollocks, ethical materials, something to help with New Scottish society. Something to help the government with a problem Jackson hadn't even known they had. Niall's project was *everything* they'd been told to aim for in creating a big, social-tech design concept and more. Christ, Jackson realised, Drew must've pissed himself when he heard it.

'So, hold on, *why* didn't you submit your work, Niall? That doesn't make sense.'

'Didn't have time, mate. I only brought it all together in my head three days ago. I haven't been great recently. Depression, PTSD, fucks up my thinking. Can't get it straight when it matters, start panicking and shit, you know how it is – or maybe you don't? Hope you don't, to be honest.'

'Couldn't you hand it in verbally or something?' Jackson was stunned.

'Yeah. I thought of that, but I shat the bed on it. I've been getting panic attacks. If I'm speaking for ages, I start overthinking it, start thinking my next breath won't come, then it all goes to shit.'

'Fuck,' Jackson replied. 'Hey, where's Hanna in all of this? You two were like, well tight, can she not type it up or something?'

'Hanna's home in Aberdeen, mate. You think your dad's bad – or mine – hers makes them both look like angels. He's inside – the jail, like. She's gone to help her mum with her little sisters. She handed in her work ages ago, typical Hanna – she's a massive sweat. She'll get the top mark of the year, betcha.'

'Oh.' Jackson felt confused, unable to imagine having a father in prison or what Hanna's mum would need help with. Rebecca never needed him for anything other than occasionally forcing him to help with unpacking shopping deliveries.

'So, you two, are you, like, a thing?' Jackson asked, keen to gain familiar parameters again.

'Me and Hanna?' Niall spluttered. 'Mate! I'm gay! Jesus, nothing gets by you, eh? Better get you signed up as a detective, like, I'm not sure New Scotland can manage without your skills, eh?'

Jackson didn't mean to be an arsehole, Niall thought. He just lived in a bubble, that's all.

'So, what about your family?' Jackson asked. 'Are they going to visit you and stuff?'

'My family are in tatters, Jackson. They're homophobic, racist, all that shit. I haven't seen them in years. They're a lot. My dad likes betting even though he's in debt, and my mum never wanted kids. Phones me to tell me every time she's pissed. They're divorced, but they both live down south now, big GBE energy.'

'Fuck.' Jackson swallowed back astonishment at how different the lives he was hearing about were to his own.

'Yeah, well,' Niall sighed. 'I'm a bit short on resilience skills, you know?'

Jackson opened his mouth to disagree, but Niall continued.

'Anyway, it's good Drew got assigned to me for EHA.'

Jackson realised Niall was crying.

'What if I never get better though, man?' Niall said, 'what if I'm depressed for, like, ten years? Or just end up in some ward, banging my head on a wall? Someone else will have thought of the same thing by then and probably better … I want this, but some days I can't even string a sentence together if I leave halls.'

Jackson felt acutely more aware of why Niall – and Hanna – might not always have been up for laughs. His mind wandered to TV adverts he'd seen about how bad depression was and the posters all over uni – another of the New Scottish government's projects to increase quality of life.

'Does Drew know about your idea Niall, for Transpariboard?'

'Nah, mate. Just you and me. Hanna and I don't tell each other anything about design ideas till we get results. We're too scared of influencing each other and getting hauled up for plagiarism. And I didn't have time to finesse my work. No offence, man, but it's weird talking to *you* about this. Like, I thought you were a wanker, Jackson, not gonna lie. But you've been decent, listening and that. Appreciate it.'

'No bother, man. No bother.' Jackson blushed, warmed by the unfamiliar territory of an offline compliment from someone he'd met in real life.

'Listen, stop worrying about uni, Niall, man. I mean, at least *you* had an idea … check me, I've got no excuse, just a half-arsed beginning. Have you seen my Jackson's Journey hashtag though? It's doing *big* numbers, man! I wish I *could* be arsed running off to the Highlands! Maybe I will – keep my dad happy and save my arse from uni. But anyway, you'll be back in a year, brand new.'

Niall laughed faintly, shaking his head and scrolling to see the latest on #JacksonsJourney. It was indeed attracting a considerable amount of New Scottish attention and hateful memes from GBE troll accounts, which Jackson apparently paid no heed to. Niall glanced through the replies, followers begging Jackson to take to the glens, clearly oblivious to Jackson's real intentions not stretching further than a trip to his parents' booze stash.

'Thanks, man. And hey, *you* were close, Jackson. I can't take my own advice but you should do whatever you can to finish, even if it's late, yeah? Put baiting your dad to the side for a couple of hours. I would, in your shoes. Listen, I've got to go, I'm forcing myself out once every twenty-four hours in the fresh air, you know? Just a walk. Even in the dark. I've got to get a call in with Hanna before morning, too. I'll be off-grid from tomorrow, so, like … see you on the other side, hey?'

'You'll do it, Niall.' Jackson replied, 'I'll see you when you get out and you'll be like, more ripped than Drew, yeah? You'll be like, Mr Health and shit! Designing like fuck!'

Jackson was pleased when Niall laughed, it felt like the right thing – a soft send-off into a hard time.

4

Niall hung up on Jackson, pulled on his beanie and his warmest hoodie, fixed his comms magnets on his ears and left his room. He walked briskly to the David Hume statue on the Royal Mile from his halls at Cowgate, generating as much body heat as possible before slowing to tap his wristband, then setting off again at a more leisurely pace while chatting on the phone to Hanna.

'Get this, I was on a call to Jackson Campbell before this,' Niall said. He followed the pavement round the corner, down onto Victoria Street. Hanna finished making a cup of tea and pulled herself up to sit on the kitchen worktop. From here, she could watch the view from the eighteenth-floor tower-block window. She looked down, taking in the streetlights, rooftops and windows of Aberdeen between her and the black of the sea where the blue-white mast and stern lights on three freighters blinked their anchored presence.

'*Jackson?*' Hanna replied. '*The* Jackson? Mint-in-my-hair-somehow-a-Blurt-star-Jackson?'

'Yes! Him!' Niall laughed. '*Weird*, right? Long story short, he was freaking on Blurt about uni, we ended up talking, and he was … I dunno … decent? More just socially incompetent. Like, you know that kind of twat at primary who wanted to be friends with everyone but tried to do it non-verbally, by tripping folk up and shit?'

'I mean, the folk at my primary did it non-verbally by smiling and shit,' Hanna interjected, 'but sure, go there with your generous assessments, I trust you.'

'I told him I wasn't finishing uni – yet – and he said some cool things. Like, completely dialled down the assholery.'

'Is this a hook-up, or what?' Hanna raised an eyebrow.

'Nah, he's straight I reckon. Reckoned he'd fucked up his final section on innovative sustainability so we talked about that and … yeah … he's like, I dunno, kinda *maybe* human?'

'Give me his Blurt.' Hanna grabbed a pencil and made a note on the corner of her mum's shopping list.

'You'll like his feed,' Niall continued, 'quality entertainment. He's just a bit clueless, bless him. Harmless though. I get him more, now.'

'I'll wait to be enlightened,' Hanna shrugged, 'I'm pretty blown away he was there for you, Ny, can't take that away from him. I'll keep a semi-open mind, promise.'

Niall nodded, determined not to let on that the profound sadness had swept into him again and now a tear was running down his cheek. He would miss her fierce friendship more than he could think how to say.

Hanna heard the catch in his breathing.

'Hey. You OK?'

'Terrified.'

'Then tomorrow is the right thing.'

'Yeah?'

'Yeah. You're strong as fuck. Admitting you're struggling is the proof. I keep having visions of you in the future – you're fully aligned – brilliant and brave, healed completely from this bio-chemical shitstorm. Stronger for having dealt with it.'

'I'll take that vision, Nowak. Thanks – for everything.'

They shared a silence as Niall climbed the steps of the vennel from the Grassmarket towards the Quartermile. Hanna heard Niall's footsteps quieten again at the top of the steps.

'Well done,' Hanna said. 'Is it cold there? It's been pretty nice here. It's definitely getting more summery.'

'I've not really been out in the day,' Niall replied, 'too many folk for my liking right now. Anyway. How are you? What's up with job applications? Any work?'

'Och, nothing exciting,' Hanna sighed. 'Internship going at a car dealership – they're so obviously trying to look like they're supporting green design but still selling big fossil fuel models into the States. A green graduate hire undoubtedly helps some target they've been told to meet. I've applied, anyway. Other than that, my mum's at the top of the list for getting a new house off Clearwater soon, so I'm helping her get ready to move. She wants to minimalise everything but doesn't want to throw anything out. It's a special kind of torture, Niall, I'm not gonna lie.'

Niall smiled, Hanna's sarcasm always made him laugh.

'Are your sisters helping too?'

'My sisters?' Hanna spluttered her tea. 'Are they fuck helping! Little shits. Honestly, the firstborn gets all the work and none of the fun, I'm telling you. They get away with murder. What I need is a big juicy holiday to run off to. I miss my freedom. Come back soon so we can get a flat together in Edinburgh, or Glasgow, yeah?' Hanna said, then worried she was being insensitive. 'No pressure though,' she added, 'I'll be fine, till you're back, I'm just enjoying a moan. Nice problems, right?'

'Maybe you should tell your mum she needs to get Zuzanna to help more too? She's old enough, isn't she?'

Hanna spluttered again, warming to her material of fondly slagging off her family.

'Zuzia? Ah, Niall, come on, I come from a family of silent martyrs, remember? We put up and shut up and take what we're given and don't complain. It's an old Polish tradition we're determined to preserve, yeah? Mixes well with my dad's Free Church vibe of pleasure being strictly off-limits, right?'

'Very John Knox with a side of pierogi dumpling.' Niall laughed.

They chatted a little more, then hung up on the count of three when Niall made it back to the Cowgate. It was Hanna's idea: say 'I love you' once, then say 'fuck off', then brace and click away. Better that way than lingering, impossible goodbyes.

Back in his room Niall brushed his teeth and looked at his wristband, its charge would last till the next evening when it would be securely packed away from him at the recovery centre while he detoxed from the online world. He picked at an old piece of Sellotape stuck to the edge of his desk then looked down at his straining suitcase, waiting on the carpet. All change tomorrow, Niall thought. A dark mood settled in his chest. How had he been laughing just minutes before? Was it real? Had he faked it? It had felt real, till now. He walked to the window and looked down at the street hoping the scene of the laughter would reconjure the feeling. Instead, an emptiness inside swelled.

'Lights off, blind shut.' Niall snapped.

His small room plunged into darkness and the electrical hum of the blackout blind started then finished. He felt his way along the desk and over to his bed, kicked off his shoes and lay down, knowing he wouldn't sleep a wink.

'Fucking useless brain,' Niall whispered to the darkness, fists clenching, 'fucking stupid useless bastard brain.'

5

Jackson passed an hour lying on his bed browsing Blurt after chatting with Niall. Damnit, but he *had* been close to getting his degree, he thought, popping the second skylight open with his toe and propping a foot out of each of the tiny windows. He hadn't been that bothered about having a degree, but now, tantalisingly close, he found he liked the idea. And here he was, just 3,000 words away from giving his mum the photo she so craved of Jackson in graduation gown and cap. What a wind-up it would've been on his dad too, Jackson thought, knowing only too well the smug I-told-you-so satisfaction Roy would take from seeing Jackson fail.

From somewhere out on the road, a jolly-sounding horn honked twice and an idea hit Jackson with almost the same force his face had met the tiny roof beam with earlier that day. Jackson's Journey, the plan he'd joked about to set off and claim his six square metres of New Scotland began animating itself in his mind's eye. He rubbed his still-tender brow and recalled the glass podium Clearwater's hologram had stood behind at the Unclearances ceremony. What was it the NSBC presenter had said while the band played? Jackson looked up the event on his iPad and fast-forwarded to the footage he was after. Gayle Wood's weird Aberdeen-cum-Glasgow accent narrated the scene:

> *Architecture students designed the glass podium at Glasgow University to symbolise the transparency of New Scotland's government. Their brief was to capture the 'nothing to hide' attitude Daniella Clearwater prides herself on winning the New Scotland general election with. This podium, which so many of New Scotland's inaugural cultural moments have been delivered from so far, is deliberate in its*

design, and I guess it says a lot that it stands here year-round, com-
pletely unvandalised, hosting so many selfies from Scots and tourists
alike …

Jackson realised that the podium was static, and being made of glass, it'd be a nightmare to move. The students at Glasgow had worked with the quadruple brief of transparency, modernity, sculpture and memorial for Glencoe, but Jackson's thoughts raced, hadn't they missed tricks regarding transportability and reusability? Wouldn't all architecture be more exciting, more modern, if it moved, too? A chill breeze blew across his tiny roof and over his feet. Careful not to bang any part of himself on any part of his home, Jackson gingerly retracted his feet back indoors. What if, he wondered, there was a tiny house, just like the one he'd planned, but made of Transpariboard, instead of sawmill wood or glass such as the type used to make the podium? And what if that Transpariboard tiny house embodied the spirit of New Scotland; nothing to hide – everything transparent, everything shareable and hashtagable. He could propose such a house would fit precisely on the footprint of the six square metres the New Scottish government were giving to young descendants of the clearances, Jackson realised, excitement building. Maybe his idea could have possibilities for portable, Green tourism, and maybe housing for homeless folk, too. *And*, what if he snuck into his parents' massive house right now, nicked some of his dad's brandy, took it out to his tiny house, logged in and battered out the missing few thousand words, turning all those 'what ifs' into a submission worthy of a degree?

Niall had handed Jackson the missing piece of his dissertation on a plate, Jackson thought, *and* he'd pretty much said he wanted Jackson to use it, hadn't he? 'Do whatever you can', he'd said. And anyway, there'd be no risk of Niall getting a whiff of it 'cos it'd be done and dusted by the time he got out of recovery and back online. And, as Niall had also said, a million other people would've patented the idea by then, and Jackson's work would be saved in a university server somewhere, long forgotten.

Arriving back at his tiny table minutes later, favourite mug charged to the lip with Hine Rare VSOP Cognac, Jackson stared at his screen and gulped, spotting a reply notification in his messages. It was from Drew. Sweat covered Jackson's upper body. He pulled his onesie down to his waist, tied the arms across his tummy, then clicked the message open and began reading.

Dear Jackson Campbell, purveyor of hysterical nonsense ...

Thanks for your good wishes.

Regarding your dissertation deadline, as we all know that passed at noon today. Come the fuck on, son. Regarding you being in Australia, as well we all know too, that's bullshit. I'm typing this from outside your parents' driveway, looking up intermittently at your massive feet sticking out of the roof of your bonnie wee playhouse. I'll toot as I scoot off, a wee farewell for now. Some hopeful part of me felt it was worthwhile giving you the benefit of the doubt, so I came up here, wanting to see your hut in darkness or perhaps sitting with a sheet over the top of it, like a budgie's cage. I was hoping you were at some poor bloody aunt's house in Australia, simply confused about the difference between winter, spring and Christmas. But no, Jackson, of course, you were literally lying your arse off in bed. Again.

We at the university wait to see what happens between now and midnight – New Scottish and Australian times. I'm not going to pursue you, Jackson. Not anymore. I'm happy to let you slip through the net and be the divergent stat until you're ready to grow a pair and try anything more adventurous than putting chocolate milk on your cereal.

Safe home, Jackson. Safe home.

Drew.

Regards,
Professor A. McAllister
School of Technological Humanities
University of Edinburgh

A long, hissing stress fart escaped from Jackson. He took a deep swig of brandy then stared down the darkness of the drive-way, half-hoping to see the scooter return, for Drew's mass to jump the gates, illuminated by the security lights. He'd been given up on though, Jackson realised. There was no man-mountain on the gravel.

Other than his dad, no one had ever given up on Jackson before.

The tiny clock on the tiny extractor fan read 21.49

'There's time,' a tiny voice in Jackson's head said.

Some copying, some pasting. Some spell-checking and adding a few mistakes so it didn't seem too perfect. Some adding of his own scant work. Then some uploading.

It would be tight, Jackson thought.

'*But there is time.*' The voice was louder now and also wanted more brandy.

Jackson took another slurp of brandy, pumped his fists and began.

6

/jacksonmcampbell /blurts/

Only handed in my final uni work, INNIT?!?!?!?! Taking the tiny
house movement forward in #NewScotland with my designs oi oi oi
WHO'S WIF ME I'm gonna be a GRADUATE suck on that #RabidRoy
#Bantz #freshbantz #Freshpantz #onlyjokingmum #sotired #brand-
ymakesmerandy #tinyhousebigboi #jacksonsjourney

Despite her forehead being very recently rejuvenated with
Botox, Rebecca could feel a twinge forming in her brow as she
lay in bed and glanced up from her iPad to see Arthur's Seat
emerge through the first light of the morning sky. She'd kept an
eye on Jackson's recent blurts about going off to claim his land,
watching with growing dismay at how quickly his stupid idea had
gained traction with idiots who consistently encouraged her son's
immaturity. And now here he was claiming to be in Australia one
minute and then finishing his university work the next. Rebecca
didn't know precisely what her son was up to, but she did know
manic behaviour like this meant one thing for sure – a clash of
the Campbell men was inbound unless she averted it or forced
Roy to take cover with haste.

Her brow twinged again as she wondered what the possibility
was of another #RabidRoy press frenzy forming. Rebecca knew
that people loved to see her husband freaking out and her son
being a buffoon. What people seemed not to care about was that
there was a human element behind it all, a mother and wife who
had to pick up the pieces while retaining a perfect figure and
holding back time from her face, hands and décolletage.

Sitting up slowly, Rebecca began thinking through her
options. She sipped some water from her bedside glass and felt a
light throbbing start behind her nose, an unwanted reminder of

last night's gin. Reaching into her bedside drawer for a painkiller then arranging herself with her iPad, Rebecca's eyes widened in horror as a screenshot of Roy's screaming face appeared in a meme attached to a blurt made by a GBE breakfast show. The blurt was then instantly shared by a late-night celebrity gossip feed from America. Rebecca felt nauseous as she watched further shares cluster. She switched off her screen and shivered. Rebecca guessed they had two and a half hours before the first of #RabidRoy-loving press might begin arriving, in the worst-case scenario.

'Roy. Psssst,' Rebecca whispered.

Nothing. Then, a deepening snore. Rebecca elbowed her husband sharply in the shoulder.

'Roy! Wake up!'

Roy woke with a start, instantly grimacing, wondering if the pain signal was, at last, the fatal and inevitable heart attack induced by his son's failure to fledge or residual stress from his country's stupidity. Perhaps both, he thought, resolving to keep his eyes shut as he slipped away. Rebecca elbowed her husband again, harder.

'Roy!'

'Jesus! Rebecca!' Roy blinked repeatedly. 'If this is about Jackson or anything to do with New Scotland, I do *not* want to know, do you understand?'

Roy growled her name in three syllables sometimes, Rebecca noticed. It had started when New Scotland had begun. Ree-beh-kah. Before that, she'd been Becs or Beccy. She remembered the feeling of the alternatives with a bolt of nostalgia.

'My love,' Rebecca restarted, 'it's *not* about Jackson or the news. It's about me. I'm starting with a migraine.'

Rebecca faked an extravagant, pained yawn, finishing with a brief whimper.

'Take a pill.' Roy moaned, closing his eyes tightly again.

'I have,' Rebecca replied, 'it's not going near it. Darling, you know Doctor Dubois says once I've entered a migraine prodrome an attack is imminent. Prevention is *not* an option at this stage.'

Roy opened his eyes a little, then propped himself on his elbow.

'Have you taken the special medication? The French stuff?' he asked Rebecca's darkened profile.

'Yes. An hour ago,' Rebecca lied, 'but the humidity in Edinburgh right now means it's likely not to work. This week, the air pressure is very much against me, I'm afraid.' Rebecca raised her hands to her temples, inhaling deeply through her nose while Roy tried and failed to recall what he was supposed to do in this situation; he'd zoned out during the last appointment with their French physician when Rebecca had diverted the conversation from headaches to a route of enquiry about jawline rejuvenation for couples.

'What can I do?' Roy asked, yawning.

'Well,' Rebecca began, 'I may be in bed for ten days from looking at the barometric forecast. If I'm lucky, it'll be a week. If you can look after walking Duchy, organising cleaners, Jackson, the gardeners, shopping and our meals ...'

Rebecca continued holding her fingers at her temples as she felt Roy flop back onto his pillow. She moaned lightly as she listened to her husband's quickening, stressed breathing. Roy stared up at the ceiling, visualising his diary for the week, wincing at the golf he would have to cancel.

'Could we, um, could we get you a nurse?' Roy tried. 'It's just, I want you to have the best care available, darling.'

Rebecca held her tongue, knowing how badly Roy coped with suspense, always preferring an argument or verbal ping-pong to the potent unknowns of silence.

'A nurse ... someone I don't know?' Rebecca replied, sounding as if she was both considering the idea and finding it impossible. 'A nurse who doesn't know our home, us, or Jackson? Someone you'd have to supervise 24/7 to help them deliver my care? Well, I suppose, if you could arrange that, it *could* work ...'

'Fuck.' Roy mouthed silently.

'Oh!' Rebecca said, her tone now lighter. 'Do you see that, Roy? The rainbows, over there, by the curtains, look!'

Roy craned his neck where Rebecca was pointing and saw nothing.

'What? Where?'

'The little dancers!' Rebecca laughed. 'Look! Little squares and circles are dancing. Some of them have legs, don't they, darling?'

Roy remembered a pamphlet he'd read while Rebecca and Dr Dubois had moved on to discuss the role of his wife's ears and hairline in a facelift. There had been a whole paragraph explaining hallucinations as a precursor to a severe migraine.

'I think you're hallucinating, Rebecca.' Roy said, defeated.

Delighted he'd taken the bait, Rebecca squealed as shrilly as she could manage.

'Oh!' Rebecca breathed, 'I've never had this before. It's quite nice! Maybe this means it won't be a bad migraine?'

Rebecca stepped out of bed and began patting the air in front of her.

'What are you doing?' Roy got up and walked around the end of the bed to stand before his wife, who seemed not to see him.

'This horse is lovely,' Rebecca chirped, a hand rising and falling as she stroked an imaginary equine neck. 'Of course, we could go to the chalet,' Rebecca seized her chance, 'the air pressure in Val D'Isère is much better than here just now, it could make all the difference in the severity of the episode, I suppose.' Rebecca smiled, then began an exaggerated mime of pleating the horse's mane.

'I believe hallucinations might be pleasant but are *not* a good sign,' Roy frowned. On making it back to his bedside cabinet, he pulled out his tablet and searched for emergency nursing services. Ads on the right of his screen flashed insistently with the price of flights to France from Edinburgh airport. Roy clicked the first link to a private hospital-at-home service. Skim-reading, he realised that a lengthy registration and vetting process was required before any nurses could be deployed.

Roy looked over at Rebecca, now saddling up her invisible horse and apparently preparing to ride. Her hands shot to her temples again, followed by a long, lowing wail.

'If I take another tablet, I can probably delay the worst of it for a couple of hours, but I shouldn't, should I, Roy?' Rebecca asked, dropping to sit on the bed. 'Can you have a nurse here by then, darling?'

Roy glanced at his screen. Flights to Grenoble had now dropped to just 100 euros, open return.

'Take the pill,' Roy barked, 'take the pill, Ree-beh-kah and I'll get you to Dr Dubois and some better air pressure. I'm sure we can minimise this, if not avoid it completely.'

'In the next hour?' Rebecca asked, careful to keep the excitement from her words.

'7 a.m., I think,' Roy said, scrolling fervently, 'if I'm fast. But we might not get first-class seats.'

Rebecca paused, torn.

'Business class then, surely?'

'Mmm,' Roy replied, 'likely.'

Rebecca recommended light wails, reaching to her bedside drawer, rummaging noisily in packets of vitamins and various prescriptions, then pretending to pop a tablet in her mouth, washing it down with water. Going to their French chalet was for his own good, Rebecca told herself, for the whole family's good, in fact. After all, if #RabidRoy kicked off on Blurt again, the days of Jackson living in the garden where she could keep at least half an eye on him would be gone. At least this way, if Jackson went viral, she and Roy would be in Val d'Isère till it blew over, keeping Roy, rabid or otherwise, none the wiser.

'Flights booked,' Roy announced, 'we better get ready if we're going to make it. Is that painkiller making any difference?'

'The horse has gone,' Rebecca looked sad, 'it looks like we've bought a window of time. You shower, my love, thank you so much.'

Roy headed for the en suite. When Rebecca heard him close the shower door behind himself she darted downstairs, snatching her handbag on the way then dashing out the back door. She stuffed a spare key and 400 euros into a limited edition Hunter welly, long since abandoned at the entrance of Jackson's tiny house, then darted back inside, retracing her steps and shielding her eyes from the steamy glow of the spotlights and Roy's gaze when they collided in the bathroom doorway.

'You've gone very red.' Roy observed.

'Oestrogen fluctuations caused by the medication,' Rebecca said, undressing with her back to her husband, then stepping into the shower.

'I'll feed Duchy before we go,' Roy replied. 'Are you safe in there, alone, while I do that?'

'Yes, I think so,' Rebecca replied, 'if you're quick.'

Roy was glad of the peace in the rest of the house. He found Duchy in the living room and carried him to the utility, where he set him in front of a generous kibble breakfast. Duchy ate, keeping an eye on Roy as he activated a secret security lock he'd had installed at the back door while Rebecca had gone to Dubai for a girls' weekend the year before. Roy had had enough of returning home from trips with Rebecca to find Jackson had moved back in or thrown parties, so he'd decided that prevention would be better than cure in the future.

It was best Rebecca didn't know, Roy decided, winking down at Duchy. Rebecca's soft spot for Jackson was unhelpful, Roy thought, and at its worst, it was downright dangerous. He opened the app on his tablet, entered the passcode, then listened to the new bolt slide from inside the door and across to the frame with a beautiful, titanium-cut, Jackson-blocking, laser-aligned clunk.

. . .

At the T-junction just before the airport, Roy and Rebecca smiled at each other while Duchy yawned on Rebecca's lap. At Roy's insistence, Rebecca was wearing her ski goggles to mini-mise all possible glare that might make her symptoms worse. A thought that Jackson might rise earlier than usual in pursuit of food niggled Roy as he turned the steering wheel to the right.

'Rebecca, darling, turn off your comms till the Alps, my love, yes? I want you all to myself – Duchy does, too – *we* want you better, as soon as possible.'

Rebecca was touched by the rare affection from Roy if also annoyed that the goggles were making it difficult to see if any familiar journalist faces occupied the traffic around them. Switching off her tablet and slipping off her wristband, she dropped both into her Gucci handbag and then squeezed Roy's thigh.

'We mustn't rush back, my love,' Rebecca said. 'I may *look* well, darling, I always do, people say, but I assure you, I feel wretched. The medication will wear off soon. I dread it, frankly.'

'Say no more, Rebecca. Say no more.' Roy replied.

7

Daniella Clearwater did her best thinking on the move, barefoot, maintaining a brisk, rhythmic pace. She was about to complete another lap of the outer track on the roof of the new Glasgow Parliament and Civic Centre when she stopped, turning to the raised herb bed at her side and rubbing the foliage between her fingers. Smelling the oils, Daniella was intrigued by how the various perfumes built on her skin. She liked working here, visiting the garden most days and looking out to the mountains in the distance while contemplating her workload. During the week ahead, she and her PA Bryce would swap offices back to Holyrood for three months in the following New Scottish parliamentary rotation, then the two of them would go onwards to Stirling and each of New Scotland's cities in turn.

Daniella pulled her dark hair into a tight, high bun to stop it from tangling in the wind. She was wearing her trusty, navy knee-length, ethical-down parka. Even though June had almost arrived, the wind on the rooftop could still be bracing.

The view from where Daniella stood was uplifting. What had been the vast multi-storey carpark for John Lewis and Buchanan Galleries was now an urban garden. Sections of micro-farming were well established on one floor, while another was home to a bee sanctuary complete with an upcycled concrete-based rockery filled with heather and succulents. There was a children's play area on the ground floor, leading to a skate park. Chill-out seating areas were generously dotted around and Daniella's heart swelled as she looked down on it all.

On warm days, the urban spaces were filled with people relaxing and talking. When New Scotland had passed the bill to pedestrianise all city centres, allowing only eco-friendly public transport and service vehicles into its cities, Daniella had foreseen the immediate impact of reducing fumes on improving the air. She hadn't expected the poignant pleasure of standing anywhere in central Glasgow, Edinburgh, Perth, Aberdeen, Inverness, Stirling or Dundee and, clear as a bell, hearing another person's laughter travel the air. Though today was quiet, a giggle drifted up, and Daniella smiled. The laugh sounded young. Maybe, Daniella thought, maybe that laugh came from the incredible student who'd submitted the dissertation her old friend Drew McAllister had urgently passed on and which had been blowing her mind since.

Hi Daniella, hope you're well.

Everything's braw with me. I'm just off a call with colleagues in Italy, amazing to hear what folk in other countries think of New Scotland – we're inspiring the world over, a great feeling.

I'll get to the point as I appreciate how busy you are. I've just received something that's made me as happy as Larry. I've got a student I thought was going to fail his degree in Soc. Tech. Instead, he's pulled a magical rabbit out of a hat and I'm sure you're going to want to see it for yourself. This young person has submitted what could be a game-changer for social housing stock, no-impact environmental tech and *even more* job creation up the Clyde and beyond. I think it's particularly impressive given the wood short- ages for new housebuilding at the moment. Have a read. With the right tweaks, I think we've got something special here.

I've taken the liberty of sending in the copyrighting and patenting applications for this on the student's behalf. I know he'll never get round to it if I advise him to do so and it'd be a crying shame to see him exploited on the one occasion he's pulled a finger out.

Give me a shout if you want more info meantime.

Looking forward to your thoughts on these designs – attached.

Best, Drew.

Regards,
Professor A. McAllister
School of Technological Humanities
University of Edinburgh

While Daniella knew a good thing when she saw one, she knew risk when she saw it, too. What this student was suggesting was excellent, but as Drew had highlighted, tweaks were needed. The main concern Daniella had spotted was the problem of toxic fumes from melting plastic. This conundrum drove her round and round the roof, challenging herself to resolve it at least partially before handing it on to an adviser.

Following the concrete sidings and tuning into the faint announcements of an electric train arriving at Queen Street, Daniella recalled a conversation with the German environment minister. The minister was running a project to maximise the production of sustainable charcoal filters, which reduced harmful outputs from manufacturing sites transitioning from fossil fuels to zero emissions. There had been talk of a plan to engage further charcoal production partners outside the EU, Daniella remembered, but more stakeholders were needed to progress development. Daniella cleared her throat and tapped her comms.

'Bryce, remember that chat about Germany's sustainable charcoal filters a few months ago?'

'Yes, First Minister, a holo-meeting with their environment minister, the virtual background was an electric train station café in Hamburg.'

'That's it,' Daniella smiled. 'Listen, I want to ask if we can become a stakeholder and add funding from New Scotland to fast-track our access to resources. Can you get onto that? Find out what they need from us to make it happen ASAP, please, and, if possible, have them send a sample supply meantime?'

'Of course, First Minister, straight away.'

Daniella listened to Bryce's fingers on his keyboard, grateful as always for his can-do brilliance, then grabbed a hose and headed to the nearest planters containing tiny shoots of green beans.

8

Jackson had tried his key four times and still, the utility room door would not budge. He started to make his way over the gravel, pulling a flower bud off the climber by the front doorsteps as he passed, rolling it between his fingers, ready to chuck at his parents' bedroom window.

'Jackson! Jackson!' a thin voice screeched from the bottom of the drive. 'Jackson! Come and talk! Where's Rabid Roy?'

Jackson froze, looking down to the security gates, spotting a small huddle of journalists and photographers, cameras already clicking away. The voice that had called belonged to Michael Templeton. Jackson recognised it immediately and groaned. He didn't want his rights to the living room to be revoked again, but if his parents woke and saw who awaited them at the gates, he knew he'd be on extremely thin ice.

'Jackson! Come and tell us about your journey?' Templeton urged. 'When do you leave? What does your dad say, eh? Is he furious again? Is Daniella Clearwater leading the youth of New Scotland away from the cities like the Pied Piper, hmm?'

Jackson scanned the rest of the group, frowning when he recognised Gayle Wood. She was standing apart from the others and looked out of place. #RabidRoy wasn't her type of story, surely, Jackson thought.

'Jackson!' Gayle called, waving. 'How does it feel to be inspiring a nation – forfeiting a life of luxury to head to the Highlands to find your roots?'

'Erm … Great?!' Jackson managed, glad for the distraction from Templeton's unnerving stare. 'I don't give permission for any of these photos to be used, by the way,' he added, 'not unless you tag my Blurt, yeah?'

Gayle nodded while Templeton and the others groaned.

'Listen, I'll, em, I'll be out again soon – I've got to, em, check on Rabid Roy …' Jackson managed.

At the mention of Roy's name, a small cheer went up from Templeton's huddle, but, Jackson noticed, Gayle Wood appeared not to notice. She continued admiring the view over the city before briefly checking her wristband, then making to an NSBC truck parked on the opposite side of the street. Jackson hurried back over the drive and round the corner of the house to the utility door, noting as he passed that his dad's big Merc was gone.

'Shit, fuck, shit!' Jackson muttered, tapping at his wristband to call Rebecca. The ringing tone persisted but, unusually, Rebecca didn't pick up. He set about messaging her instead.

Mum

MUM THO!!!!

I'M CALLING CHILDLINE

Mum I can't get in the house

RabidRoy's fan club are at the gates

let me in Dad's at golf

Jackson, we're not home. We're at the chalet.

the fuq!!!??!?!??!

DO NOT SPEAK TO THE PRESS
You revived #RabidRoy on Blurt.
You left me no choice.

how am I supposed to get into the house??!?!?!?!

You have your key and a spare in the welly.

The key's not working
My key's not working either

Omg I can't believe yous have done this?!?!?!

Do you have the euros from the welly?

Yeh
Omg Dad's changed the locks!!!

Don't be ridiculous.

Where am I supposed to say Dad is?

You say NOTHING, Jackson!

Not even to the one from NSBC?
I've seen you watching her when Dad's at golf.

Gayle Wood? But she's intelligent – it can't be her.
Why would she be there?

Dunno. But she is.
Maybe she got demoted.

Oh god. This is escalating.

When are you coming home?

We can't keep living like this, Jackson.
We're lurching from one crisis to another!
You're ageing me unnecessarily!
I read your blurt – you said you'd finished your dissertation.
Do something with your life, Jackson!!!

Jackson hated it when Rebecca got all earnest on him. It was easier to deflect her emotions face to face, less so when she put them on a screen. Words in the air were ephemera, just like blurts, you said what you were thinking at that moment, and then, poof, they soon disappeared. Messaging was medieval by comparison, Jackson thought, dashing from the back door to his tiny house, locking the tiny door behind him.

The only place Jackson couldn't see the press was from his mezzanine, so he lay up there and checked his tablet. His notifications were going mad; messages ranged from enthusiastic support for #JacksonsJourney to hatred from Brit-Nats, mainly calling him a sheep-shagger. There were also a fair few offers of sponsorship from companies, Jackson noted with interest. They offered everything from rucksacks, walking boots, tents, stoves, hats with wifi antennae, drinking water bladders and midgie sedation gas cylinders. People, it seemed, really did think he was going to bugger off to the Highlands and claim his land. Jackson scrolled back to his profile info, smirking as he saw he'd gained another three thousand followers, but the shine was taken off by one of Rebecca's messages drifting back into his head, spoiling his fun.

Do something with your life, Jackson

He could message his mum and get her back home, Jackson thought. What would she say if he flipped the table on her and asked what *she* was doing with *her* life? He could tell her he was following *her* bad example – shopping and chilling and sticking keys and money in wellies, keeping secrets from Dad. Ha! That'd get her apologising and making his tea, he thought, smiling. Yes. He'd make himself feel better by making his mum feel bad.

But as he pulled the conversation with Rebecca back up on his tablet, the usual magic wasn't there in Jackson's thumbs. He imagined his dad, hospitalised by stress, hooked up to monitors, near-death by stress. Jackson recalled his conversation with Niall and how it had made him think that perhaps Roy wasn't the worst possible father to exist. Jackson stared at his screen, then pulled up his private messages with Niall. Niall's profile photo was now ghosted out, indicating his new offline status, but their messages remained. Niall's words were kind and patient, contrasting sharply with Jackson's hyperactive interjections of emojis, lols and staccato rants.

Keen for distraction, Jackson clicked his uni app and felt his stomach career into his bowel when he saw three messages waiting – one from Professor McAllister and another two from the New Scottish Government – presumably more, 'Your Nation, Your Future!' spam. He'd save the spam till last, Jackson thought. It'd be a nice transition away from trauma after reading whatever death threats Drew was making. Steeling himself, Jackson clicked on Drew's message:

Well Jackson, what can I say? You shocked us all and you did it!

I'm not a man for wasting words, as you know, so I give you my hearty congratulations and confirmation that, despite the late hand-in, the university is delighted to accept your submission under the Every Human Actualising guidelines, which, as always, prioritise effort and positive change over compliance.

Further, also according to guidelines which I'm sure you've read, I'm delighted to tell you I felt your work was so exciting that it warranted sending to New Scotland's government under our Bright Lights Fast Track Scheme (BLFTS), wherein educational custodians can highlight important work to our country's leaders when they believe it to be in the national interest. I am only doing this with one other student this year. I have taken the liberty of also applying for patenting and copyrighting your idea to protect your intellectual property.

In short, you're onto something massive here, Jackson. Well done! Your documents confirming your ownership of your Portable Tiny House Design™ and your process regarding the manufacture of Transpariboard™ should be with you in the next month.

I suggest you prepare yourself for talking to some officials; what you've come up with could be nothing short of revolutionary for the next phase of New Scotland's development, particularly for young people struggling to get on the property ladder.

If I can help, message me. I'm pretty busy, but I'm here if you need me, son.

Here's to happy endings, Jackson Campbell!

Can't believe I'm getting to type this, but – get this – I'm proud of you!

Best,

Drew

Regards,

Professor A. McAllister

School of Technological Humanities

University of Edinburgh

Jackson stared at the screen in horror. This was *bad*. This was *really bad*. His stomach let out a yowl, followed by another; it sounded like foxes were beginning to contemplate mating inside his onesie. He could hold it no longer. He jumped from halfway down the ladder then crawled across the two feet of tiny house floor to pull the cords down on each set of tiny blinds at his tiny windows. Then, doubling with a cramp, he pulled himself up and made for his tiny toilet.

Afterwards, physically empty and mentally filled with terror, Jackson clicked back into Blurt. Scrolling through hundreds of replies, hoping his breathing would soon slow, he recognised a name and face among the strangers:

/HannaNowak/blurtsTo/jacksonmcampbell
Hey stranger. #JacksonsJourney, huh? Exciting. Congrats on getting your work in. Sounds like you surprised yourself ;-) Hope you make it thru the press and out to the wilds, very inspiring. Got my #unclearances e-certificate today. I'm tempted …

Hanna had attached a photo of herself holding her screen up to show a certificate awarding her a symbolic plot of land on the Isle of Raasay. She was pulling a puzzled expression. Jackson realised that he'd never seen her without make-up or looking anything but hostile. The warmth of her words – and Drew's – felt so *new*. So welcoming. And, Jackson found that if he took a small swig of vodka from the half-empty bottle on the dish drainer, he could forget all the reasons they felt terrible.

. . .

Rebecca sat on the reindeer-skin sofa with an Irish coffee in hand in front of the chalet fire. A most unladylike sweat had developed underneath her cashmere leisurewear. She wondered, was Jackson perhaps trying his best already? Was her son's best terrible, but his best, nonetheless? Staring at the flames, Rebecca pictured her son's lolloping gait, wandering between his tiny house and the back door. She saw in her mind's eye how he still ate coco pops clutching the spoon as if it were a bike handle, just like when he was a toddler. 'My little caveman' she'd called him back then when even Roy had been so delighted with everything Jackson did.

'A proper boy,' Roy would chip in, grinning as he and Rebecca lent on the granite kitchen island, watching Jackson launch Coco Pops, toy cars, the salt and pepper mills, avocados, antique coffee grinders and whatever else he could get his hands on from the table to the floor.

Jackson had always been good at entertaining himself, Rebecca remembered. He'd done it every morning before his nanny, Anya, arrived to battle him out of his pyjamas and into his smart little uniform for private nursery and, later, prep school. Where on earth had it all gone wrong? How, Rebecca wondered, *how* could she get father and son back on track? How could she wean Jackson from the online world? How could she make him care as much about what his dad thought as he did about the approval of strangers? She sipped her drink then picked up her phone.

> Darling, I'm sorry. I was harsh. Take your time.
> Growing up is hard.

omfg chill out muthaship lol

> You're not upset?

you might've been rite mum

I do need to do something with my life innit

                                        Well. Plenty time yet.
                                        Did you talk to the press?

No.

                                        Good! Thank you!
                              Jackson, you know we love you, don't you?

ok

                          Darling, can you unblock Dad's number?

Yeah. as soon as he admits he's
changed the locks on the back door

                          Maybe you just need to try the key again?
                                    Fresh start? Great big effort?
                          Open mind? Open door?! Open sesame!

right
when are you coming home?

                                        When the press go away.
                                        Love you, poppet xxx

Rebecca smiled, placing her tablet down and looking over at Roy, who lay on his zebra-skin recliner, open-mouthed and snoring, his favourite book about Britain's heyday as a golfing empire rising and falling on his stomach with each snorty rasp. A seed had been sown, Rebecca thought. Now all she had to do was plant another, then carefully cultivate both.

In the tiny house, Jackson moved the blind an inch and

peeked out of the window. There was still someone at the gates, despite the late hour. Normally this attention would have thrilled Jackson, but his guilty conscience about the theft of Niall's work made him want to lie low until life (or Drew McAllister) had moved on to a completely different topic. The dark figure gestured up, hailing Jackson to come and talk. Templeton. Jackson switched the tiny house light off and sank back into the half-light of his laptop screen and the milky glow of a full moon shining through the tiny skylights. He was trapped in all possible ways.

Bored, his hand moved to the touchpad and clicked on the first message spam from the New Scottish Government. He tutted as he scanned the shmaltzy opening sentences congratulating him on being a crucial part of New Scotland's future. He scrolled down to see an embedded certificate, just like Hanna's but stating that Jackson's patch of land was on the Isle of Eigg, wherever that was.

Jackson rolled his eyes, clicked through to the following message, apparently from the First Minister herself, and began scrolling to the unsubscribe link when four lines caught his attention, stopping him dead:

'... I've read your dissertation in full and would like to discuss it and a proposal I have for your immediate future. I therefore warmly invite you to attend a meeting at Holyrood this Thursday, at 2 p.m., my PA Bryce will arrive at your home at 13.30 to collect you, if this all sounds agreeable ...'

'*Fuck!*' Jackson screamed. He jumped back, desperate to get away from the tiny table, smashing his head on the mezzanine as he went. The First Minister's words stared up at him as he backed away, taunting him as the back of his head began throbbing.

'No, no, no, nooo, no!' Jackson whimpered, sitting down slowly on the floor, then lying back and staying very still to mitigate the risk of further injury. This, Jackson realised, as he stared up at his tiny pots and pans hanging on the tiny piece of wall above the tiny extractor fan, this was *really bad*.

9

Brilliant morning light poured through the panorama of windows into the group therapy session on the top floor of the recovery centre. Strung out from withdrawing from the online world, Niall was making a beeline towards the huge blue armchair he'd sat in during the previous two sessions. Fin, one of the recovery centre's wellness coaches, raised his hands then clapped them into prayer pose, his signal for everyone to stop and listen.

'Morning, everyone,' Fin said, his expression serene. 'Welcome to your third group therapy session. I want you all to sit in a different place when you come to group from now on, OK?'

Niall's heart sank as he watched Jim, an elderly man claiming to be suffering from grief and gambling addiction, jump up from an old church pew and make for the blue chair, grinning when he claimed it.

Fin continued, seemingly oblivious to the dark stares of most of the group around him who were not yet seated, '... To prepare for living in a different way when you leave, you'll learn through disrupting comfort zones that your capabilities are bigger and more secure than you've ever understood before.'

Niall scanned the room and realised that by the time he made it to the remaining empty seats he was going to be the last standing, and, therefore, the enormous purple LazySack which looked like a huge, bruised, hairless testicle would be his for the session.

'Neil, you seem to be faltering,' Fin observed. 'Do you have an affirmation from yesterday's session that might help at this moment?'

Fin approached Niall as everyone else scuttled past the LazySack. He placed a warm hand on Niall's tensing shoulder. Niall fought back tears and a surge of aggression.

'Tell us how you feel, Neil,' Fin said. 'Remember, all feelings are permitted, no one's judging, everything is valid in group.'

'*Neil* isn't valid!' Niall spat. 'My name's *Niall*, for a start, so I'd fucking like to be called that, yeah?'

'Oh,' Jim piped up from the blue chair, its squishy bulk surrounding and protecting him, 'Niall,' he pondered, 'like … *pile*. Not Neil, like … *a feel*. Feel Neil! Pile Niall! Ha!'

Niall's cheeks coloured to match the LazySack.

'Ah. Apologies,' Fin made a brief prayer gesture with his hands, 'Niall. To rhyme with *reconcile*. I'll do my best not to forget again.'

Niall was not soothed.

'I feel fucking angry,' he hissed, glowering at Fin. 'It's a stupid idea, moving folk about. We should get to sit where we want, where we're comfy.'

Fin nodded.

'Go on, Niall.'

Niall rolled his eyes.

'I don't *want* to go on!' He was shouting now, he realised, 'I want to go back to my room. I'm sick of this place already. I want my tablet. I want my wristband. I want to speak to a normal fucking human. I don't want to sit on a fucking ballsack. You can't make me be something I'm not. I hate this. I hate *you*. I hate you *all*. You're fucking weirdos. Some of you are clearly fine and have families at home and everything, I don't even know why you're here.' Niall looked around the room at the shocked faces staring back. Shame immediately plunged into his chest. His voice dropped to a shaky low, 'and I hate myself even more now for saying that, so how the hell is any of this exactly helping, *Fin*?'

Fin bent with Niall as he crumpled to the floor. A woman on the hanging chair nearby leant forward, offering a tissue, then swayed back when Niall had taken it from her hand. Fin looked around the room, his soft smile encouraging.

'Can anyone think of an affirmation from yesterday's Alternative Thinking Session with Claudia that might help re-ground Niall at this moment?'

Niall sniffed back snot.

'Everywhere I go, I am enough,' a quiet voice said. It came from a woman with a cheek grommet piercing on either side of her face. She'd chosen a black leather recliner which remained upright under her tense, bulky frame.

'Excellent, Sadie,' Fin replied. 'Niall, can you repeat that when you're ready, even just in your thoughts?'

Niall blew his nose loudly on the tissue then shook his head, mortified.

'You're doing so, so well, Niall. I'm proud of you for your honesty.'

'I'm fucking breaking down even further though!' Niall wailed, tears flowing down his cheeks. 'I feel humiliated! And now I'm being a fucking monster to folk I don't even know! You're turning me into everything I hate! You've singled me out and all I ever want to do is blend in. I bloody told you that when I got here!'

Fin nodded.

'Maybe you're not breaking down, Niall. Maybe you're breaking through. Rock bottom often feels like humiliation, but it's not a destination, it's simply a waypoint.'

Fin gave Niall's shoulder a final pat, then stood and returned to the middle of the space. Niall glanced around the room. Anyone who met his eye was smiling as if they cared, or was also crying. Everyone else was staring out of the windows, pretending they didn't care. Denial was a move Niall knew well. He stood up and walked to the LazySack then dropped onto it, belly first, groaning as the landing winded him. It was the first movement of his body he had made without thinking about it in years. He realised that it was possibly the most natural movement of his body he'd made in years. Fuck it, Niall thought, wiggling his chin to create a small pocket of air he could breathe easily in as he lay face down. Never mind keeping up appearances anymore. If rock bottom was a LazySack, it was surprisingly comfortable.

10

Jackson had spent the previous day hiding out in his tiny house. He'd reached for alcohol every time he remembered the First Minister's message and tried to distract himself between sips by blurting photos of himself balancing different things on his head, a game his followers always seemed to love.

Following an uncharacteristically early breakfast, Jackson now stared at the map on his screen, struggling to accept the reality that no matter how much he begged in the taxi chat window, no drivers were willing to take a part-cash payment for an immediate lift to his family's chalet in France. His hands hovered over his keyboard, about to message his mum and ask for an emergency bank transfer, then drew back. Flashes of his last conversation with Rebecca still smarted when he looked at their messages; Jackson knew if he asked for money now his mum would respond within minutes, squawking a million questions down the phone like a demented chicken, wasting more precious time. He scanned his tiny kitchen, mentally sweeping for a hidden credit card or discount voucher he might've somehow forgotten, before resting on his tiny clock. The minutes were motoring towards the time Daniella Clearwater's PA was due to turn up, and a new, leaden sensation in Jackson's chest was beginning to settle. He called up the message from Clearwater again, staring at it then snapping open the ring pull of another cappuccino cooler and downing it. Jackson had already ruled out Plan A – simply packing a bag, walking to Waverley Station, and catching the first train to France. He'd got as far as stuffing two of his spare onesies into a rucksack before realising that he'd have Templeton and several members of the press and their camera drones pestering him all the way, thinking they had the scoop on him setting off to the Highlands.

Re-reading Daniella's message for the millionth time, Jackson visualised the PA turning up. He'd probably be driving some kind of hippy eco-bus that ran on recycled chip-shop fat, Jackson thought, or perhaps he'd have an electric scooter like Drew's. Wincing at the thought of another close encounter squashed against the back of someone he wasn't on intimate terms with, Jackson plumped for the image of the eco-bus and let the caffeine begin to work its magic in his mind. How about if he took the lift to Holyrood as Clearwater had planned, playing along and getting past the press before they even knew what was happening? Then, when they arrived at Holyrood, he'd leg it instead of following the PA into the building; he'd escape, running as fast as he could up Canongate, onto The Royal Mile, then down Jeffrey Street to Waverley, then jumping on the first train south. That way, Jackson figured, the press would be off his scent, and the First Minister would decide he was insane, dropping whatever her idea was and never contacting him again. He closed his eyes and imagined himself climbing the stairs to the bus, every part of the vehicle painted in shades of green, Templeton in shades of red at the foot of the steps, screaming up at Jackson to go with him instead; then again Templeton, this time in the distance behind the bus, a puff of cloudy chip oil catching his throat, quieting him at last.

Relief at finding a workable plan spread through Jackson's body, and muscles relaxed in his long limbs for the first time in twenty-four hours. He pictured his arrival at the chalet doorstep, adorable scenes of his reunion with Duchy, and the beginning of his new life as a super-famous French influencer. It was possible, Jackson fantasised, that while they were all in the chalet he might not wind up his dad at all so that when his parents returned home, there would be nothing but good feeling all round. And in time, *voila*, a degree certificate to hang in the hall.

Jackson began scouring the drawers under his tiny corner sofa, and finding a pair of black jeans and a t-shirt that wasn't too badly stained, pulled them on. He ate a second bowl of Coco Pops and gulped back another tin of coffee before brushing his teeth and splashing his face with water, gasping as his bruises reminded him of their presence.

1.25 p.m.

Jackson's stomach made a small, trumpeting noise as he brushed his blonde hair into middle-parted curtains, shrouding as much of his face as possible. He then selected the most enormous, darkest pair of sunglasses from a stash of sponsored goodies he'd been sent the previous summer, positioning them high on his nose, almost completely obscuring the bruise on his forehead. Finally, at 1.28 p.m., he pulled on his denim jacket and baseball boots, grabbed his keys and stepped outside, instantly rousing Templeton and the other members of the press at the gates. Jackson lingered at the tiny house door for a second, fingers reluctant to turn the little key as he looked lovingly inside at his rucksack. There was no way he could take it without arousing suspicion.

'Au revoir, tiny life,' Jackson whispered as he closed the door. The finality of the lock turning reminded him of the gravity of the stunt he was about to pull. 'Goodbye forever.'

A long black car slid silently into view outside the gates as Jackson began the walk over the gravel. Templeton marched over to the vehicle, pressing his nose against the blackened windows when it stopped. Bryce Cooper emerged from the far side of the car, smaller than he seemed on TV but just as pristinely suited and styled. Jackson hurried down the drive and vaulted the gate, his significantly sized soles slapping the pavement, announcing his arrival. Templeton spun, pushing past his colleagues to get to Jackson, rat-like features contorting with surprised pleasure as he whacked his comms badge to summon his drone.

'Jackson?' Bryce craned his head above the huddle, his tone cautious.

'Yes! Hi!' Jackson replied, waving at Bryce as he made his way through the gathered bodies and camera tripods.

Gayle Wood emerged from the back of the NSBC truck and stood at the top of the small set of stairs, half frowning and half smiling as she stretched her neck and arms, all the while coolly regarding the excitement at the Campbells' gates.

'Well! About time!' Templeton roared. 'We jolly well thought you were all dead, young man! Where are you going, Jackson? Where is your father? Has he lashed out at your mother? Not a soul has moved in that house for thirty-six hours! What the *hell* is going on? And why is Clearwater's dubious little sidekick here, hmm? On behalf of the people of Great British England, we demand to know!'

'Excuse me,' Bryce squeezed between Templeton and a low-flying GBEBS drone to get to Jackson's side. 'Is everything OK? I mean, we weren't expecting a reception …'

'Everything's fine!' Jackson said, eager to leave. 'This is just a stupid thing about my dad … could we? Could we just *go*?'

Uncertain, Bryce looked Jackson up and down, checked his wristband, smiled tightly and nodded, gesturing towards the car.

'Do you think this is wise, Jackson?' Templeton screeched. 'Is that bruising on your face a result of your father's violence? Are you going to Holyrood, Jackson?' Templeton followed, hot on Jackson's heels. 'Jackson, has your mother restrained your father? Which way is the wind blowing? You haven't blurted in hours. What's your father behaving like? You're the younger man – have you tossed him from the arena, Jackson? Are you the head of Clan Campbell now?'

Templeton's hysteria was instantly muted as soon as the car doors shut.

Bryce nodded at the driver to leave, then watched while Jackson fastened his seatbelt.

'Why on earth is there a press pack outside your house? We haven't publicised this at all, are you somehow linked to the GBE press?'

'No, man,' Jackson replied, oblivious that Bryce had no idea who he was, apart from a student with an idea. 'Nah, like, don't worry about it. It's 'cos of my blurts. Rabid Roy and that? Hey, I thought you'd be in an eco-bus, by the way, nice wheels.'

Bryce sat back as the penny dropped, eyes wide.

'*Your* father is Rabid Roy?' Bryce was horrified. 'Campbell. Oh, yes, I see. J Campbell. Jackson Campbell. Goodness. Well. We completely failed to connect the dots here. I mean, the context did not suggest …'

'Yeah. I mean, he's not that bad,' Jackson went on, 'I mean, he's like … mad, obviously, but … well, it's funny, isn't it? All of it? I mean, it's just bants, isn't it? Roy – Dad –freaking out and stuff? Templeton loves it.'

'Bants?' Bryce shivered. 'I, um, I don't know what to say. He – your father, I mean – he certainly has only ever appeared to me to be *very* distressed and very *distressing*, but … has he hit you? Have you fought? Physically?'

Jackson pulled off his sunglasses and shook his hair back.

'Oh. This? No! I banged my head on my house!'

Bryce pulled back, gasping in horror, his hand clamping his mouth as he took in the mottled purples, fuchsia and blues of the butterfly bruise covering Jackson's brow, the bridge of his nose and the skin around his eyes.

Jackson stared, surprised at Bryce's reaction, then leant forward to look at himself in the driver's mirror.

'Oh,' Jackson laughed, 'it looks worse in here. I've only got a tiny mirror under my mezzanine, so the light's not great.' Jackson flashed a megawatt smile at Bryce. 'My parents are in France. We've got a chalet there for skiing. That weirdo at the gate's just making stuff up. Honest, this was an accident. I live in a tiny house. The mezzanine's cool for space but not cool 'cos I'm tall. I bang myself off it a lot. Like, chill, honestly, man, this wasn't Roy, yeah?'

Bryce nodded slowly, secretly scrutinising Jackson's body language. He seemed genuine enough, Bryce thought.

'OK. Well. I need to brief you,' Bryce said, 'on the meeting today – the Bright Lights FastTrack Scheme – Drew McAllister will be attending too, in holo, he's unable to attend in person. I'll need to brief the First Minister, too now when we arrive, about your full, um, status.'

The mention of Drew's name made Jackson push his shades back onto his face and nibble a thumbnail. He glanced out the window, pleased to see they were almost at Holyrood Park. It wouldn't be long now until he was free, Jackson told himself, his heart quickening. Bryce continued speaking – something about protocol and security – while Jackson, pretending to listen, nodded intermittently until the car slowed outside the parliament. Jackson held his breath, a hand hovering over his seatbelt, waiting for the moment.

'Damnit,' the driver said.

'What is it, Jane?' Bryce frowned.

'GBEBS drones. Look.'

Jackson copied Bryce as he looked up through the panoramic roof, spotting two decrepit drones, jerking spasmodically, attempting to position themselves either side of the car.

'Would you rather avoid?' Bryce asked Jackson. 'Templeton always has a couple of tricks up his sleeve, drones on standby in a few places.'

'I'd definitely rather avoid!' Jackson said, fear rising. Drones like these looked slow, but they were possibly still fast enough to tail him to Waverley and have Templeton on his arse again, ruining everything.

'Can we shoot at them with lasers, or what?' Jackson asked, hopeful.

Bryce laughed.

'Not quite, Mr Campbell, not quite.'

'FM's entry?' Jane asked.

Bryce nodded, then gestured for Jackson to sit back, deep into the car seat.

Jane made a quick selection on a dashboard touch screen. The car sped off, flinging them all through a dramatic 180-degree turn before snaking effortlessly back past the drones, through the first turns in the park roads, then up Holyrood Road, abruptly rounding a corner into a close through to the Royal Mile. They paused briefly while a wall panel on their right slid open, revealing a large, dark chamber. The car entered, the wall closing again behind it, engulfing them in blackness.

'*What the fuuuck?!*' Jackson whimpered.

'Computer, parking bunker lights, please,' Jane said.

Jackson watched as lights outside the car lit up one by one, a blue ring of glow making its way around the inside of a concrete dome. The only break in the surface was a wide glass door, the panel they'd entered through having now disappeared entirely.

'Cool. Huh?' Bryce said, 'I guess you'll get quite a kick out of this as an applied tech student?'

'Does that door go up to the main entrance?' Jackson's voice caught, his throat parched.

'Nope,' Bryce replied, 'that door goes straight to the FM's wing. We're right on time, despite Templeton's shenanigans. Let's go and introduce you to the boss, huh?'

II

'C'mon son! No like you to be shy! Daniella's all right! Just be yourself. You've done the hard bit already!'

Drew's voice boomed from his hologram in the corner of the vast, triangular-shaped meeting room to where Jackson now stood frozen between Bryce and the First Minister. Daniella Clearwater was extending her right hand to shake his, which was still gripping his tiny house key so hard that his fist now resembled a large chunk of corned beef. He stuffed his hands into his pockets and stared at his baseball boots, willing the ground to melt beneath him, sucking him away.

Bryce cleared his throat and politely repeated his introductions in an attempt to jumpstart Jackson out of what appeared to be starstruck awe. Jackson looked up, flashing a brief, terrified smile. Daniella was radiant in the flesh, and Drew, in Jackson's first close-up experience of a hologram, was a Shrek-like shade of green. Glancing between the faces staring at him, Jackson wondered if it hurt if holograms hit people. Where exactly was the line between technology and reality? It was the sort of question that a technology graduate should have the answer to, he realised.

'Your parents must be so proud of you?' Daniella asked, withdrawing her hand and trying a different tack.

Bryce moved to Daniella's side, cupped her ear, and whispered fervently. Daniella's expression changed to a look of mild shock. When Bryce finished, Daniella took a deep, contemplative breath.

'My, erm, parents are on holiday,' Jackson managed, 'they don't actually know I'm here … yet … I thought I'd wait and, erm … surprise them.'

He removed his sunglasses and pushed them into a chest pocket without thinking. Daniella gasped.

'Your face!'

Drew strained to see, then looked horrified, too.

'Oh, don't worry!' Jackson laughed awkwardly, 'I just bumped it on my roof in my tiny house. It's a bit small in places.'

'Oh,' Daniella looked relieved, 'and you're extremely tall, unlike me. Design considerations, yes?'

'Jackson's dad's a big man, too, Daniella,' Drew chimed in, 'in a way. And quite well known. You've heard of Rabid Roy, aye?'

Daniella nodded.

'Indeed. Bryce has just brought me up to speed. I had no idea you were Ra— I mean, Roy, Roy Campbell's son. Till now.'

'Aye!' Drew replied, a twinkle in his hologram eye. 'Sometimes the apple falls plenty far from the tree, eh?'

'Yes, Rabid Roy is my dad. Apologies for, erm, that.' Jackson winced, then shrugged, feeling himself relaxing a little as the heat of the limelight shifted to his absent father.

'J Campbell. Oh, my goodness, yes, I see. I'm putting two and two together now. Jackson Campbell, with the huge Blurt following – yes? I've heard you've been quite taken with Unclearance, planning a journey, is that right?'

Jackson reddened, his mouth opening then shutting, carp-like. Daniella Clearwater was lovely, he realised, genuinely lovely. She radiated a calm that helped to loosen his tight shoulders. He'd play along further, he decided, then after the meeting, he'd ask to be let out the secret door and scarper to Waverley from there. That way, he wouldn't have to see the disappointment in the First Minister's face – or admonishment in Drew's.

'I'm not really planning that,' Jackson replied. 'Sometimes I just say things for bants. I don't even know where the Isle of Eggs is. I was just trolling my dad up 'cos he hates all that New Scot— I mean, well. You know, I suppose?'

Dimples appeared then vanished from Daniella's cheeks before she spoke, 'And are you in pain?'

Jackson stared at the First Minister. Had she hypnotised him? Just looking into her eyes he felt he could tell her anything.

'Yes,' Jackson half-whispered, 'sometimes, I keep myself busy so …'

'Then you must get some arnica,' Daniella replied, 'works wonders for bruising. And you should probably be checked for a concussion. Did you lose consciousness at all when it happened?'

'No, I'm OK, really.' Jackson managed.

'OK,' Daniella continued, 'but don't be a hero about it. Never works out well.'

Jackson watched as Daniella tapped at her gleaming wristband, narrowed her eyes as she read something then swiped it away and smiled back up at him. She was dressed head to toe in navy, even her fingernails were painted to match, a tightly tailored bullet of efficiency accessorised perfectly with warmth in her eyes and smile.

'Hey,' Daniella continued, 'did you know my comms team use various social media accounts as zeitgeist trackers to help us keep an eye on what people in New Scotland are motivated by?'

Jackson shook his head. A wayward, leftfield thought that he should confess as soon as Clearwater stopped talking, was refusing to be shushed by his previous plan.

'Yours is one of the accounts,' Daniella went on. 'It's a wild card, sure, but good ideas often spring from spontaneity, don't they, Drew?'

Drew gave a lime-tinted glowing thumbs-up.

Daniella gestured for Jackson to sit at one of the chairs tucked behind a generously proportioned V-shaped desk.

'Is that, like, spying on me?' Jackson asked.

'Jackson!' Drew laughed, 'how can it be spying when you're putting that information out to millions of people yourself? Think aboot it!'

Daniella shrugged.

'I'd say you're both right, I guess.'

'Daniella,' Drew continued, 'it seems Jackson's one of those special kinds of geniuses, the type who can't see the common-sense things in front of him, then drops into meta-thinking as if it were a wee Jacuzzi, know what I mean?'

'A bit like you at that age, eh, Drew?' Daniella's retort solicited a concession of an amused nod from Drew before she addressed Bryce. 'Bryce, 4D plans, please.'

Bryce tapped his wristband while Jackson continued watching Daniella, mildly aroused, when a bright blue flash caught the corner of his eye from the middle of the room. He looked at the space between the desks, gasping as a series of laser lines began crisscrossing the area. A large planter standing beneath them was elegantly swallowed by a motorised opening in the floor and replaced by a platform. Jackson had seen something similar happen at a concert before, but the swiftness of it all right before his eyes seemed infinitely more impressive. Looking up again, he tilted his head one way then the other as it slowly dawned on him that the lasers were creating something; they weren't just random lines, they were plans – *his* plans – his tiny house plans, forming right before them.

Daniella looked to Drew, discreetly placing a finger on her lips for a second. Jackson gaped at Daniella as she stood, then walked around the desk to the edge of the tiny laser house, stopping when she reached it.

'Surprise!' Daniella's eyes twinkled with delight.'This is one of the ways we test things before moving onto physical prototypes. Good, isn't it?'

Jackson got up, jaw hanging, sat on the desk then swivelled on his bum to the other side. He stood in front of the house, the buttons on his denim jacket catching the laser light as he stared.

'Touch it.' Daniella instructed, watching as Jackson raised a shaky arm, one finger extended. When he made contact with the lasers, the house slid slowly away from him by a few millimetres, as if he'd pushed it.

He jumped back, dumbstruck.

'Take a minute.' Daniella said. 'This technology is brand new. No rush, ask us anything you like. It won't hurt you. Explore.'

Jackson watched as Daniella strolled over to a vast window perfectly framing Salisbury Crags, then stood with her back to the room, making it clear she'd meant what she said. Jackson looked to Drew, then Bryce. Both of them nodded encouragingly toward the house. Jackson walked around the laser structure, admiring how well the different angles worked as it hovered in front of him.

'If a hologram bumps into a laser, em … tiny house,' Jackson said, 'do, em … does anyone get hurt?'

Bryce and Drew laughed while Daniella watched two dunnocks pecking through succulent plants on the rooftop of the parliament offices below. An idea crystallised in her thoughts. She rejoined Jackson, simultaneously beckoning the laser structure downwards from where it had been hovering a little above the platform.

'It's exactly to scale,' Daniella said. 'You can step inside if you like, it should be true to the Transpariboard experience. We have noticed a few problems with layout, placement of a shower, for example, could be closer to the kitchen sink, minimising plumbing. However, a bigger challenge is surely how to keep this baby cool in sunlight? You don't mention how you think Transpariboard would deal with heat transfer. I'd be keen to know if you'd like to share?'

Jackson gestured a swiping motion with his arm and the sliding door of the laser house swept open, just as his plans had shown. In terms of proportions, he realised he'd produced something cool; tiny living had paid off, he knew what door needed a slight movement here or a cupboard located there. An image of his parents proudly watching him as a kid popped into his head. He swallowed slowly, his mouth parched and his eyes filling with tears.

'Listen … First Minister, Professor. Bryce. I've got to tell you that, that, I, I don't—'

'You've no clue about that heat question, have you, son?' Drew's interruption captured Daniella's attention. 'Honestly, Jackson, that's understandable; your skills lie in eagle vision; we see a distinct split these days, Daniella, between the eagle vision and the mouse vision, know what I mean? The mouse does details. Product Design from an interrogation perspective, it's a specialism. Jackson's your big ideas man, do you see?'

Daniella nodded.

'I have the budget to bring in that specialism, if necessary. But …' Daniella paused for a second, 'But I also now want to make a shell version of this, nothing inside at all. Just walls, door, floor and roof. Max minimalism. A clear, tiny house that can be folded up and down with no more effort than a pop-up tent. And with a transportable component too. For a journey. An eco-friendly journey, on foot or bike.'

'You're not actually going to build it though, are you?' Jackson asked, incredulous.

Daniella looked the laser structure over, then straight back through it to Jackson.

'Oh, I definitely want to build it,' she replied, 'in fair quantities, too. First in Transpariboard and then other materials for the iterations where privacy's needed, if we can come to the necessary agreements on usage, of course. We haven't done anywhere near enough on small dwellings and I think you've provided the impetus for change.' Daniella leant back on the table behind her.

'Jackson, could you be convinced to be serious about a journey to Eigg?'

Jackson stared, ashen.

'I know the island well,' Daniella continued, 'have you been before?'

Jackson shook his head. Daniella began slowly walking the perimeter of the room.

'Your design is excellent. And the suggestion for an interim material to use during the timber shortages is – truly – a gift. But now I know who you are, I can't ignore the serendipity of it all.' Daniella stopped, eyes focused on Jackson's face with a hawk-like bearing as her head tilted almost imperceptibly. 'What I'm asking, Jackson, is not just to be able to make this product and use it in initiatives with social housing, but also, to give it an *adventure*. A reality adventure with you live-blurting it, helping me push Unclearances, really engaging folk with the idea of accessible eco-travel, history *and* future?'

Drew's hands slapped together in slow, painful-sounding spanks as he applauded Daniella, his teeth glinting a dark, emerald green.

'Told you this could be big, Jackson, didn't I?' Drew boomed. 'Didn't I say that?'

Jackson moved his feet further apart so the sweat in his groin could form a rivulet down his thighs rather than an embarrassing stain. When he looked back to Daniella, her head was full cocked, her smile waiting to broaden with his answer.

'I want to help you,' Jackson half-croaked, 'I really want you to … to like me, I mean *it*, to like *it*.' An unstoppable tear slid down Jackson's nostril, settling in the shadow of its curve before anyone could notice.

'You do?' Daniella asked, unsure. 'I mean, I know these things are nerve-wracking, I do, honestly. But, well, we're only here once, as far as we know, aren't we? Sometimes we need to push through the fear, don't we? To get to the good stuff. I believe we should make life count, and make it fun, every time we get the chance.'

Jackson sniffed.

'Like, to do something, with our lives?'

'Yes,' Daniella replied, touched by what she understood as Jackson's beguiling innocence.

'I can help as well,' Drew said. 'That Product Designer, Daniella? I've just the lass. Hanna Nowak, from Aberdeen, classmate of Jackson's. Anything you want made portable, she's yer woman.'

'*Hanna*?' Jackson spluttered. 'As in *Niall* and Hanna?'

'Aye,' Drew replied, proudly, 'she's amazing, Daniella, incredible ideas for alleviating the impact of poverty, a lot of stuff that'd be transferable to GBE. I was going to tell her to attend the open conference on initiatives for resource sharing, but this is an even better fit.'

'Right then,' Daniella said, 'ask her, Drew? We'll pay a living wage to everyone involved, obviously. Round the clock. I feel like time is of the essence here. As fast as possible, we should run with this and tag it onto the hype for Unclearance while it's building.'

Sweat gathered at Jackson's hairline. Bryce shot up from his chair.

'First Minister, sorry to interrupt, we're running over, your 3.30 with Greenland is about to be on screen in your office.'

'Right, thank you.' Daniella looked to Drew, then Jackson. 'Same time next week, all of us – with Hanna Nowak, or, if she's not available, Bryce and you put your heads together on an alternative, Drew? Yes?'

'Aye,' Drew replied, 'shouldn't be a problem.'

Jackson's stomach lurched as Daniella waved then left the room, chatting animatedly into her comms badge as she went.

'I'll be back to show you out as soon as possible, Jackson.' Bryce called over his shoulder, following in Daniella's wake.

Jackson looked at Drew, closed his eyes, took a deep breath then spat the words out.

'Drew! Don't kill me, please, but I, I, can't … I … Transpariboard … it's not; it's not *mine,* I stole the idea … from Niall.' Jackson braced. When the punch didn't come, he opened one eye. Only the vaguest green outline of one of Drew's massive hands remained, leaving a slight haze of waving luminous dots as the holo-link closed. Gone. Deactivated. Drew hadn't heard a word.

Turning away from the laser house, Jackson made his way to the window. He missed his mum and Duchy, he realised. A sting of nostalgia for his dad sprung up too. He looked at his wristband, unblocked Roy's number, hesitated, and then pressed call. He listened as the ring tone stretched to France and back again. Halfway through the third ring, Roy picked up, his voice terse.

'Jackson? What do you want?'

'Dad … hi … em, listen, there's this thing, and, em, I'm not sure what to do, like, it's kind of a mess and—'

Roy interrupted.

'Like *what*, Jackson? Run out of money? Set your tiny house on fire? Played skittles with the cars? Broken seventeen windows, have we? Not your fault though, no doubt. Hurry up, out with it, why let us have one *single* trip away without ruining it somehow?'

Jackson listened as the ski lift clanked nearby. He could hear his mum in the background, loudly explaining to someone that her ski gloves had been made specially to match her diamanté poles.

'So?' Roy demanded.

A ripple of adrenaline prickled Jackson's damp skin.

'I was just phoning to say thanks for locking the back door, you massive bellend.'

'Don't you dare call me that you … *you* … parasite!' Roy snarled. 'You're a lazy, feral, hyperactive toddler and I—'

'How can I be lazy *and* hyperactive, you twat?!' Jackson spat back, then hung up and immediately blocked Roy's number again.

Jackson looked back at the house, now shimmering in the afternoon sun. What was the worst thing that could happen, he thought. Niall had said he hadn't told another soul about Transpariboard, hadn't he? So what if he just went with all this journey stuff? That was what he'd done so far, after all. What if he kept riding the wave, popped over to this island of Eigg for a few nights, made a hashtag or ten, had a laugh with Hanna then, when it was all over, buggered off to the chalet? Yes, neither Niall nor Hanna would ever speak to him again when they found out what he'd done, but he didn't need real friends, did he? Jackson scrolled through his Blurt followers, thousands of them. They were friends, weren't they? And they loved him, whatever he did.

Jackson pushed his sunglasses back on, stuck his tongue out and pushed it against the window, snapping a selfie with the top of Arthur's Seat just in view behind.

/jacksonmcampbell /blurts/
that feeling when you've just met the First Minister and she's, like, shown you all her lasery shit and she's, like, WELL COOL and, like, wants to get, like, well down wif da yoooooooooooooooooooof on tech!!!!!!!!!!!! Paging HannaNowak, innit?!?!?!!!!!! #JacksonsJourney #NewScotland #WHIT #fuuuuuuuuuuccccckkk #RabidRoy #Unclearances #DaniellaCanClearMyWaterAnyDay #UpBeforeMidday #SexyBunkerLife

/ZuzannaN/ blurtsTo/jacksonmcampbell
Why are you blurting my big sister HannaNowak? She hardly uses blurt. She probably won't see this. Can I get a selfie with you on you and Hanna's graduation day? #JacksonsJourney #NewScotland

/TheJacksonCampbellAppreciationSoc/blurtsTo/ZuzannaN
Hi if you want a selfie with jacksonmcampbell it's best to become a junior member with us. We're not official but there is, like, a hierarchy in fans to be observed. X

/ZuzannaN/ blurtsTo/ TheJacksonCampbellAppreciationSoc
Omg you are too funny/lame. Fuck off.

12

Jackson's window-licking had been reblurted with the hashtag #Unclearance by Daniella and begun racking up viral momentum with each engagement the collaboration inspired. His blurt from his birthday about going off to find Campbell bones on ancient land was still viral, too; Jackson had been alerted to both facts by Rebecca's screechy call from the chalet at nine-fifteen that evening once he was back home. He'd put the call on speaker and stretched his arms and legs as far as the roof of the tiny house would allow.

'Jackson Montague Campbell! Why the hell is that *woman* blurting you and saying you're going on a journey? Explain yourself immediately!'

'What woman?' Jackson replied, keen to spin out his mother's outrage as far as possible.

'Daniella Bloody Clearwater! The Fascist Dictator!' Roy's voice joined Rebecca's, booming into the tiny roof space.

'Why mother, you sound so gruff … what a deep voice you have.' Jackson chortled.

'This takes the bloody biscuit, Jackson, it really does! I forbid you from liaising with nationalists, do you hear me? I could be banned from the golf club for this. Do you understand how serious that is? Your mother's bereft. This is lunacy too far, how bloody dare you?'

Jackson pictured his father, purple from the collarbone up. The thought delighted him.

'Settle, Dad, nobody at the golf club blurts. They've got a written petition on a clipboard to reverse the Gender Equality Act, for fuck's sake. I honestly don't think you're in any danger of being outed in the never-changing lawn-porn fantasy land of birdies and bogeys, you know?' Jackson picked his nose, half-listening to his mum while she rabbited on but paying significantly more attention to a surge in Blurt followers on his account. Jackson smiled, pleased life was balancing again.

'Jackson! Jackson, are you listening?' a higher pitch in Rebecca's voice tuned Jackson back in. 'Whatever you're up to, stop it immediately, do you hear? I'll have the Wi-Fi cut off if you don't start behaving, do you understand?'

Jackson rolled his eyes. His parents still hadn't understood that New Scotland had a free Wi-Fi cloud cover over the entire country; every time he tried to explain it Roy would interrupt with a rant about how the nationalists didn't control the weather. The time Jackson had spent in the slick ambience of the First Minister's world now held a mirror to Rebecca and Roy's reflections that Jackson hadn't seen before. How could they fail to be impressed by Clearwater? And how, by association, was there still an absence of even the tiniest smidgen of pride for Jackson himself? Their imperviousness began to irritate him intensely.

'Jesus, Mum, remember you said I should do something with my life? Yeah? Well, here it is. I'm doing something! It's something you don't like, yeah? Well, I don't like The Spice Girls, but you don't see me sabotaging your trips to see them every time they reunite, do you?' Jackson heard Rebecca gasp. 'And Dad, stop giving yourself a heart attack. You're always going on about wanting me to grow up, yeah? Well guess what? If I go on a trip for Daniella, I'm not going to be living in your garden while I'm doing that, am I? Isn't that what you want?'

Rebecca spluttered, Jackson's easy use of Daniella's name made her feel faint. She steadied herself on Roy's arm and remembered Jackson's most hurtful comment.

'What on earth do you mean *you don't like* The Spice Girls? When I put them on you were always the first to dance to "Spice Up Your Life"!'

'Mum, I was the first up to dance right out of the door of whatever room you were playing them in. They're fucking awful!'

'Jackson! Don't bloody swear at your mother!' Roy bellowed, triggering Duchy into a frenzied yapping at a stuffed Beaver lamp-base in the chalet hallway.

'Mum, Dad, Duchy … I've got to go,' Jackson cut in, thrilled by the chaos he had caused. 'I've got things to do, gotta keep my FM happy, innit?'

Rebecca cut in, 'Why?! *Why* have you got to go, Jackson? Are you going to her at Holyrood? Are you? Tonight? Is she molesting you?'

Jackson rolled onto his side, farted loudly, then hung up.

Rebecca's desperate eyes implored Roy at the chalet window as she spoke, 'What are we going to do?' Roy stood, hands on his hips, staring out at the mogul run and the fir trees flanking the mountainsides.

'We're going to do *nothing*, Ree-beh-kah, absolutely nothing at all, which is exactly what we should've done a bloody long time ago. That child is a car crash in slow motion. I wash my hands of him. He's a disaster.'

Rebecca collapsed back onto a leather sofa.

'We can't just stand back and watch him go further off the rails, Roy. He's our *son*, for God's sake.'

Roy watched with increasing revulsion as Duchy began mounting a goat-horn objet d'art next to the log basket.

'He's twenty-five, Ree-beh-kah,' Roy rolled his eyes, 'he should be finding a wife, buying shares, settling into the unfurling of the disappointment of proper adulthood.'

Rebecca flinched, an icy stab of hurt jolting her. She stared over at the little dog now working away at the ornament, inching ever closer to the flames of the fire with each thrust.

'Duchy! Stop it!' Rebecca yelled.

'Leave him,' Roy said coldly. He walked across the shagpile to the drinks cabinet. 'He doesn't listen to a bloody word we say either.'

13

Bored by being unable to get back to sleep at ten the following morning, Jackson decided to take a wander. He crunched down the driveway wearing his onesie, sunglasses, one croc and one welly and the bright sun felt good on his skin.

Templeton spotted him first and pushed to the front of the small press horde. The news was slow elsewhere so staying to capitalise on the excitement caused by Jackson's blurts was an easy gig. Templeton gabbled into his comms badge then tried to get Jackson's attention.

'I say! Jackson! Over here! Look! Shiny thing! That's right, Jackson, here I am! Tell us about where you're going and when Jackson! And where are your parents? What does Rabid Roy think about Jackson's Journey? He can't be too pleased about you fraternising with Clearwater. Have you recorded any good rants from him recently, Jackson? Tell us everything! I have a lifetime's supply of GBE jam for your mum if you'll give me the exclusive, what do you say, let me in, there's a good chap?'

Jackson stopped ten paces from the gates and fished a stone out from inside his croc.

'Woah, Templeton, man,' Jackson ambled closer as he spoke, 'I've just come down to say hi, I haven't even had a coffee yet, come on, you're like, way too much, know what I mean?'

Jackson noticed Gayle Wood appear at the back of the huge white NSBC truck with its enormous purple and green thistle logo across the street. She waved, checked both ways for traffic, then crossed. Jackson waved back, licking his lips as he stared at the coffee in Gayle's hand.

'Jackson, hi, Gayle Wood,' Gayle extended a hand over the gates and Jackson shook it. 'I'm with NSBC,' Gayle continued, 'listen, no one's been answering your buzzer. I've got a load of parcels for you in the truck, there've been a fair few deliveries. Merch, I guess, from the companies who want to kit you out for the journey? Anyway, they're safe and ready when you are.'

Gayle's handshake was strong, and, Jackson thought, she was more attractive in real life, up close. Jackson was wishing he'd changed into jeans or the least dirty of his three onesies when he noticed Gayle giving him a tight smile, her eyes crinkling slightly at the corners for a second, like his mum's used to. He felt like she'd read his mind and viscerally disapproved.

'We have good coffee, too.' Gayle added, then left.

With his usual up and over vault of the pillion post, Jackson landed on the pavement, the Croc flying from his foot in mid-air. Gayle had already begun crossing the road and Jackson called after her, hopping to catch up. When she didn't respond, he decided to go barefoot, kicking off the welly, too.

'Jackson! Your shoes!' Templeton shrieked. 'Are you feral, young man? Rabid, too, perhaps?'

Jackson glared at Templeton, frozen on hearing an echo of a word his father had spat into his ears when he had called him from the Holyrood meeting room.

'*You're* feral!' Jackson snapped, turning to Templeton. 'Hanging around out here, flapping about like a big tweed vulture.'

'Do you want to hit me, Jackson?' Templeton hissed, hopeful. 'Or perhaps you want to bite me, getting a bit foamy round the young Campbell chops? Chip off the old block, are we?'

Jackson glanced up at a rusty GBEBS drone hovering above Templeton, its camera lights blinking back at him, making him wince. He looked down at the older man again and as his eyes adjusted, he saw Roy for a second, in Templeton's place. A man full of anger and indignation. A man who was quick to fury, slow to kindness. Jackson struggled to remember what his father's face looked like when he laughed. Had he ever seen it?

'You're more like him than I am.' Jackson said.

Gayle pulled the door to the truck shut behind Jackson and gestured for him to sit on a large box. She poured coffee from a thermal carafe and handed Jackson a mug. All around her stood an array of cardboard boxes in different sizes, each with a label addressed to Jackson or to 'Jackson's Journey'.

'Here they are,' Gayle nodded, 'you're merched up for …

well… something you know more about than us, right? The mysterious journey. I take it you've been in touch with all these companies privately?'

'Nope,' Jackson replied, 'lots of folk just send me stuff 'cos of my Blurt following. I've got a PO box that redirects it all here. I wear it or use it, or whatever, they share my blurts about it, everyone's happy. Sometimes I sell stuff afterwards or give it away. Depends if my mum's moaning about me getting a job or not.' Jackson shrugged then took a long slurp from his mug. 'Jesus, this coffee's good.'

Gayle moved to lean back on a worktop, careful not to upset any of the tidily stacked recording equipment behind her.

'You sleep in here?' Jackson asked.

'Sometimes,' Gayle replied, 'not so different from a tiny home, huh?'

Jackson's eyes took in the control panels and equipment lining the walls of the section of the truck he could see. The rest of it, towards the driving cabin, was out of sight behind a narrow black curtain. A large leather swivel chair in front of a bank of screens turned and a young black man smiled up at Jackson, removing massive headphones so they hung about his neck. Jackson spluttered a little in surprise. He'd assumed Gayle, like himself, to be completely alone in her miniature quarters.

'Sorry, man,' Zach Scott, Gayle's colleague, said, 'didn't mean to give you a fright.'

Jackson removed his shades, setting them down on the box at his side and making Zach and Gayle gasp when they saw his bruises.

'Don't worry,' Jackson said, 'and no, it wasn't Roy. Tiny house injury. I've fixed it now – the house, I mean, I taped a pillow to the rafter so I couldn't headbutt it anymore.' Gayle and Zach stared, speechless. 'It's not sore,' Jackson explained as a blush formed on his cheeks.

'You need to get arnica on that, man.' Zach said.

'That's what Daniella Clearwater said,' Jackson was eager to change the subject. 'So, em, Gayle, is this your son?'

Gayle frowned, '*What*?'

'Your son?' Jackson repeated, 'Is he hanging here while you're working?'

'Um, this is my colleague,' Gayle replied, 'Zach Scott. Why on earth would you think he was my kid?' Jackson looked from Gayle to Zach.

'I don't know. Em, I guess because he looks my age, so I thought he was too young, or something, to be, like, working? And you're, like, older and that …,' Jackson flashed a grin at Zach, hoping he'd validate him. 'How old are you then, Zach?'

'Me?' Zach stifled a giggle. 'Twenty-six.'

'See?' Jackson said to Gayle. 'Kinda my age. Are you, like, an intern or something?'

'Um, I was,' Zach replied, 'four years ago. Straight up NSBC Production Assistant now. On track to be a co-ordinator in two years.'

'Oh. Right.' A pang of inadequacy toured Jackson's gut. He decided to change the subject. 'So, do you have kids, like, in the other bit Gayle, through there?'

'Wow,' Gayle laughed bitterly, 'I do have kids, Jackson, but they're with their father right now. Opportunity of a lifetime, apparently. He's taken them to New Zealand to see his new life. And his new wife, the whole shebang. They'll be home with me again once his time off is up, or when he's decided it's all too much effort again. Whichever comes first.'

Jackson raised his eyebrows, unsure how to respond other than to return the conversation to himself.

'My mum's in France,' he said, 'with my dad. He hates me. Like, *really*, hates me. They're not coming home till you lot are gone. I have no idea what I'm doing – with any of this,' Jackson gestured to the boxes, his mind filling with a familiar feeling of rejection. 'Or with anything, really. I think your kid's dad might be a prick if he's moved to New Zealand when you've still got kids to share. That's shit, like.'

Zach nodded. 'It is shit.'

Jackson dared to look back at Gayle. Her expression had softened.

'It is shit,' she replied. She poured them each another coffee. 'Thank you both for that. Luckily I have lots of work to keep me distracted from it.'

Jackson watched Zach give Gayle a small salute then copied him, making Gayle laugh. All of it was a welcome change from the confines of recent life in the tiny house. The sleek lines of the truck's interior were interspersed with digital displays, shelves brimming with gadgets and there were enticing panels of buttons and switches too. Zach's headphones were cool as well, Jackson thought, as was Gayle's directness. He wanted to stay, Jackson realised, to be part of it all, just like Zach.

'So, Jackson,' Gayle said, watching him carefully, 'I'm going to cut to it. Zach and I have sat here rather than in the office all week for two reasons. One, it's a nice view outside and we both hate hot desks, and two, we've been waiting to speak to you and find out if my hunch is right – that you'll be our next big project.'

'Me?' Jackson asked, confused. 'How?'

'Your journey?' Zach replied.

'I was interested in your blurt about going off to find Campbell land back on the day of the Unclearance ceremony,' Gayle explained. 'You caught my imagination. Clearly I wasn't the only one. We asked Bryce Cooper this morning if you had a media team in place now, through the government,' Gayle continued, 'he said you hadn't. So here we are. Pitching to assist you in what your blurt said you might do. Interested?'

Jackson was taken aback.

'I don't understand. What would you do?'

'Depends what the plan is,' Gayle shrugged. 'I checked the public database; your Campbell ancestors are from Eigg, right?'

Jackson nodded.

'And I'm assuming Clearwater wants to marry it with her Unclearance objectives? You go there to have your Braveheart moment and take your tiny house with you?'

'Sort of.' Jackson blinked away a mental image of Niall's face scowling at him as he thought of what Gayle didn't know, his plagiarism of Transpariboard. 'Not with my tiny blue house though, with a different one.'

'Right.' Gayle continued, 'Well, we're proposing that we come with you, film the whole thing, blurt and promo from all NSBC channels, report on the journey along the way; fly on the wall. Possibly license the idea of the documentary and sell it to other countries—an insight into New Scotland and Jackson Campbell. We discover you as you discover your history and make Clearwater's vision for the future come true. Social commentary.'

'Folk love it,' Zach chipped in, 'reality TV with an integrity mission. Honestly, it'd be huge. Bagpipes and heather and sunsets on the coast. I can see it now. Beautiful.'

Gayle smiled at Zach, then looked at Jackson, eyes narrowing a little.

'And I guess …,' she went on, 'from what you said about your dad just now, whatever's going on there, I sense you want to change the narrative on it?'

Jackson swallowed. Parasite, his father had called him. Lazy. Hyperactive. Feral. Do something with your life. The words passed in front of Jackson as if they were a chyron below Gayle's face.

'I mean Rabid Roy is literally so last year,' Jackson heard Gayle say. 'But, you know, maybe I'm picking that up wrong? Sometimes you still seem into it? Maybe you like all that Templeton crap, in a way?'

'Nah, not now. I used to,' Jackson's voice was quiet, 'and I do want to – what did you say? Change the thingy, on Rabid Roy. Stop the thingy, actually. But I legit don't know how. Like, I try. I do. Sometimes. But—'

'*We* know how,' Gayle said. 'It's our job, Jackson. Zach's and mine. We tell stories. We direct the focus. I'm not interested in your dad, to be brutally honest. Folk like him get enough attention, always have. I want new stories. Stories about change. Stories about where New Scotland's going, especially if other countries haven't been there already. Stories about reparations and how we don't repeat mistakes once we know we've made them, not more stories about a vortex of virtue-signalling or flat-out bitching and warmongering, like Templeton.'

Jackson watched Gayle's face light up as she talked. She was passionate, like Daniella Clearwater, but slightly scary, too. He wanted to hear more.

'There'll be a fee, obviously,' Gayle continued, 'it won't be huge, NSBC is almost not-for-profit, but, we could … I guess you could use the help with journey organisation too, right? Help make an inventory for the merch, and, uh, maximising your exposure, help you plan a route, deal with the logistics. It's a simple concept, but there are complex things to consider too, right?'

Gayle and Zach watched Jackson wiggle his toes and tip the last of his coffee back. He pulled his feet up beside his bum so he sat, ape-like on the box, making a steeple shape with his hands, thinking hard, frown lines coming and going. At last, he spoke.

'The fee might be a problem,' he said, 'but I can give the first 400 euros today if you like, and—'

'No!' Gayle interrupted, 'Jackson, we pay *you*, you don't pay us! Well, NSBC pays you – and me and Zach.'

'Oh,' Jackson said, 'really?' Gayle nodded. 'And do you think, honestly, like, you could make me look, well … nice and, like, show another side of me? Show I'm making something of my life, that I'm not lazy?'

There was a deep sadness about him, Gayle observed; a private grief she would be devastated by if she saw it in the face of one of her children.

'Sure, Jackson. What you're talking about is 100 per cent on brand for NSBC. My speciality. It's a chance to tell a story about growth rather than fear. It'd be an honest story – warts and all – but more than anything, a story about change, humanity and realness and how that connects with New Scotland's impact.'

Jackson listened intently, his eyes growing wider.

'But you'd need to tell us the full thing, Jackson,' Gayle continued. 'You'd have to open up, bare all, share the plans, everything. Because we'd be a team?'

'Does that mean you'd come with me?' Jackson asked, a huge surge of excitement bubbling through him. 'On the journey, the whole way, to the meetings at Holyrood and everything? You'll help me?'

'Everything,' Gayle said, 'as long as we have exclusivity and I can tell Templeton and Co to hop it, today. Maybe your parents would even feel OK about returning then? We could move your tiny house to the NSBC studios if that'd make them more comfortable about you working with us. We'd be totally out of their hair.'

As Gayle spoke Jackson pictured himself as a huge nit, jumping free of Roy's thinning silver-black spikes. Zach grinned up at Jackson, giving him an encouraging thumbs-up. Gayle extended her hand, ready to shake. Jackson grinned, then grabbed it.

/MichaelTempletonGBEBS/blurts/
BREAKING: #RABIDROY'S BOY SAYS 'IT'S ALL TOO MUCH!' HINTS

AT COLLAPSE OF CLEARWATER'S NEXT PLANS FOR NEW SCOT-
LAND. BEGINNING OF THE END? Obviously!

/MichaelTempletonGBEBS/blurts/

#RABIDROY'S BOY HAS GONE MAD. NEAR NAKED ON STREET.
SO MUCH FOR CLEARWATER'S MENTAL HEALTH POLICIES! THIS
PLACE IS FULL OF NUTTERS! #NEWSCOTLANDFAILS #JACKSONS-
JOURNEY #GBESUCCESS #REUNITETHEKINGDOM #ROYALBABIES

14

Niall's eyes were shut as he conjured the image of his mum getting on the Megabus as she left for Great British England. He remembered the yeasty smell from the Edinburgh breweries wafting through the air between them. She'd stood on the first step of the bus, her feet already leaving him, every part of her but her face angled away as she blew a big gum bubble, let it snap, before reeling the gum back into her mouth with her tongue, then had looked Niall up and down one last time before puckering her lips into an air-kiss. A second later she'd stepped into the bus's darkened aisle.

The feeling of abandonment swirled behind his sternum. Claudia, one of the recovery centre's senior therapists, prompted Niall for more with her honeyed Canadian accent.

'Keeping your eyes closed, mentally place the image memory of your mum onto a big piece of paper; an A3 piece, say. Do you understand, Niall?' Niall nodded, briefly spreading his fingers. 'Good, Niall.' Claudia continued, 'I see you reprogramming those responses. Well done. Now make that sheet of paper smaller, all right? Make it half the size. Fold it down the middle. Can you do it, Niall?' Niall folded the image of his mum in his mind's eye and nodded. Then the image sprung back open, making him frown. He watched his mother's foot leave the tarmac and rise onto the Megabus step again and shook his head vigorously. He folded the image again, imagining it glued shut along the edges this time. Again, it sprung back open. His mother's disenchanted glance ran over the length of him again, apparently not finding anything pleasing.

'It's back. It opened again. I can't keep it folded.'

Niall heard Claudia's pen on her clipboard as she made notes. He imagined what she was writing – probably that he was beyond repair. Or that he was so thick his brain couldn't do the simplest thing.

'I'm going to count you back now, Niall,' Claudia said. 'It's perfectly fine that the image popped open again. All is well. Now we have more information and that means we have progress. You're bright. Very bright. And very traumatised. So, your conscious mind is resisting. Well done on a fantastic effort. And five, your eyes are lighter, ready to receive the light of the room. Four, your limbs feel wakeful, bright, ready …'

Niall played along with being counted back, keeping his eyes shut till Claudia reached zero. He found Claudia out of her chair and standing behind her desk, her hands holding up two highly patterned boxes of tea bags.

'Borage and wood sorrel or chamomile and viola?' Claudia smiled expectantly.

'Just water, please.' Niall replied, utterly sick of the disappointment of recovery centre teas which smelled great but tasted how he imagined wrung-out fluid from dishcloths would.

'Mint?' Claudia was undeterred. 'Wonderful for the digestion. I don't think you've tried my mint yet. Try a mint, Niall, it rarely fails.'

'Fine,' Niall smiled tightly. He crossed his arms and legs as Claudia flicked the kettle on. When the drinks were ready, Claudia placed Niall's on a small cork coaster on the table at the side of his chair then rearranged the papers on her clipboard before handing it to him before sitting down.

'That's your treatment plan, Niall, all right?' she said, watching Niall scan the information before him. 'Your initial assessment period with us is over, and today's exercise, and your recent cortisol, serotonin and nutritional test results consolidate our team observations. As you can see, we're suggesting several continuing interventions, an anti-depressant medication, MDMA therapy, continued group work for renewing processing pathways and continued solo sessions for solution-focused perspectives. Fortnightly B12 injections, too. All of this, we feel certain, will enable you to move forward positively. It's a biopsychosocial approach. This is a great plan, Niall, I promise.'

'Why is the chemical stuff all underlined in red?' Niall asked, staring at the list.

'Because it's urgent,' Claudia replied. 'Your biochemical profile is telling us very clearly the neurotransmitters you need to be happy and well, are, right now, unable to repair themselves. To put it simply, even if you won EuroMillions tonight, after an initial burst of elation you'd probably return to depression tomorrow. Your battery's run too low, Niall. You need a top-up. A reset. It may be that you'll always need help to keep those levels up. Or it may be that this top-up is enough and your body will take over once you stabilise. We can't predict how that'll look until we gather the data over the year ahead.'

'Am I going to be in here for a year?' Niall asked, panic flashing in his eyes.

'Highly unlikely,' Claudia shrugged, 'but your work on your mental health doesn't stop in sync with your stay here ending, all right? We will collect data with you about your health for as long as you'd like us to, and we can have future consultations online. That way you get ongoing specialist care outside of the centre and together we recalibrate medicines and therapies, if necessary. Understand?'

Niall tried to imagine feeling better – happy, even. What was that like? Had it ever really happened for him? A memory of laughing with Hanna at university popped up. Had he meant that laughter or had he been faking it? He waited for an answer but nothing came. He lifted his mug and blew across the minty steam, then sipped.

'How's that?' Claudia asked, her eyes bright.

'Good, thanks,' Niall lied, sitting the mug down again, 'so when do I start on the drugs?'

'As soon as you'd like,' Claudia replied, 'but not before we've addressed any questions you have about them – and about the entire plan. These are our suggestions, remember, and they're well informed. But this is your body, your life. You're in control. If you hate this plan or feel strongly even about one part of it being wrong for you, we can change it. There's no heavy-handedness, all right? No coercion or pressure. You have agency – completely.'

'Will I get worse before I get better?' Niall asked, 'I've heard heaps of folk get that.'

'It is a possibility,' Claudia replied, 'particularly for people like you whose levels have become so badly depleted. It could be a real rollercoaster. But it may also go extremely smoothly. We'll be with you every step of the way, monitoring you daily, either way. This is where the MDMA therapy can come into its own – where folk are particularly resistant to a reset, we can speed progress, hack into it if you will. That's not something that can truly happen outside of licensed centres. Not yet anyway.' Claudia took a long sip of her tea, mystifying Niall with how she genuinely appeared to be enjoying it. 'It is possible you'll sail through it, Niall,' Claudia continued, 'maybe the worst will be a little uptake nausea, easily treatable with a touch different nutrition. It happens more often like that.'

Niall looked at the clipboard again, willing himself to feel something.

'It won't happen like that with me,' he stood and held the clipboard out to Claudia, 'I can guarantee that. I'm a disaster, really.'

'You most certainly are not.' Claudia frowned, then rose and took the clipboard back. Niall let go of it with one hand but held on with the other.

'Can I see what you wrote when I was hypnotised? I heard you writing when I couldn't fold the paper.'

'Of course,' Claudia nodded and backed away to lean on her desk. 'Page four. The session notes are there.'

Blood swooshed in Niall's ears. He was about to be confronted with an awful truth. Why had he asked for it, he wondered, why on earth would he wilfully request something that was going to hurt so badly? His fingers flipped the sheets of paper to page four. Claudia's handwriting was an artwork of curls and extravagant strikes in teal fine-liner crammed into a black box entitled 'Observations'. Niall squinted as he made out the words:

Lovely young man. Truly. Trying very hard but remains resistant to hypnosis. Suspect hypervigilant due to current biochemical profile. Desire to please/freeze in 1:1 setting is high e.g. does not report hypnosis isn't working. Struggles enormously to express honest preferences and also to trust that inconsequential & more significant truths will not yield punishing consequences. Learned suppression behaviour from dysfunctional parent relationships? Seems likely. Discuss compliance vs assertiveness with Fin for group & individual work.

Embarrassment broke Niall's numbness and coloured his cheeks.

'OK?' Claudia frowned.

'I don't know,' Niall whispered. 'I think so. God, I'm a pathetic arsehole, amn't I?'

'Not at all,' Claudia said, 'that's some very dark self-talk right there, Niall. In lay terms we might do better to say something like you have issues with people-pleasing. Less so in group though, I hear, which is great.'

Niall blushed again.

'Niall, we're human,' Claudia continued, 'it's an imperfect experience. We travel a spectrum of emotions and reactions most days. The needle readings on that change much more frequently when we're ill. It's hard. And it's also fixable.'

'Shall I go now?' Niall asked, 'I've got group soon.'

'Finish your tea first?' Claudia nodded at Niall's mug. Niall looked up at her and considered necking the mug, down in one. Quick and painful. Claudia would be pleased with that, he was sure.

'I don't like herbal teas,' Niall said. He watched Claudia as the words tentatively left him and wondered when her face would turn to anger or resentment.

'Good that you told me,' Claudia replied, 'all progress is powerful, isn't it?'

Niall stared at his trainers. Inside his left sock, the red, angry area of athlete's foot between two of his toes stung as he sweated. He looked up at Claudia again and saw her smiling at him. She looked peaceful, Niall thought, the way someone might look if the person they were with was not too much bother, not too much anything. How strange.

15

The huge NSBC truck now sat at the top of the Campbells' drive, its rear door facing Jackson's tiny house door with a few metres of gravel between. It had been Gayle's idea to unpack the boxes into the triple garage which stood nearby, at the top of the driveway.

'How will we get in though?' Jackson asked, absentmindedly scratching his groin through his onesie.

'Have you tried the doors? Are they locked?' Gayle tried the nearest handle. The door began tilting open.

'Jesus, I didn't know you could do that without a pleeper,' Jackson exclaimed.

'A pleeper?' Zach looked baffled.

'Yeah – a key you press and it goes "pleep",' Jackson replied, distracted now with trying the other garage doors and finding they opened too.

The triple garage was about half full, most of its contents stacked neatly against the walls on large metal shelving units. Only a third of the floor space was used up by larger items covered in dust sheets. Gayle spotted the feet of an antique mahogany dining set standing on the grey carpet-tiled floor. Between the table and a garage door stood three of Roy's older golf bags on wheeled caddy stands. The covered heads of golf clubs protruded in different shades of burgundy and bottle-green velveteen and leather.

'Don't your parents lock this?' Gayle asked. 'Big haul here for burglars.'

Jackson shrugged.

'Dunno. I mean, I thought it was locked. I don't think they worry about stuff like this, it's just old. My mum gets the charity folk to come sometimes and clear things out that she's put in here from the loft, or whatever. My Dad keeps his best clubs in his study. He's got a hole in the floor in there for practising his putting, sad bastard. I bet I know the alarm code though.' Jackson indicated a panel on the wall beside an array of light switches, a fuse box and a motorised door control panel. 'It'll be two, zero, zero-seven, nine-six. The date of the Spice Girls' first number one.'

Zach winced.

'You don't have to give us the code, man, like, it's private, isn't it?'

Jackson shrugged again, nonchalant.

'Fan of the Spice Girls, are you?' Gayle tried to keep a straight face.

'No. I hate them. My mum loves them. Girl Power, innit?' Jackson made a peace sign with his right hand and pouted, cod-like. Gayle and Zach laughed.

'If we put some flattened boxes on the table to protect it that could be a really good workspace, couldn't it?' Gayle said. 'And you're sure your parents are OK with us being here, Jackson? They're not going to rock up and evict us, or want to park out there?'

'They're fine with it,' Jackson lied, sure in the knowledge his mum was watching his every move on Blurt and would keep Roy away for as long as any press at all remained. 'They never park in here anyway,' he continued, truthful this time. 'Dad's big Merc's too big to get under the door and Mum hates reversing. She can't look over her shoulder properly since her last facelift.'

Gayle and Zach flashed a glance at each other.

'And we'll use the alarm code to lock up,' Zach added, 'you can do that with this control panel, from inside the garage. Keep everything safe, for them, and our cameras and your stuff too, Jackson.' Zach took a few steps towards the back of the garage, 'I'll mostly film from here, and if we keep a path clear round the outside of the merch and over to the table, I can walk with the camera too, OK?'

Gayle gave a thumbs-up.

'Yes, great, much better than trying to do it all in the truck. Let's start getting boxes in.'

'Is this a good time for me to go for a nap then?' Jackson asked, yawning and stretching so his fingers almost touched one of the strip lights hanging from the rafters. 'I didn't get my lie in today, so …'

Gayle glared at Jackson.

'Peanut energy bar?' Zach asked, waving a snack from his chest pocket in Jackson's direction.

Jackson looked from Gayle to Zach as he took the snack. Zach's eyes bulged at him, flickering briefly in Gayle's direction.

'Jackson, when's the next meeting with Clearwater?' Gayle's voice was terse.

Jackson watched as she wrapped a scarlet ribbon hanging from the truck keys back and forth around a fingertip, reminding him of a tiny noose.

'Thursday,' Jackson replied.

'So, from tomorrow, we only have five days to get you and us organised, inventory this merch, plan your journey in out-line form and do a load of research into logistics, history, routes, weather, everything, really, so we can start to shape the narrative into something you're happy with?'

Jackson swallowed.

'Or would you prefer to fly by the seat of your pants?' Gayle shrugged. 'Shut it all down till the meeting, see us at Holyrood then let Clearwater dictate the whole thing, running the risk of the journey coming across like a *Blue Peter* spin-off series where you recite poetry to a windmill here and there and me and Zach pull out 'cos that's not our aesthetic at all?' Jackson shook his head. 'Do you see what I'm getting at, Jackson?' Gayle asked. 'If

you're doing this with us it means work, remember? *Teamwork.*
No naps for you, while Zach and I graft.'

Jackson stared down at the carpet tiles, his fingers gripping the
energy bar so tightly it began to disintegrate within the wrapper.

'No, no, of course,' he managed. 'I don't want yous to go, I
want to do it as a team. Sorry, like, I just … as soon as I see my
tiny house I just think of lying down. It's not that easy to stand up
in a lot when you're me, see? It's kind of conditioned me, I think.'

Gayle frowned.

'Well, maybe decondition yourself? Sleep in here if it helps.
I'm not your parent, Jackson, Zach and I aren't going to keep
reminding you of how to be an adult, you do get that, don't you?
You must at least match our effort, if not exceed it?'

Jackson nodded vigorously, turning and briskly making to the
truck. Inside, he piled smaller boxes on top of the big one he'd
sat on previously. When he stepped, laden, back into the doorway
Gayle and Zach were waiting at the bottom of the steps.

'Careful.' Zach smiled, holding a hand out in case Jackson
needed help.

'Thanks, man.' Jackson felt relieved Zach appeared not to hate
him.

'After we've unloaded, can you talk us through your dissertation, Jackson?' Gayle asked. 'We'll order food and you can hook
your laptop up to our projector. The back of one of the garage
doors will work for a screen surface, won't it Zach?' Zach nodded.
'We'll need to know everything Clearwater knows already,' Gayle
continued, 'and you can give us notes on what was discussed at
the meeting too?'

'Yip,' Jackson replied, head craning to see round the boxes as
he set off towards the garage, 'no problem.'

A thought of Niall tugged at Jackson's conscience as he bent
then dropped the boxes where Zach had said they should go.
Gayle's footsteps were crunching on the gravel as Zach passed
boxes to her from the truck. Jackson cast a quick glance around
the garage walls, reminders of his parents staring back at him.
His eyes caught on a fat strap of diamanté and baby-pink leather
hanging over the shrouded shoulder of a dining chair – Rebecca's long-abandoned golf bag. His mum had tried to partner Roy
on the course when he'd first retired, Jackson remembered. Then

she'd given up after a string of arguments with the club captain about suitable golfing attire. The entire episode had mortified Roy.

'This is my chance,' Jackson whispered to himself, '*I'm* not giving up.'

'Good,' Gayle replied. She placed three smaller boxes next to Jackson's pile. 'That's the spirit. Come on, the rest are smaller and lighter. Zach will chuck to me, I'll chuck to you, you stick them here, OK?'

Jackson followed Gayle back under the doors, glad her disapproval seemed to have dissipated.

'Is anyone else involved so far?' Gayle asked as they walked. 'Who else was at the meeting with the FM?'

'Drew McAllister,' Jackson replied, 'my EHA guy, he's one of my professors.'

'Oh, yeah, I've written about him before. Cool.' Gayle nodded, 'Is that it?'

'They're inviting another girl from my course to the next meeting. Hanna. They want her to do some of the detailed design for the tiny house.'

'They're modifying your house?' Zach asked. 'What's wrong with it? It looks perfect.'

'No,' Jackson replied, 'I've designed a new house – Daniella Clearwater wants me to take the new one on the journey – not that one.'

'Oh,' Zach replied, 'wow.'

'Wow, indeed,' Gayle added, intrigued. 'I'm going to need the other designer's details, in that case. Ideally, we get a video call in with her tomorrow, see what she's thinking, make sure we're as up to speed as possible, and share whatever we need to before we meet Clearwater. I know what the FM's diary's like – back-to-back. Bryce Cooper can have her whirling away before you cover everything you need to, in my experience. We have to be as prepped as possible for when we get her in front of us.'

'What does everyone fancy for dinner?' Zach asked, passing one of the final boxes to Gayle.

'I could eat ramen?' Gayle replied, tossing the box to Jackson.

'Good shout,' Zach answered, 'you good with that, Jackson?'

'Yeah, cool,' Jackson replied, an uncomfortable image of Hanna's face reading his dissertation appearing in his thoughts. Would she instantly recognise something of Niall's in the plans, he wondered. 'You two choose,' Jackson tried to sound carefree, 'I'll go along with anything.'

16

'I want to go home now.'

Roy announced the following day after disembarking the ski lift and arriving at Rebecca's side.

Whilst waiting, Rebecca had caught up on Blurt and now stood adjusting her Louis Vuitton ski goggles so her fringe sat perfectly between them and the brow of her Hermès bobble hat.

'We'll go after this run,' Rebecca answered. 'Duchy will be fine for another hour. If we're quick, we'll have time for a little cocktail at the bar before we go back for lunch.'

'I mean home to Edinburgh.' Roy pushed his poles resolutely into the snow.

'Oh,' Rebecca flashed a brief sympathetic smile, 'no, you don't want that, Roy, I promise you.' Rebecca pushed off.

'Actually, I bloody *do*!' Roy shouted, struggling to dislodge his poles before following. 'I'm bored. There's no driving range. My swing's being affected by too much skiing. I'm sick of the mountains. I'm sick of picking snowballs off Duchy's legs after every walk. I'm sick of the bloody EU putting subtitles on everything from America and GBE when I try to watch telly. I'm sick of the French. There, I said it.'

Rebecca skied on, starting the first downhill section, trying to get far enough away to drown out Roy's whinging. However, private tuition sessions in the last week had already greatly improved Roy's technique and he caught up quickly.

'Well, I fancy the entire summer here,' Rebecca called back, affecting a throwaway lightness. 'Maybe Christmas too, Joyeux Noel, et cetera. Let Jackson go through his little phase, then return home and say no more of it. Much wiser.'

Roy's lips pursed into a small purple anus.

'And Duchy likes the quality time when you thaw his little legs out,' Rebecca continued, determined to flatter her husband back into compliance. '*And* your skin looks radiant, darling. I don't know *why* you want to rush back; it's probably been raining the whole time in Edinburgh. The golf pitch will be waterlogged. You're better off here – go to the little driving range, the VR thing, you'll love it.'

'It's a *course*, Rebecca, not a pitch,' Roy spat, 'and I don't want to play computer games; I want real-life games! And we can't bloody ski all summer. The snow will be completely gone soon. They're carting stuff down from the tops every morning as it is.'

'Well, then we'll go walking.' Rebecca was undeterred. 'We'll walk to the peaks. We'll take Duchy. It'll be marvellous, we'll be so fit!'

'But I don't want to walk!' Roy barked, 'I want to bloody golf, woman!'

Rebecca snowploughed to a stop, planting her poles with indignant vigour.

'And what about me, Roy, hmm? What about what I want? What about my health? Hmmm—?'

Roy let out a menacing laugh as he slowed.

'Don't even think about it!' he snapped. 'You only bring your health up when I mention Jackson or home. I'm watching you. You bloody *knew* he was plotting something. I said it and you denied it. I won't fall for it again! It's my bloody home, bought with my family money. I have more right to be there than him. I'm not bloody dead yet!'

'Oh, I see!' Rebecca shrieked as Roy took off, fast picking up speed. 'I see! I take you out here, reduce your blood pressure, wean you from your tablet addiction, get you a lovely tan, book tables at all your favourite places for dinner, save you from yourself with that horrific Templeton man, and this is what I get, is it?' Rebecca was struggling to keep up now, so she shouted louder.

'Reduced to some *woman* who lives in your house, am I? And Jackson, a guest of yours, too, is he?' Rebecca's cheeks coloured as she caught up behind Roy, both slaloming furiously, 'He hasn't asked for a cent from us since we left! Not one cent … but yes, I'm the villain here, attempting to get you a relationship with your son. Oh, absolutely, *I'm* awful!'

Roy veered to the edge of the run, braking with a spray of snow at his side as he stared at his wife, his face curdled to confusion. Rebecca sensed the change and executed a perfect skid-stop of her own.

'Did you just say Jackson *hasn't* asked for money since we left?' Roy asked, pushing his goggles onto his forehead.

'Yes,' Rebecca answered, eyeing Roy up and down, 'I did say that. Glad you heard me since you were so determined to get away.'

Roy was flabbergasted.

'How much money did you leave him, Ree-beh-kah?'

'Just 400 euros,' Rebecca snapped, 'I only thought we'd be gone a few nights.'

So far, Roy realised, their resort services bill for nightly trips to his favourite restaurants was several times that amount.

'Have you sent him some other type of currency?' Roy knew if he didn't pose questions carefully his wife would lie effortlessly by omission.

'No,' Rebecca frowned, 'no other money in any currency. Wait. Do you think Clearwater's giving him money?'

'More likely she's found a way to steal it from us, via him, the idiot.' Roy shook his head.

'Well, you'd know,' Rebecca said, 'you check the accounts every morning, don't you?'

Roy nodded.

'Nothing is missing. There couldn't be anyway. Jackson has absolutely no access to any of our accounts. Neither of us can allow him that without sign off from the other, as you very well know.'

'Well, there you go.' Rebecca pulled off her Stella McCartney mittens to check her manicure. 'Why on earth are you throwing horrible accusations around then? You two are as bad as each other at times.'

Rebecca looked up and stared at her husband, issuing the direct challenge of a rare truth.

'Well, maybe it is good if he buggers off on his journey,' Roy said. 'Better on Clearwater's buck than mine, that's for sure. How long till he goes?'

'Our buck, thank you, not *yours,*' Rebecca corrected. 'And I don't know when he goes. But it's not imminent. Not this week anyway, by the sounds of it.' Rebecca looked at the mountains behind Roy and remembered the first time she'd seen them, just a year before Jackson was born. She and Roy had only put their skis on once on that trip; the rest of the time had been spent indoors, mostly nude and almost constantly smiling. Even though they were only a little over an hour away, she felt very far from home. Loneliness had crept into her marriage somewhere along the years and moments like this held it aloft, cold and undeniable, and no Jackson to distract from it. Who was looking after her baby? Behind her silicone implants, her breast tissue swelled. But damnit, Rebecca thought, they couldn't go back now if she was to preserve any hope for Roy and Jackson's relationship.

She'd gathered from Templeton's blurts that he was now staging a Make England Great Again protest at Holyrood, something he did regularly. His continuing presence in Edinburgh meant he could be back at the Campbell gates at any time, too. And then there was the fact that Jackson's blurts showing pictures of NSBC's Gayle Wood camping in their driveway were making her feel lightheaded. If she could just keep Roy distracted until Jackson disappeared on his stupid journey, she thought, all would be well, even if it meant her blood pressure rocketing meantime.

'Well …,' Roy said, 'I do feel *well*. You might have a small point about being here rather than there. And if we're saving money by not being drained by Jackson for once, well …'

Rebecca watched Roy's face. It saddened her that his change of heart had come via the news about saved euros they could well afford to spend rather than for genuine affection for her or their son.

'You look pale, Becs,' Roy frowned, 'are you all right?'

'You called me Becs,' Rebecca whispered, startled.

Roy placed a hand on Rebecca's elbow.

'I did, didn't I? Well. Is it your head?'

Rebecca observed that Roy was more handsome with a bit of colour on his t-zone.

'Maybe just a little tired,' Rebecca replied. 'It's all the stress. It's bad for me. For all of us. And not just because of wrinkles.'

Roy's gaze fell to his boots.

'Sorry,' he muttered.

'Your stop was perfect, very James Bond.'

Roy looked up, blushing and pleased.

'Race to the bottom?' he asked, wiggling a hairy eyebrow suggestively before pulling his goggles back into place.

Rebecca giggled and pulled her mittens back on.

'You're on!' she squealed. 'To the bottom! First one there books the private tuition and hot-stone massages for a fortnight!'

17

Hanna Nowak was hungover from a night of impromptu clubbing with school friends who'd walked in on her pub shift the previous evening. She sat up in bed and looked at the notes and doodles she'd made in her small sketchbook while talking to Drew McAllister on the phone the day before.

'Working with Jackson?!' she'd written, then she'd swapped from her 4B pencil to a black Sharpie and written 'EUROS??? Pay???' in the centre of the page, with a small line extending from it to the words, 'some to Mum'.

'I'm surprised this isn't a no-brainer for you,' Drew had said following Hanna's silence when he'd outlined his meeting with Jackson and Daniella. 'Think of the exposure, the contacts, it's a bloody dream situation, Hanna, so it is.'

'I know,' Hanna had agreed, 'but working with *Jackson Campbell*? Like, not all of us want that energy or twenty-four-seven level of attention, do we? Going to uni with someone like that's been intense at times. His house idea sounds good and all, and his trans-board stuff, but, like, do I want to get on his crazy train? The guy doesn't do privacy, and if he fucks … I mean, if he screws up, do I sink with him? Like, it could be great, but it could also be awful, couldn't it? Depending how he behaves.'

'You're overthinking,' Drew had countered. 'I promise you. No publicity is bad publicity when it comes to actual design experience. And, yes, he can be a muppet, and he's high maintenance, but you know what, Hanna? You should be blatant about using the opportunity to your advantage. This is potentially a once-in-a-lifetime experience. And you'll always have a glowing reference from me. So, what do you have to lose?'

The blaring of her youngest sister's favourite show's theme tune from the TV in the living room had broken Hanna's concentration. She could handle losing that, she'd thought.

'Don't think about it for too long, Hanna,' Drew had urged, 'First Minister's moving fast. Really, what have you got to lose?'

By the time she'd hung up, Hanna had added 'nothing to lose?' to her sketchbook, and beside it, a small stick drawing of herself from which emerged a thought bubble: 'something to do till Niall gets better?'

Now, hours later and with a dull headache starting, Hanna reached for an aspirin packet in her make-up bag and reflected on her doodlings again. She knocked back three tablets with a glug of water then tapped her touch screen. A message from Jackson appeared in her notifications.

> Hi! Drew said he'd spoken to you but you're not sure if you want to get involved. I have signed up with NSBC so they can livestream the whole thing and, like, handle all the stuff I'm crap at ;-) Gayle Wood (!) is asking if we can do a video call with you. I've attached the plans and stuff here for the tiny house/Transpariboard so you can have a look. Let me know what you think about speaking to Gayle?
>
> See ya! J ☺

Hanna tapped open the documents and skimmed over Jackson's plans. To her surprise, she was immediately absorbed in what she saw. Her heart quickened as she spun an image of a clear tiny house on her screen. Good design was Hanna's first love, she often joked, though she wasn't embarrassed by its truth. She sat up and messaged back.

> OK. Video call? What time?

To Hanna's surprise, Jackson replied immediately.

> ACE! 7 pm?

Hanna tapped a confirmation then attempted to forward the files to Niall, but when she tried to select his name from her contacts, it was ghosted out, made inaccessible by Niall or the rehab centre's choice. The oddness of it made her feel abruptly untethered. She took a sip of water and looked back at Jackson's work, honing in on notes about Transpariboard. A memory of being alone with Niall in the uni archive a few months before flashed; they'd been trying and failing to juggle three vintage plastic Coke bottles. Niall had stopped abruptly and the two bottles he'd been holding had dropped to the vinyl floor, bounced a little, then rocked by his feet before stopping.

'What?' Hanna had asked, watching Niall's eyes sparkle. Hanna knew something interesting was happening behind them, but he'd given nothing away.

'Processing,' he'd whispered, then picked up the bottles and stared hard at them.

Hanna felt intangible doubt rise about Jackson again. She added an addendum to her last message.

> not committing to anything apart from a chat tonight to find out more – 7 pm sounds good.

She hit send, then flicked through her photos to find the most recent ones she'd taken with Niall.

'What do you think, Ny?' Hanna asked her screen. 'Would you, if you were me?'

Niall's mute face smiled back. What he might say wasn't as clear to her now as it once had been. Depression fragmented people, Hanna knew. Sometimes they'd say something they meant, while other times, they'd sound definite about something unexpected, swearing they meant it with every fibre of their being, then swerving away from it mere hours later.

Hanna called up photos from a couple of summers before when she and Niall had gone to a festival in Perth. They'd laughed so much her jaw had ached for days afterwards. She found a video of Niall in a crowd, looking up to a DJ on an unseen stage. That was the real Niall, Hanna knew. Could she work with Jackson and take one for the team, she wondered? See if she could get contacts for her *and* Niall? She pressed play on the video and smirked as Niall bounced, his fist punching the air in time to beat-heavy techno.

'Yessssss!' Niall yelled, his energy infectious, 'Come on!'

Hanna laughed as she turned the volume down. The aspirin kicked in on one side of her head but not the other. Patience, she thought, and probably less vodka in future, too. And nothing to lose indeed.

18

The following evening Jackson, Gayle and Zach each sat in branded camping chairs, staring at the back of the garage door they'd set up as a projector screen. Jackson and Zach ate noodles from takeaway cartons while Gayle finished an apple, dropping the core into an empty NSBC mug in her armrest's cup holder then covering a yawn. At Jackson's side he'd positioned one of his MacBooks on a camping table. On its screen, Hanna could be seen sitting cross-legged in jogging bottoms and a vest on her bedroom carpet. She'd muted herself while she ate a large bowl of cereal. Her hair was pulled into a bun with two pencils jutting out and design books and sketches littered the floor around her.

The Campbell garage had taken on a distinct feel of a hybrid of an outdoor pursuits company's stockroom and an army field HQ. Gayle had taped an Ordnance Survey map of New Scotland to one of the garage's gable walls. A large ring had been Sharpied around Edinburgh and another around Eigg. In the North Sea, Gayle had stuck a Post-It note with the words 'EIGG – 30.49KM2 vs EDINBURGH – 264KM2'. Underneath that, directly onto the sea, Jackson had scrawled 'YOU CAN FIT 8.7 EIGGS INTO EDINBURGH', then drawn eight and a half huge eggs with smiley faces beside his intel. Sharpie routes in green and red each marked what Zach had understood as the two most viable routes for the journey. He'd written '332K?' in red on one Post-It note above Ireland and in green on another Post-It '349K?'.

The 7 p.m. meeting the night before had gone well. Jackson had been silently relieved to hear no challenges from Hanna about Transpariboard being his work. He'd gone to bed feeling philosophical and excited afterwards, telling himself the same thing his mum said when confronted in a designer shop by an eye-catching handbag: whatever happened next was fate, outside of her control, the work of a higher power.

On hearing more from Hanna about her placement experience in designing eco-friendly vehicles, Gayle and Zach were impressed. Jackson had also appeared to swiftly recognise the boon to team competency Hanna provided by suggesting she take the lead on simplifying the house design, allowing him to concentrate on keeping his presence buoyant on Blurt. The suggestion suited Hanna well; it gave her the clear delineation between Jackson's work and her own that felt critical for her CV, and she felt relieved to know it was now dealt with without any awkwardness.

Hanna un-muted her comms and gave a thumbs-up when Gayle asked if they all wanted to watch a YouTube video about Eigg. The four of them sat transfixed by the story of the island's historic chaotic transition out of feudalism, culminating in a people-power buyout to community ownership in 1997. Since then, they learned, Eigg's community had blossomed every year; the island now sported everything from a hydro-electric scheme to a micro-brewery, adventure centre, gin distillery, wicker-weaving studios, several organic farms and crofts and music festivals.

'I had no idea,' Zach said when the titles rolled. 'Helluva place to call your genetic home, Jackson. They're like, so bohemian and cool but, like, sustainability gurus, too. Mad.'

'Tell me about it,' Jackson agreed, 'they were the first community to be completely sustainable for electricity in the former UK, did yous hear that bit?'

'I remember my parents talking about it,' Gayle said. 'They went out there once, maybe even to the buyout party. It was a big deal at the time. The islanders basically stuck a keystone in for Scottish independence; showed that little places can do big things. *And* that the old system really, really sucked for Highlanders, by comparison.'

Hanna sent an image to the group chat. They all looked at a farmhouse with cheery-red window frames and a wide track running along the hillside behind it towards to a windfarm.

'There are the wind turbines,' Hanna said, 'so we'd follow that same track to Grulin then, yeah? Then there's nothing else in terms of development? No proper roads or buildings, yeah?'

Gayle nodded.

'Grulin's split into two; Upper and Lower. The track passes through Upper Grulin first, then onwards to where Jackson's descendants lived – Lower Grulin. I can't find much footage online about anything after the wind farms so far though. Just the odd photo of ruined houses.' Gayle frowned, 'I'm guessing vehicle access to the Grulins is bad, if not impossible. There are a few videos from drones, but they tend to focus on the peak or the coastline. I'd like to see more of what's between them too. We'll need to look into it some more. See what's possible with NSBC satellite imagery tomorrow, maybe.'

'I've got an image and info here that says there's a well-worn foot and sheep track to Upper then Lower Grulin,' Zach said. 'I'll post it. If you zoom right in you can see it, I make it about a metre, at the widest. Half a metre mostly though.'

'Tight,' Hanna frowned, 'interesting.'

'No chance for the truck,' Zach added, 'I reckon we'd have to park up at the windfarm and leave it there, G. What do you think?'

'Agree, unfortunately' Gayle said. 'That's only three-point-five kilometres from Lower Grulin, right?'

'Less, I think. I'll find out.'

'Thanks, Zach,' Gayle tapped her chin as she considered livestream logistics. 'We'll need batteries for the cams every morning, or we can set up photovoltaics. Either is good, if we know before we go. I can pick up whatever we need from stores before that.'

Failing to grasp the last noodles in his box with his chopsticks, Jackson opened his mouth and tipped the contents into his mouth. He was about to force a post-meal fart when he thought the better of it, having faced disgust from Gayle and Zach about that habit the day before. He looked around the garage now and felt happy. If this was work, he thought, he liked it.

Earlier in the day, Gayle and Zach had shown Jackson and Hanna how to research historical census information online. Between them, they'd taken an hour to identify where Jackson's blood relatives who were cleared from Eigg had lived. Looking at satellite images, they'd found what was left of the townships with difficulty – corners of a few remaining blackhouse walls forming the only clues between bracken and boulders. What was easy to see was that at the edge of Lower Grulin, sheer cliffs fell away to the Atlantic Ocean, while behind the ruins, the land rapidly gathered gradient so extreme it ended vertically, forming the south face of the Eigg's high point, a long-sided, formidable basalt block: An Sgùrr, a name which meant sharp, steep hill.

Further investigation had shown that most of Eigg's current residents lived in a broad basin bay sloping away from breath-taking cream and turquoise beaches on the island's west shore. This modern village, Cleadale, lay eight kilometres from Grulin and the same distance again from other clutches of crofts on the island's east coast. Hanna had felt a sting of poignancy reading that Lower Grulin was similar on many fronts to where her Unclear-ances certificate said her dad's forebears had lived – Hallaig on Raasay, a calf island to Skye. She'd found both Grulin and Hallaig described in a blog as being 'violently silent' in the aftermath of human habitation, and the description had sent a chill up her spine.

Hanna opened a large, board-covered sketchbook on her lap and poised a pencil; she wanted to get a few questions on product design answered before they all got too tired to do more.

'So, a couple of things, I'll be quick,' Hanna blushed a little. 'Transpariboard, it's a composite material, made of all sorts of waste plastics, is that right, Jackson? What sort of strength are we talking, per sheet?'

Gayle and Zach looked to Jackson.

'Um, at least as tough as polycarbonate,' Jackson replied, his cheeks matching Hanna's as he remembered a reference Niall had noted.

'Impressive,' Hanna rubbed her chin. 'No problems for drill-ing, joining, dovetailing then?'

'Should be fine.' Jackson agreed though he hadn't a clue.

'Drew says the FM wants to make the tiny house transporta-ble, an empty shell?'

'Yip,' Jackson nodded, 'I think we should pull them with bikes. I've tried moving a tiny house before by hand in the garden. It's not fun.'

'Have you distance cycled before, Jackson?' Zach asked. 'With luggage?'

'Kind of,' Jackson shrugged, 'I've cycled up Dundas Street once. I had a six-pack on my handlebars. It's really steep. But we can get eco-engines, can't we?'

A thought occurred to Gayle as she and Zach glanced at each other.

'Come on the journey, Hanna,' Gayle said impulsively. 'Having the Product Designer along for the ride too – in case of kit emergencies – it's a no-brainer. But also, it'd be good to have you there; it'd enrich the visual story.'

Jackson turned to stare at Gayle. The thought of keeping the lie up in front of Hanna, in person, for weeks on end was alarming. Gayle felt Jackson's stare, but kept talking.

'One guy travelling alone, no matter how entertaining he might be … well, it's a tough shout to keep drawing stories from. And Jackson will need the company. Zach and I won't always be able to be that for him – we'll be tied up with the livestream and truck sometimes. NSBC would pay you, Hanna, naturally, just as we will with Jackson, and maybe it's a nice thing to do with some of your summer? Eigg's incredible, by all accounts …'

Hanna watched Jackson while Gayle spoke. Along with a surge of excitement about what was being offered, she felt a mix of offence and amusement at Jackson's reaction. He had certainly tried hard enough to get her attention at uni, and now here he was, hogging opportunities for himself, despite his life already oozing with privilege. Hanna took a deep breath. A once-in-a-lifetime opportunity, Drew had said, and now here that opportunity was, improving again.

'Would I be meeting the First Minister and stuff like that?' Hanna asked. 'I've still got my job here, too. They've been good to me. I couldn't just leave.'

'The meeting with the FM's in four days,' Gayle replied. 'Can you make it down for that? It'd be good to meet in person. We can do most of the rest online until the journey itself, and you'd need to go to Faslane too. Oversee elements of the Transpariboard manufacturing.'

'That's all a bit terrifying!' Hanna gulped as a jolt of anxiety hit. Jackson watched, surprised to see her shoulders slump and her suddenly vulnerable expression. 'I've only done stuff like that before as an observer. This is a new material; it's not even my design.'

'Hey,' Gayle's tone was warm, 'you can always sense check out loud with Zach and me, you won't be alone. We're not experts, but we're not daft either. And Jackson'll help too *if* you need him, won't you?' Gayle elbowed Jackson lightly. He looked at Hanna again. Her self-doubt reminded him of how he often felt but never showed.

'You're the class sweat, Hanna,' Jackson's voice was soft, 'you'll ace it.'

'You give me whiplash sometimes, Jackson Campbell,' Hanna replied, 'but thanks for that, I appreciate it. There's something else, too. I'll just say it. If I came on the journey, I'd want absolutely no questions about my private life on the livestream, especially about my dad. He has … some, well, issues. And they're private – no offence … but, well, I handle that side of things differently from Jackson. I can't talk about it online.'

Jackson remembered what Niall had told him about Hanna's dad being in jail; a frisson of fear about entangling the daughter of a possibly violent convict in his lie startled him. However, he thought, Hanna now stood to gain a lot too, surely that'd take some heat off him; maybe it'd even impress a criminal? And surely a convict wouldn't be able to track him down in another country once he'd buggered off to live in the chalet? He could barely find the place on Google Earth himself, after all.

'Understood, Hanna,' Gayle nodded. 'My family's off-limits to the public too. It's not a problem.'

'Thanks.' Hanna blushed again, hoping for a quick subject change.

Gayle looked at her wristband.

'I'm going home, folks. I want to get in a gym session, food, and an early night. Then I can video call the kids first thing. I don't get much out of them unless it's evening there, and their dad's usually out of earshot then too, which is better.'

'I'm going too,' Hanna said. 'I've got a shift till the death starting at half eight. I'll catch up on anything new in the workspace tomorrow, yeah?'

'Yeah,' Jackson and Zach said in sync.

'It's already tomorrow where my kids are, right now,' Gayle said, gathering up her tech.

'That's a mindfuck,' Jackson said, mulling over the time difference.

'Indeed.' Gayle slipped her hand under the fabric of her wide-necked t-shirt, grabbing the muscles between her neck and her right shoulder, then squeezing and pulling as if she was single-handedly kneading dough, her eyes shut against the pain of a muscle refusing to yield.

'I have my foam roller in the truck if you want it?' Zach said.

Gayle gave an exhausted sigh, then relaxed her hand. The skin on her neck where she'd pummelled was a furious, broad blotch of red.

'Thanks, Zee,' she said, 'I'm meeting my trainer. I think she'll work it, then tape it. Should help.'

'Worked before, didn't it?' Zach's eyes were kind.

'It did,' Gayle said. 'I get neck tension when I'm stressed,' she explained, turning to Jackson then Hanna, 'or when my kids are stressed, like now.'

'Yikes, sorry, Gayle,' Hanna said, 'my mum gets that, too. She can't sleep if something's up with one of us.'

'My mum gets migraines,' Jackson frowned, 'it's probably my dad that causes them though, eh? Not me. I'm no bother.'

'The body keeps the score.' Zach's face remained sympathetic. 'Your mum's probably like that too, Zach?'

'My mum's dead,' Zach said. 'Sorry man, no pretty way to say it. My dad gets stressed, though, for sure. He always checks in to see I'm OK.'

'Man, I … shit, sorry, I—' Jackson spluttered, his eyes wide with shock.

'It's all right,' Zach said, 'I hate it when it comes up like this, I feel bad for you more than me right now, but if I don't say it now, it's worse for everyone when I have to say it later …' Zach nudged Jackson's elbow till he met his eye, helping bridge the moment from mortification back to normality.

'You staying here again tonight?' Gayle asked Zach.

'Yeah. I'm gonna show Jackson how to set a drone to specific coordinates, amn't I, JC?'

'Jesus Christ!' Hanna laughed. 'You have the same initials as Jesus Christ!'

'I do,' Jackson grinned 'it's like I'm destined to be famous, innit?'

'It is, man.' Zach laughed too.

'OK,' Hanna smiled, 'thanks for that parting image.' She gave a wave, closed her laptop and was gone.

Gayle ducked under the garage door.

'Night.' she called behind her, then crunched down the drive.

19

/jacksonmcampbell /blurts/
Hitting up the #HOLYROODBOI massive again today, making dem plans for #JACKSONSJOURNEY ☺)))))))))) #NewScotland #NSBC #ImOnTheToilet #morning #daylight #greenjuice #swallow

/ZuzannaN/ blurtsTo/ TheJacksonCampbellAppreciationSoc
Hey there just let me know if you want to apply for junior membership for my club that knows more about #JACKSONSJOURNEY than you. Must warn you though, there's a rumour an application from anyone in your club would be rejected by my club, and it's true. HAHAHA ☺

Hanna used the train journey four days later to read up on Daniella Clearwater, hoping it'd calm the butterflies in her stomach about meeting the FM in person. She shaded her eyes from the sun as she read on. A feature in *Time Magazine* explained that Clearwater described herself as 'in a monogamous relationship with my job, for at least eight years'. The FM then explained that after her role at the head of the New Scottish government, she planned to adopt a child, take a year off, then pursue her next career goal of sitting on the EU Environment Taskforce while living in Lisbon. According to the article, none of Daniella Clearwater's goals had missed targets yet. Hanna counted back the years since Clearwater had become FM; if everything went to plan, she'd be off to Portugal by 2040. Without her, the concept of New Scotland seemed impossible, Hanna thought, staring out across the water to the distant outline of Edinburgh Castle's toothy silhouette.

The train arrived on time and Hanna made her way through Waverley's bustle, up the stairs from the station to the Fruitmarket exit, then crossed the road to the slow curve of Jeffrey Street. She stopped halfway and leant on the iron railings, admiring the views of Calton Hill. It felt good to be back in Edinburgh, Hanna thought, taking a deep breath of the brewery's malty scent in the air. She tapped off her music and the familiar sound of unseen bagpipes carried to her. Rounding the corner from Jeffrey Street onto the Royal Mile the bagpipes were replaced with a loud chanting.

Hanna remembered seeing a few mentions of the MEGA demonstration outside Holyrood on Blurt over the last few days. She hadn't paid it much attention; demonstrations about one thing or another came and went often, after all. On her right, an elderly passer-by with Nordic-walking sticks slightly lost his footing, brushing Hanna's arm before righting himself, casting her an accusing glance as he did so. Hanna stopped for a moment, watching the back of his red MEGA baseball cap as he made his way into a swell of tourists.

Reaching the plaza in front of the Edinburgh Parliament a few minutes later, Hanna surveyed the scene, taken aback by the scale of the gathering before her. Drones buzzed overhead; some were private – covered in stickers or custom spray-painted. Like the one now hovering and zooming into her face, others were instantly recognisable as the decrepit, logo-emblazoned kit of GBEBS. Someone had already grabbed this drone and drawn a cock and balls onto its domed underbelly. Hanna smirked and gave the drone the finger, holding her position until it closed its camera lens then buzzed away. Hanna made for the empty half of a nearby concrete bench and placed her rucksack in front of her, a hand gripping it tightly. She looked around the swarming colony of red-capped heads filling the concourse. The faces beneath the caps were almost all heavily lined and florid, many framed with grey hair or beards.

About fifty huge St George's Cross and Union Jack flags swayed on tall poles waved by protestors. In the middle of the crowd, Hanna spotted Michael Templeton heaving his tweed-clad frame to the top of an unstable stepladder, cheers from the crowd around him growing louder as he ascended.

Hanna stepped up onto the concrete seat so she could see better. Templeton was being handed new MEGA caps by someone on the ground, then throwing them into the crowd. Pensioners leapt upwards with all the grace of salmon with partial rigor mortis, trying to catch the merch. Templeton laughed uproariously with each throw, almost toppling his ladder several times. Beyond him, before the paving slabs stopped and the grassy area started, Hanna saw a huge line of camping tables with attached stools. More protestors sat at them, chatting, eating, and watching the scene. Many of the tables had Union Jack tablecloths clamped on while a banner declaring 'REUNITE THE UNION' hung taut above the tables, strung between two thick metal poles, their ends wedged into weighted cones.

Hanna looked to the entrance to the parliament and noticed protestors sitting at the foot of each of the concrete columns supporting the overhanging roof. The protestors' arms were connected by sections of wide plumbing pipes, inside which their wrists were presumably cuffed. Dotted at intervals around the plaza perimeter were small huddles of New Scottish Police Officers, all apparently relaxed, despite the muddle of activity. Hanna listened discreetly as the officer closest to her talked into her comms badge.

'All equipment appears benign. Weaponisation of flag poles is low, very cheap plastic, bendy. Average age is approx. eighty-one, first-gen Brexiteers, classic GBE boomers, Ma'am. No imminent threats or breaches detected. They just seem to come and go from the Saint Mary's Travelodge – nature calls, I imagine. Or naps. Over.'

On Hanna's other side, three protestors began setting up what appeared to be a tall tent which soon revealed itself as a puppet show and immediately drew keen attention from the crowd. Hanna stepped forward to see the stage better when the show began. First, a Krankie puppet appeared. Hanna rolled her eyes at Clearwater's predecessor's all too familiar effigy while audio feedback whistled from a giant speaker, then settled. The crowd booed the Krankie as she danced a little, waving the saltire flag in one of her little puppet fists. Half an egg sandwich flew through the air towards the puppet but missed, catching the edge of the tent instead.

'Bitch!' a protestor yelled, closely followed by cheers as they erupted for three heavily maned lion puppets now manically bobbing too.

'Death tae the English!' the Krankie screamed, her voice relayed so loudly through the speaker it made Hanna wince. 'Death tae the royals and everyone at Westminster! Batter them all like Mars Bars! Death tae the Armed Forces! Haha ha!'

Hanna watched as a climax was reached; the lions leapt on top of the Krankie, growling and pulling its limbs and head in different directions. Hanna noticed twists of delight and menace on the faces of the crowd. A tall man at the back caught her eye. He was moving through the mob at pace towards the front. His red-capped head was down, and his denim jacket collar was up, shrouding his chin. He both fitted in and stood out, Hanna noticed, watching him change course slightly as if he was now headed straight for her and not the puppets. Hanna stepped down from the concrete seat and hoisted her rucksack onto her front, side-stepping closer to the police officers.

'We had it all!' one of the lions screamed while the other two stayed pinned and snarling on their prey, 'We were set to rule the world again! England doesn't need Europe! Empires don't need permission! They simply lead! But Scotland's jealousy grew! Oh, yes! They had to stop us. But we will be victorious again! Reunite the Union!'

At this, the crowd went mad. The Krankie was launched through the air, flags were thrust higher and vicious jeers and picnic missiles were hurtled at the stage. Hanna watched as the puppet master opened the curtain behind the stage and stepped out, sweaty and delighted. The Krankie doll, now decapitated, landed at Hanna's feet. Hanna stared down as the end of a flagpole speared the puppet's hollow fibre abdomen. An elbow nudged her left arm, and when she looked to see whom it belonged to, she jumped at the sight of a red-cap grinning down at her, nodding back towards the parliament building. Jackson. He winked at Hanna, beckoned, and headed away, his head down again as he snaked towards the parliament entrance. As they approached the doors, Hanna watched them slide open, revealing Zach, Gayle and several security guards inside. Jackson pulled Hanna in and the noise from outside was drowned completely when the doors closed. Jackson, Hanna, Zach and Gayle looked at each other, then burst out laughing, relieved to have Hanna safely extracted from the mêlée.

'Quite a start getting through that, hey?' Gayle wiped the corner of her eye with the back of her hand.

'Did you all wear the hats?' Hanna asked, incredulous.

'We did,' Zach opened his jacket and showed Hanna a red cap stuffed inside a webbed interior pocket. 'Jackson's idea. We bought them from a vendor up by Pollock Halls. I feel dirty, but it had to be done. Can you imagine if Templeton heard JC was approaching?'

'My God,' Hanna laughed, trying to comprehend precisely how fit Zach was in the skin compared to the brief flashes she'd seen on screen. 'I hadn't realised how many there would be. And I don't want a hat, but now, wow, I mean, shit – I feel super under-dressed.'

Hanna took in Gayle's pristine white high-waisted flares, black flats and fitted sleeveless black blouse. A toffee-coloured jacket hung over Gayle's arm and she held an elegant charcoal laptop sleeve with a small NSBC enamelled badge on a corner. Gayle's hair was also immaculate, smoothed back in a chic clip, and her eyes twinkled under an expertly applied brown liner. Zach was equally impressive in navy jeans and a thick white cotton shirt highlighting an understated but expensive navy jacket. Jackson, by a welcome contrast, looked blasé as ever in holey black jeans, a washed-out blue t-shirt, flip flops and his denim. His hair at least looked as if it had been washed, Hanna clocked, and that was significantly more effort than she'd ever seen him make for uni. Hanna looked down at her own fading black maxi skirt, DMs, silver vest and biker jacket. Only that morning, her outfit had looked *too* smart in the mirror, particularly in comparison to the joggers and jeans she'd lived in since returning home. Hanna patted her hair self-consciously, grateful now for her mum's intervention urging her to pull her hair back from her face in loose waterfall braiding in place of her usual ponytail.

'You look fantastic,' Gayle issued a level stare at Hanna, 'every inch a product designer. Zach and I are in TV, remember? And a bit of power dressing never hurts when you're trying to convince a First Minister to let you have everything your way on a reality show, right?'

'Right,' Hanna smiled, grateful for the reassurance. 'Are these MEGA things getting bigger?'

'Not in winter, they're not,' Gayle replied. 'You only get the coachloads of pensioners from GBE coming up in spring and summer. They might seem hardcore terrifying but show them a bit of New Scottish weather and they soon blow back home.'

'I think it's a holiday for some of them,' Zach added. 'I heard GBEBS lays on the buses and food for free to make it look like heaps of folk up here are still against independence too. Rent-a-mob. Sad buggers.'

Gayle nodded then checked her wristband.

'Come on,' she said, turning to the security desk, 'I've already stuck my walking shoes in a locker. Let's get through the scanners, yes?'

Jackson watched Hanna as Gayle and Zach began chatting to the security staff. Mischief danced in Jackson's eyes.

'You all right, Hanna? Seen something you like in Zach, have we? Bit of a heat coming off of you, know what I'm saying?'

'Oh, my God, you total fud. Shut up.' Hanna laughed. Jackson reminded her a lot of her seventeen-year-old sister, Zuzia. They were both smart and funny, and consistently work-shy, too. She wished she'd realised earlier.

'You fancy Za-ack,' Jackson leaned into Hanna's side and sang quietly in her ear, 'Zach's melted the ice Queen.'

'You're *such* a twat,' Hanna smiled as they approached the security desks, placing her rucksack into a large black tray.

'Any sharp objects with you?' the security guard moved Hanna's tray onto the conveyer belt.

'Just this prick,' Hanna pointed at Jackson.

The guard laughed.

'We heard you were coming today,' the guard said to Jackson. 'How's your dad? Still angry?'

'Yeah,' Jackson grinned. 'Roy's always fuming about something.'

'Not out there with that lot, is he?' the security guard nodded towards the MEGA demo then held out her hand for Jackson's jacket.

'Nah. He's in France, shouting at Europe from the top of a ski slope. I might get him a megaphone for Christmas. Get it, a MEGA-phone?!'

'Ha! Better there than with that bunch, eh? Can I get a selfie?'

the security guard beckoned over a colleague from the sliding door controls.

'Course!' Jackson grinned. 'I'll catch you up, Hanna. Maybe you'll be less purple by then, yeah?'

Hanna lifted her bag from the tray on the other side of the scanner.

'Speaking of purple,' Hanna narrowed her eyes and leant in towards Jackson and peered at the now faint bruised arcs under his eyes. 'Are you really tired, or … have you had a wallop from someone? Looks a bit sore?'

'Nah!' Jackson grinned, 'it's fine, standard tiny house injury, don't worry about it, I'm not!'

'OK.' Hanna replied, unsure, then watched Jackson climb onto the loading table and into a tray himself, before assuming a half lotus position. He steepled his hands, nodding his finger-tips piously then grinning for the camera as the guard's colleague obliged, pretending to run his handheld scanner over Jackson's upper body.

Hanna spotted Gayle and Zach in the middle of the light-filled foyer. Zach was filming Jackson on his mini tablet, a top of the range model with built-in flight and film capability Hanna recognised from fantasy shopping for tech. Hanna made a whistle of admiration as she crossed the polished concrete.

'Nice camera,' she said. Zach smiled, glad he had the device to hide behind till he worked out how to deal with remaining professional while fancying Hanna at the same time. Watching her at the door he'd kept finding his eyes drawn to her neck where a tendril of blonde hair had slipped from her braid and disappeared under her jacket collar.

'He actually can't stop himself, can he?' Gayle whispered to Hanna conspiratorially.

Hanna looked surprised.

'Jackson,' Gayle explained, looking to where Jackson now stood running the handheld scanner over both the security guards' heads, the three of them giggling like toddlers. 'He performs, doesn't he?' Gayle went on. 'Can't help himself. A natural, I suppose. Probably should see if he can break through to present-ing at some point, don't you think? Lots of reality stars do, don't they?'

'He'd actually be good at it,' Hanna agreed, smirking as Jackson pretended to turn and run with the scanner then heading back, handing it over and giving an almost elegant bow.

Gayle checked her wristband again.

Zach stopped filming and nodded to Gayle, drawing her attention to a sweeping concrete staircase on the other side of the foyer. A short man in a pale grey three-piece suit and gleaming patent brogues had stopped halfway down, tapping his wristband with a dexterous speed neither Hanna nor Jackson had seen the like of before. The light flashed on his kingfisher-red crew cut when he stopped tapping and began walking again.

'Here comes Bryce Cooper,' Gayle's voice was low.

Hanna watched as Gayle rolled her shoulders, to stand instantly taller, her stance adjusted as if she were about to confidently dive from a great height.

Zach leant into Hanna's shoulder.

'FM's PA,' Zach whispered, leaning in briefly to Hanna's shoulder.

'Oh,' Hanna nodded, 'thanks.'

Bryce stopped again, made another flurry of taps on his screen, then looked up, double-taking when he spotted Jackson waving at him with both hands in the air.

'Game faces on,' Gayle whispered, her eyes trained hawk-like on Bryce's face as he approached. 'It's time to make the magic happen.'

20

Niall and Fin had taken a bark-chipped path through a willow bed and away from the recovery centre, finishing at the neighbouring reservoir's edge. Fin indicated a bench he'd sat on with many patients before.

'Good contemplation spot.'

Niall picked up a windfall branch and ripped a leaf off.

'I'm super fucked-up.'

'Really?' Fin replied. 'How so?'

'I'm the youngest,' Niall sat down. 'All the others have been through heaps more. I'm here already, twenty years earlier.'

Fin watched the water. The shore was calm but further out a wind pushed waves onto inky darkness.

'Ah,' Fin replied, 'using logic to create equivalence where none exists.'

'How?'

'Is what you're saying true?'

An urge to poke Fin in the face with the stick struck Niall.

'Yes. I'm here. They're here. I'm the youngest.'

Niall followed Fin's gaze to a large, dark bird on a floating log.

'Shag?' Fin's eyes narrowed. 'Yes?'

Niall pulled back to the end of the bench, almost falling off. Fin blinked, confused.

'Well, what kind of bird is it then, if not a shag?'

'Oh!' Niall blushed, 'Oh, God. Sorry. I—'

The bird elongated its neck. Huge wings stretched out and away.

'So, where were we?' Fin fiddled awkwardly with his cuff. 'Equivalence where none exists?'

'No!' Niall's thoughts spun, 'I proved it *does exist.*'

'So the criteria for being in rehab's the same for everyone?'

Niall's neck tensed.

'Judgements are about unique situations,' Fin continued. 'Remember, older people talk less about mental health. Do you think it's possible they've been where you are now several times already, with no help at all?'

Niall looked at the branch. It was flexible enough to bend into a circle. Long enough for its ends to tuck in then out.

'Wreath?' Fin asked.

'Or a noose,' Niall muttered.

'Or a ring,' Fin was undeterred, 'to represent a new bond to truth? Hang it up to remind you?'

'Could you *be* more cheesy?' Niall rolled his eyes.

'Oh, definitely,' Fin smiled.

Niall stared down at the branch, crushed by the embarrassment of being wrong. Wrong assumptions. Wrong mental health. Wrong child in a family. Wrong approach to uni. Wrong, wrong, wrong.

'Come. Let's walk back,' Fin stood. 'You're doing great, Niall. You're not, how did you put it? Super fucked-up, wasn't it?'

Niall shrugged.

'You're not that, Niall. You simply need supported time out to acknowledge and recover after trauma caused by inadequate parental support.'

Niall shot a glance at Fin. It hurt to hear his parents skewered by anyone but himself, but the clarity resonated too.

'We'll support you in catching your breath and taking stock. We'll help you identify how you want your life to look and feel, outside of trauma. You're a fast learner. I'd like you to lead this evening's reflection session. How does that sound? You could share what happened for you here – the parsing of truth from brain chatter, ask others if they relate?'

Niall shook his head.

'Not ready for that. Sorry.'

Fin stood, briefly mirroring Niall's frown. He was eager to return to the centre and brief a colleague on the shag misunderstanding.

'Do some parents just not love their kids?' Niall squinted up at Fin. 'Unconditionally, like?'

'I'd say that's true, in my experience,' Fin replied. 'Parents' love is not universally unconditional. It's a bit of a lottery, sadly. But no matter what bad luck befalls us, we *can* all learn how to make a good life, Niall. I promise you that.'

Niall nodded, pretending to agree. As they headed back to the centre Fin began explaining the bi-annual willow cutting cycle. As Niall listened, anger like spots of molten lava, gloopy and destructive, called for his attention to an unnamed, gathering rage. He was supposed to tell someone if he was feeling strong emotions, Niall knew. Yet he'd been feeling them a lot and saying nothing. He opened his mouth to speak but again, couldn't conjure words that felt right. More wrongness, Niall thought, pretending to itch his arm through his hoodie, pinching his flesh hard between his thumb and index fingernails as immediate punishment.

21

On arriving in the First Minister's vast, triangular meeting room Jackson made straight for the window. He pulled out his tablet and took selfies, feigning busy Blurt interactions and photo-editing in order to delay acknowledging Drew McAllister's holo-hulk form for as long as possible. Hanna, by contrast, had been drawn straight to the holodeck in the corner as she entered the room, immediately spotting Drew chatting to Daniella Clearwater.

'Yes, Aberdeen. This morning.' Hanna replied, desperately trying not to gush when Daniella asked her if she'd travelled that day.

'Do you know I grew up in Aberdeen?' Daniella's cheeks dimpled as she smiled.

'Yes,' Hanna nodded, 'I read your wiki on the train. You were on the other side of the Don from me, we're just off Great Northern Road, up from Grandholm Bridge.'

'Ah. I know it well,' Daniella nodded.

'And the train was OK, was it Hanna?' Drew asked, unaware that the edges of his hologram were flickering on one side of his head so his left ear and shoulder came and went as he spoke.

Bryce appeared behind Daniella and tapped a control panel on the wall, his finger like a woodpecker on speed again. Drew's image immediately sharpened.

'Train was great,' Hanna's eyes widened as she tried to take everything in. 'No bother at all. Whole table to myself. It's nice to be back in Edinburgh though. You forget the tourist madness till you see it again, don't you?'

'You do,' Drew agreed, then frowned down at a tablet someone outside the hololink had handed him. 'I'm sorry, Hanna, Daniella, I have to go.' Drew said after a few seconds of reading. 'I'm wanted on a call about an EHA student. Mature woman. Her childcare's been dropped again, and she thinks she should jack it all in today. The risk of us losing her is just too big, sorry. I'll need to go and help.'

'Let's get you off, Drew,' Daniella replied. 'I know you'll not rest till that's sorted. NSBC have added me to the workspace for the project with Hanna and Jackson. We'll get you added too, OK?'

Drew nodded, smiled, and was gone. Daniella gestured to the seats. Gayle and Zach chose chairs in front of the window while Hanna made her way to a chair one along from Jackson, hanging her jacket on the back before sitting. Daniella remained standing.

'Where's ogre-features gone?' Jackson whispered, scooching closer to Hanna. But before she could reply Daniella spoke.

'Gayle, thank you for adding me to your workspace, everything looks good. Professor McAllister's had to log out, unfortunately.' Jackson fist-pumped under the table. 'I've promised we'll add him to the workspace, too,' Daniella continued, 'his role's purely support-based for Jackson and Hanna via EHA, he's there to support them for another twelve months post-graduation. It's important they – we, rather – all have that link.'

Gayle nodded to Zach who opened his laptop and made a few quiet keystrokes then gave Daniella a thumbs-up.

'Thank you,' Daniella said. She unbuttoned her suit jacket and fixed a serious expression at Gayle. 'I think its best if we understand everyone's objectives first, ensure we have common ground to move forward from.' Jackson tipped himself forward over the desk and stared at the planters on the carpet, then looked up at Daniella and Bryce, struggling to mask his boredom with formalities. 'I'll be super clear,' Daniella continued, 'I *love* this project. But from a legal standpoint there's more that I *don't* need from it than I do. Let me elaborate.'

Gayle leant back in her chair, one arm crossed her chest while her other hand cupped her chin. Zach watched Daniella, alert to an unspoken tension between the FM and his boss.

'Can we get the lasery house out?' Jackson asked.

'Not yet, Jackson,' Daniella replied, 'let's get the less fun stuff out the way first.'

Jackson flopped back into his seat with a sigh.

'Go ahead, First Minister,' Gayle replied, 'tell us what you don't need.'

Daniella began walking slowly around the edge of the room.

'What we don't want is any public or legal liability,' Daniella started. 'The New Scottish government's role in this is, ideally, mostly very similar to that of a regular viewer in terms of Jackson's actual journey to Eigg. In complement to his take on Unclearances we'll offer commentary on ours via Blurt, especially if Jackson's experiences meet, exceed or challenge our vision for Unclearance.'

Daniella stopped at an enormous touchscreen on the wall by the door and tapped it. The word *Unclearance* appeared on a screen on the wall beside where Drew's hologram had stood. The huge white lettering was superimposed onto a video of blue sky. The roofless ruin of a blackhouse sat amidst swaying grasses below. Daniella walked on again.

'We want no say over how you organise yourselves and we have no interest in logistics. We need regular signal boosting of all our blurts and we'd expect full right of reply *and* very fair warning on any unforeseeable circumstances that arise and might shine a negative light on Unclearance. From our side, we'll fund the production of a test run of Transpariboard to amp the open-minded, exploratory nature of the whole project – and of the Every Human Actualising programme.' Daniella stopped at the window, turning to smile at Hanna, 'Naturally, I hope Jackson will love Eigg and feel bonded to his story there. I'd like to see you all go hard on smaller footprint travel and the detail of what you see and feel along the way, particularly the great stuff, obviously.' At this Daniella nodded at Zach, pleased to see him touch-typing notes as she spoke. 'I also massively hope Transpariboard will turn out to be a go-er for more than just Jackson's Journey or dissertation development, but that's for another time. *If* it's viable as a building material Jackson will have to think long and hard about how he wants the product to go forward.'

Daniella looked at Jackson. His chair was tilted onto the two rear legs and he was scrolling his tablet, oblivious. Gayle cleared her throat and rose from her chair.

'OK.' Gayle walked towards Daniella, stopping a couple of metres in front of her. Arthur's Seat was perfectly framed through the window in the space between them. Jackson looked up and banked an idea to mull later about picturing himself, Daniella and Gayle in the same positions, but naked. 'I'll level with you right back,' Gayle said, 'NSBC wants total project ownership. We'll take all liability and expense, apart from the Transpariboard development. We plan to make a franchise series we can sell the rights for globally. We won't link to the Unclearance name or concept globally, it'll simply be "Journey" outside of New Scotland. Depending on how Jackson gets on we may or may not ask him to be involved as a social media ambassador across the brand. We'll see on that, too.'

At this Jackson almost fell off his chair. The only future he had considered recently had been lying low in France, followed by a later domination of French social media. Now another carrot had been dangled he found he wanted it. But was that realistic, he wondered, given the lie? Hanna reached out and shoved Jackson's chair back forward, redressing the balance.

'We won't use Transpariboard tiny houses elsewhere either,' Gayle continued, 'our contract re the journey production will be with Jackson and Jackson alone. We'll hire Hanna for the New Scottish production. I propose Jackson and Hanna each travel with a tiny Transpariboard house to Eigg; Zach and I will accompany in the NSBC truck, maybe rotating one of us cycling, without a house in tow. If there are two Transpariboard houses we can better emulate the feeling of a crofting village when we set up on the island, among the blackhouse ruins. We'll stay there for a week, exploring a different part of Jackson's ancestor's lifestyles each day, taking perspectives of both fly on the wall and immersed observer.' Hanna's eyes opened wide. 'We have no interest in Transpariboard outside of whatever Jackson's doing with it himself after the journey,' Gayle continued, 'our interest is in the story of people leaving one life and taking a literal and metaphysical journey to another.'

'But—' Jackson interrupted, only to be shushed by Hanna, Bryce and Zach.

'A moment please, Jackson.' Gayle held out an open palm gesturing for Jackson to stop.

Daniella lifted her chin then walked away from Gayle. Hanna looked to Zach who gave a quick smile then then went back to typing.

When Daniella arrived back at her chair she bent, lifting a large brown unmarked cardboard box from the floor, then placing it on the desk. The box looked to Jackson to be the right size for a pair of women's knee-length dog walking boots. Rebecca had several just like it in the boot room.

Daniella caught Jackson's eye when she lifted the lid from the box. A flash of something shimmering was just visible inside. Daniella carefully lifted out a sheet of material, about a centimetre thick. Was it a chopping board, Jackson wondered? Daniella walked towards him then handed him the object.

'Thanks?' Jackson said. 'That looks really designer. My mum would probably like it, she likes bling. But she doesn't eat bread. Can you cut salad and that on it, too?' Daniella smirked, presuming Jackson was joking as she watched him hold up the board, noticing how the particles inside it caught the light; it was iridescent when he held it one way, then transparent the other way.

'*Jesus*. Is that …?' Hanna stood, beckoning for Jackson to pass her the board.

'Are you still calling me Jesus?' Jackson muttered, busy admiring a cross-section edge of the board.

'Yes,' Daniella laughed, 'it's Transpariboard, Hanna.'

Jackson threw the board from his hands as if it had burned him, sending it clattering to the desk in front of him.

'*Fuck*!' he breathed, staring at the material.

Hanna reached then ran a hand over it, disbelieving. She bent to crouch beside Jackson and stood the board on its short end, looking through it to Zach. Hanna waved wordlessly and watched Zach wave back. She then tilted the Transpariboard so it stood at a slight angle. At once the material appeared iridescent, transforming Zach to an indistinct blur.

'My God,' Hanna was half-hoarse. 'Did you know?' she stared at Jackson. 'Did you know it'd be *this* good?'

Jackson stared down at the desk in front of him, his fingers twiddling wildly.

'The privacy?' Hanna blurted. 'Did you know it would do that, at an angle?'

Jackson shook his head. He dare not speak. It was like the Transpariboard had stolen his voice; the lie now trapped inside

Niall's material itself, shimmering and glimmering out at them all – unexpectedly beautiful, painfully innocent.

Hanna headed to Gayle, passing her the Transpariboard. Gayle held the board like a tray then swivelled so she was facing the window. Zach stood and craned a little to see over Gayle's shoulder and share her view. A group of minute people on Arthur's Seat were visible then obscured, melding with the hill into an abstracted khaki blob when Gayle tilted the board. Daniella cleared her throat.

'Hanna, what did you mean by privacy?' she asked, smiling encouragingly.

'Oh!' Hanna grinned. 'When it's angled, the transparency's compromised, yes?

Daniella nodded.

'So imagine placing that in this window frame, tilting it slightly. Then you'd have privacy glass, yes? No use to see out of, but no one can see in, either?'

Daniella's eyes narrowed.

'Yes,' she replied. 'Goodness. That's interesting.'

'So if you put this in a toilet window,' Hanna continued, 'the opacity at tilt means you have privacy. Good when you want light but no view in or out.'

Daniella smiled widely at Hanna, inspired by her passion. She reminded Daniella of herself, in years gone by. It was good to spend a meeting like this, Daniella thought, a welcome break from more difficult matters.

'And,' Hanna went on, mouthing a quick thanks as Gayle handed the Transpariboard back, 'if you made the back half of, say, a tiny house with the material in slight tilt, and a slightly tilted wall inside … well, you'd have a Transpariboard house with a private area, do you see? For sleeping. Or the toilet, or a shower.'

Jackson watched Hanna. He couldn't remember ever seeing her so animated. Her eyes were wide and bright, she verged on laughter with every word. Had Niall seen her like this before, Jackson wondered, or had he stolen this from him too?

'So.' Daniella leant back in her chair and gave a chuckle. 'As we can see, initial feedback for Transpariboard is good. We've got a batch lined up for manufacturing and testing at Faslane, whenever Jackson says go, we start on panels. All this in less than a week,' Daniella laughed. 'I've always said, our achievements rise to match our expectations of what we're capable of, and here it is in motion. From there we set up a laser-cutter for a tiny house design, once it's finalised. Then it's wherever Jackson wants to take it. And I suggest a conversation with Drew on that before you have a conversation with NSBC or anyone else about it, Jackson.'

Daniella's tone was protective, Gayle realised. A pang for her own kids hit her chest.

'I completely agree.' Gayle's shoulders lowered.

Hanna handed the Transpariboard back to Jackson and returned to her chair, hurriedly pulling her rucksack onto her knee so she could find her tablet and begin making notes.

Daniella looked to Gayle, her features notably softened, 'Hearing your agenda, knowing your work, Gayle, I have no objections to your proposition of project ownership. It suits us well and seems to give everyone else what they need. You'll do this justice, I know.'

Jackson's stomach creaked like a set of rusty door hinges.

'Maybe we shouldn't use Transpariboard?' he said. 'I mean, honestly, it's a lot of hassle, isn't it? All this manufacturing and stuff. And, I mean, well, even *I* thought it was a chopping board.' Jackson held the Transpariboard aloft with one hand, pulling a face at it before setting it down to shimmer in a ray of afternoon sunlight. 'I think when the public see it they'll just be like, "that's shit", don't yous?' Jackson scanned the blank faces staring back at him. 'It'll be meme'd to death after, like, four hours,' he continued, 'honestly. Trust me. I know Blurt, don't I? Like, no offence, but I'm basically the Blurt expert, amn't I? And do you know what? We could just use sheds for my journey, from B&Q? Like, put them on trailers. Or wheels, maybe. Or tents? Oh, my God! Yeah! Tents? They already *exist*. You get ones you just wear on your back, like a rucksack, like a turtle shell on your back.' Jackson gesticulated wildly, his hands grabbing an imaginary shell on his back, 'They're, like, a big circle, you just unzip it round the edge and out pops a tent. Then you pin it down if it's windy. Yous must've seen them? Yeah?' Jackson looked desperately to Zach for support, but Zach dove behind his tablet screen. 'I could easily blag us tents from ScotSports,' Jackson went on, bending his neck to try and force Hanna to look at him. Hanna swatted Jackson away like a fly and continued battering notes into her keyboard.

'It's up to you, Jackson,' Daniella said evenly, keen to calm what she understood to be something akin to stage fright, 'but first, let's show the others the laser form?'

Bryce tapped his wristband and catalysed the swapping out of the plant pots in the floorspace between the desks for the platform. Jackson covered his face with his hands then splayed his fingers slightly, unable to resist. Hanna, Gayle and Zach's faces lit up as the lasers once again began crisscrossing, forming the tiny house outline firstly in bright pink then, as the model finalised, changing to a radiant, gently pulsing, electric blue.

Just above the windowsill a small light flashed a burst of red, white, then blue amongst a taller section of succulent plants on the living roof outside. Bryce rushed to the window, tapping his wristband as he crossed the room. The huge windows darkened. Bryce pointed.

'I've raised the security shield, First Minister, if I'm not mistaken that's a GBEBS drone sitting out there in the sedum, it's battery's fading, I just saw the alert sequence.'

Gayle and Zach spun round. Bryce stopped a few centimetres from the glass, just able to make out the camouflaged edge of the drone's elliptical top half.

'Are we safe? Should we get down?' Gayle asked, alarmed.

'We're safe,' Bryce assured everyone. 'Nothing's getting through that shield, believe me. And we scan all GBE tech – none of it's weaponised, don't worry. But that thing's got footage. Shall I get it netted, First Minister?'

Daniella breathed deeply. The others watched a smile play slowly on her lips.

'You know …,' she got up and walked over to Bryce, 'that demo. The MEGA folk. It somehow always ends up being an opportunity for us, rather than the crisis they hope for. I was just about to say we have to move on to my last topic – how to launch this project. But I think …,' Daniella raised an eyebrow at Gayle.

'Oh!' Gayle said. 'Ha! Are you …?'

Daniella nodded.

'Oh, wow!' Gayle grinned. 'You want to let Templeton run with the footage?'

Daniella smirked, delighted.

'I mean *come on,*' she said, 'it's *perfect!* The footage will be grainy, sure, it's a GBE drone. There'll be no audio. But they've got the whole picture otherwise. It'll save us a press conference. He'll think he's kicking up a scandal, we keep quiet for a day or two, let the curiosity build …'

'Then off we go, take back the narrative,' Gayle added. 'You talk about Unclearance and we talk Jackson's Journey. It's genius!'

'What do you say, JC?' Zach asked.

They all watched Jackson standing inside the laser tiny house, Transpariboard clutched at his chest.

'He's stunned,' Hanna laughed. 'Totally in love with his design babies, look!'

Jackson looked at everyone now gathered by the window. His cheek muscles were pained by the force of holding tears in and pushing a huge, fake smile out. There they were, Jackson saw, a group of people each so rich in skills, ideas and talent. And here he was, the odd one out, wishing he could go to the same place as the plant pots. Or France.

22

/MichaelTempletonGBEBS/blurts/
BREAKING: CLEARWATER IMPRISONS NEW SCOTTISH VIRAL
BLURT SENSATION IN LASER PRISON. GO TO OUR WEBSITE TO
SEE EXCELLENT HIGH-QUALITY PHOTOS #GBEBS #ReuniteTheUn-
ion #GBEGlory #FightOnPatriots #EmpireStateOfMind #Winning
#NewScotlandLosers

/RebeccaCampbell/blurts/
Rebecca campbell search

/RebeccaCampbell/blurts/
Rebecca Campbell age search

/RebeccaCampbell/blurts/
Rebecca Campbell weight search

/RebeccaCampbell/blurts/
Blurt beginner instructions for blurting? Search

/RebeccaCampbell/blurtsTo/jacksonmcampbell
How do I know if I blurted? search

/MichaelTempletonGBEBS/blurts/
BREAKING: CLEARWATER HAS CREATED A NEW CHEMICAL
WEAPON WHICH SHE IS TESTING ON NEW SCOTLAND'S IDIOT
HUMAN MASCOT JACKSON CAMPBELL. RABID ROY LIKELY
ALREADY DEAD. #NewScotlandsWar #ClearwatersDirtyConscience
#DirtyDaniella #ReuniteTheUnion #EmpiricalEvidence #SitDown-
Scotland

/RebeccaCampbell/blurtsTo/MichaelTempletonGBEBS

Blurt How dare you! Roy Campbell is not dead! He is alive and well in Val D'Isère! Look! Stop calling him Rabid Roy or we will sue you! He is Rejuvenated Roy! See attached photo!

/MichaelTempletonGBEBS/blurts/

BREAKING: NEW SCOTLAND HA HA HA HA HA!!!!
#ReuniteTheUnion #DirtyDaniella #GBEGlory #GBEBS

/MichaelTempletonGBEBS/blurts/

BREAKING: JACKSON CAMPBELL'S MOTHER – #RABIDRE-BECCA?!?! HA HA HA HA HA!!!! #Desperados #ReuniteTheUnion #DirtyDaniella #BeggingToComeBack #GBEGlory #GBEBS

/MichaelTempletonGBEBS/blurts/

BREAKING: NEW SCOTLAND CRUMBLING FROM TOP DOWN. CLEARWATER'S EVIL REGIME VISIBLE TO ALL AT LAST. #DirtyDaniella #GBEBS #ReuniteTheUnion #GBEGlory

/MichaelTempletonGBEBS/blurts/

BREAKING: MEGA DEMO CATALYSES THE END OF NEW SCOTLAND. UNION WILL BE REUNITED THANKS TO GBEBS DEDICATION TO TRUTH. #ReuniteTheUnion #WinningTheBattleAndTheWar #GBEBSHolidays #GBEBSCares

/RebeccaCampbell/blurts/

Blurt Good evening world! Here is a photo of Duchy Campbell getting his nails done! #littlecutie #bigbonednotfat!

23

where did ancient Scottish crofters shit?

Jackson typed the sentence and hit search. He looked over the top of his screen at Hanna as she tapped diligently at her keyboard, her mouth pulled into a tight pout.

'When you type your lips look like a cat's bum,' Jackson smirked.

'I'm so glad the painful flirting you used to do at uni is over, Jackson,' Hanna said, briefly breaking from typing to raise her middle finger.

'I still flirt with the other girls,' Jackson winked, 'you've lost your mystique, you see? I can't fancy you now we're friends. It's the chase I love. You should see my messages. Smokin' hot. You might have turned down your chance, Hanna, but your peers like the game.'

'What a loss for me.' Hanna smiled and stretched out to pick up a whistle on a lanyard from a box of hiking safety kit Jackson had received in the morning post. Hanna had made good use of some of the camping equipment already, sleeping in the Campbell garage all three nights since the meeting at Holyrood. By day she'd workshopped changes to the houses, including the design of harnesses to link to the trailers for pulling them by bodily force, where conditions might leave no other option.

Jackson looked back at the selection of links for historical organisations, blogs and chat forums listed on his screen. He clicked on one which included a selection of colourised images of blackhouses, then searched the site content for 'shit'. No results. Next, he tried 'toilet', yielding three results. He scrolled through to the first mention – a paragraph which suggested some crofters toileted in the byre where they kept their cows during winter. Jackson baulked at a vivid memory of walking round vast, stinking khaki pancakes on a track in the Pentlands during a school trip. He scrolled again and came to a quote from the son of a Paisley man who'd been evacuated to a crofting family on Islay in 1942, which stated that his aunt's croft had included a lean-to over a pit for toileting. The last reference to toilet claimed that al fresco toileting in rotated pits far from water supplies had been the done thing in many places. Jackson read on, intrigued with a comment that the topic of crofter's sanitation was heavily stigmatised because of the disgust about these aspects of crofting life projected by landowners and other occasional interlopers.

'So, right, they shat in their byres – maybe. But maybe they shat outside, in a pit. Or maybe they shat in wee sheds, over a pit? It's not crystal clear, to be honest.'

Hanna nodded.

'Thought as much. So what's your preference? I'm not sure I can do it – shit, I mean, free range, can you?' Hanna picked up a pencil and began outlining a picture of the tiny house design in her sketchbook. She drew a bucket next to it, then a large, two-dimensional question mark above, the mass of its dot stretching into a drop shape, ready to splash into the bucket.

'I've never shat outside before,' Jackson said. 'I piss outside a lot. My mum doesn't mind, she says it keeps the foxes away.'

'I wish it was as easy for girls,' Hanna replied. 'Don't suppose the neighbours would appreciate seeing me squat on the grass next to our flat.'

Jackson considered for the first time that no neighbours at all could see into his garden.

'You ever been camping?'

'My mum took us every year. Cheap and cheerful. You know that campsite at Mortonhall, up and over the golf course up there?'

'Yeah?' Jackson recalled the place vaguely, but hadn't strayed much on foot beyond the clubhouse in over a decade, maybe two.

'Ace fun. They had Highland cows in a field and everything. A wee shop. Massive washing machines and tumble dryers in an old stable. The *best* playpark. We were filthy all day long, playing outside. Mum hosed us down every night. Good times.'

Jackson stared out of the open garage door, struck that at several points in their childhoods he and Hanna had been nearby each other. Maybe they'd passed on a walk. Jackson blushed realising that if that *had* happened, Rebecca would almost certainly have rushed by. She was never one to share airspace or small talk with people in a different social orbit from her own.

'Tell you what,' Hanna continued, 'we'll stick with the sloping option for each of the walls, that way if one of us wants the loo, or privacy to sleep or change – whatever – we just tilt that wall into a secondary stable roof notch with its base levering off the hinge between wall and floor. Et voilà, Transpariboard magic. Done.'

'We'll take a bucket for each of us,' Hanna went on, 'I'll make a note in the workspace for Gayle to add a question for the ranger on Eigg about historical sanitation points. I've seen a burn on the map, so sluicing will be possible, I guess, if we take a clean supply for drinking and cooking upstream. We'll take a shovel, too. Low tech but effective. Fine for a short trip. What do you think?'

'I never went camping,' Jackson mused. 'Is that weird? It's weird, isn't it?'

Gayle and Zach disembarked from the back of the NSBC truck where they'd been preparing in earnest for the technological considerations of the livestream for most of the day.

'How's it going?' Gayle grinned. 'Managed to resist blurting?'

'I'm gaming it,' Jackson's eyes twinkled, 'the longer we wait the more Templeton puts himself in the shit, right?'

Zach stretched an arm out and Jackson stood to high-five him.

'Have you contacted your mum?' Zach asked. 'She hasn't blurted since this morning.'

'Yeah,' Jackson replied. 'I messaged and told her we're just playing with Templeton. She wants to know when they can come home though. Apparently they've both had some facial tightening thing. She wants to get a photo of them in *Edinburgh Life* before it wears off.'

'Nothing strange there,' Hanna said. She glanced at Zach, pleased to see him pulling out the chair next to hers to sit on. She made a series of clicks then projected her screen onto the back of the garage door. A freeze frame of a cycle-powered trailer appeared, complete with a trailer box in tow, about two metres long by the same in height and a metre in width. They all watched as an ecstatic-looking Swede made his way through the colourful streets of Stockholm riding a bike which was apparently effort-lessly pulling a trailer, stopping occasionally to deliver parcels.

'This is by far the best option to efficiently re-spec,' Hanna said. 'Electric hybrid bike, combined with an electric-assisted flat-bed trailer, we swap out his delivery unit with the fold-out tiny house design to form an updated twist on trailer tents. There's an extreme terrain option for all the wheels and chassis, plus the trailer can be hitched to other vehicles, both ends, so if there's an emergency, someone can't ride, whatever …,' Hanna shrugged, 'there are options. Options are good.'

Gayle moved closer to get a better look.

'We can charge all of that from the NSBC solar panels on our truck roof,' she said. 'If I can park up and turbo charge the spare batteries along the way too this'll work, no problem.'

'Each unit has a battery with decent capacity,' Hanna explained. 'Even without top-ups at charging stations we should be good for uphill assistance throughout, thanks to all the banked charge from downhills.'

'And a real sense of adventure for the narrative, too.' Gayle added. 'This is great Hanna, well done. Are they interested in sup-plying this for us, the Swedish makers?'

'Almost bit my hand off,' Hanna said. 'They've got an outlet in Edinburgh. They've already sent me a photo of two units they've got in stock which fit the brief. And a third on the way if we want it, for Zach or you. All they've asked for is inclusion of their logo. We can get a camera rig onto the bike, no bother. And they know to stay quiet meantime.'

'Perfect!' Zach said, excitedly rubbing his hands. 'Absolutely perfect!'

'And,' Hanna went on, 'I messaged with the contact at Faslane this afternoon. I reckon with the tiny houses on we can get each trailer down to sixty-five kilos. It's coming out super light. There should be scope to rope some kit onto the houses when they're folded away too.'

'Wow!' Gayle said. 'That's impressive. When can Faslane sign off on designs?'

'Tomorrow, if we want,' Hanna replied, 'any chance of a lift?'

'Every chance of a lift,' Gayle smiled, 'we'll all go.'

'I don't mind not going.' Jackson tried to sound chilled.

'What?' Zach stared at Jackson. 'Are you mad? Why would you want to miss that? You'll see the first big sheets of Transpariboard coming off the line! That's going to be so awesome. And it'll be good for your game of staying off Blurt, innit? You shouldn't be embarrassed about getting emotional, if that's what it is. We've got your back.'

'And from there we'll work out a date for leaving,' Gayle added, pulling on an NSBC hoodie. 'And Jackson, we can clear out of here anytime. Your parents shouldn't be waiting for that. Say the word.'

'How much longer will we be?' Jackson asked. 'How long will the Transpariboard take? A month?'

'A month?!' Hanna laughed. 'More like a week! It'll be laser cut. Once it's cooled it can be put together like a big Lego set. Easier, in fact, 'cos the pieces are big. The worst of it is a few hinge dowels to hammer in for the folding pieces and even that's less than an hour's work for the pair of them.'

'Seriously?' Jackson whispered.

'You're an anomaly, do you know that?' Hanna leant back in her chair, unaware of Zach breathing in the smell of her hair as she removed her bobble, then shook out her ponytail. 'Don't you remember predicting that timeframe?' Hanna asked. 'It's all in your projections in your dissertation.'

Jackson's eyes darted from Hanna to Zach. He picked up the Transpariboard sample from where it sat, shimmering in the middle of the table and held it mid-air, tilting it in front of his face to cover his blushing.

'I'll have to head home tomorrow after Faslane.' Hanna scrolled her diary. 'I said I'd do a few more shifts at the pub. Then I'm free to go. All in with you all.'

'Perfect.' Zach spoke without thinking.

Hanna smiled at him, then looked away.

'Zach means he thinks *you're* perfect, Hanna,' Jackson said, dimples dancing, 'but he hasn't seen your typing face.'

'Zip it.' Zach rolled his eyes, trying hard to style out playing his hand, 'Or I'll withdraw your shower rights, got it?'

Jackson shrugged.

'I don't care,' Jackson pulled his onesie underarm fabric towards his nose and took a deep sniff. 'I can go for days without showering sometimes. You stop smelling yourself after a while.'

'Till the morning,' Gayle called as she left the garage. The peace of her evening walk home had become a welcome decompression ritual from days in Jackson's world. When she reached the main road a few streets away from the Campbells, she felt a vibration on her wrist and looked down to see a new group message from Bryce Cooper.

In the garage, Zach spotted the message too.

'You two!' Zach said. 'Look at the workspace.'

Jackson reopened his laptop and Hanna tapped her screen back on.

'FM Clearwater proposes we launch news of the journey tomorrow evening,' Hanna read. 'Oh, my God!' she whispered, 'It's happening!'

Jackson picked up where Hanna left off,

'… we have received information that Michael Templeton departs New Scotland tomorrow night (11/06/35) on the 18.32 from Waverley. We therefore plan to post our first announcement on Blurt just after 19.00, allowing us to capitalise on any further dispatches of misinformation Templeton makes into the GBE early evening news just before he boards. This timing will also reach our own Unclearances target demographic in one of their most active Blurt windows, between 19.00 and 23.30.' Jackson rubbed his hands together and his thumbs began tingling, already keen to blurt.

Jackson scrolled to reveal another paragraph.

'FM Clearwater would also like Jackson to consider giving Faslane permission for a larger batch of Transpariboard tiny houses to be made immediately in addition to the two houses for the journey. Her idea is that one be gifted to each New Scottish city to display in a civic space from the journey's launch date. Additionally, there would ideally also be one for the Isle of Skye (for the sake of rural accessibility), one for the national archive and one for the EU archive. Lastly, she would also like to send one to the GBE government as a gift of neighbourly goodwill. This would mean an additional eleven houses with no requirement for trailers as they would be fixed in situ for safety reasons. Please let us know your thoughts ASAP. With thanks and very best wishes, Bryce Cooper.'

A wide grin spread across Hanna's face as she tapped the love heart icon next to Bryce's message.

'This is *epic*!' she said, her fingertips drumming the edge of the dining table. 'Folk will be able to go and touch them, get in them, take selfies with them. What a brilliant idea!'

'Well?' Zach asked Jackson. 'What do you say, man? Gonna share your toys?'

'Course he is! Who wouldn't?' Hanna nudged Zach playfully.

Hanna's certainty pricked Jackson's conscience. His attention wandered to a sticker on the back of her laptop screen; a simple outline drawing of two cat's faces in motorbike helmets, the words 'ride or die' in an elaborate italic typeface underneath. He'd seen it before at uni on Niall's laptop, Jackson remembered.

'Would Niall?' Jackson asked, 'Share, I mean?'

'In a heartbeat,' Hanna replied. 'Why?'

'If me – and you – if we do well from this, we, I mean *you*, anyway, you can help *him* too, can't you?'

'Definitely,' Hanna replied. 'That's 100 per cent my plan.'

'Who's Niall?' Zach tried to sound casual, but anxiety edged his question.

'My best friend,' Hanna replied, 'he was at uni with me and Jackson. He's in a recovery centre right now, his mental health got rocky. He's getting help.'

'And he's massively gay.' Jackson flashed a knowing smile at Zach.

Zach tried to hide his relief while Jackson leant forward and began typing.

'I say yes to all that Bryce Cooper, you absolute ginger genius,' Jackson read aloud while he typed. 'Sounds ace. We'll tell them at Faslane. Can't wait. We're pumped. S'later. Love, J-Dawg.' Jackson gave himself a little round of applause then remembered to click send. 'Sent!' he announced, triumphant. 'Check me, getting shit done!'

24

/RebeccaCampbell/blurts/
Rebecca Campbell Edinburgh Life photos search

/RebeccaCampbell/blurts/
Why is my dachshund so fat will he die search

/MichaelTempletonGBEBS/blurts/
BREAKING: COMING TO YOU LIVE FROM 'WHOLE CASTLE VIEW'
– THE CAMPBELL MANSION. JACKSON CAMPBELL STILL BEING
HELD IN A NUCLEAR PRISON AT HOLYROOD?! WHERE ARE HIS
RABID PARENTS? WHY DO POLICE NEW SCOTLAND NOT CARE?
#GBECares #GBEBS #StateTorture #NuclearWeapons #ReuniteTh-
eUnion #War

/RebeccaCampbell/blurtsTo/MichaelTempletonGBEBS
Send Blurt I am reporting you and your drones to Police New
Scotland for trespassing round my property! How dare you! #rude
#manners #getout!

/MichaelTempletonGBEBS/blurts/
Memo and reminder to final brave patriots leaving corrupt New
Scotland after our highly successful #MEGA demo – DO NOT
DRINK NEW SCOTTISH WATER! Return to safety, patriots. #Effluen-
tEdinburgh #GBEsafety #NewScottishDanger #NewScotlandLosers
#MEGA

/MichaelTempletonGBEBS/blurts/
Police New Scotland have attended Campbell Mansion and
removed me from the grounds where I was simply checking in the
windows for bodies. They tried to trick me into drinking 'coffee'

from a tartan flask with them in order to sedate me and presumably then take me to the secret Holyrood nuclear prison. I have wrestled free from their evil clutches. #ReuniteTheUnion #KnowThineEnemy #NewScotlandPoison #MEGA #GBEBS

/RebeccaCampbell/blurtsTo/MichaelTempletonGBEBS
Blurt Why are you saying 'effluent Edinburgh'! Edinburgh is affluent! Not Effluent! #Report #Rude #nottrue!!!! #NewScotlandhasgood-plumbing!!!! #Villeroyandboch

/MichaelTempletonGBEBS/blurts/
BREAKING: CAMPBELLS STILL MISSING. REPORTING FROM THE SAFETY AND CIVILISATION OF LONDON IN THE MORNING. #ToryGlory #GBECares #NuclearNuisanceNeighbour #EffluentEd-inburgh

/NewScotGovtFMClearwater/blurts/
I am excited to announce a brilliant collaboration between #Unclearances, #NSBC and Jackson Campbell! Jackson will leave Edinburgh this Saturday to journey to see his Unclearances land on the stunning Isle of Eigg in the Inner Hebrides. We'll all be able to join him throughout on a livestream to see New Scotland's past, present and future join up in a new chapter of our country's story! #JacksonsJourney #EcoTravel #EdinburghToEigg #EHA #Adventure #Transparency #NoKidnap ;-) #NuclearFreeZone ;-) #EU #Progres-sivePolitics #NewScotland #GreenNewDealDelivered

/NewScotGovtFMClearwater/blurts/
Jackson and his Journey crew will be travelling with tiny house kits to shelter in along the way. The tiny houses are designed from a rev-olutionary new upcycled material Jackson has invented – Transpar-iboard™! Enjoy this photo of #Transpariboard™ and Jackson here (image credit GBEBS, with thanks). #JacksonsJourney #NewScot-land #GreenNewDealDelivered

/NewScotGovtFMClearwater/blurts/
We're gifting a tiny #Transpariboard™ house to each New Scot-tish city and to the Isle of Skye to exhibit while Jackson journeys. So, you too can climb in and discover the wonder of #Transpar-

iboard™ and use it to frame your own view of New Scotland's safe, inspiring and eco-friendly environment! Don't forget to tell us all about your own eco adventures and share your selfies too, using #Unclearance and #JacksonsJourney! #NewScotland #GreenNewDealDelivered

/NewScottishBroadcastingService/blurts/
NSBC are delighted to partner the New Scottish Government for Jackson's Journey! Following FM Clearwater's announcement tonight re #JacksonsJourney and #Unclearances please follow our new Blurt feed /NSBCJourney/NewScotland/ for updates! #NewMedia #NewScotland #EUBroadcasterOfTheYear #QualityQuantityQuestions #NSBC

/jacksonmcampbell /blurts/
Surprise! Guess where I've been all day? Here's a clue, it used to be a naval base and I dry humped a decommissioned submarine. #DesigningLikeFuq #JACKSONSJOURNEYBITCHES!!!!!!! #JacksonsJourney #Unclearances #DodgyCroftersToilets #Tartan #history #bikes #Sexy

/NSBCJourney/NewScotland /blurts/
VERY EXCITED to get #JacksonsJourney moving THIS WEEKEND! We'll be taking an NSBC truck, three bikes and two folding #Transpariboard™ tiny houses on an adventure of several lifetimes as Jackson Campbell takes transformative steps into his future on #JacksonsJourney! #NSBCJourney #NewScotland #EUBroadcasterOfTheYear #NSBC

/RebeccaCampbell/blurtsTo/jacksonmcampbell
Private Message Jackson! Remove the pornographic photograph of you on the end of that submarine at once! For goodness' sake! Just as I was making progress for you with your father!

/jacksonmcampbell /blurts/
BACK IN EDINBURGH looooooong day at Faslane with the NSBC massive and /HannaNowak making tiny houses so sorry we missed you, Templetots ;-) #Faslane #GBEBS #WasThatSubADomIFeelBruised #JacksonsJourney #Unclearances #BigSexyNSBCTruck

/jacksonmcampbell /blurts/
PS keep the merch coming we are feeling it big timeeeeeee ☺
#Bikes #Trailers #TinyLife #Snacks #merchMeUpBeforeIGoGo
#JacksonsJourney #Unclearances #MyHelmetYourLogo

/jacksonmcampbell /blurts/
Ps thanks #GBEBS for all the great publicity innit, could not be
doing numbers like this if it wasn't for my favourite stalker Michael,
like, lysm baby but the only weapon I've been handling is my OWN
☺☺☺ #StopShoutingMikey #AngryBoi #BrightRedBoi #Steamed-
Gamman #JacksonsJourney #GBEBS #NuclearBoxers

/HannaNowak/blurtsTo/jacksonmcampbell
wtf I now have 17k Blurt followers, your life is MAD. So tired. Good
day

/jacksonmcampbell /blurts/
OMG WE WERE GONE FIVE MINUTES TO ORDER FOOD AND
CAME BACK TO #JACKSONSJOURNEY TRENDING ACROSS THE
EU lol lol loooooool #lol #TinyBedtime #SoCool

/MichaelTempletonGBEBS/blurts/
Speechless. Speechless and disgusted. The 'First Minister' of 'New
Scotland' has embarked on a project with a halfwit who simulated
sex with a submarine which was, just over a decade ago, the
nuclear warhead pride of Great Britain and the Commonwealth.
That nation of tartan reprobates truly could not have fallen lower.
Clearwater is an international disgrace. #GBEBS stands with union-
ists all over SCOTLAND on this dark, sinful night.

/jacksonmcampbell/blurtsTo/ MichaelTempletonGBEBS/
Aww Mikey babes that is so cute you are standing with my dad
tonight. I thought you hated him but no, you're feeling the love.
#MichaelLovesRoy #JacksonsJourney #MEGA #GBEBS #LoveIsAll-
MichaelNeeds #TartanReprobates

/jacksonmcampbell /blurts/
OHMYGOD just opened the post thank you so much Armstrongs in
Edinburgh for the kilts!!!! Me and Zach are going to be WELL SEXY

in them. Defo wearing on journey!!!! #JacksonsJourney #Tartan
#RateMyCalves #Commando

/HannaNowak/blurts/
Going out training on my neighbour's bike tonight. Switching from
my usual running. Gotta get the bum ready for the BIIIIIIIIIG cycle, I
guess. #JacksonsJourney

/jacksonmcampbell/blurtsTo/HannaNowak/
Training? Wot you on about? We don't need to train. It's just a bike
ride innit. Chill oot Macleod. Me and Z aren't training. #JacksonsJour-
ney

/HannaNowak/blurtsTo/jacksonmcampbell/
Zach runs and does burpees every morning while you lie in, you
clueless bam. You better be match-fit for what lies ahead, Campbell. Slackers will not be tolerated ;-) #JacksonsJourney

25

The bedrooms in the recovery centre were on the first floor. Leaning against the wall beside the thick glass of his floor-to-ceiling bedroom window, Niall realised why they were not higher. A hopper window could be opened above him and pushed outwards; it was big enough to let air in and out but too small to let a body through. And even if the window had been bigger, Niall saw, the drop wouldn't be enough. The windows down in reception started at waist height and the grasses beyond them were set back by a smart ring of pebble landscaping, making every view to the outside of the vast, circular, semi-subterranean recovery centre entrance look like part of a panoramic screen saver.

Some of the grasses had grown long sheaths at their tops in the last week, Niall realised. Inside the sheaths would be seeds, he presumed, growing longer and fatter, squeezing together until they pressed against the sides of their papery pod, making it burst. Then, Niall assumed, the seeds would be picked up and eaten by a bird or a mouse; taken inside a digestive system then shat out, surrounded by their own fertiliser, destined to grow in literal crap.

But what if they didn't make it out of the sheath at all because the sheath was dysfunctional, or somehow underdeveloped, Niall wondered. In his mind's eye he watched the sheath turn from green to pale gold to brown to black, buckling slowly; curling and drying and dying. Whatever plan they had once possibly seen for themselves would not be happening in the tight, cold dark.

Containing a growing darkness had become a twenty-four-seven stealth operation for Niall. He ruminated on the hurtful details of his life, replaying memories over and over. Today, his sixteenth day in the centre, he had focused on forgotten birthdays, birthdays followed by cards with 'sorry, son' and a card once delivered with the envelope barely sealed. And twice, the wrong age on the card. What had previously been an ebb and flow of pain was now just constant pain. Now there was no tide, but a tsunami in the making.

Niall had become a master of subterfuge. Or so he thought. He used misdirection to throw people off, asking questions about them in reply to questions about him, always putting the heat elsewhere. He was doing it, he told himself, for the greater good. After all, what use was it to anyone if they realised Niall needed *all* the help on offer, that his case was much worse than anyone else's, despite what Fin had said?

He couldn't remember the last time he'd slept, but no one else needed to know that. The upside of insomnia, he'd decided, was time to process, maximising the efficiency of his own counsel.

At some point during the previous night Niall had lain, watching the moon shining like a bright white penny over a distant Glasgow, and a realisation had arrived in his neuronal nightshift. It had initially proven hard to reckon with, but in the light of day the gist was clear; there was a point to the lives of everyone he knew, and yet there was no discernible point to *his* life. If he too was worth something, life would've intervened to stop him having to be dealt with by sandal-wearing strangers reeking of patchouli and constantly proffering weird drinks.

Niall felt the glass grow cold against his forehead. He watched as Jim, the grumpy chair-thieving bastard, wandered out of the centre and took a puff on his vape, then stowed it back in his pocket and wandered back inside. Even Jim had shown he had worth at the previous evening's group therapy session, Niall thought. He'd brought out a picture of himself with his grandkids, four of them, draped all over him in an armchair. Then he'd shared a letter they'd sent, co-signed in four different examples of terrible handwriting, wishing Jim better and telling him to try hard not to be sad about Grandma dying any more.

I'm such a cunt, Niall thought, embarrassed by all the hateful names he'd been privately assigning to a brave old man because of a selfish desire for sole rights to a comfy chair. It wasn't just the chair though, Niall thought, it was also because men who looked like Jim were most commonly the ones who gave Niall and other young folk strange looks on the street, in normal life. But now Niall knew more. This same man inspired outpourings of love from children – the ultimate apparent diviners of human goodness or badness – while Niall, well, he couldn't even inspire his parents to love him.

A beater seemed to strike Niall's heart, the blood rising to the bruise of it; a molten metal of hurt swinging in the cage of his ribs.

He was a zombie grandfather clock, Niall thought, pressing himself against the wall by the window. He pinched the skin on his forearm hard and waited to feel something. Two small white lines where his nails had dug in stared back at him.

He closed his eyes hoping it would slow his thoughts.

Cunt, his mind hurled at him. You're a cunt, Niall.

Niall Cunt Horn. He said it ten times, so he wouldn't forget.

Niall's life, he understood perfectly now, was worthless.

He had no worth.

There it was.

He was a rotting seed. A doomed sheath.

He pinched the skin on his stomach, hard.

Nothing. The sheath was half dead already, he realised.

26

The night before the launch Gayle picked up a last energy bar wrapper from underneath the dining table in the Campbell garage and pocketed it. She took a last look around the immaculately cleaned space before giving the nod to set the alarm and moving to the door, ready to close it behind Zach.

They had packed everything they needed for the journey into the truck's storage hold earlier in the day and the remaining boxes were stacked under and on the mezzanine inside Jackson's tiny house. As a gesture of goodwill to Jackson's parents Gayle had had NSBC deliver a large replica vintage bathtub planted generously with lavender to the Campbell's back door. Now, just before they vacated to the hotel at Holyrood, she hoped the gift would pass muster with Rebecca and Roy on their return.

Jackson sat on the bottom step of his tiny house and watched four fat bumble bees on the lavender flowers. Some of the stalks bent with the bees' weight as they harvested pollen, pinging back up when the bees hovered, hanging in the air for a moment while selecting their next landing spot. He was like a bee right now, he thought – his tiny house step was his hover and France was, after Eigg, his destination. He'd thought about taking a photo of the bees, of the whole scene at the back door, in fact. However, as he'd drawn his tablet from his denim jacket pocket and framed the shot the pretty image had unsettled him. With the inclusion of the lavender from Gayle his parent's home looked picture-perfect; somewhere he wanted to be. Somewhere he wanted to be happy, too. The physical resonance of it made his belly feel bruised. He was leaving, after all, and he'd be gone for as many years as it took for the inevitable GBE-spun scandal about his theft to die down; or until the long arm of Interpol, pursuing him on Niall's behalf, reached out and grabbed him.

The garage alarm tones brought Jackson back to the present.

'Nailed it!' Zach declared with a grin as Gayle pushed the garage door closed behind him.

'I never manage that alarm,' Jackson called over, 'I always trip up or something. Then I have to start again. Or I just turn it off.'

'Tiny house locked up?' Gayle asked as she and Zach approached.

'Yeah. Yous have to check it though. I've never totally locked up before, like, with no one else home. It's weird.'

'It is.' Gayle stretched over Jackson's shoulder to try the tiny house handle. It held fast when she tried it either way.

'Locked,' she announced. 'Well done. Now I'll worry because no one checked mine after I left this morning, damnit.'

'Oh.' Jackson pondered it as he stood. Till then he hadn't really given any thought to Gayle's situation when she wasn't in the garage. The driveway fell almost silent in the early evening air. On impulse Jackson grabbed Gayle and hugged her. Her body felt rigid, like an ironing board, then softened when she decided to hug him back.

'Thanks, Gayle.' Jackson was earnest when he released her. 'For everything, like.'

Gayle nodded. Jackson's hug was the first close contact she'd had with anyone since her kids had left for New Zealand and though he smelled, as ever, not completely sanitised, his innocent warmth disarmed her. She breathed a long sigh.

'I miss my kids,' she said at last. Jackson and Zach nodded, neither of them able to think of what to say. Gayle waited, hopeful for a sliver of wisdom, then checked her wristband when none came. 'And now we need to go and meet Hanna, and *her* extremely busy mum, don't we?'

Zach checked his wrist.

'We do. They'll be there in five minutes,' he agreed. 'Say good-bye to the homestead, JC. Next time you're here you'll have ghost stories to tell, huh?'

'What?' Jackson searched Zach's face. 'Who's going to die, like? Why would you say that?'

'Mate, I mean from Eigg.' Zach clarified, 'The ancestors, innit?'

Gayle was already making her way to the truck. She stopped at the door.

'Eigg was on the news the other night,' she called to the others. 'Did you see it?' Jackson and Zach shook their heads. 'It was the anniversary of the community buying the land and turning the island into a trust,' Gayle continued, 'twelfth of June. Thirty-eight years since it happened. Apparently, they had a secret donor at the eleventh hour who gave them almost a million pounds. The secret of who she is – or was – has never been revealed. Intriguing, huh?'

Zach raised his eyebrows.

'Did it mention us?' Jackson asked.

'Briefly,' Gayle laughed, 'it said we'd just missed a really good party for the celebrations.'

'Balls.' Jackson tutted.

'Come on,' Zach nudged Jackson, 'we don't want to be late.'

. . .

Hanna, her mum, Alicja, and sisters Zuzia, Ana and Amelia arrived at the meeting point just off Holyrood Road five minutes before the NSBC truck drew up. Bryce had posted specific instructions into the workspace about where Gayle should park and she followed them to the letter. His reasoning became clear when, moments after turning off the engine, what Gayle had thought was an unremarkable granite wall on their right slid two silent metres to the left and revealed the bunker, its location perfectly hidden to any passing public by the truck. Bryce hurried everyone in, looked both ways outside then pressed a control pad to shut the door again.

Under the bright bunker lights Hanna excitedly introduced everyone. Alicja thanked Gayle profusely for enabling the family's visit to Edinburgh, while Bryce bent to compliment pre-schooler

Amelia on her zebra-striped cabin baggage suitcase. He had spotted that she looked mildly traumatised by her new subterranean-like status. Her three much older sisters now stood talking to Jackson, Zuzia and Ana giggled at every word he said while Hanna pretended to listen but was clearly much more interested in what hid under the dust covers nearby.

'Would you like to help me pull the covers off the special bikes and tiny house trailers?' Bryce asked Amelia.

Amelia looked over Bryce's shoulder to two long, white draped shapes beyond. She eyed Bryce suspiciously. He was the first completely pristine-looking person she had ever met, and she wasn't entirely sure she trusted him yet. She cast a glance at her mum and, reassured she was nearby, cautiously let go of her suitcase and offered her small, warm hand.

'Come on,' Bryce said, 'lots to do tonight, isn't there?'

'Ahem, everyone!' Bryce called. Spotlights rotated and sent a wash of brighter light over the bunker walls. Jackson, Gayle, Zach and Hanna looked up, trying to spot a control room, but everything at the top of the bunker was reflective, holding its secrets tightly.

'Thank you,' Bryce continued as a hush fell. 'I suggest we get on, I'm sorry to rush you, but I know the little ones will want to get to bed at a decent time.' Bryce smiled down at Amelia then over at Zuzia and Ana. Zuzia and Ana stared coldly back at Bryce, horrified that he clearly thought they qualified for an early bedtime. Bryce caught their expressions and, realising his mistake, his face began to glow dark pink and moist. He cleared his throat and pressed on, 'So, yes, em, let's see this kit, shall we! Please, pull off the sheet, Amelia!'

Amelia stared at Bryce, mesmerised by how the bright pink of his forehead almost merged with the bright ginger of his hairline. She tugged at the nearest sheet which rippled easily towards her then slid down the trailer and bike to the floor. Delighted gasps filled the bunker. Amelia bent to pick up the silky cover, then her face lit up as she looked up to Bryce and over to the other sheet, her expression posed the question.

'Yes!' Bryce said, delighted. 'Go on!'

Amelia ran the few steps to the other trailer and pulled the edge of the second sheet, this time keeping hold of it and stepping back, a miniature bridesmaid in reverse with a voile train. Another gasp went up as the folded sheets of Transpariboard caught the lights and spectral refractions lit up the bunker in thin, beautiful rods and prisms of rainbow.

'It's like my mum's disco ball,' Jackson whispered. His eyes darted around the dark walls, trying and failing to keep up with fleeting patches of light transforming the bunker into a magical cave.

Hanna opened her mouth to speak, but no words came. She walked towards the nearest trailer and knelt, her fingertips light on the Transpariboard. It felt smooth and cool. She ran an index finger over the precision-cut hinges, marvelling at their perfection.

'Beautiful,' she whispered, 'absolutely beautiful.'

Amelia wandered back to Bryce.

'Can I get in?' she asked, now grasping a sheet in each hand. When Bryce failed to understand she shot a look backwards at the seat on the nearest bike.

'Oh,' Bryce replied, 'yes, of course. Climb up! The brakes are on.'

Amelia climbed into the bike seat and grinned across the bunker at her mum. Alicja waved excitedly then carried on chatting to Gayle.

Jackson joined Hanna.

'So these are a bit nice,' he said, crouching beside her.

'They are,' Hanna agreed. 'You must be *so* proud.'

'Nah,' Jackson nudged Hanna so she had to grab the trailer to steady herself, 'teamwork makes the dreamwork, innit?'

'You are remarkable, yeah?' Hanna replied.

Jackson pretended he hadn't heard and stood up, following the twinkling reflections again. Hanna stood too and moved nearer, closing the small gap between their elbows.

'Jackson,' Hanna almost whispered, 'I think I get it now, that for someone who is an absolute attention whore online you also don't like the spotlight in person, weirdly. Am I right?'

Jackson looked Hanna up and down.

'Guess so.' Jackson shrugged.

Hanna nodded, her face serious. Jackson leant into her ear.

'Since we're getting real,' he said, matching Hanna's hushed tone, 'isn't the real question how are *you* going to shag Zach in a half see-through box, especially while your mum's watching at home with your mini-me Russian doll collection, hmmmm?'

Hanna shot Jackson a fond, faux-withering glance. She had been waiting for a comment of this nature to arrive since the introductions, as it always did when the four sisters and their mother, all uncannily alike, were seen together. Even though Zuzia had dyed her hair black and was wearing an appalling amount of eyeliner, the resemblances were still striking. Hanna waited for a reference to the Polish Von Trapps, or a Slavic Jackson Five. She was relieved no one had so far thought of the latter, or had tried yet to turn her and her family into a Blurt hashtag sideshow complete with photos of them all in descending height order.

'Shall we test this, then?' Hanna nodded towards the trailer. 'I'd rather not make a total arse of it when the cameras are on tomorrow, you know?'

Jackson pulled off his denim jacket, scanning for somewhere to hang it. Zuzia grinned back at him from mere centimetres away, a beckoning finger waiting to be a coat hook. Jackson jumped, surprised.

'I'll hold it, Jackson,' Zuzia said, 'as long as you follow me on Blurt.'

'Oh, right,' Jackson replied, 'are you old enough for Blurt, like? I thought they were really clamping down on under-agers?'

'I'm seventeen!' Zuzia hissed angrily, then added an awkward giggle.

'Oh.' Jackson replied, 'Cool then. Hanna'll give me your deets, yeah?'

Zuzia hugged the jacket tightly as Jackson moved back to the trailer.

After a successful assembly of both tiny houses, the second one going up much faster than the first, Amelia set in motion a contagion of yawning which had everyone, apart from Zuzia, agreeing to call it a night till an early, pre-launch breakfast together in the morning.

. . .

'That Zach looks at your big peach *a lot.*' Zuzia said to Hanna at midnight, both of them too excited to sleep. Their mum, Ana and Amelia had conked out on the huge bed on the other side of a vast bedside cabinet while watching cartoons.

'Does he?' Hanna smiled in the glow of her tablet, 'I haven't noticed. But good.'

'Well obviously you haven't noticed,' Zuzia replied, 'he's behind you when he's doing it, idiot.'

The sisters giggled until Amelia stirred with a long moan, sat up and glared at them, then left the crook of her mum's arm to walk zombie-like to the fold-out bed on the other side of the room. Hanna got up and padded after Amelia, tucking her in then re-joining Zuzia, shushing her with a finger at her lips.

'He's sweet,' Hanna whispered. 'I like him. A lot. But. He lives in Glasgow, normally. And he works in telly. Folk will throw themselves at him all the time.'

Zuzia yawned.

'You don't need to be scared, trust me. He's into you. He doesn't seem like a prick, does he? Like the type who'd tart around? He's quieter than that. And sweet. And geeky. Geeks are drawn to other geeks. You're in, I'm telling you. Me, on the other hand, with Jackson …'

Hanna rolled her eyes. 'Oh, *no*. Zuzia. Seriously. That is *not* happening. He's almost ten years older than you. Come on.'

'I know!' Zuzia glared at Hanna. 'Fuck's sake. It's forsaken love, isn't it? But mentally he's *not* eight years older, is he? If anything, he's eight years younger. It's not fair. He talks to me as if I'm the same age as Ana, too. It's disgusting. I wore my crop top and everything.'

'I don't see the journey going down well if some drone catches Jackson checking out girls in the crowd who were so recently children at the launch, Zuz, do you?' Hanna pulled the covers up from the bottom of the bed, kicking them out from where they were tucked under the bottom of the mattress.

'Fuck off!' Zuzia hissed, 'I'm hardly a kid.'

'Night, Zuz.' Hanna shuffled round to face the view of Salisbury Crags silhouetted against the night, but her sister pulled her shoulder back.

'I'm just saying you could put a word in, that's all,' Zuzia urged.

'He's following you on Blurt now.' Hanna sighed. 'If you guys are meant to be, down the line when age gaps are no longer relevant, you'll be, right? *Night*, Zuz.'

Zuzia flopped back on her pillow and refreshed her tablet. She'd been scrolling the Jackson's Journey hashtag since they'd parted in the hotel corridor, checking in vain for anything new from the object of her desire in the suite next door. She zoomed in again on Jackson's profile picture, he was pretending to fellate a ScotsSports bike tyre pump that Zach was holding out. He looked so gorgeous, Zuzia thought, jealousy that she was not going on the journey coursed through her as she regarded Hanna's back.

'You're evil,' Zuzia whispered, scrolling again, 'I hope Zach's secretly married. With seventy-two children and a supermodel wife.'

Hanna feigned a snore as her wristband buzzed lightly. She pretended to yawn and cover her mouth, then snuck a peek at her screen so Zuzia wouldn't see. It was a message from Zach.

Nite through there. Jackson's conked. Sugar low. He just bolted three cheeseburgers, a pint of Irn-Bru and two knickerbocker glories off room service. Thank God the bathroom has a window and a fan, you can imagine the aftermath. Anyway. I'm just lying here looking forward to the adventure – with you. Xx

Hanna's stomach flipped. She tapped the heart icon. Damnit, she thought, closing her eyes tightly, seventy-two children and a supermodel wife or not, she was falling. Hard.

27

/jacksonmcampbell /blurts/
Have binged, will travel. Gonna power us to Auchterfechterbogle on farts alone. #PARP #BrownNoise #Ow #Waffles #JacksonsJourney #JacksonsGurney

/NSBCJourney/NewScotland /blurts/
Day 1! We leave from the New Scottish Parliament in Edinburgh at 10 a.m., taking stops along the way, but where will we camp tonight? Join us on the livestream and wave along the way if you can, we'll keep you updated, wherever you are! #adventure #JacksonsJourney! #NSBCJourney #NewScotland #EUBroadcasterOfThe-Year #NSBC

/NewScotGovtFMClearwater/blurts/
I couldn't be prouder to watch #JacksonsJourney set off today! Follow the hashtag and @JacksonsJourneyNSBC! Have a great day, everyone! #Transpariboard™ #EHA #TransparentGovernment #unclearance #GreenNewDealDelivered

/RebeccaCampbell/blurts/
Private Message Jackson Campbell: I don't know if you know that Michael Jackson had a monkey called Bubbles and they lived in an oxygen tent together. The pictures of you and your little blonde friend in your houseboxes remind me of that. Hope you left the garage tidy. Bon voyage!

/HannaNowak/blurts/
Can't believe #JacksonsJourney's actually happening! And to my BFF, I know you can't see this, but I love you, Niall. #ProductDesign #NSBC #NewScotland #TransparentLiving #Unclearance #ProudEHA :'-)))))

/ProfDrewMcAllister/blurts/

Gutted to miss the launch, but important work continues with the #EUKnowledgeCrew in #Berlin. My heart's in #NewScotland, as ever. GO FOR IT #JacksonsJourney! #NSBC #TransparentEducation #EHA

/MichaelTempletonGBEBS/blurts/

Morning all, I have eyes in Edinburgh on the vulgar, classless #JacksonsJourney. Weather is heinous, kit disastrous. I predict high death toll. Another vanity project from vicious Nationalist Clearwater. #ReuniteTheUnion #AtomicEdinburgh #NuclearNeighbour #GBEBS

Gayle took a morning run then breakfasted with the others. While Jackson finished the fifth fat waffle he'd dared himself to eat from the buffet, she'd wheeled in a large luggage trolley borrowed from the hotel and handed out small bales of branded NSBC and Jackson's Journey merch to everyone. Afterwards, leaving everyone delightedly trying on hoodies, caps, jackets and helmets she made to the truck to stow a few items for her kids, then carefully moved the truck to the centre of the parliament plaza. The night before, Bryce had sent Gayle an exact position to park at for the launch, advising that once the truck was in position New Scottish Police Officers would bring the bikes and trailers from the bunker. Gayle noticed a wide area for them to drive through had already been sectioned off to keep pedestrians at bay when the time came. Looking around, she saw press colleagues setting up drones and kit with rain covers. The forecast predicted a dry, bright day – perfect for cycling – but a concrete-grey hue in the morning sky and a chill nip in an unexpected wind suggested nature was going off script.

Gayle heard an excited whoop and spotted two New Scottish Police Officers riding Jackson and Hanna's bikes and trailers onto the plaza. The Transpariboard houses were standing, just as Jackson and Hanna had left them the night before and, even in the overcast conditions, still managed to twinkle.

The nearby journalists stopped what they were doing and stared then hastened their efforts to finish prepping.

'What the hell, Wood?' an ex-colleague of Gayle's called over, nodding towards the houses.

'Good, huh?' Gayle called back, 'But you knew they would be if I was involved, surely?'

The man shrugged a friendly concession. Gayle watched as he adjusted his tripod to point straight at the houses now parked next to each other, perfectly angled to include the huge NSBC thistle logo on the back of the truck from every possible perspective.

Jackson's Journey flags had been made by the NSBC comms team, four of whom now rushed out from a heavily branded pop-up marquee at the edge of the plaza. Two of them were carrying microlite telescopic step ladders and wearing safety helmets and tool belts. Gayle and the police officers watched as they moved like a troupe of circus gymnasts, fitting two enormous flags on metre-high poles to the rear corners of the truck, then busily attached a much taller, rigid flagpole into the rear tow-loop of each house trailer. The flag on Hanna's trailer was a section of a map of New Scotland, Gayle saw, with the journey she'd planned in the workspace with Zach marked in red from one corner – Edinburgh – to another – Eigg. On Jackson's trailer, the flag matched the two on the truck; bright purple, with Jackson's Journey in large white capitals and the hashtag in green, the three colours of NSBC's brand.

'You've ridden these more than Jackson and the product designer now.' Gayle told the police officers.

'Well, they're great!' one officer replied with a grin. 'Seriously. I'd take that on holiday to the highlands. No bother. Light as a feather!'

'I'm glad to hear it,' Gayle said. 'I've had a few sleepless nights thinking it all through, I can tell you.'

'The brakes are great, too,' the second officer added, 'we put them through their paces.'

Gayle spotted Zach making his way down the steps at the parliament's walkway from Holyrood Road. He was wearing the branded rain jacket from his pack, and she watched as he zipped it up, shooting a small grimace at the sky.

'Slightly crap weather,' Zach said as he neared. 'We ready to get my bike out?'

'Yes,' Gayle replied, 'on both counts'. She smiled at the police officers, 'Are you folks here till the off?'

'Affirmative,' the second officer replied, 'we're sworn to protect all your kit till you go. I believe you're even getting a subtle escort out of the city, courtesy of the FM, in case any MEGA vehicles decide to come alongside and make things difficult. You shouldn't know our people are there, if they're doing their job right. FM prefers not to alarm the public wherever possible, you know?'

'That's brilliant.' Gayle smiled. 'Thanks, to all of you. We'll unload Zach's kit now too, then go and meet the others.'

As Gayle and Zach carefully reversed his modified bike out of the NSBC truck and parked it next to the trailers they checked over its cameras and handlebar drone controls. Gayle then talked through the route which Bryce had arranged special permission for them to take.

'Straight onto Canongate, take a right down Jeffrey Street onto Market Street followed by another right onto Waverley Bridge,' she told Zach, 'then a short section on Princes Street, then up to St Andrew Square, then a right down to Queen Street.'

Zach half-chanted the waypoints back as Gayle said them.

'You'll have a trickier job than me,' Zach said, 'betcha anything there'll be taxi and bus drivers who haven't read their memos and blast their horns. Not often they see alien vehicles in The Green Rectangle, is it?'

'They'll cope,' Gayle shrugged. 'Don't underestimate the goodwill with you folks out in front. There's something about Jackson that just makes folk laugh, isn't there? Even on a bleak Edinburgh morning.'

'True,' Zach agreed, 'then it's over to the Dean Bridge and down to Queensferry Road?'

'Yes. Then from there we get the city behind us.' Gayle looked up at the sky, now a much more foreboding grey, 'But if the weather gets really crappy we'll find a place to pull in and take cover so you guys don't get soaked. I've got a few ideas in mind, we'll play it by ear and keep chatting on comms, OK?'

'OK,' Zach agreed, 'I better go and check on Jackson, I think his gut is rejecting about seventy per cent of the food he's eaten since last night. How long have we got? Half an hour?'

'Yes, just about,' Gayle replied. 'Where did you leave him?'

'Hauling himself across the hotel bedroom tartan carpet after we'd packed,' Zach said. 'He got a friction burn on his thigh from his kilt, but that didn't stop him. He said he was too bloated to walk, but he made me blurt it, too. Standard, really.'

Gayle laughed, glad she'd already packed her stuff. The thought of returning to the aftermath aroma of Jackson's bowel activity was a sensory experience best avoided whenever possible, she now knew well.

'And Zuzia?' Gayle smirked. 'Still tracking him?'

'Hanna's mum came out to the corridor and pulled her inside. I don't speak Polish, but I don't think she was asking her nicely.' Zach chortled. 'So, he's escaped, unless she's trailing him to here, now. Or digging a tunnel with a teaspoon through the wall between the suites.'

Gayle laughed then checked her wrist. The plaza was now two thirds filled with people, most of them swarming the promotional stands NSBC had set up selling Jackson's Journey sweatshirts, t-shirts, caps, rucksacks, bike helmets, sustainable water bottles and a selection of other items Gayle couldn't make out. A few groups had begun noticing the Transpariboard Houses and were breaking away from good vantage points around the podium for the FM's speech, curiosity and wonder getting the better of them.

Gayle pulled an NSBC baseball cap from her pocket, put it on then raised her collar, affording her a perfect disguise as a regular crew member alongside Zach. A New Scottish Police Officer was ushering a pipe band into place on a reserved spot alongside the podium.

A gaggle of young teens wearing leopard skin print hoodies with 'THE JACKSON CAMPBELL APPRECIATION SOCI-ETY' emblazoned on the backs in white lettering strained against each other at a stall.

Back up in the suite, Jackson checked the time. Zach would be back for him at any second, he realised. He opened the door to the corridor and popped his head out to check for Zuzia who had sent him almost hourly messages since midnight offering to go for a walk with him, or to film him for Blurt while he did ridiculous things in the hotel corridors. When he saw no one there, he stuffed the Jackson's Journey jacket Zach had left out for him into the top of his rucksack, grabbed up the straps and snuck out of the room. Arriving at the elevator he pressed the button and was dismayed to see the lift light up at the ground floor while he was on the tenth. He jogged to the fire exit stairs behind a heavy door and began his descent. Two floors down he looked up and out of a long lozenge of window on the half-landing. Through it he could see rooftops and one of the closes leading through to the Royal Mile. Beads of sweat pinged into his armpits, immediately dampening his t-shirt. He could go, he realised. For the first time in weeks, he was alone – this was the chance he'd been waiting for and it had arrived with a whisper. He placed a finger on the glass and felt his heart beat faster in his chest. The sky outside was darkening and the lead along the slate rooftop ridges took on a blueish glow. His eyes darted down the side of the nearest building where a slimy gloop of algae and rust clung to the stone faces of the random rubble from a crack in a black gutter pipe above. Jackson winced. It was going to rain, there was no doubt about it, in fact it was probably going to rain the whole way to the Isle of Eigg, he thought. In France his parents had got cracking tans, according to their photos. And it never rained there, as far as he knew. The universe was telling him something, Jackson thought, surely this was a sign? He pulled his rucksack onto his back and took off, round and down and round and down till he was at the bottom of the stairs facing a fire exit into a back lane. Sitting on the floor by the door was a huge, open umbrella, someone must've left it there to dry, Jackson thought. He bent and grabbed the handle then pushed the emergency exit bar with his bum, dragging the umbrella sideways through the doorframe then righting it and hiding underneath it. He could see a few steps in front of him which was all he needed but, more importantly, no one could see him. He heard the door slam shut and felt his nostrils flare with adrenaline.

'Just go,' he whispered to himself. 'Just. Go.'

A message buzzed on his wristband. He ignored it. An image of Zach, Gayle and Hanna, all waiting for him with the kit, formed. He felt sick. He tipped the umbrella upwards slightly. At the other end of the lane on Holyrood Road, small clutches of people were passing, making their way to the parliament. He looked up the lane and found it empty. A sign above caught his eye. 'Jackson's Entry' it read. Jackson stared at it, disbelieving.

'It *is* a sign,' Jackson muttered, 'it has to be, to go to France.'

'Is it, aye?' came a sarcastic voice.

Jackson spun round and saw Zuzia in the fire-exit doorway. He pulled the umbrella lower again and stared at her feet, which remained resolutely still.

'Peek-a-fucking-boo, is it?' Zuzia half-laughed, but her tone was bitingly cold.

Jackson tipped the umbrella backwards and stared at Hanna's sister.

'Fucking off, are you?' Zuzia asked.

Jackson shrugged, trying to look unphased.

'Nice,' Zuzia said, 'just make a complete arse of my sister then, yeh? Who gives a shit about her, or the others? Opportunities like this one come along all the time, don't they? For folk like you, anyway.'

Jackson stared, speechless.

'Say something!' Zuzia spat. 'God, you big prick. Here was me thinking you were alright. But you're just a coward, aren't you? Fuck's sake.'

Jackson shook his head. This was not a story he wanted to hear about himself. It felt wrong – too harsh, too sore. Tears swelled in his eyes.

'I ... I got scared,' he managed. 'Don't you ever get scared? I hate all the attention. It's fine online and that. But all *that*.' Jackson waved his free hand towards the door, 'I don't actually deserve it. Hanna does, yeah, Gayle and Zach, yeah, totally. They've all worked their asses off. But me? No.'

'You're a narcissist.' Zuzia ran her eyes up and down Jackson with disdain, 'I looked up your star sign last night. I couldn't understand it then, but now it fits. How could I not have seen?'

Jackson's wrist buzzed again. Something in the Jackson's Journey hoodie pocket Zuzia was wearing buzzed too. She moved her foot to hold the door open and pulled her tablet out.

'They're looking for you,' she said, 'apparently everyone thinks I'll know where you are. So what's it going to be? More of the amazing disappearing man? Or, actually thinking of another person for once? I don't mean me, obviously. You're dead to me now.'

He considered for a second that he could shove Zuzia inside the door, slam it and leg it up the close, but the coolness of Nowak eyes staring at him again stilled him. He pulled the umbrella shut then grabbed the door. He nodded to Zuzia to go in.

'Come on,' he said, 'you're right.'

Zuzia's eyes widened, her mouth making a small O. She re-entered the stairwell and, before Jackson could change his mind, raced to the fire door leading to the hotel's vast reception area and flung it open. A mob of about thirty members of the Jackson Campbell Appreciation Society stood in front of the lifts, eagerly awaiting Jackson's imminent appearance. Jackson dropped the umbrella back on the floor where he'd found it and sighed deeply.

Zuzia regarded the fans; they mostly looked like teddy bears crossed with teenagers in their onesies. Three of them appeared to be in charge and looked older than the others, maybe Hanna's age. Zuzia narrowed her eyes as she watched them, wondering which of them was behind their Blurt account. One of them looked in Jackson and Zuzia's direction then quickly alerted the others. Squeals of delight followed. Zuzia looked at Jackson. His hair was shrouding his cheeks but still, a damp sadness in his eyes was unmistakable. A pang of guilt hit Zuzia's chest and made her frown, confused. She turned and saw the fans approaching

'Showtime,' Jackson whispered as he walked past her and out of the stairwell towards the swarm. Zuzia watched as he set his bag down, threw his arms open for hugs then posed for selfie after selfie. She snapped a photo, making sure to get the reception desk in shot, then sent it to Hanna.

28

Jackson and Hanna stood in matching jackets on the podium waiting for the First Minister's launch speech. Jackson's kilt skimmed his knees, but the cold was making him wish he'd worn a onesie or, like Hanna, the branded leggings to keep the chill off. At the back of the gathering amassed in front of them, an enormous inflatable baby with a cross face bobbed on three ropes. Jackson recognised the blow-up's face immediately – a rubberised Rabid Roy. An inflatable arm flailed in the wind with a pointing finger waggling, seeming to give the entire crowd a telling off. Jackson glanced up to the clouds, wondering if his parents would be able to see it if their plane came in over the parliament.

Hanna followed Jackson's dark gaze to the effigy of his father. One of the people holding its ropes was standing exactly where the MEGA puppet booth had been before, she realised. She imagined an inflatable of her own dad alongside Roy and shivered; they'd have made him with one hand balled to a fist, she thought, her throat dry. She averted her eyes from Roy's frothing lips and looked to Jackson.

'You all right, JC?' Hanna asked. She wished she'd made the time to chat more with him before they'd moved on the stage, but she'd been swamped by friends then rushed to the podium at the last minute.

Jackson rubbed his chest with the heel of his hand.

'Couldn't we just have done this on social media?' he asked. 'Isn't this all a bit stupid? Real-time stuff, like? It's so meta.'

'Not long, then we're gone,' Hanna said, 'and I'm here, OK?'

Jackson's eyes glistened.

'Do you know what Drew would say right now?' Hanna's tone was playful as she switched to a gruffer pitch. 'He'd say chin up, Jackson, this isn't aboot *you* – or Hanna – or *anyone*. It's aboot the future! Aboot New Scotland being a better place, so you can take a few minutes of crowd pain and a sore arse afterwards without moaning, can't ye?'

Hanna's face had contorted to echoes of Drew's while she tried to deliver his barbed Glasgow accent.

'Urr you listening?' Hanna went on, half-barking with a final, comical grimace.

Jackson giggled, rocking towards Hanna then nudging her with his elbow.

Daniella appeared at the parliament's main entrance, flanked by Bryce and her sign language translator. Four New Scottish Police officers walked around the trio in kite-point formation, pleasantly urging the crowds to make room for the First Minister. After making her way up the stairs to the podium and shaking hands warmly with Jackson then Hanna, Daniella faced the cheering crowds, both hands waving. She wore a perfectly tailored white woollen coat with a matching polo-neck, trousers and pumps. As a nod to the collaboration with NSBC she had attached a felted thistle to her lapel, alongside an enamelled badge of the New Scotland flag. She beamed at the cameras and drones aimed at her then tapped the mic. A hush fell.

'Welcome, everyone!' Daniella's tone, unlike the weather, was warm and bright. 'We're here today to take another step along New Scotland's path of discovery and this step, this'll be an easy one, I think. Don't you?'

An approving response rose in answer from the crowd then was interrupted by a lone voice through a loud hailer.

'I say Jackson, you say Journey!' the leader of The Jackson Campbell Appreciation Society shouted from the middle of the crowd. 'Jacksiiiiiiiiiiiiiiiin!'

Jackson waved awkwardly.

'JOURNEY!' the other fans' returning volley was immediate.

'Jacksiiiiiiiiiiin!' the leader yelled again.

'JOURNEY!' the throng cried, this time louder.

Daniella held her hands out, palms down, bouncing them for a second, a gentle appeal for quiet. Jackson's Appreciation Society's leader lowered her loud hailer and smiled coyly while blowing kisses to Jackson with her free hand.

Daniella looked down to her shoes, hands clasped, suggesting she might pray. When she looked up after a pregnant pause, her expression was grave.

'Three hundred and forty-three years and five months ago – to this *very* day,' Daniella's voice boomed, 'the families of Glencoe, save a small clutch of escapees, were murdered.' A phone rang in the crowd and was immediately hushed. 'They were murdered,' Daniella looked up, her eyes steely, 'by people they thought were their *friends*. That event is now known as the Glencoe Massacre. It happened in 1692 because the elderly chieftain of the MacDonalds of Glencoe was late in delivering an official oath; the oath was his and his people's paperwork signifying their reluctant but critical bending of the knee to William of Orange. The chieftain couldn't help being late with delivering the oath, he was told to deliver it to Fort William, but when he arrived there on horseback he was informed he was expected in Inveraray, instead. Despite the significant challenges, this elderly man made it expeditiously to Inveraray where nobody at all bothered to deal with him for several days. The chieftain then returned home. Shortly afterwards, he and his people were visited by fellow countrymen in the uniform of redcoat soldiers of the King's army. The soldiers, many of them Campbells, made camp with the MacDonalds while they awaited orders for *their* next mission. They stayed for a week or so with the MacDonald folks and their animals, their hospitality. They even slept inside their homes until the order arrived with their leader, one night under darkness. Then, before the break of the next day, the soldiers rose and began slaughtering the clan.'

The leader of The Jackson Campbell Appreciation Society looked around, horrified, her expression mirrored in the silent faces of many others across the crowd.

Daniella swallowed hard, then continued, 'It will forever be a symbol of what happens in countries and cultures where, unlike New Scotland, most people are far from power; alliances are ephemeral. Coin comes before culture. All is war, strategy, greed, title. Lies. Theft. The patriarchal, egotistical focus.'

Rabid Roy's front-fixed rope was pulled low at this, giving him the appearance of looking down in shame. Jackson tried to swallow, but his throat felt completely parched. He opened his mouth, inhaling a large, humid breath but his chest was immediately desperate for more. Unsure where the First Minister was going with her unexpectedly sombre speech, Hanna slipped an arm through Jackson's and pulled him closer to her side.

'We cannot travel back and make it right – more's the pity.' Daniella's voice softened, 'The division, pain and suffering caused by that day runs through us still, just like the river in Glencoe that Jackson and Hanna will shortly ride alongside. Its banks saw and heard everything on the day of the massacre. That pain speaks still to our hearts now, to all New Scots, from here and from everywhere. And those riverbanks? They're here with us still too – wider – bursting now with life that feeds the glen and the skies, all of New Scotland and the oceans beyond. Persisting. Pushing new paths through the soil. Opening, to change.'

Hanna bumped gently against Jackson as the hairs on the back of her neck stood on end.

'This morning I paid tribute to Glencoe privately.' Daniella raised a hand, loosely indicating her office window, 'I hologrammed in. I couldn't stop thinking about the massacre – reason being Jackson Campbell here, of course, who proposed this very journey the day I was at Glencoe last, launching Unclearances. I saw the river, this morning. I saw the glen. I saw the sheep enclosures made of stones from destroyed blackhouses broken up to pen in ever-absent rich men's stock. The weight of it all felt so huge, so *present* and yet so *unpresent*, so difficult to decipher.' Daniella gestured to Jackson and Hanna to come closer.

'Oh, fuck,' Jackson whispered.

'But also today,' Daniella adjusted the mic, 'today before I came down here to see you all, I looked out of my window up there and my melancholy was interrupted. I looked down and I saw a young Campbell man, Jackson, the mastermind behind not just Jackson's Journey but also Transpariboard, a product set to make its own resonant mark on history. Here *he* is, this young descendant of Campbells. Maybe even related to some of the same Campbells who orchestrated the Glencoe massacre. Or maybe related to one of the few redcoats present on that day who reportedly didn't have the stomach for what they were ordered to do, so risked it all to help a handful of MacDonalds escape instead.' Jackson's eyes bulged, astounded, while Daniella continued, oblivious.

'Jackson, *our* Campbell, is literally here today wearing the colours of conciliation, resplendent in MacDonald Glencoe tartan.' Daniella indicated Jackson's kilt and smiled, tearful, 'Well, when I saw that *I knew* – once again – as I have known at various constellation points throughout *my* journey, that everything – right now – is just as it should be, that we *have* learned, as a nation. That we learn *still*. That all of our journeys in New Scotland are underway, because of full circle moments like this.'

Daniella dabbed a tear and the crowd let up a long, heartfelt applause. Daniella watched for a few moments, then applauded Jackson's kilt below his bewildered face. After what felt like the longest thirty seconds of Jackson's life, Bryce removed the microphone from its stand and handed it to Daniella.

'Now, everyone,' Daniella beamed, 'let me properly introduce NSBC's Product Designer who'll be accompanying Jackson on his journey. Hanna Nowak, folks!'

Zuzia, Alicja, Ana, Amelia and Hanna's friends all screamed above polite applause from the rest of the crowd.

'How do you think you'll fare on the journey, Hanna, and on Eigg?' Daniella asked.

'Well, a lot depends on the weather and how the Transpariboard performs,' Hanna replied, her cheeks burning bright red. 'We're pretty sure it'll do well, but as with all field tests there's always something unexpected that'll crop up. We'll just play it by ear, you know?'

Daniella nodded. She'd decided deliberately to speak to Hanna first, suspecting it'd put Jackson's stage fright at greater ease.

'And you've a symbolic patch of land yourself, is that right Hanna?'

'Yes, that's right, First Minister, up on Raasay.'

A small cheer rose from a few people in the crowd, evidently Raasay fans.

Hanna laughed a little. She crossed one leg in front of the other and then back again, her body language shouting as loudly as it dared that it did not want to have the conversation the First Minister sounded like she was now starting.

'Shit,' Gayle said under her breath, 'I don't think Bryce passed on my notes about not asking Hanna about her dad.'

'She probably thinks she's been allocated a random patch, like me,' Zach replied. He moved the NSBC livestream drone's view-finders away from Hanna's face to scan the crowd instead.

'Will you go there too, one day?' Daniella asked.

'Maybe.' Hanna made sure to keep smiling, but her eyes fixed past Daniella onto her mum. 'From what I've read – the place on Raasay – Hallaig, I mean, it sounds quite a lot like Grulin, on Eigg.'

'Many similarities,' Daniella smiled, 'and the origin of a lot of beautiful poetry too, I'm sure you'll discover.'

Daniella held the mic to Jackson now. Hanna stepped back and gave a sigh of relief.

'Jackson, our modern Campbell! What do you say to it then, you good to go?' The crowd cheered and applauded. Knowing Jackson's tendency to stage fright, Daniella had been careful to pose a question requiring only a one-word answer.

A New Scottish Police Officer stepped forward from behind Jackson. Daniella followed the officer's interest out to above the crowd, to where a GBEBS drone had begun jerking sporadically about twenty metres from the podium. The drone shot a foot upward then released a speaker which dangled from two tangled wires from an underside hatch. A screech of ancient modem interference erupted from it and hands shot up across the crowd as people tried to cover their ears.

'It's all right, everyone,' Daniella said, 'GBE press, that's all.'

A low groan followed from the crowd and inflatable Rabid Roy began bouncing with added vigour as the wind and rain picked up. A tinny echo of the sound of someone clearing their throat from the speaker became audible.

'One two, one two, Saint George's Cross, testing, *testing*.' Templeton's voice became clearer as he moved through the crowd towards the podium, holding a small mic to his lips. People beneath the drone ducked and swerved out of its way while the New Scottish Police Officer behind Jackson spoke into her comms badge.

'Net that. Fast. Clear and present dronefall danger. Over.'

'Clearwater! Jackson, son of the pathetic Rabid Roy!' Templeton shouted. 'Since you're all about reparations and design nowadays, what do you intend to do to repair the damage you did to the United Kingdom, hmm?'

Hanna looked nervously to Daniella and found the First Minister completely calm, the only sign of heightened emotion being a light tapping of one of her feet. Raindrops began falling, softly at first, then splattering. Three officers with nets darted through the crowd towards the drone.

'You're a fraud, Clearwater!' Templeton roared with robotic distortion, 'A nuclear fraud! We know you want to take over England! We see your disgusting gestures, trying to make out you're nice, that you want to be friends! Did you know the GBE government are − as we speak − writing "Return to Sender" on that disgusting tiny house you sent? *Did you?*

Daniella raised an eyebrow.

'I didn't know that about the tiny house, Mr Templeton, no,' Daniella looked wounded. 'That's obviously upsetting. I hate waste. However, that news marks the first time I've learned *anything* at all from you, so, for that, I'll count a positive.'

The crowd went wild with hilarity. Daniella gave Jackson and Hanna a quick wink. The net was raised to the drone and it was deftly captured then pulled to a cleared space where an officer straddled it and tasered its charging socket, abruptly ending Templeton's live broadcast and drawing him from the centre of the crowd. Back on the podium, Bryce hovered behind Daniella with a huge New Scottish government umbrella, attempting to shelter her from the now heavy rain.

'Now!' Daniella beamed, 'Rather than us all getting soaked, I say we get going with sending these wonderful young people and NSBC on their way with Jackson's Journey. What do you say, New Scotland?'

The crowd yelled approval and several Jackson's Journey umbrellas bounced upwards. Inflatable Roy tipped backwards and forwards, rain bouncing off his livid face every time his head rope was yanked backwards. Daniella linked arms with Jackson and Hanna and the three of them made their way slowly through the crowds to where the bikes and trailers waited.

'That GBE guy is terrifying,' Hanna whispered. 'I don't know how you stay calm around him. When he's going off … it's … well, it's surreal.'

'Don't worry about Templeton, he's toothless, I promise.' Daniella's voice was reassuring. 'Barely makes a ripple anywhere these days. I am so proud of you two, and I feel I should apologise for the rain. It likes to keep me humble every time I attempt a speech anywhere, doesn't it?'

Arriving at the bikes and trailers, Hanna saw her Mum and youngest sisters waiting. She blinked back tears, thanked Daniella and excused herself.

Jackson looked up for Zuzia, but she was nowhere to be seen. He pulled on his helmet then looked to Daniella and realised she was speaking to him but he hadn't heard a word. His cheeks blushed furiously.

'Thank you,' he said, hoping it was an appropriate response. He grabbed a bemused Daniella's hand and shook it before turning and making to his bike. The crowd around him created a wall of noise. As he sat, Gayle appeared at his side, bending to bring her face level with his. Jackson watched her lips move, but again heard nothing. He nodded, repeating his pretence of taking it all in. Gayle squeezed his arm then walked away. Jackson watched her disappear into the cab of the truck. He looked to Hanna at exactly the second the pipe band struck out the first notes of 'Scotland the Brave'. Hanna raised an arm and pointed to the cleared passage of plaza. Jackson watched as Hanna mouthed 'Go! Go!', while gesticulating wildly. He was watching himself in a movie, he realised, the music crashing into his chest and bursting his heart; the bright shock of it making him splutter, barely aware of the zoom lenses shooting close-ups of his face.

'Jackson! Go! You go first!' Hanna's voice broke through at last. The taillights of the NSBC truck flickered behind her. Jackson twisted in his seat to see Daniella and remembered her hologram at Glencoe, on his birthday. Was he lucid dreaming, he wondered? He'd read about that somewhere. His hand moved to his chest – the movement felt like pulling a limb through treacle while everything around him ran at double speed. Were there ghosts after all, he wondered? Is this what cleared Highlanders did to their ancestors – grabbed their hearts with their hands and infused their veins with hallucinogenic bagpipes? Breathless, Jackson looked to Hanna again; she was still gesturing wildly for him to move out in front of her. The drums started and the heavens opened more, as if also instructed to cry. A slower movement at his right caught his eye. Zuzia – drenched

– wearing *his* denim jacket, a black rivulet of eyeliner working its way down her cheek.

'Just pedal, Jackson,' Zuzia urged, 'that's all. Just pedal. You can do it. It's OK. It'll all be OK. Don't be scared.'

Jackson pressed his right foot then his left and the bike responded immediately.

'Go on! That's it!' Zuzia was walking alongside him now, the heat of anger gone from her words. Jackson sniffed and swallowed back snot. He was moving, he realised. The noise of the crowd and the music were loosening a finger or two of phantom grip on his brain.

'Let's do this thing!' Jackson heard Zach call as he whizzed by on his other side, gleaming drones flanking his tech-laden bike. 'Auto-assist on for the hill, Jackson, hit that button, baby! Just follow me! And smile for the livestream, this journey is a-go-go!'

29

On the last leg of the drive from Edinburgh airport to Whole Castle View Rebecca quietly watched a clip on Blurt of Jackson crossing the old Forth Road Bridge on his bike, pulling the Transpariboard house. He looked happy, she thought, watching him pedal and chat to Hanna, then pull a silly face at the camera. All of this was a welcome contrast to how he'd looked when she and Roy had watched the launch that morning. Roy had been appalled by the anatomical inaccuracies of the omnipresent inflatable and then equally as intrigued as Rebecca by Jackson's apparent aversion to attention after the First Minister's speech. Rebecca looked up and realised they were turning into their street. She pushed her tablet into her bag then patted the significantly cushioned girth of Duchy on her lap.

'I must say I feel incredibly conflicted when we sail through French customs while Great British England's queues look so miserable,' Roy said. He tapped the leather steering wheel while they waited for the driveway gates to open. Rebecca made a sympathetic-sounding murmur while applying a final coat of her new Chanel lipstick, *tarte aux clémentines*, which she felt set off her tan perfectly. She wanted to be ready in case Michael Templeton and a drone were about to jump out from behind a rhododendron as had happened so many times during the Rabid Roy crisis, making her swear never to be caught unprepared again.

'If they'd just rejoin the EU,' Roy muttered, manoeuvring into his usual spot by the garages, 'but there's a stubbornness, isn't there?'

Rebecca slid a surreptitious glance at her husband. This was the fourth time in a fortnight she'd noticed a shift in Roy's commentary. Empathising with people in queues and taking a borderline philosophical approach to political difference was a leap indeed, Rebecca observed.

'You didn't drink at all today, darling?' Rebecca asked.

'Not a thing.' Roy looked out through the windscreen at Jackson's tiny house, the reflection of his car gleaming in the darkness of the tiny blue-framed windows. 'I'm driving, I thought that'd be obvious, darling.'

'Hmm,' Rebecca replied, wondering if Roy had snuck a whisky warmer when she'd popped to the priority passengers' powder room before baggage collection.

'Gosh!' Roy looked around the driveway, unable to spot anything broken. 'I feel *so* relaxed. The holiday *has* done me good, Becs, it really has. And now here we are, home, and everything's peaceful. Remarkable!'

Rebecca checked her wing mirror for Templeton but not one leaf quivered on the specimen azalea behind them. She stared at Roy, annoyed at his apparent lack of rush to disembark and open her door.

'Get out, yes?' Rebecca prompted, heaving Duchy upwards as she waited. When Roy opened the car door, she was careful not to catch the car's paintwork with her heels when she swung her legs from the footwell. Once clear, Rebecca placed the dog on the ground, glad she'd dressed him in an alpine-styled Gucci sweater which offered some nipple protection now that she could see his substantially swollen chest and gut resting on the gravel.

'Roy,' Rebecca feigned cheer in case of an audience. 'Darling! Go and open the back door, please, see what all the key fuss was about, hmm?'

Roy stared, then remembered his deception, and about turned.

'Yes, yes darling, off we go!' Rebecca sung, a vision of camera-ready Stepford perfection as she walked slowly behind Duchy.

'Is it open?' Rebecca asked when she and Duchy eventually made it to the back door.

'Not yet,' Roy fibbed. 'I waited for you, so you can see there's not a problem. Do you have your key?'

Rebecca tutted. She was getting sick of having to be the one to do everything since they'd got home. She opened her bag's clasp with a loud sigh, then stopped. The lavender bathtub planter from NSBC at Roy's side catching her eye.

'What on earth is that?' Rebecca lurched backwards.

Roy looked down on the planter.

'Ooh,' he replied, 'that's rather pretty actually. Very French, non? Must've been the gardener. Or a raffle prize I'd forgotten about from the club.'

'Pretty?!' Rebecca squawked, 'It's hideous! It looks like the sort of thing you'd see at a tired old National Trust property. It'll have to go.'

A huge black bee with an orange bottom made a small wiggle on the middle of a lavender stalk then flew off slowly, its back legs laden with ovals of pollen.

'Who the bloody hell puts an attraction for venomous insects so near a house? That's very strange! Honestly!' Rebecca stabbed her key at the keyhole ready to wrangle it, but the door opened easily, activating the warning tones of the house alarm. Roy stepped inside and, delighted, disarmed the security system with six stabs of his finger.

'And he really *hasn't* been in the house in …? How long …?' Roy looked around the utility room. 'How long have we been away, Beccy?'

'Days. Months. Weeks,' Rebecca answered dryly. 'I don't know! Roy Campbell I am *not* your keyholder or your calendar!' Rebecca pushed her key into the lock and tried it again, watching the mechanism work easily back and forwards. 'What's that?' she asked, gawping at the top of the door where the new lock sat in its perfect slot. Roy cleared his throat, looking everywhere but Rebecca's face as he inwardly cursed her thoroughness.

'Oh, it's … it's, well, it's just part of the five-lever mortice system, darling,' he replied as breezily as he could manage.

'So why isn't it poking out when I turn the key, like the other bits?' Rebecca pointed to the other levers on the door's edge with a *tarte-aux-clementine* fingernail. 'And there are five already – that's a sixth.'

Roy gave a blasé wave of his hand.

'It's a *six*-lever mortice we've got,' he said. 'I forgot. I didn't think the five-lever was secure enough, you know, after partition when we were expecting the looting and pillaging by SNP louts? I had it replaced with a six-lever superior model. And look how well it's done! But obviously one is broken now. What a shame! I'll get onto that soon, I expect.'

Rebecca stared at Roy, watching as he avoided eye contact, then smiling at an unopened case of Champagne on the floor by his wellies. It was the first resemblance between her husband and Jackson that Rebecca had seen since before Jackson had become a teenager.

'Look how safe everything's been!' Roy said, taken aback. 'Every time we've been away before we've come home to utter carnage, broken windows, beds slept in by partying strangers, stuffed pheasants and badgers from the shelves and walls set "free" into the garden. And this time, if what you've told me about our son's escapades are true, not only has he *not* screwed up our home, he actually appears to have got himself a qualification *and* gone off with a sensible friend. This is nothing short of a miracle!'

Rebecca stared at Roy from beneath perfectly blue-eyelinered lids, wishing she had a point to make in retaliation. A rasping sound began emitting from Duchy as he continued heaving himself, claw by claw, over the utility floor in an attempt to get to the kitchen.

'And,' Roy continued, sensing advantage, 'it has to be said, Rebecca, while you *haven't* had Jackson to contend with it *may* – just *may* – be possible you've redirected time and energy you'd normally spend on Jackson to Duchy. And, *one must ask*, given Duchy's current inability to breathe at the same time as walk, is that *healthy*?'

Rebecca's orange lips pursed as she looked down at the dog, now collapsed and panting heavily.

'It was the fondues!' Rebecca knelt down. 'There was also possibly the matter of a small impala skin – a very, *very* petite one. Do you remember it, Roy? It was on the bath pillow in the jacuzzi. I noticed it wasn't there yesterday. And I don't think Duchy would've *meant* to eat it. I thought maybe you'd put in on your chair as an antimacassar. I forgot about it till I saw your chair this morning, and no antimacassar. But, well, surely, he'd … you know … pass it? But there's been nothing, has there? Not yet, anyway. Surely he didn't eat it though, don't you think?'

Roy regarded Duchy's bulk with fresh alarm.

'Darling, I'm going to take Duchers to the New Town Animal A&E,' Roy said. 'You get settled here, yes? Pour a gin. I'll call once we've got a medical opinion.'

The colour ran from Rebecca's face. She watched as Roy scooped Duchy up, carefully removed his sweater and hung it on a coat hook, then carried the dog like a helpless, miserable, oversized baby back to the Merc. When she heard the gates clank shut behind them Rebecca went to close the back door but was unexpectedly struck by the view of Jackson's tiny house. The blue of its paintwork looked beautiful in the late afternoon sun, but the boxes inside were absorbing all of the light and life from its interior, leaving its tiny windows like empty eyes staring back. She looked down at the bathtub of lavender again and realised how well it complemented the tiny house's woodwork. Maybe the planter wouldn't be so bad if she got the gardener to stick a few large diamanté studs to it, she thought. A small bird called from somewhere inside an acer on the first terrace and was answered by another beyond the garages. Rebecca watched an incoming bee land on the tallest, most violet of the lavender heads then spotted the corner of an envelope on a bamboo skewer sticking up at the back of the pot.

She plucked the envelope from its holder. It was addressed to 'The Campbells' in beautiful handwriting with a small NSBC logo printed in a bottom corner. Rebecca opened the envelope and pulled out a thick piece of white card with a pale lilac and green thistle printed as a subtle background. The same handwriting in expensive looking black ink read, 'Thank you for the use of a great HQ to plan #JacksonsJourney. All best, Gayle Wood & NSBC.'

Rebecca's hackles rose. She sucked in her stomach then clicked furiously over the slabs to Jackson's tiny house where she pushed the card and envelope through his tiny letterbox, bending a long orange nail perilously far as she did so. Cursing under her breath, she spun on her heel and looked up, confronted by her empty driveway and enormous, empty house. Save the birds and bees she was quite alone, possibly for the first time in years. A honey-bee took off from the lavender and buzzed slowly into the utility room, hovered a second, then buzzed back out to the plant, apparently also preferring Gayle Wood's offering. Rebecca took a deep breath, clicked back to the house, slammed the door behind her and clicked straight over the travertine tiles to the kitchen. She removed a can of pre-mixed gin and tonic from the drinks fridge and, since no one was bothering to accompany her – not even a GBEBS drone – she took a long, deep glug straight from the tin.

30

/jacksonmcampbell /blurts/
NO, MY GOD NEVER MIX A KILT AND A BIKE WITH NO UNDER-
WEAR. I HAVE ACTUAL BALL AND ARSE BURN. #NSBC #JACK-
SONSJOURNEY #CANTSTOPSHOUTING #SOREAF #HELPME
#WILDERNESS

Jackson's Appreciation Society had followed on bikes out of
the city, eventually petering out at Barnton when the rain had
become almost unbearably heavy. They were replaced shortly
afterwards by a new, smaller group of eight teens who had cycled
from Dunfermline and were waiting on the middle of the Forth
Bridge enjoying a completely different weather system than the
wet grey cloud overhanging the city. They followed the team and
made up a large, loose peloton all the way to Inzievar Woods
where Gayle decided they would make camp for the night. She'd
hoped they'd reach Stirling before quitting for the day, but Jackson's frequent outbursts on the comms link about severe arse pain
had forced a reconsideration to lessen the risk of injury. The Dunfermline teens lingered in the background of the livestream after
a photoshoot session with Jackson. After positioning cameras and
camping chairs around a clearing in the woods by the car park,
Hanna and Zach manoeuvred the bikes so the tiny house doors
faced into the clearing opposite the long side of the truck. In
between it all Gayle began assembling a campfire.

Jackson lay face down on a sleeping mat between the door of
his tiny house and the truck.

'I'm going to die of a broken arse. I swear. I'm going to die,'
he half whispered.

A drone buzzed in haphazardly between the treetops, lowering
slowly over Jackson. On hearing it Jackson reached round, pull-

ing his kilt upwards, revealing bright red chafed buttocks to the camera. The teenagers huddled by the back of the truck snapped pictures, giggling.

'G, are we concerned about this drone?' Zach asked.

Hanna looked up from where she knelt locking the wheels into place on Jackson's trailer.

'GBEBS?' Gayle asked, removing her baseball cap and squinting against the evening light filtering through the treetops.

'Must be.' Zach noticed the flaking paintwork on the drone's underside, 'It's defo old.'

'Nah, don't worry, nothing to hide, right?' Gayle shrugged. 'But Jackson, make a smart choice about getting bites on your ass, won't you? Because if you think it's sore now, your flesh definitely does not want to meet the aftermath of a horse-fly's teeth …'

Jackson farted loudly then pushed his bustle of kilt back into place.

'You are *such* a minger!' Hanna winced, crossing the short distance from Jackson's trailer to her own.

'Thanks.' Jackson extended his arm and shot a selfie.

Zach waved at the drone as it began scanning the clearing, then sat in a camping chair and pulled a tablet from his inside pocket to check the feed to the livestream. Hanna watched the drone close in on the teenagers, pleased to see one of them pick up a stick and poke it at the camera, forcing the drone to retreat upwards and into standby mode on the branch of a nearby pine.

'Didn't someone send us arse cream, Zach?' Jackson croaked. 'I'm sure they did. Chafe-safe? Nut and butt? Something like that, or were they all energy bars?'

'Oh, aye, some aloe-vera stuff. It's in the hold. You'll see the box,' Zach replied.

Jackson wailed, dismayed by Zach's lack of offer to get the cream for him and unable to imagine standing upright ever again.

'I'll tilt in the walls in the houses,' Hanna said. 'I really don't fancy waking up and staring into the camera of someone taking photos of my drooling gob, know what I mean?'

'Good idea,' Gayle replied, 'nothing we can do about the roofs though, is there? That drone could decide to take a bird's eye view.'

'I'll set a motion sensor on one of our drones,' Zach said. 'I'll code it to intercept the camera view of the other one if it starts hovering over the camp area. Only flaw might be the GBEBS one getting noisy, obviously, and waking you two up. But it'd only be for a minute till whoever's remote operating it realises they're beaten.'

'Jeez.' Gayle knelt to drop a small bundle of pre-chopped kindling next to Jackson's mat then tapped her wristband to activate the birdsong sound screen on the livestream. 'I didn't think of this till now. Can you two lock the tiny houses from inside? And, if you can, how would I – or Zach – or emergency services, whoever, how would we get in to you if you were unconscious or something?'

Hanna walked over then knelt next to Zach's chair.

'When the doors slide shut there's a press lock mechanism that pushes up from under the floor, jamming the door so it can't be slid open again without the button being depressed from inside.'

Gayle nodded.

'In an emergency,' Hanna continued, 'kick or shove in the door panel. It'll give on a high impact strike. I designed in a slightly thinner section of Transpariboard in the middle.'

Gayle nodded.

'I'm happy to sleep out too,' Zach tried to sound casual. 'I could go head-to-toe in a house. In my sleeping bag, like, if anyone's scared.'

'*Anyone,* like, Hanna?' Jackson sniggered.

Gayle smiled as she pulled a fire steel from one pocket, then a fistful of tindersticks from the other.

'Putting the comms loop back on now, OK?'

Jackson, Hanna and Zach nodded and Gayle tapped her wristband.

'What did yous just say?' a voice called from the huddle.

Gayle rolled her eyes.

'That I want a sausage roll,' Jackson called back, 'and the arse cream.'

'I'll get you a sausage roll!' one of the teenagers replied.

'I'll put on your cream!' shouted another.

Gayle loosened the bundle of tindersticks and struck the fire steel. Sparks jumped from the metal to the wood.

'They've got sausage rolls at the Sawmill Café,' the first teenager called, 'it's just through those trees. Will I get you one?'

Jackson rolled onto his side to face the teenagers and grinned.

'If you get me four I'll give you the money and love you forever.'

The teen and a pal hopped onto their bikes and were gone.

'I'm disgusted with myself,' Jackson sighed, pulling a sad face.

'For exploiting infatuated youth?' Hanna asked. 'You bloody should be.'

'No,' Jackson frowned, 'for being near sausage rolls and not smelling them. What the hell's happening to me?'

'I've got beans and toast for us all in the truck,' Gayle smiled, 'and veggie sausages. If you guys want anything else from the café, go try to grab it now. Says online it shut five minutes ago at seven.'

'Maybe you should go and wash off your ass, Jackson, get the woolly bits from the kilt out of it,' Zach suggested. 'They've got to sting. Then put on the cream, then your boxers. That's what I'd do.'

'And wear the gel-padded pants tomorrow.' Hanna patted her bum through her leggings, 'They're ace.'

Jackson moved onto all fours pointing his rear towards the others.

'Need a firelighter, Gayle?' he asked, only half joking.

'If you even think about it,' Gayle laughed, 'you will regret it, I promise.'

Jackson stretched then rose and wandered to retrieve his rucksack from the truck's hold.

'I'm going to the toilet block,' he called over his shoulder. 'I'll wash my arse and put on my onesie. Then I'm going to eat my sausage rolls. Then I'm getting in my tiny house and I'm not coming out again till morning.'

'Don't forget the cream,' Zach called back.

The GBEBS drone buzzed from its place in the tree to follow Jackson from the truck to the toilet block, then waited a careful distance above the teens while Jackson went inside.

Dramatic screams emerged from the toilet block's open window when Jackson saw his behind in a mirror.

Zach tapped his tablet screen to direct Jackson's audio only to the livestream.

'Was he worse than you thought he'd be today, or better?'

Hanna asked. 'He really frightened me at Holyrood. I thought he was going to leg it, did you see him? He was a wreck.'

Gayle and Zach looked at Hanna, surprised.

'I thought he was nervous,' Gayle replied, 'but I didn't realise it was worse than kinda average nerves. Shit. I was preoccupied with everything else, I guess.'

'Yeah, same,' Zach frowned. 'That's a shame. It's a bit 'the boy who cries wolf' sometimes with Jackson, isn't it? He does drama so much I guess sometimes we might not realise when it's real.'

More screams were emitted from the toilet block, followed by a peel of laughter.

'Seems OK now though, doesn't he?' Hanna asked. 'And there were only, what? Four big tantrums about his bum?'

'Yeah,' Gayle agreed, 'Queen Street was the first? Then the request to overnight at that big bit of grass beside the road in Blackhall, bless him.'

Hanna and Zach giggled.

'Big tantrum just before the bridge,' Zach joined in, 'but there was a good bit in the middle too, when he got right into it. He definitely buzzes off attention, as long as he's in control. It was good he had fans there. Then he moaned again after we were over the bridge, but he was quieter about it then, audience in earshot, I guess?'

'I mean,' Gayle fanned at the small flames now licking round the larger pieces of kindling she was dropping onto the fire, 'do you think he has any idea most folk would do a bike ride like that in two hours? And it took him what? Seven? How long do you think those kids were waiting on the bridge?'

Hanna shrugged then scooched onto Jackson's sleeping mat. She slipped off her trainers and crossed her legs.

'There's heaps of folk talking about it on Blurt,' Zach said. 'If he doesn't know already he will soon.'

'I hope I haven't massively underestimated the timings,' Gayle said, 'or his work ethic. Maybe I've been too optimistic?'

'Aye aye.' Hanna nodded towards movement across the car park, 'Here he comes.'

Zach tapped his wristband to change the audio back to the group setting. Jackson reappeared at the side of the truck wearing one of his leopard skin onesies. His kilt was slung over one arm and in the other hand he carried a large picnic basket. Two of the teenagers followed, pulling his rucksack, heaving it to lean on the truck beside the hold. The drone situated itself back in its tree.

'Look what they gave us!' Jackson grinned. 'The café folk, they gave us everything they had left over from today – for free, like! They're watching the livestream! How cool is that?!'

'Have you given the kids something, Jackson?' Gayle asked. 'They've been standing for ages.'

'Will we let them come over?' Jackson asked.

'Fine with me.' Gayle smiled.

Hanna and Zach nodded too.

Jackson backed himself carefully into a camping chair then gave a long, relieved sigh as he sat with far less pain than expected. Within seconds the teens had joined them at the fireside, blurting pictures and messages.

'The cream's helping,' Jackson announced. 'I used a whole tube.' He stretched down and scooped several of the paper bags from the basket into his lap. 'Help yourselves,' he said to no one in particular, pointing a trainer toe at the food. Jackson tucked his hair behind his ears then took an enormous bite of sausage roll. The teen who'd poked at the drone began passing bags of baked goods to the others.

'I'm feeling the big Jesus vibes again,' Zach laughed, glancing from Jackson to the basket. 'You've got a heavy loaves and fish look going on right now, man.'

'What time do you all have to be home?' Gayle asked the teen sitting nearest.

'Ten,' the girl replied.

'Half nine,' came another reply, accompanied by a long sigh.

'You all need to head together, OK?' Gayle replied. 'Safer that way.'

'Do you have lights on your bikes?' Zach asked.

Only one teen nodded. Zach stowed his tablet back in his jacket pocket and got up, making towards the truck.

'I'll get you all some' he called over his shoulder, 'we've got heaps of freebies.'

Hanna enjoyed the view of Zach as he walked away and felt her heart race.

'Why don't you have bike lights on?' Jackson asked, pastry

from his sausage roll spraying out of his lips as he spoke. 'You have to have them, don't you? Zach says it's the law now.'

'We didn't think we'd be out this late,' one of the teens replied, 'we thought you'd get to the bridge at noon then just pass through here. Everyone thought you'd be in Stirling for the night, or Bridge of Allan.'

Jackson broke a thick square of millionaire's shortbread in two then shoved half of it into his mouth. He chewed and pondered. Gayle cleared her throat then stood.

'I'm going to put on a ton of beans and toast,' she said. 'Pop another bigger bit of wood on in a minute, will you, Hanna?'

Hanna nodded.

'Why did you think we'd be at the bridge by then?' Jackson asked, spraying shortbread crumbs into his lap this time. 'We cycled all the way from Edinburgh, do you know that?'

The teen winced apologetically then grabbed a doughnut and started nervously picking hundreds and thousands off the icing.

'We went past Dundee and everything,' Jackson continued, gazing into the flames. 'We've been everywhere, it's a massive journey we're doing, like.'

'Dunfermline,' Hanna corrected.

'What?' Jackson asked.

'It wasn't Dundee. It was Dunfermline,' Hanna explained. 'It's pretty close to Edinburgh.'

Jackson frowned at Hanna then popped the rest of the shortbread into his mouth.

'You're from Aberdeen,' Jackson said between chews, scrunching empty paper bags into balls before lobbing them at the fire. 'That's practically the North Pole, so maybe you don't really get the distances down here, in the bigger part of Scotland?'

'So wise.' Hanna nodded up at Jackson with as pious an expression as she could manage. 'Truly, our modern messiah has spoken.'

31

The following morning Niall lay in the thick, aerated tog of a pristine white sleeping bag with a hood fitting snugly around his face. He looked up at massive puffs of dense clouds passing far above the skylight window from the huge reclining chair. When he'd entered the MDMA Therapy Room he'd sat down, then watched while soft cuffs were Velcroed round his ankles and wrists before the sleeping bag was zipped up the middle to just below his chin. Fin had been by Niall's side for the last three days, after finding him alone at the reservoir's edge and spotting a haunting look in Niall's expression. The light buzz of thermostats and comms tech whirred as they began auto-calibrating the sleeping bag to keep Niall perfectly comfortable, removing any risk of him becoming overheated or dehydrated during the session.

'So. How do you like the cocoon?' Fin asked. 'Is it what you expected?'

'I mean, it's a strong look.' Niall heard his own voice somewhat louder inside the hood. 'I hadn't expected it to be quite this astronaut-without-a-spaceship vibe, but massive maggots are in this year, are they?'

A dimple flickered on Fin's cheek as he pulled a clear piece of tubing from a pocket on the side of the cocoon.

'Straw,' he explained, tapping the tube with his finger. 'Remember it'll let you sip water, but it'll limit how much you can drink over ten minutes. If you feel thirsty or hot at all you tell Claudia straight away. Clear, Niall?'

Niall nodded.

'You'll be monitored throughout,' Claudia said as she entered the room wearing pale blue scrubs. Niall regarded her as she smiled at him. Next to the chair and cocoon she matched the skyscape perfectly. She tapped her wristband and Niall's chair began a slow rise and deeper recline. Niall felt momentarily nauseous as his centre of gravity adjusted and a childhood memory of being in a dentist's chair flashed by.

'OK, Niall, just like we discussed,' Claudia's smooth lilt was reassuring. 'If the treatment is working, you'll experience everything from pleasurable, possibly mildly orgasmic sensations throughout your body to euphoric, blissful, transformational thoughts and feelings. You and I will be in informal conversation throughout this first treatment, understand?'

Niall nodded then stared up at the sky with resigned mortification.

'If you are not susceptible to the dose of MDMA we've selected for you,' Claudia continued, 'you'll likely feel nothing at all. We'll understand that within fifteen minutes of the dose being administered and at that point we'll get you out of the cocoon and have a chat about what to do next as part of our crisis intervention. I don't anticipate that will be necessary, however. Any questions before we begin?'

Niall closed his eyes and moved his awareness to his genitals. As had been the case for almost a year now, there was nothing he could imagine happening to that part of his body that would awake any function aside from toileting.

'No,' he replied, 'no questions. And I'm pretty sure I'll be completely unresponsive in every way. Sorry, because I know you're putting in a lot of effort, all of you. But I don't see me coming back from rock bottom. I think it's just the way my brain's wired – to get more and more depressed.'

'OK,' Claudia replied. Fin patted Niall's arm through the suit then turned and crossed the room. Niall raised an eyebrow at the underwhelming reaction to what he'd just said. 'Fin's gone to the observation area behind the screen,' Claudia continued, 'if you open your mouth when you're ready I can administer your dose.'

Niall opened his mouth. An image of the extremely hungry caterpillar flashed in his memory as he felt a tablet on his tongue, which immediately began to dissolve. He closed his mouth and swallowed, listening as Claudia pulled a wheeled chair to beside his feet. She sat, placing one of her hands on the cocoon so he felt a gentle pressure on his calf. In the silence that followed, Niall sensed a kernel of realisation. No sooner had he registered it, it transformed, redoubling, then exploding into a bloom of knowing. He was a pod bursting with life. A current of intrigue cloaked his skin, tickling pleasantly so the soft hairs on his limbs stood on end.

'I'm a pod!' Niall exclaimed, finding it impossible not to laugh, 'But I don't know if I'm full of peas or beans.'

'Go on,' Claudia urged.

'My dad's allergic to legumes. I'm having a flashback of being at a burger van with him.' The words rushed out of Niall, 'He's telling the women at the van that he's fine with seeds.' Niall wrinkled his nose, 'Oh! She's asking if he's allergic to sesame buns. He's not. Oh! *I'm* not a seed, Claudia!' Niall's voice cracked. 'Oh, God. I can join it up. Right now. I'm not a seed or a sheath. I'm a pod. And it's OK if my dad's allergic, isn't it? It's OK!'

'It is OK.' Claudia squeezed Niall's calf through the cocoon, then released it. A fizzling, shivery pinball of an urge to stretch ran down Niall's spine to his coccyx, then shot pleasingly back to his neck. He arched his back, then released. The pinball touched the base of his skull and then divided in two, weaving a symmetrical crown of warm, liquid-like pulsing under his scalp. Niall felt the reverberation of his own appreciative moan in his throat. He spread his fingers wide, pulling the pinballs immediately back to his neck, round and through his shoulder blades then shooting down his arms to his wrists where they subdivided again, yet lost no momentum. From there they seemed to light up each bone and tendon of his hands as they went, deepening his bliss. All the while, images from his past played like movie trailers in his mind.

'What's happening now, Niall?'

'I'm watching my dad, and he's watching me.' Niall smiled. Without opening his eyes, he could tell the clouds above the skylight had gone; the sun shone through the glass and every cell of skin on his face tilted like a microscopic solar panel to catch it, drinking it in.

'Sunflower skin,' Niall whispered. 'Turn to the sun. Tournesol, they call them in France, don't they? Turn to the sun. God. We're all like that, Claudia. That's what we're like, isn't it?' Claudia squeezed Niall's calf again. Inside the cocoon his fingers opened then closed. He pictured catching his dad's hands and holding them.

'There's a rainbow over us,' Niall said, 'you're on one end, Claudia, and my mum's on the other. Oh. Good. *Everyone's* here. Fuck! Everyone's here but we're all doing our own thing! It's OK that we're not connected, we can just ... we can just *be* – apart or together.'

'Tell me how it feels Niall, for you.'

Niall breathed slowly and thought about it. His consciousness rolled over the velvet of Claudia's words which hung, ribbon-like, between and around everything. It was a velvet that was both a concept and a thing. A perfect textile which existed everywhere. The fibres of connection, seen and unseen. Niall became aware that jigsaw pieces were sliding and clicking together. The picture they were making was an exponential sky of *freedom*.

'I feel *good,*' Niall said, a wide grin now unstoppable. 'I feel *so* good. Dad is *love*. I am love. The rainbow is love. Mum's thoughts are in Dad. Dad's thoughts are in me, and Mum. We're perfect, Claudia. It's like, every colour in the rainbow is also a bit of the colour before it, isn't it? And the colour after it, but normally, we can only see one at a time but, it's *so* different to that really. So, *so* different.'

Claudia squeezed.

'What is the value of the rainbow, Niall?'

Niall swallowed. Inside the cocoon his chest rose then fell, slow and steady.

'The rainbow's value is the whole world,' he answered, 'the whole world is in the rainbow. It never ends. It is beautiful – always – even in the night when it can't be seen. It exists. When the stars are there instead the rainbow is in them, when the stars are gone they are the rainbow – or the sky. Everything is energy and love. Even maggots. Caterpillars. Fin. You, Claudia! Me. Mum and Dad. Everything is connected and love. It's infinite. The value is infinite. It's the highest possible value of all things.'

'Tell me why you are here with me, Niall, with the world, with the rainbow?'

'I'm here to live.' Niall's smile grew. 'I'm here to do what only I can do, with my energy. Just like everyone. Everything.'

'Tell me about the dark times, Niall,' Claudia's voice was soft. 'The truth will set you free. What happens in the dark times, why do we go there sometimes?'

'It's so we can go here, after,' Niall answered immediately. 'I'm walking now. I'm walking on the rainbow, to my mum. She's walking towards me, towards me and my dad.'

'Good,' Claudia said, 'beautiful.'

'We're abseiling soon. When we get to the top of the rainbow we're going to abseil down and then we're going to go up again and then abseil down again.'

'Good,' Claudia said, 'you're doing so well.'

'We're *all* doing so well!' Niall replied. 'We're all doing really, *really* well. We can all be safe. We can all be free. I can let go! I think that!'

'I second that, Niall.' Claudia brushed a tear from her cheek with her free hand. 'I validate all you say.'

'I know,' Niall answered. 'I know. I was so busy before, I couldn't see where all the lines ended up together, could I? But on top of the rainbow it is the highest. The clearest. No lines. Just love. Just colour. Just freedom. Everything.'

Claudia squeezed again.

'Abseil, Niall. Be free. Play. I'm right here. Take your time.'

Niall opened his eyes. High up he spotted a bird. It would have a seed in its belly, he knew it. He closed his eyes and breathed the sky, the bird and the seed. He pictured another seed, spinning and dancing on the breeze till it came to rest on a faraway lake. He heard the seed land. It sung inside, all about love. It didn't matter anymore whether he was a pod or a seed. Either way, all was well. Niall understood it for the very first time: there was abundant time for everything. No rush, no panic. The pinball arrived back at his coccyx and split again, this time weaving its magic round his pelvis then doubling, flashing through the muscles of his thighs, then all the way down to his toes. Niall smiled. There was nothing to fear in his own body, even the fact that parts of it could now once more hold the possibility, should he want it, of doing more. He – and everyone – was a work of complete perfection, journeying always to exactly the right place. Niall laughed out loud. All was well, with all the world.

32

/NSBCJourney/NewScotland /blurts/

Today's plan: Tullibody, Doune, Callander. Can we get that far? Further? And are you coming too, New Scotland? ;-) We hope you'll step into the beautiful sunshine and wave us along if you can ☺ #JacksonsJourney #Day2 #NSBC #adventure #NewScotland #Summer35 #Beauty

/RebeccaCampbell/blurts/

Rebecca Campbell young dancer

/TheJacksonCampbellAppreciationSoc/blurts

Are NSBC working Jackson too hard? ☹ Cycling is hard for anyone to start. We hope NewScotGovt are not exploiting him ☹ jacksonmcampbell please remember what you blurted when you walked away from your other degrees – quitting is OK when it feels right! #LoveWithJackson #Solidarity

/MichaelTempletonGBEBS/blurts/

About two miles after Inzievar Woods this AM our GBEBS drone fell into a roadside ditch and lost signal with GBEBS HQ. We suspect it was tampered with by thuggish New Scottish teenagers, causing it to malfunction. A reward will be given to anyone helping to relocate this piece of equipment. #HugeReward #PatriotKlaxon #Mission-Truth

/jacksonmcampbell /blurts/

Lolling like a lolligator at folk thinking I was tired yesterday! People! That was just a lil warm up, I was taking it easy! Catch me if you can today, bitchez ☺ #JacksonsJourney

/Deli-ciousOfCallander/blurts

Jackson, pop into our bakery in Callander today and try one of
the Coco Pop slices we've made to celebrate #JacksonsJourney!
Crunchy coco pops lusciously bound together with a velvety sauce
of caramel and butter, topped with a slab of milk chocolate and
decorated with #JJ in creamy white chocolate. #BakeNewScotland
#FlyCup #FancyPiece

/jacksonmcampbell /blurts/

Right Deli-ciousOfCallander you better hold about ten of those
beauties for me because we just stormed thru Tullibody and Doune
and we are coming in so HOT for your highly sexual snacks. Hanna
and Zach can't keep up with me. I am the fastest. #JacksonsJourney
#JacksonsCalfMuscles #Sweaty #IFancyYourPiece

/RebeccaCampbell/blurtsTo/jacksonmcampbell

Private Message Jackson Darling Poor Little Duchy ate an impala
skin at the chalet. Do you remember the one? It was a baby impala,
on the pillow in the jacuzzi bath. You'd think a baby one couldn't
do any harm, wouldn't you? But it did. Poor Duchy has a large scar
and may not be able to wear any of the autumn/winter outfits I had
planned for us to twin in. Anyway, now he doesn't need his summer
colonic. Your father is watching your livestream. It was on in the
vet's waiting room. Then he turned it on at home as soon as they got
back. I don't know what to do.

/MichaelTempletonGBEBS/blurts/

Young Campbell clearly on performance enhancing steroids.
Shameful. Thank you very much to RoryTheTory, a kindly local from
Perthshire and a member of the Scottish Unionist and Conservative
Party who drove all the way to find the vandalised #GBEBS drone
and set it on its way again – all in service of truth and empire. Well
done Rory, your rewards of a GBEBS egg cup and bumper stickers
are on the way. #NewScottishLies #DirtyDaniella #RealScotsSup-
portGBE #loyalty

/jacksonmcampbell /blurtsTo/RebeccaCampbell

poor Duchy ☹ ☹   ☹ poor Dad ☺   ☺   ☺ ha ha ha ps your
messages are still not private

/RoryTheTory/blurtsTo/MichaelTempletonGBEBS
my pleasure Michael, anything for Britain. #DirtyImmigrantsOut #MEGA #BetterTogetherBitterApart #ClearwaterHatesMen

/TheJacksonCampbellAppreciationSoc/blurts
So proud of Jackson, he is so humble! He's totally pushing through, omg we love him so much and his mum is so cute, welp! #love #hero #JacksonsJourney #ThePerfectHuman

/ProfDrewMcAllister/blurts/
Absolutely pining for home, what have yous done to me NSBC-Journey/NewScotland ?!??! Loving it all. Beautiful footage, I know I'm biased but you just can't beat the routes to the highlands in the sunshine, can you? They've got everything. The trees, the fields, the wee villages with all their flowers … My kids insisting on replicating the journey ourselves before the year's out! #EHA #EveryHuman-Actualising #NewScotland #EU #OnYerBike #EcoTravel #Jacksons-Journey

/RebeccaCampbell/blurtsTo/jacksonmcampbell
Private Message Jackson stop overdoing it. I know your pain face even when you're hiding it and I've been seeing it all day long. At the very least get hold of some painkillers, for goodness sake. You're going to burst a blood vessel in the white of your eye at this rate. It's one of the real downsides of exercise and exertion and should be avoided at all costs.

/NewScotGovtFMClearwater/blurts/
Glorious weather! Well done #JacksonsJourney team! How those #Transpariboard™ houses shine in the sunlight! And what a joy it is to see our cycle lanes in action – we never doubted they were the right thing to do and now it's almost impossible to imagine it was different! What skill, consideration and talent we have in our New Scottish infrastructure teams! #Unclearance #cycle #Transpari-board™ #EHA #GreenNewDealDelivered

/MichaelTempletonGBEBS/blurts/
Disgusted to see discussions from pockets of #GBE citizens discussing moving to New Scotland and falling for Clearwater's

propaganda. Traitorous behaviour, frankly. Never forget the immigrant swarms in New Scottish cities and villages. Stay safe. #GBEBS #Breaking #TrustGBEBS #KeepControl #EmpireSafety

/HannaNowak/blurts/
Thought we'd peaked beauty-wise at Callander!!! OMFG New Scotland is beautiful!!!!! #NSBC #HappyHanna #ProductDesign #JacksonsJourney #AirInYourHair

/TheJacksonCampbellAppreciationSoc/blurts
OMG GBEBS have streamed Jackson having a pee that is a VIOLATION OF HIS HUMAN RIGHTS!!!! Answer our emergency poll should we start a crowdfunder to sue GBEBS? #TempletonIsAPerv #GBEBSCreeps

/MichaelTempletonGBEBS/blurts/
GBEBS apologises to our viewers for the brief flash of Jackson Campbell's genitals during this evening's footage. We thought Campbell was going to hide in a copse of hazel to take drugs, but he switched plan and decided to force urination instead. The resulting footage fell below the superior moral standards we at GBEBS pride ourselves on and unfortunately our genital filter detection and auto-blurring software were clearly hacked by Clearwater. #ProstheticPenis #CyberHack

/ZuzannaN/blurts/
I AM DYING – Jackson's KNOB!!!!!! And, SIDEBAR – #MySistals-Hanna and she is KILLING it on #JacksonsJourney!!!! The girl is #FITASFUCK, swear to God, every km makes her #GLOWUP more. #NSBC

/NSBCJourney/NewScotland /blurts/
We've made camp at Strathyre for the night! 63k today! Inzievar Woods seem like a lifetime ago already! A cooling wind, no midgies, HannaNowak awestruck by the views. jacksonmcampbell eating us out of tiny house and tiny home ;-) ☺ #JacksonsJourney #NSBC #adventure #NewScotland #Summer35 #Beauty #GetSome

/jacksonmcampbell /blurts/

Made it 4785642328434948 km to a campsite on the edge of the planet. HannaNowak having her 40th solo orgasm of the day, this time about the colour of a flower and some pheasant she saw up a hill. I know what I want on my headstone: JACKSON'S JOURNEY COCO POP SLICES ARE BAE. Callander snacks have set a HIGH bar, people. I hear my manhood went viral. You're welcome. #Free-ThePython #NSBC #JacksonsJourney #JJCocoPopSlices

/HannaNowaksMother/blurts/

Hello RebeccaCampbell I am Alicja, the mother of Hanna. I want you to know everyone can read your blurts. Also when you type your name you are not making a search you are making a blurt. They are not private. It was sad not to meet you in Edinburgh. Maybe when they come back? Good wishes.

/RebeccaCampbell/blurts/

Private Message HannaNowaksMother thank you but please note I have paid for the enhanced golden Blurt package with the extra letters and the privacy. Your English is very good, well done. Clappy Hands Emoji send

33

Rebecca appeared in the lounge at Whole Castle View at 9 a.m. the following morning to find Roy still sitting in front of the livestream. Duchy lay on Roy's lap, still sporting a tubigrip bandage protecting his surgery scar. Both Roy and the dog were snoring gently while the television screen was divided into four, showing each member of the journey team silently scrolling their tablets in various states of repose. When the image on screen changed to a camera pointing at the Transpariboard houses they seemed at first to be floating, Rebecca thought, then she realised Scotch mist had struck again.

Sensing Rebecca's presence, Roy awoke and looked to his wife.

'Has it been on *all* night?' Rebecca asked.

'Um, yes. I suppose it has.' Roy stretched the arm that wasn't supporting Duchy, then smacked his lips together. 'Have you just woken?'

'No,' Rebecca snipped. 'I've been ordering the shopping and organising the gardener and cleaner. I hoped you'd gone golfing.' She tried and failed to read Roy's expression as he picked up the remote and pressed rewind. When he pressed play they both watched Jackson cycling through a small town the day before. Rebecca frowned at the pedestrians clad in practical outdoor clothing and in serious want of a hairdresser while Roy zoomed in on Jackson's face, watching intently.

'Don't you want to see the golf?' Rebecca asked, struggling to keep a pleading note from her voice. 'It's better when you take a hands-off approach. With Jackson I mean, isn't it? You don't want to ruin the benefits of all that relaxing time away, do you? It wouldn't represent good value for money, would it?'

Roy raised an eyebrow, amused by Rebecca's attempt to conceal her agenda with an uncharacteristic concern for spending.

'Actually,' he said, 'I'm not drawn to the golf today. I may well stay here. For Duchy, you know? He's comfortable. The vet said rest would be critical.'

Rebecca flushed, exasperated.

'What's going on?' she snapped. 'If you're going to explode just do it, will you? This calm act is unsettling. It's revenge, is it? For me taking us to the chalet and you missing some stupid golf match or something, is that it?'

As a cloud moved in front of the sun outside the window Roy caught a reflection of himself on the TV screen. He'd thought his face was mellow, much like his mood, but on seeing himself he realised his nostrils were flared and his eyes were intense and dark. The severity of his expression took him aback. He shook his head, vaguely hoping it would rearrange his features.

'You're wrong,' he replied quietly. 'There's something strange, Rebecca, something I'm not quite sure about yet. I'm having peculiar feelings, thoughts … I—'

'Anger?' Rebecca interrupted. 'Or have we moved on to loathing now that you're addicted to this … this … *journey*. Or is it a bit of fury? Outrage and disgust? What have you settled on?'

Roy looked Rebecca up and down.

'Do you really think that?'

'Why not? You two are ridiculous.' Rebecca tutted. 'You should think about *your* father, Roy, and what he was like as a dad. You were never good enough, were you? No matter what you did. If you carry on like this, you'll end up the exact same way with Jackson, mark my words.'

Roy's lips tightened into a tiny, momentarily furious clench. Duchy roused, glared menacingly at Roy, then tucked his head away again.

'Coffee, then?' Rebecca offered, her tone cold. 'Maybe that'll help you get up and at something normal?'

Roy nodded, refusing to meet Rebecca's eye. She'd hit a nerve. A strange sensation had been building in Roy's consciousness most of the night before. It had peaked after he'd replayed footage of the launch several times while Rebecca slept.

Rebecca left the lounge as Roy placed the remote gently on his thigh, careful not to disturb the dog. Jackson's panic-stricken face as the journey began had reminded Roy of an event in his own life he'd avoided thinking about for years – the death of his father. Staring at the mist-shrouded Transpariboard houses and listening to the distant noises of Rebecca and the coffee maker from the kitchen, Roy's memory wandered to the withered outline of his father's upper body propped against a crinkled ocean of white Egyptian cotton pillows. The rest of the old man had been weighed down underneath an oppressive grey brocade bedspread.

'Royston, my son,' Roy remembered his father croaking, 'you must now be a guardian of the empire, a fighter for the realm of all that is good and right in Edinburgh. Do what you must, son, to protect Scodland. And the monarchy, and the firm. You must keep it all. At all costs. Keep the ties that bind – the finances, the union, Roy, keep them united.'

Roy had known then it would be the last time he'd hear his father say their country's name in that nasal way that he'd been assured since childhood was a hallmark of class. Pain had pierced his gut as grief performed a swan dive. Roy cringed as he remembered what had come next.

'Dad,' he'd sniffed, 'I hope you're proud of me, I hope you …,' he'd hesitated, fumbling with his pinky ring. The words that were on the way did not adhere to the well-worn script of Campbell discourse. But he'd closed his eyes and they had spilled over, stupidly forsaking all tradition.

'Dad, *I love you* and, well, it would mean the world to me to hear you say, just once, while you still can—'

When he'd looked up he'd been sure he would find softness in the eyes looking back at him. Instead, he'd met with death's shocked glare; his father's lips twisted in repugnant horror, nostrils flared, eyes bulging, the top deck of his false teeth hanging free of his gum. The private doctor who'd stayed discreetly in the corner until then rushed over, gently smoothing Roy's father's features into a more peaceful pose.

'Is that … *normal?*' Roy had whispered, bewildered.

'Yes! *Yes!*' the doctor had trilled too quickly while pouring Roy a large brandy from the bedside decanter. 'A brief rush of adrenaline and, erm, really, it was the best way for him to go.'

Duchy snarled at something in his dream, as Roy's mind began drawing lines between events he'd never considered connected before. Life at Whole Castle View had got really strange after the death – combative, even – while Roy had been taking over the firm in the months directly following the funeral. Rebecca had wanted Roy to retire early and only attend annual board meetings, but Roy had found the idea abhorrent, shameful, even. As he progressed steadily in taking over his father's clients, he'd arrive home in the late evenings to a feeling that it was them – Rebecca and Jackson – against him. He was never overtly excluded from whatever they were doing but, equally, he was never invited to join in.

Then Jackson had begun playing up, and Roy and Rebecca had united against him for a spell; a phase that was characterised by meetings with teachers, formulating punishments and consequences, a string of appointments one of them always seemed to miss, about the possibility of a diagnosis of ADHD. Then all of that had been interrupted for Roy by the more pressing matter of the United Kingdom to fight for, the promise he had to upkeep for his father, and in not just one but two referendums. Fighting for the union had stretched his eight-hour days at the office to include four hours every night at the club, strategizing and lobbying about how to move away from what Templeton and the like wanted – that Scotland should stay submissive and cowed to England's might.

Instead, Roy and his cronies wanted what had proved to be the impossible; an upgrade for Scotland, a fairer say at Westminster with no need for a painful breakaway from the union. After the last referendum, Roy's failure had turned his grief to a concentrated anger, shortening his temper for all frivolity and closing his mind to a positive view on anything about his country's reinvention. At first he had locked himself in his study or sulked at the club. Then slowly he'd merged back into home life and work, bringing an aura of tension everywhere he went. The United Kingdom had been destroyed and the union between himself and Rebecca had suffered a blow too, he now saw. Conflict had been normalised for everyone railing against New Scotland.

His son had passed through his teenage years and increasingly barbed sparring and division in the Campbell home now reigned. A slow sadness bloomed in Roy's chest while he watched the tiny houses shimmer in the mist. Somewhere in the last year, in a tiny house in his very own garden Jackson had made the leap from being solely a haphazard jackass to a maverick revolutionary of eco-manufacturing. Roy frowned, trying to pinpoint moments in recent months that stood out and possibly marked when this genius had been occurring so nearby, but nothing stood out. None of it made sense. Had he really been so bound up in his own anger that he'd missed every clue about a monumental shift in his child? And now, now he'd had a little distance, was he really able to see something he would've missed before when he watched Jackson?

Rebecca returned with a thermal carafe of coffee and two mugs on a tray. She set them down on the marble table between their chairs.

'Do you think Jackson is OK?' Roy asked. 'I mean, have you noticed anything, you know, different?'

Rebecca stared at the highlights reel now playing from the day before. Jackson seemed to be near constantly shoving small bricks made of Coco Pops into his cavernous mouth.

'He's happy as Larry, darling. Look at him!' Rebecca nodded towards the screen. 'Look at that dentistry. Wonderful. Nothing wrong with him at all apart from the fact he's pretending to be fit and doing himself multiple muscle mischiefs. I'd know if there was more, trust me. His bottom is obviously going to be in want of a resurfacing treatment, and I suspect he's using a hellishly cheap SPF, but, well. Good genes allow for a spell of caretaking deviation, don't they?'

'He wasn't right at the launch though.' Roy frowned. 'Come on, Becs, he's usually a total buffoon. Jumping all over the place. Winding folk up. Shenanigans. Anything to keep the attention on him. But then, he looked, I don't know? Frightened? Broken, even?'

Rebecca shook her head.

'Please never, *never*, ask me to think of that launch again. If you do, I'll get a private investigator to find out who owns that inflatable baby, then I'll go to their nasty little abode and fly my own inflatable modelled on their undoubtedly awful image, twice the size of their inflatable, right outside their house.'

Roy pictured the scene and felt touched when he noticed the defensive anger breaking through Rebecca's Botoxed brow.

'No, darling,' Rebecca said, carefully pouring them each a coffee, 'Jackson's fine. Trust me. Mothers know.'

'My mother was bloody clueless,' Roy muttered, his attention drawn to a photo on the wall beyond of Jackson on his first day of school. Jackson had skinned his knees badly the week before the photo had been taken when he'd come off his balance bike on to the pavement. Roy remembered feeling frustrated that the little boy was still making errors in his cycling. The thought embarrassed him now. After all, just yesterday Jackson had cycled further than Roy had ever managed in a lifetime.

Rebecca was missing something, Roy knew. Jackson was *not* OK. Something with his son's journey and Clearwater's Unclearances scheme didn't add up. And where there was money and national pride at stake there would be blame waiting ahead, not to mention bitterness and pain.

34

Jackson wrested a hand from deep inside his sleeping bag, where it had nestled in his groin all night. He pushed hair from his lip, looked up from his screen and listened to the sounds of the morning. Somewhere nearby Zach was tuning his guitar. And there was rain, rivulets running down the tiny house roof. He unzipped the side of his sleeping bag and lifted his right leg, pushing the tiny house wall so it left its sloping privacy mode. Hanna's tiny house was still hidden in a dense white cloud. He scooched over to the left and stuck his left foot out to move the wall on that side too then propped himself on his elbows. He could make out the slightest sight of NSBC's purple thistle logo through the mist. He craned his neck to look down at the ground around the tiny house and saw only half a metre of grass in any direction, each verdant blade hanging with miniature globes of moisture. Daisies stood refusing to open, their petals held tightly shut and upright, the yellow of the pollen within kept dry, waiting for the sun.

'Wow,' Hanna's sarcasm and a long yawn arrived through the comms link, 'so this weather is boring.'

'Morning,' Gayle replied.

'I'll teach you some chords later, if you like, Hanna?' Zach offered.

'Sure.' Hanna yawned again, non-committal.

A movement outside caught Jackson's eye just as he was about to tease Zach about leaving him out. He screwed his eyes up and tried to see better. An odd, dark barrel shape formed then loosened to an abstraction a couple of metres from where he lay. Jackson blinked hard, listening intently to a light swish of grass now accompanying Zach's tuning.

Two dark holes surrounded by a shiny, almost fluid cylinder emerged above Jackson's eye level. Jackson thought of an old photo of Roy holding a shotgun which stood on top of the piano at home. The dark holes twitched. Jackson held his breath. A breeze revealed the rest of a stag's wide grey-brown face topped with thick velveteen antlers, his eyes already locked on Jackson's. For a millisecond the memory of Niall's face merged with that of the stag; the fluid intensity in the centre of the eyes mesmerising Jackson like a glimmering knifepoint where he lay, frozen and terrified. The stag stepped silently backwards and was gone.

Jackson's breathing spluttered back into life.

'Did yous …? Did yous *see*?' he whispered, glancing frantically around while his fingers scrambled on the floor either side of his sleeping mat for his tablet. 'There was a stag, like, a *proper* fucking *Narnia* thing, with massive antlers.'

To Jackson's disgust no one responded.

'HELLO?!' he bellowed.

'It was probably just a rabbit, Jackson,' Zach replied.

'It wasn't a rabbit!' Jackson snapped, 'I know what a bloody rabbit looks like. I'm telling you, it was a moose. Do you get moose in New Scotland? Or Elk? Do you get them?'

Hanna rolled onto her side and pushed the wall in front of her into see-through position. She squeezed her eyes open and shut hoping it'd bring Jackson into better focus, but the weather defeated her.

'What time is it now?' Hanna asked.

'Half nine,' Zach said, the sound of his feet slapping on the truck floor accompanying his reply.

A rush of powerful hooves beat the ground nearby then petered out.

'See!' Jackson shouted.

'Shit, man!' Zach laughed. 'OK. That wasn't a rabbit. Fair play.'

Hanna shivered and pulled her sleeping bag over her head then tightened the drawstring so she was encased and cosy.

'OK,' Gayle cut in, 'computer's saying there should be a break in this low visibility very soon; between about ten and one. There's going to be some very heavy rain then, but the mist will lift for a few hours. If you guys are up for it, I say we bolt, blast through the rain, then hole up in a campsite at the end of Glen Coe. Red Squirrel, it's called. Then we can wait there again knowing we've made a little progress. It says here they've got a drying room, showers, all the essentials. And there's a pub next door. The cycle lanes are about half a K off the road right up until the last section, I expect they'll be really quiet. What do you think?'

'I'm down.' Jackson grinned and blurted a selfie, immediately energised by the possibility of alcohol.

'How dangerous will it be on the bikes?' Zach asked.

'The tyres should handle it fine,' Hanna replied. 'We've been under-utilising them so far, to be honest.'

'And we can add some high-vis vinyls to the backs of the trailers and houses. We can carb load with some toast and leftover pasta now and stuff some unwrapped energy bars in your pockets for along the way. No stops. Proper hardcore. We'll set up a nav course to guide you in. It's not ideal, because we won't be in convoy, but it's safer. And less boring than this.'

'It'll be an adventure, that's for sure,' Zach added.

'Definitely,' Hanna agreed. 'What do you think, Jackson?'

Jackson released a large fart.

'Jackson?' Gayle sighed. 'What do you think?'

'About what?'

'About Gayle's idea?' Hanna said. 'She's just asked if you're OK to cycle off-road, fast, through a glen, Glen Coe, in fact. In torrential rain. While also keeping an eye out for me and Zach incase anyone comes off.'

'I think hardcore sounds very me,' Jackson replied, 'don't yous think? Blurt'll love it. Maybe I should just wear a t-shirt so my nipples are, like, popping through it in the rain? What do yous think?'

Gayle and Zach pulled exasperated faces at each other in the truck.

'You'll be head to toe in reinforced waterproofs, Jackson,' Gayle replied. 'Safer, in the unlikely event you do come off.'

'Sexy,' Hanna joked, liberating herself from her sleeping bag.

'Sexy on me, that's for sure.' Jackson replied.

. . .

'Fuckin yas!' Jackson yelled, eyes wide as the bikes bounced down the last of the section of track Zach had informed them was ominously called Black Moss.

Jackson thrust his feet out from either side of the bike and freewheeled, while Hanna, cycling in second place looked up to a drone Gayle had set to track them as it zoomed backwards, capturing the three of them and the track in the middle of a panorama of wildness, while stones and sand under their tyres spat and leapt into the heather at either side. The GBEBS drone lagged behind them all, struggling to keep enough altitude for filming its targets at the same time as keeping its lens clear of rain.

'I *love* this!' Jackson yelled. 'This is so much fun!'

'Come on, race you to the bridge!' Hanna shouted as she picked up speed.

Jackson stood tall on his pedals, powering forwards. Hanna made chase, then slowed allowing Zach who'd been filming from behind to easily catch up by her side.

The mist had lifted, and the rain had not yet amounted to more than a few spits but a grey and foreboding promise of both hung above, obscuring the top half of the terrifyingly inhospitable mountains.

'You good?' Hanna smiled.

'I'm good,' Zach replied, 'hard going on the way up, huh? But it's paid out on the way down.'

They both watched Jackson arrive at the other side of the bridge ahead, skidding to a halt and giving the trailer a violent jolt, then turning to shout victorious obscenities before realising he was alone.

'Bastard!' Jackson's voice echoed across the landscape. 'You knew I was too fast, Hanna! Where now?!'

Hanna then Zach crossed the bridge.

'Altnafeadh,' Zach replied, pointing beyond where Jackson waited, 'up that way to the main road, then into the bike lane on this side and ten km along till we see a cottage on the left, after a loch. Then it's a right to the road to the campsite.'

Jackson stared blankly as he tried to remember which instruction had come first.

'Up to the main road,' Zach said again, 'then left. I'll tell you the rest as we go.'

'OK!' Jackson grinned, then headed off.

A strong wind brought a chill as they pedalled on. Hanna looked up and realised the storm had lowered its hem significantly. Huge raindrops began spattering their backs and helmets.

'Hope this wind doesn't change and put it in our faces,' Hanna grimaced, 'let's make this fast *and* safe. Yeah? And if visibility gets bad, we pull in, yeah? No fucking about, OK? This is serious.'

'Yeehah!' Jackson shrieked back, his eyes wide with coursing adrenaline, 'Let's fucking do it!'

'Loving the scenery, Hanna?' Zach asked, sure the question would help Hanna relax. But instead, there was a long pause.

'I feel bad saying this ...,' Hanna said at last, 'but do you know what? I'm really shocked that, well, I *don't* love it.'

'Oh?' Zach felt deflated.

'I can see it's awesome,' Hanna continued, 'of course I can see that, and I do mean awesome in the full sense, like, I am *in* awe, the scale is *crazy*. But, well ... it's lonely, isn't it? And desolate? I see what that word means now, properly. I had no idea how much I loved trees till there wasn't one in sight in any direction, you know? It's the first place I've ever looked around and thought fuck, you know? I could actually die here if I was alone.'

Zach considered it.

'There's a lot of other stuff growing though, right? I mean, you couldn't say it's, like, barren, could you?' Zach tried.

'No, not at all,' Hanna agreed. 'It's not that. I think maybe, well, it's a bit spooky?'

'What do you think, Jackson?' Zach asked.

'Yeah,' Jackson called, 'it's fully murder-y, innit?'

'Your family's from here too, aren't they Jackson?' Hanna asked. 'Can you feel your kinfolk, or what?'

Jackson took a brief look around, trying and failing to picture people in the landscape. 'Nah. I don't see it,' he said. 'I mean, where the hell would they have lived? There's no houses, are there?'

'Remember the clearances, Jackson?' Hanna laughed, 'And Unclearances, Daniella's project? Folk's houses were knocked down; their roofs were burned, the land was given over to sheep—'

'Bummer!' Jackson called back, then started humming. A large clank behind Zach made him stop and turn round to see the GBE drone had fallen to the cycle track and now lay blinking in the middle of the lane they had just traversed.

'Jackson, right turn ahead,' Zach said. He dismounted and pulled his own bike back onto the cycle track's merging lane, raising a hand to wave at a car that had slowed on the now slick, wet road to allow them plenty space. 'Ok. Safe to turn,' Zach instructed, 'signal right, Jackson, then move right into the middle, and make sure there's absolutely nothing coming towards you before you turn, OK?'

'OK!' Jackson jutted his left arm out.

'God help us,' Hanna muttered. She stuck her right arm out as she too pulled over the road. Gayle was waiting in the NSBC truck just after the bridge over the River Coe, the trucks windscreen wipers were swishing nimbly from left to right while she checked nothing was approaching.

'You're good, folks,' she said, 'follow me, I've booked the pitches at the campsite already. I've managed to get a booth reserved for food at the pub, too, they've got the fire on, everyone doing OK?'

'I'm going to get drunk, Gayle!' Jackson announced, waving as he pedalled past the truck, spotting a sign with a huge red squirrel at the end of the roadside ahead.

'I guessed that,' Gayle replied as she clicked the truck's engine back on.

'I'm just getting Templeton's drone off the cycle track,' Zach's voice came through the comms link once more. 'It's collapsed again. I don't want it to cause an accident.'

'Good job, Zee,' Gayle replied.

'I need to be healed by alcohol,' Jackson sang excitedly. 'I've escaped death twice today already – a killer moose *and* a storm. So, so hardcore.'

'Hanna, you doing all right?' Gayle asked.

'Yeah,' Hanna replied, 'doing fine. Pumped to see the drone footage later. That was intense. How're you?'

Gayle opened the truck window but pulled back from the rain as Hanna drew alongside.

'I'm fine, my kids are hooked on the livestream,' she beamed, 'I feel properly connected to them again. It's lovely. And the footage is magnificent, you're gonna love it. Folk are going mad for it. We're lucky we got what we did given the conditions.'

'That's so cool about your kids!' Hanna watched a new light in Gayle's eyes as Zach caught up and stopped at her side. 'Glen Coe's making me feel weird though.'

'Lots of people relating to that,' Gayle replied, 'it's not everyone's cup of tea, very much its own thing. There are bits quite like this further north but nothing else quite has this mood, I think.'

Hanna glanced down at the river running alongside the road and watched the browns and greys of the stones under the clear water. A memory of a painting her dad had been given by his parents of their home island, Raasay, was still hanging behind the sofa at home in the flat. The painting depicted a depressing scene; a brown bulk of land behind a dark, thrashing stripe of sea. A thin strand of smoke wound up from the chimney of a grey cottage with a battered-looking wooden door set between black window eyes. She had barely noticed it until she'd seen her Unclearances certificate. Since then it had seemed to catch her every time she'd entered or left the room.

Gayle pulled out from the lay-by and drove the short distance to the campsite with Hanna and Zach in convoy. They found Jackson with a small crowd gathered around him, parked the truck and houses then rushed through a gap in the trees which lead them through to the pub's car park. When Hanna looked up at the pretty white inn she felt her mood lift. Faces were pushed against the bottom panes of the sash and case windows downstairs and a small, excited huddle waited at the door, one of them holding a silver tray with what looked like four glasses of whisky on it. As they made it through the door the heavens opened behind them.

Zach smiled at Hanna, holding his hand out to take her helmet.

'Seems like a good time to ask,' he said, 'all eyes on Jackson and that. Fancy a date?'

Hanna blushed but couldn't hide her delight, 'Who with?'

'Just this guy I know,' Zach replied, 'single dad to a suddenly-adopted kid who's only a year younger than him. Shite on guitar. Likes tech. Funny as fuck.'

Hanna looked towards the inn's anaglypta papered ceiling, pretending to wonder.

'Sounds like my type,' she said, 'and I'm pretty good on guitar, so maybe I can help him?'

Zach grinned.

'You play guitar too?!'

Hanna nodded.

'Well. He just thinks that makes you even hotter, to be honest.'

35

As the clock approached 11 p.m. Roy and Duchy watched the owner of the Clachaig Inn teach Jackson how to pull a pint. A row of eager punters waited on the other side of the bar; some grabbed selfies with Jackson in the background and all seemed keen to be served by him. Roy had been flicking between GBEBS and NSBC coverage all day with increasing frustration at the feed from south of the border which, much like American TV, seemed riddled with ads and dramatic pauses and replays to build tension where none existed. By 6 p.m. he had settled reluctantly on NSBC which, by comparison, was consistently upbeat and engaging. He'd even allowed the audio from NSBC's brief news programme to wash over him when it briefly interrupted the livestream. To his surprise, he'd found himself agreeing with a clever comment a Green MP had made about the New Scottish economy while on his knee Duchy stared lustfully at Roy's leather slippers while enjoying a light massage.

His son had touched the nation's heart, Roy realised as he watched on. And, seeing the cheery faces on screen of staff and customers alike, Roy also saw that what he'd hitherto thought of us as a great annual evening outing in his local pub, The Canny Man, now looked God-fearingly sedate compared to a Glen Coe session.

Jackson placed a pint of mainly froth onto a beermat, grinned, then bowed out from behind the bar. He was instantly approached by four young women each holding two shot glasses of a luminous green fluid. One of the women wore bright red lipstick. She thrust a shot glass at Jackson who grabbed it and, in unison with the women, knocked the shot back. Another of the women took the empty glass from his hand and replaced it with a full one which Jackson also immediately dispatched then slammed onto the bar before sticking his tongue out and shaking his head wildly.

A four-syllabled chant of 'Jack-son's Jour-ney' started up from a crowded table nearby and hastily spread. Jackson grabbed another shot from a row being poured on the bar then beckoned the four women to join him in a conga. Others hurried to join in and Jackson lead them all, snaking between tables and chairs, sticking his tongue out as he passed the now recovered GBEBS drone, then out through double glass doors to the inn's reception area, through the busy dining room, into the inn's kitchen and back through to the hallway. By the time they arrived back in the bar the staff had pushed the tables and chairs to the edges of the room and rolled away a section of tartan carpet to reveal a rectangle of worn wooden dance floor. A ceilidh band finished tuning-up next to an enormous fireplace, and Jackson was grabbed and propelled into leading a Strip the Willow with the landlady.

Fifteen minutes into the dancing Jackson broke off and, reeling with dizziness, lurched towards a jug of water at the end of the bar. He glugged half of it down, ice cubes and half slices of lemon hitting him in the face as he did so, then poured the remainder over his already soaking head before making a wobbly path to the toilets. Roy saw that Hanna and Gayle had tied their hoodies round their waists to help cope with the growing heat as they were whirled and skipped by locals through the steps of the dancing while Zach sat with the band, playing alongside two other guitarists. Ten minutes later, the dance floor was all but cleared when the opening notes of a waltz had the bar heaving again.

Jackson reappeared at the toilet door; the skin around his lips had an aura of red lipstick and an angry-looking love bite had appeared by his Adam's apple. The lipsticked shot-bearer left the toilet behind him and rejoined her friends to uproarious applause. An unexpected chuckle escaped Roy at the sight of Jackson amidst the happily chaotic mêlée.

Rebecca arrived in the lounge following a long retail therapy browsing session on the iPad at the kitchen island. She held a hi-ball tumbler of gin and tonic in one hand and a small crystal bowl of popcorn in the other. When she spotted Jackson on screen the bowl dropped to the carpet, bounced on the thick creamy pile and sent popcorn in every direction. Roy muted the volume as Duchy jumped from his lap, launching himself at the fallen food.

'Mind your stitches, Duchy!' Roy winced.

'What the *hell* is that?' Rebecca spat, zeroing in on Jackson's neck.

'I thought you liked that kind of thing?' Roy said, getting up from his chair.

'Love bites?' Rebecca glared, 'How *dare* you?!'

Roy bent to pick Duchy up but pulled his hand back when the dog turned, ears pinned, teeth bared and eyes bulging, his intention to snaffle every possible snack made clear. Roy looked from the dog to his wife and felt the skin on his back grow clammy.

'Werewolves, darling,' he attempted, settling for picking up the empty bowl instead, 'your favourite film. *Twilight*, isn't it? Vampires, all that. It was a joke, Becs.'

Rebecca's eyes darkened. She raised her glass and took a sip.

'Shall I get you more popcorn?' Roy tried to sound cheery, 'In a new bowl?'

Rebecca's nostrils flared.

'*I'll* get me more popcorn,' she replied, snatching the bowl from Roy's hand.

Duchy clawed at a last piece of corn trapped between the heel and midsole of one of Rebecca's baby pink slippers.

'And I suggest you get yourself a *life*, Roy Campbell!' she continued. 'Maybe if you watched more *art*, more stories like Bella and Edwards', and *less* reality television, maybe then we'd all understand each other – and the world – better!'

'Yes,' Roy frowned, 'well. I think I'll just watch the livestream for now,' he said. 'Perhaps the, um, *art* – perhaps that can come after Jackson's travels? No rush, is there?'

Rebecca tutted and left. Duchy followed for a few steps then gave three short, scornful barks before trotting back to Roy. Roy lifted Duchy onto Rebecca's recliner and winced slightly as the dog scratched at the leather then turned three tight circles before lying down, to fall instantly asleep. Seconds later Roy's tablet screen on the side table flashed with notifications from the bank, alerting him to a spending spree now taking place in the kitchen. He rolled his eyes and increased the volume on the livestream.

In the moonlit glow of the car park the livestream drone captured Hanna, Zach and five French backpackers waving good-night to Gayle then helping a very floppy Jackson into a wheelbarrow lined with jackets and bedding.

'Jackson, please,' one of the backpackers said excitedly as they left the car park for the campsite, 'tell us 'ow you are inventing the Transpariboard. Where did you seek l'inspiration?'

Jackson blinked several times then pointed up at the dark mass of mountain on his left.

'Sssshhhh,' he slurred, 'there's s'elk. Issa elk. Ish him. He did it. He's a killer elk now. Or a moose, innit?'

'Ooo?' replied the backpacker, 'Ooo is eee?'

'S'niall,' Jackson replied, his right arm flopping as his left rose, pointing down at the silver glint of the River Coe running silently at the bottom of the bracken-covered banking.

'That the Nile, is it, Jackson?' Hanna giggled.

'Yeah,' Jackson replied, 'I mean, *aye*, Hanna. S'down there. He's everywhere. S'waiting. He's s'waiting, to get me—'

Zach held up a hand indicating everyone to stop. He pulled a bottle of water from his pocket and crouched next to the wheelbarrow.

'Hold his head up more for me,' Zach frowned.

One of the backpackers stepped behind the barrow, hooked an arm under each of Jackson's and heaved him up to sitting.

'Drink, J-dawg,' Zach instructed. He cupped Jackson's hand round the bottle and guided both to his face.

Jackson looked like an enormous baby with a sippy cup, Roy thought. His son was spilling as much as he drank but it was good of the others to make sure he was getting fluids down before bed, nonetheless.

When Jackson had emptied most of the bottle he slouched back down, and the others began pushing and walking again.

'Time, the deer, is in the wood of Hallaig,' Hanna said, looking across the river to a stand of silhouetted Scots pines.

'What's that, Han?' Zach asked.

'Poem,' Hanna replied. 'By Sorley Maclean. He's quite famous. Gaelic. Died before we were born. Kept coming up when I googled Raasay. He's from there, like my dad's folks. Jackson's moose-elk reminded me. I only remember that first line – and the feel of the last bit – it's crazy-sad.'

'Fu'sake, Han,' Jackson slurred sarcastically.

'Oh?' Zach smiled. 'Go on.'

The backpackers nodded enthusiastically. Hanna shrugged.

'It's about how when the sun goes down the deer in the wood will die and lie with the remains of the homes of folk from a bit of Raasay called Hallaig, another area which was cleared. Some of my family's folk, turns out, lived there. And I think about how we'll never really completely know who was there, but they – and the deer, *they* see who we are, and what we do. They see *us*, always.'

Roy felt the small hairs on the back of his neck rise. In the silence after Hanna's words it seemed the entire world had fallen silent, save the odd squeak from the barrow's wheel.

36

/ZuzannaN/blurts/

heavy, heavy jealous about missing that session. According to my blurt feed half of New Scotland are heading to the Glen Coe for a piss up next weekend now haaaa ha ☺

/TheJacksonCampbellAppreciationSoc/blurts

Jackson should not be sleeping alone after drinking that much ☹

/RoryTheTory/blurtsTo/MichaelTempletonGBEBS

Michael I am standing by in case you or the monarchy want me to intercept the journey at any point and begin the rebellion to get the UK back. Now the world has seen what new Scotland is really like and what folk like me have to put up with. Rain and bikes and parties and immigrants. It's disgusting. Just let me know, OK? Also when do you think my egg cup will arrive? I have boiled some eggs and I'm not sure whether to crack them before the postie comes.

/TheJacksonCampbellAppreciationSoc/blurts

Jackson is still breathing. Thank God. Gayle Wood should probably be looking out for him more.

/ZuzannaN/blurtsTo/TheJacksonCampbellAppreciationSoc

omg you fuds he's absolutely fine!!! they've given him heaps of water to drink and he's puked the shots into the river. Gayle Wood's not his mother FFS!! Get a life! He sat up and ate six energy bars ten minutes ago then was straight back to snoring. You lot are weird.

/MichaelTempletonGBEBS/blurts/

Never in my life have I seen such a classless display of foul manners as what NSBC broadcast last night with the New Scottish First Minister's blessing. We knew that New Scotland would be regressive but I think we underestimated just how fast a return to fully animalistic behaviours would occur. #JacksonsJourney? Jackson's mental hospital gurney would be more apt! Disgraceful! #ZooScotland #DaniellasChimps #GBEBS

/NSBCJourney/NewScotland /blurts/
Hanna is at Signal Rock, a short walk from the Red Squirrel campsite! This is apparently where the message was relayed from one Campbell to another for the Glen Coe Massacre to be carried out ☹

/jacksonmcampbell /blurtsTo/HannaNowak/NSBC-Journey/NewScotland
um hello, why the fuck did you not wake me? #AbandonedByLovers

/HannaNowak/blurtsTo/jacksonmcampbell
we tried! You sleep like the dead! We came in and opened your vents and everything. It was absolutely stinking in there, JC. Dunno how you live thru that tbh. You're welcome, etc.

/NewScotGovtFMClearwater/blurts/
I believe the #JacksonsJourney agenda today is to get to the mesmeric shores of Loch Shiel, from Glen Coe to Glenfinnan. Is it possible this is the most beautiful bike ride of all time? I think so ;-) I am so proud of how people are embracing #Unclearances and leaning into their curiosity about New Scotland's past, we have so much to learn from – together. Happy cycling today, team!

/Deli-ciousOfCallander/blurts
guess where we are this morning?! Clue – it's not Callander and we're setting up a pop-up stall not far from where a modern-day Snow White is lying in a see-through chamber looking gorgeous as ever ;-) We have a queue of happy campers forming already! #JacksonsJourney #CocoPopSlices

/jacksonmcampbell /blurtsTo/Deli-ciousOfCallander
omfg is that you? Is that you I can see over by the shower block? Are u here? Are coco pop slices here? Is this a mirage? I love you so much please let this be real I need, like, 12 slices. Minimum

/TheJacksonCampbellAppreciationSoc/blurts

omg what is that bruise on jackson's chest? Did he need to be Heimliched in the night because he was choking on his own vomit as we suspected would happen? What are NSBC not telling us? Are they taking care enough? They are way too casual with him. Answer our poll – should Jackson be given a bigger team and should a rep from JCAPS be there to properly represent his needs?

/RoryTheTory/blurtsTo/MichaelTempletonGBEBS

the postie has been. Egg cup not there. Eating my eggs now, awaiting instruction. Will put on my camos, just in case. Hello to all my new #MEGA Blurt friends. We are as one. Let me know if you want me to swap out the drone's photovoltaics. It seems to have old tech that doesn't store much charge.

/ZuzannaN/blurtsTo/TheJacksonCampbellApprecia-tionSoc

it's a lovebite you fucking noobs

/RebeccaCampbell/blurts/

has Rebecca Campbell had surgery Search

/RebeccaCampbell/blurts/

why are my thighs still wobbly after skiing so much search

/NSBCJourney/NewScotland /blurts/

It's #Day3 of #JacksonsJourney and we're super grateful for better weather ☺ No sunshine but no rain or mist – we'll take it and run (or cycle) with it! Thanks so much to the lovely staff last night who looked after us all so well with great food and hospitality! Here we come, Ballachullish, Onich, Corran and Fort William! Can we make it all the way to Glenfinnan too? Let's see ☺ #NSBC #TinyAdventures #NewScotland

/ProfDrewMcAllister/blurts/

I love that bridge at Ballachullish. Just look at it. Stand on it and look in any direction and you've got a view to rival any of the seven wonders o' the world. Loch Linnhe one way, Loch Leven the other. Our two most incredible lochs, perhaps. Hard to comprehend the millions of ways they each touch and influence our whole ecosystem. Absolutely love the NSBC drone work showing the seabirds and otters. I'm getting no work done! Too beautiful! #EHA #Humility #JacksonsJourney #HannasJourney #together

/jacksonmcampbell /blurts/

Thank you so much for all the roadside love at Onich and Corran. Yous are the best. Also well done for living on a flat bit of road. I cruised it all on e-power. You should see some of the other hills in New Scotland. Not cool. Anyway I loved the calf massages the best when I stopped to refuel on #CocoPopSlices #JacksonsJourney

/TheJacksonCampbellAppreciationSoc/blurts

how do you pronounce Onich?

/HannaNowak/blurts/

hello Fort William, you're a bit lovely ☺ So is your McDonald's ☺ I keep hearing the Road to the Isles is going to be something else. Excited ☺ Also super weirded out that I never had a clue about how stunning the west of New Scotland is till this journey. Anyone else?

/ZuzannaN/blurtsTo/HannaNowak

me, obvs. But at least we've seen Krakow. That's nice too.

/jacksonmcampbell /blurtsTo/HannaNowak/ZuzannaN

I've seen mountains before. France has them too. #JacksonsJourney

/ZuzannaN/blurtsTo/HannaNowak/jacksonmcampbell

gosh you're such an everyman, aren't you?

/ProfDrewMcAllister/blurts/

That wide, stubborn hulk of Ben Nevis behind #JacksonsJourney as they headed out of Fort William and past the Caledonian canal locks of Neptune's Staircase. Wonderful camera work from NSBC! Iconic scenes! I'm welling up! #EHA #NewScotland

/ZuzannaN/blurts

omfg how cute are my sis and Zach cycling side by side?!??! And #ZannasJourney is trending too now! Ha ha haaaaaaaaaa! ;-))))

/RebeccaCampbell/blurtsTo/jacksonmcampbell

Private Message Jackson darling is it possible you have picked up a disease from the sexual assault you encountered in the hostelry? Where was the woman from? Glasgow? Who is Zanna? Is that the assaulter's name? Glad you had more flat bits to cycle today. Better for your fitness level.

/NewScotGovtFMClearwater/blurts/

I'm watching between meetings; from the awe of Glen Coe to the fairy tale of the lush greens of the Road to the Isles. I feel like I'm there! I extend my warm thanks to the #JacksonsJourney team for helping me envisage my own future adventures! #NewScotland #OnYerBike #EconomyOfHealth #WealthIsHealth #TinyHouses #Transpariboard™ #OnePlanetLiving #GreenNewDealDelivered

/HannaNowaksMother/blurts/

#ZannasJourney! My heart!

37

In contrast to the blue and white medicalised vibe of the MDMA treatment room, Claudia's office was a bohemian heaven. Two walls were painted pale pink and another was a lightly polished pale concrete which also formed the floor and ceiling. A huge, creamy, textured rug with thick twists and knots massaged the undersides of Niall's feet as he walked across it in just his socks, then sat in a large wicker chair. Claudia sat facing Niall behind her glass desk, the ends of which were supported by chunky oak trestles. To her left, a thick driftwood stick hung horizontally from thin ropes attached to oversized steel ceiling hooks. A selection of plants in macramé potholders hung from the stick, leaves trailing and stems spiralling, soaking up light from the window wall and jasmine-scented vapour from a vast aromatherapy diffuser below. Steam rose in a thin spiral from the tea brewing in a wonky earthenware mug in front of Claudia as Niall pictured one day having his own flat, styled in just the same way.

'It's been seventy-two hours,' Claudia smiled, 'three whole days and nights since your MDMA therapy. How do you feel?'

'Great!' Niall couldn't help grinning, 'I feel *great*. It's amazing. It's like … I dunno? Everything's just … just *different*, you know?'

Claudia observed Niall's stance. The way he sat and moved now was almost childlike in its fluidity. The animated gestures he made with his hands as he spoke conveyed a new and happy ease.

'And now tell me about group yesterday. It went well?'

Niall raised a hand to his head and brushed his fingertips from the hairline at the nape of his neck all the way up to his crown. He hadn't shaved his hair since arriving at the centre and it was now half a centimetre long. He enjoyed the sensation of the softness of it though he suspected he looked a lot like a mad baby bird.

'It went *really* well. I think I actually really enjoyed it. Jim's had the MDMA, too.' Niall tutted lightly, then laughed. 'Well, *you* know that. It was surreal, like, comparing notes. He looks like a new person, he's ordered himself a pair of jeans to try and everything, says he's modernising!'

Claudia bobbed her nettle teabag in her mug before raising it, letting it drip its last, then placed it on a speckled blue dish.

'You've had an awesome result,' Claudia said, 'as has Jim. I think you're very good for each other. You're really broadening each other's perspectives, aren't you?'

'*Yes!*' Niall gushed, 'I thought he was a right old dick. But, like, honestly, he's pretty cool. He's done some impressive shit in his life as well. Like, he's been to Egypt and everything. You don't really think of old folk like that, do you? Till, you know, you really speak to one?'

'Intergenerational perspective is everything.' Claudia nodded. 'It's a guiding tenet of how we work here, I'm glad you can see why, Niall. It's something we lost in old Scottish culture in so many ways, and we really feel like it's a hugely healing thing to foster growing it back, for everyone's sake. And I know Jim loves your company too.'

Niall sighed happily.

'All right,' Claudia continued, 'I asked you here today for two reasons, Niall. The first was to reflect on your MDMA experience; we're on that already. The second is to raise the idea of a first trip away from the centre. An opportunity to test your learning in different scenarios and see where it holds up well or needs reinforcing.'

Niall's smile disappeared.

'With Jim?' he asked, 'Or you and Fin?'

'Well, possibly none of those options,' Claudia replied, 'and certainly not Jim. You two are a great support to each other here, but it'd be too much to expect you to support another person outside of the centre just yet.'

Niall gulped.

'It could be with someone of your choosing whom you trust from your normal, everyday life, however.'

Niall resisted the strong urge to pull his hoodie up and shroud his face and began fidgeting with the threads of the friendship bracelet Sadie had made for him during the previous day's Craft-ernoon. Hanna's face arrived in his mind's eye but then, to his horror, her image brought a sharp jag of anxiety. How on earth, he wondered, could he ever convey to Hanna everything he'd been through since they'd spoken last? And what if something triggered him out of the blue and made him feel unwell, suicidal even, and Hanna had to be responsible for him? The thought made him feel nauseous.

'What were you thinking there?' Claudia asked.

'Hanna,' Niall half-whispered, 'my best friend. She's got a lot on though, she looks after her little sisters a lot and stuff. And she's up in Aberdeen.'

'Ah.' Claudia shifted slightly in her chair. 'I hope this isn't patronising, Niall, but I don't think that would be a great idea. It could be better for you to be with someone with a little more life experience, hmm?'

'But not Jim?' Niall frowned.

'Correct,' Claudia nodded, 'but your files tell me we do have Drew McAllister on your team.'

Niall considered it; the tapas night out with Drew and Hanna sprang to mind again. No pull of anxiety followed.

'It's a big ask, though,' Niall said, 'Drew's nice, but it's the summer holidays. He's got kids — of his own.'

'EHA counsellors are employed year-round, Niall,' Claudia replied. 'With annual leave, of course. But that differs from the usual academic holiday schedule.'

'Is it just for a day?' Niall asked.

'Maybe. Three nights, max. Whenever you have a sense you're ready. You're the boss.'

Another wave of nausea moved in Niall's stomach. He remembered a technique of positive visualisation Fin had taught them in a recent group session. 'How would this situation look for me if anxiety wasn't in control?', he asked himself, closing his eyes briefly. He pictured himself looking curious instead of scared. He opened his eyes again.

'Would I take my tablet?' he asked, trying to resist his brow knitting at the thought of being back online.

'No,' Claudia answered, 'we're not *there* yet. Online re-entry takes preparation we haven't begun at this stage. You'd take a wristband from here, so you can open a link to Fin or me at any time. And if you wanted to return speedily, you'd let us know, and we'd organise that.'

Claudia opened a small wooden box on her desk, lifted out a glossy blue wristband and matching comms magnet then laid both gently on a tassel-edged miniature prayer mat.

'How many folk need the emergency return?' Niall tried to hold Claudia's eye

but found himself constantly drawn back to staring at the glimmering lure of the bracelet.

'Percentage wise?' Claudia tapped her fingertips together as she brought her hands to a steeple under her chin, 'Oh, very few. Maybe one a year. I mean, it's low because we take such care that people are ready and that they'll handle whatever they encounter because of the skills they've put in place. But of course, circumstances *can* throw a curve ball, and that can lead to an acute feeling of crisis.'

Niall nodded. He felt like a balloon was repeatedly inflating then popping in his stomach.

'I don't think I'm ready, Claud,' he heard himself reply. 'My instinct says no. I just want to stay in my happy bubble, for now.'

'All right.' Claudia nodded. 'But, rather than thinking that you are *not* ready, I would like you to reframe it over the next forty-eight hours till we next meet as you being on the path to being ready. Sometimes anxiety is a useful thing for telling us what our fears are. Then, once we've identified them, we can sit with them and offer objective challenge. Are they each real, do they have a basis? Are *some* real, and giving us helpful information about where we are, what's important and what we need to make ourselves feel safe and re-centred in a new situation?'

Niall took a long breath out then stood.

'I'm going to …,' Niall rolled his shoulders backwards twice, 'you know?'

'Yes,' Claudia replied, 'good, quite right.'

Niall lifted and rolled one ankle after the other, then his wrists, then slowly tipped his head backwards then forwards, resting his chin on his chest for a second.

'Where was the tension this time?' Claudia asked.

'Shoulders, still,' Niall replied, 'and all down my back.'

He bent from the middle, slowly bringing his hands to the floor, his fingertips touching the creamy bumps of a crocheted section of rug while another section cushioned his soles.

'That's it, lengthen the spine, well done, Niall, *perfect*. All is well in this moment.'

Niall walked his hands backwards to his feet, then stood again, mindfully focusing attention on each vertebra as he unfurled.

'That's the thing, isn't it?' Niall looked back to Claudia, his cheeks flushed, 'Staying in the moment?'

Claudia nodded, closing her eyes for a moment. Her deepest sign of approval, Niall knew.

Niall sat again, leaning back in the chair, letting it take all of his weight.

'Remember, even as something difficult is happening, by the time we've realised it, it's already becoming part of the past,' Claudia said. 'If we can ground ourselves, welcoming the future as it appears, we know that by meeting everything with honesty, love and an open heart, we can handle *whatever* happens, don't we?'

'I'll be ready soon, I think,' Niall said.

'I think so, too,' Claudia replied, 'you're ready for the holodeck now, too. Have a go in the morning, the staff down there will get you acquainted with how it works. Fin will set different programme choices for you, things he thinks will be most helpful.'

Niall felt a frisson of excitement. It'd been three weeks and two days since he'd surrendered his tablet and wristband. The idea of being around tech again appealed.

'Now, reframe the feelings as part of a process of readying, add in the holodeck work and come and see me again, tell me how you're feeling then.'

Niall nodded.

'Thanks, Claud.'

'Always.' Claudia smiled, 'And thanks for your honesty, Niall, and your commitment. You're doing so well.'

A warm glow spread through Niall's body. Love. MDMA residue too, perhaps. He crossed the room and gently placed a hand on the door handle.

'Niall, one last thing,' Claudia called.

'Yeah?'

'Do I have your consent to enquire about Drew McAllister's

availability tentatively, but nothing more for now? It'd be good to give him some notice, even if we've no specific dates in mind, wouldn't it?'

Niall considered it. It was OK to say no, he knew. But was it OK to say yes, perhaps? A sleek black and beige flash of a darting bird through the massive window behind Claudia caught his eye. Niall recognised it as a swallow, thanks to listening to Fin and Jim at the reservoir on their daily wander together. He blinked and the bird was gone, off again on its business. Living. Trying. Thoroughly in the now.

'Yes,' he replied at last, meeting Claudia's eye again. 'OK. That sounds fine, for now.'

38

The gently vibrating alarm on Roy's wristband woke him the next morning. He left the bed as stealthily as possible, careful not to disturb Rebecca or Duchy from their deep slumbers. He grabbed his housecoat from its hook in the en suite and tiptoed out, closing the bedroom door quietly behind him. Pulling on his housecoat as he went, he made his way down the sweeping staircase to the WC off the hallway. He lifted the toilet seat lid carefully, then pulled several sheets of toilet roll from the gold-plated holder and dropped them into the toilet before sitting to relieve himself. He thought of Jackson peeing in the River Coe the day before and chuckled as he hastily washed and dried his hands, promising himself he'd remember to return later to flush.

Next, he headed down the hallway to the kitchen, where he removed a bottle of water from the fridge and a freshly brewed thermal carafe from the coffee machine he'd set the timer on before going to bed. He set out a wide, dark green wicker tray from a shelf under the kitchen island, then retrieved two mugs from hooks on the wall above the kettle. He checked the time and a frisson of fear sparked; more minutes had passed than he'd realised. He carried the tray through to the lounge, placed it on the coffee table in front of the television, then hurried to the alarm control panel. There, he deactivated the house's security settings then tapped in another code to open the gates at the end of the driveway. Wincing as the barrel lock made a heavy click when he unlatched the door, he wedged his knee between it and the frame, casting a glance back upstairs as he did so. The double doors to the master bedroom suite remained reassuringly shut. He took a deep breath, then pivoted to reach the brass umbrella stand before pulling it across the doormat towards him, then propped the door with it.

He stepped out onto the semi-circle front step and looked down the drive. Right on cue, a smart van drew alongside the gates, then reversed a few metres, then indicated to turn up Whole Castle View's drive. Roy winced as tyres crunched on the gravel then drew to a stop. Fearing that the delivery driver might be a noisy, over-friendly type from Glasgow or Fife, Roy improvised an urgent sign language through the vehicle's window, placing a finger on his lips, then pointing to an upstairs window of the house, then mouthing a long 'shhhhh'.

The van driver nodded before quietly opening her door and taking long, tip-toeing steps past the van's grille to approach Roy.

'A surprise, is it?' the driver whispered. Roy nodded and watched as she waved her hand over a motion sensor on the wing mirror and the van's side door slid silently open. The cheery blue of the edge of Jackson's tiny house peeping out at the head of the driveway caught the driver's eye. Her brow furrowed, her expression shifting as she wondered why where she was standing felt familiar when she knew she'd never made a delivery to this address before. Eager to throw her off, Roy flashed a generous smile and affected a West Coast lilt.

'I want to get it in before my wife wakes,' he whispered.

'Aw! That's nice!' the driver smiled. 'Everyone's getting them. It's that Jackson's Journey, isn't it? Making us all want to get fit and be even more eco-friendly. She'll be well chuffed, will she, your wife?'

'Yes,' Roy lied, 'can we, um … hurry? *Please*?'

The driver slipped inside the van to where the Stat-Fly 6000 waited, tension-tethered by haulage straps to prevent it from moving in transit. Roy was reminded of a day he'd spent at the races as a young man with his father. They'd watched a gleaming thoroughbred being unloaded from a pristine trailer onto an AstroTurf lawn before being led to its stable. Roy had expected, hoped – perhaps – that the horse would be wild and uncontrollable. But instead, the animal had stood stock-still when the hydraulic ramp lowered and everything about its muscled, equine perfection had seemed somehow defeated as it was moved from one cage to another.

Roy was pulled back to the present by the van driver gesticulating at the bottom of the box with one hand as she unclipped transit straps with the other.

'The box has wee wheels on the bottom,' she whispered, 'just like in the ad. Did you see the whole ad, the long one?'

Roy nodded. The advert had been impossible to miss, it was one of three playing on the hour every hour of the livestream. On seeing it for the forty-second time yesterday, Roy, like hundreds of others across New Scotland, had grabbed his tablet and made his order, selecting an express delivery time Rebecca was almost sure not to be around to witness.

'Once we've lifted it into your hallway, you'll manage alone. Roll the whole thing to where you want it,' the driver continued, 'then press the button on top, and bob's your mother's brother, the box springs open and your bike's inside, ready to go. You can leave it standing on the base and just pull off the sides, they're attached with Velcro, yeah? Easy, does it.'

Roy grabbed the handle on the front of the box while the driver pushed it from behind. Roy took the weight over the threshold then set the box down carefully on the polished limestone tiles before waving the driver away, relieved the interaction was over. He carefully repositioned his knee at the door again while he moved the umbrella stand and made sure the latch closed with only a small, soft click.

'What the hell is that?' Rebecca's icy voice echoed from the top of the stairs where she and Duchy stood staring down at Roy. Duchy barked disapprovingly, then shifted his attention to the delivery with a low warning growl as he assessed the imposter.

'I asked what that is, Roy,' Rebecca spat. A chill breeze seemed to pass through the hallway from where she stood in the glacier white of her silk pyjamas, their diamanté buttons glinting in the light from the soaring stairwell windows at her side.

Roy eyed the open double doors to the lounge.

'It's a static bike, Rebecca,' he replied, then energetically began pushing the box towards the lounge. 'I'm missing the exercise from the skiing.'

'You have your golf!' Rebecca shouted, beginning her descent. Duchy's breathing gave a short rasp as he jumped down each step at Rebecca's side. 'Golf's exercise! And the gym at the club. I have told you before, Roy, exercise equipment does *not* make a home. If you want it here, we bring in the architects and build a fitness studio. I refuse to compromise the integrity of our spaces. The look of our home is in constant service to its photogenic nature. And when are you ever going to go outdoors again, hmmm? This is getting ridiculous. I think you might be depressed. Or having a midlife crisis. *Oh, my God!*' Rebecca gasped, her hand shooting to her mouth as words she hadn't planned to say resonated deeply. 'That's what this is, isn't it? A midlife crisis!'

'Golf isn't *really* exercise,' Roy called back.

The box snagged on the wide brass threshold bar between the limestone hallway and the creamy shagpile of the lounge. Roy darted to the front of the box and lifted it by the handle, then pulled again. He glanced up and saw Rebecca closing on him, she'd now reached the bottom of the stairs. As soon as he was alongside his recliner, Roy whacked the button on the top of the box and jumped backwards as the sides of the packaging fell. Roy leapt towards the bike and onto the seat, a triumphant 'ha!' marking his establishment of squatter's rights, exactly as he'd planned on seizing them.

Rebecca stared from the lounge doorway. She looked at Roy, sweaty and red in his housecoat and sporting a menacing grin. Tears began to well in her eyes. She took in the aggressive lines of the black and red exercise bike now standing with devilish contrast in her cream, champagne and rose-gold-accented lounge. Roy looked at the tray before him then at Rebecca and decided it was too soon to ask her to pour him a coffee. Instead, he tapped at his wristband and activated the livestream on the television. Jackson appeared, almost life-sized, walking out onto a short wooden jetty then stopping and squatting at the end of it, staring down into the blackened mirror of a loch. A vast lawn swept down from a pretty, cream-coloured hotel with red window frames behind him. Beyond that, the thick leaden silver of Glenfinnan Viaduct cut through the middle of the shot, blue sky and sunlight shining above and through the arches and treetops surrounding it.

'The Harry Potter railway!' Roy shouted, delighted. 'Do you recognise it, Becs? Such a classic!' Roy looked at Rebecca again and found her blotting her undereye with the cuff of her pyjama.

'Can't you buy another sports car?' she half-whispered, 'Or a racehorse? Something … something, I don't know … *normal*, Roy? You have always said, no matter what happened, you said our home was *my* domain. *My* speciality. That, and my style, Roy. And my looks. My memories of modelling. They're all *I've* got.'

Roy got off the bike.

'It's not a midlife crisis, Rebecca,' he said as he poured two cups of coffee. 'I promise. It's just till this livestream's over. I want to stay fit while I watch. And the bikes are exciting. Have you seen the ad? Everyone's talking about it, apparently.'

Rebecca shook her head although she had seen the advert tens of times and had also been inspired by the messaging about joining the journey from the comfort of home.

'When the journey's finished I'll give the bike to charity,' Roy continued, 'or we'll get the architects in if I want to keep it. And I'll go outside again. I will. Deal?'

Roy held a mug of coffee out. Rebecca crossed her arms and stared down at Duchy.

'Do you promise?' she tried and failed to stop her lower lip trembling. 'All that *and* you won't go rabid? Promise it.'

'I promise.' Roy frowned. He was surprised Rebecca still thought rabidity was even a slight possibility.

Rebecca took the coffee then gave the bike a wide berth as she made for her recliner. Duchy sniffed suspiciously at the cardboard then followed. Roy placed his coffee in one of the bike's cupholders and got back on, arranging his housecoat so it tucked under his bottom rather than dangling near the pedals. On screen, Gayle appeared behind Jackson on the jetty. She was wearing running gear and her skin sparkled with perspiration. Jackson's parents watched as their son heard her approach.

'Hey,' Jackson smiled, 'been running?'

'I have,' Gayle smiled back, 'you're up early, mister.'

Jackson nodded.

'Want to sit?' he asked.

'Up to you,' Gayle shrugged, 'what do you fancy? Breakfast or sit? I'm good with either. I can leave you alone again, if you'd prefer? No offence taken. Mornings alone are special. What feels natural?'

Rebecca rolled her eyes as she sipped her coffee and her son pondered.

'What do you mean?' Jackson asked. 'Like, sit on something that's the oldest thing here, in nature?'

'No!' Gayle laughed, 'I mean, what's your urge, right now, about what you want to do?'

'Oh,' Jackson replied, 'I don't know. Sit a bit? Then get coffee? And food.'

Gayle pulled her shoes off then sat, dangling her feet into the water, enjoying the cool on her hot skin. Jackson copied.

'Something on your mind?' Gayle asked.

'*Something on your mind?*' Rebecca mimicked in a hammy Scots accent. 'As if! He's fine!' Rebecca asserted. 'Absolutely, perfectly fine.'

Jackson shrugged, then looked unmistakably sad. Roy unconsciously mirrored his son's expression.

'I'm not fine, to be honest,' Jackson replied, 'I get a bit jealous of Hanna. And of Zach. And you. I mean, who wouldn't, right? I feel a bit stupid next to yous. And a bit lonely, sometimes. You've got your kids to talk to at nights. Hanna and Zach have got each other now. I've usually got Duchy, our dog, at home. Stupid, isn't it?'

Gayle raised her eyebrows.

'You? Lonely? I guess I was thinking Blurt prevented that. All your fans. Sorry, Jackson. I missed that.'

Jackson smiled, trying hard to minimise what felt enormous inside.

'If it helps,' Gayle continued, 'I get lonely, too. Yes, I have the kids, *if* they're about. But being a parent is work as well as love. And it's lovely to see Zach and Hanna being all loved up, very sweet. Lovely, but also a reminder of … well. Loneliness, I guess.' Gayle shrugged. She looked as though she might say more, then glanced at the drone and thought better of it. Roy watched and felt the unspoken words meld with the birdsong in the trees at the loch's edge.

'Know what I realised?' Jackson asked.

Gayle shook her head.

'I'm not very good at feeling stuff if it isn't stuff that makes me laugh,' Jackson explained. 'So when I feel stuff that isn't, like, *nice*, it all kind of swirls about inside me, and I try to get rid of it as fast as I can. Sometimes I just enjoy making other people feel like shit too, like, as bad as I feel, you know?'

Roy heard someone take a sharp intake of breath then realised it was his own.

'I felt like that this morning,' Jackson went on, 'so I got up, to do bants or whatever. And there was no one there. You were running, obviously, Hanna and Zach were … I dunno … they're not here, anyway. So I walked over to the hotel bar, but it was shut. Then I walked over here, thinking maybe there'd be fans. But there was no one here either. And there's only, like, four folk awake on Blurt – and even they're all just tagging "Zanna's Journey". And that's when I realised it; I'm not very good at being alone, am I?'

Gayle watched Jackson's eyes searching her own. She delivered neither validation nor disagreement and simply listened instead.

'Maybe that means I'm a bit psycho?' Jackson added.

'No!' Gayle laughed, 'It means you're gaining self-awareness. Perspective. Empathy comes next. It's a good thing, Jackson. It means you can get on with more folk. Everyone needs to develop it. It's part of growing up. Then comes emotional freedom. So I'm told, anyway.'

Jackson listened, unsure how to respond.

Roy gripped his coffee cup so tightly his knuckles began to hurt. He recognised exactly what his son had described; that maelstrom of emotion. The impulses to self-medicate it all away, or to lash out and implicate someone else. The drone camera panned to just Jackson.

Duchy looked to Rebecca, then Roy, and barked angrily. He'd been waiting to be lifted onto Rebecca's lap for several minutes and was growing increasingly irritated at being forgotten. Rebecca jumped a little and spilled coffee on her pyjamas. As she stared at the stain Roy saw her bottom lip wobble. He stepped off the bike and scooped Duchy up. Duchy protested, shocked, then succumbed and gave Roy's neck a little lick. Roy looked back at the TV. Hanna and Zach had appeared behind Jackson and Gayle. They too were in exercise gear and were both sweaty, their faces lit to happiness by endorphins. The GBEBS drone followed behind them, emitting loud buzzing noises that suggested a service was long overdue.

'JC!' Hanna called, making Jackson turn. 'We tried to wake you. Say you'll come running one day, hey? We miss you. And beating Zach is *fun!*'

Jackson looked surprised, then pleased. Zach playfully give Hanna the Vs. She stuck her tongue out in answer.

'What do you think, Jackson?' Gayle asked. 'Are we worth setting an alarm and getting yourself up for? I beat them both, that was fun, too.'

Jackson stared at Gayle, impressed, then nodded.

'Yeah,' he replied, tucking his hair behind his ears, 'yeah, I reckon so.'

Jackson got up and walked to Hanna and Zach. When he reached them he touched Hanna on her arm, shouting 'tag!' before legging it away. Hanna gave instant chase, followed by Zach. Gayle pulled on her shoes then picked up Jackson's. Roy watched as they reached where they'd parked the night before. There they all were, he thought; New Scotland's darlings, laughing – joyful even. The Glenfinnan Monument commemorating the beginning of the Jacobite uprising in 1745 loomed over them. He looked down at Duchy and spotted a softness in the little dog's expression. Maybe everyone was a bit psycho – or just misunderstood, sometimes. Feelings arrived in Roy's chest, the difficult variety. Though he wasn't holding Duchy tightly he realised his knuckles, wrists and shoulders hurt from gathered tension.

'What the hell have we taught Jackson, Rebecca?' he whispered.

'Everything,' came Rebecca's answer. 'We've taught him absolutely everything he knows.'

Roy waited for Rebecca to say more, bracing for the following statement that would surely pin blame on him like a rippled cravat to a tailor's mannequin. Duchy looked from Roy's frozen wince to Rebecca dabbing a tear then broke the silence with a sorrowful whimper.

'Duchy doesn't know whose side to take,' Rebecca sniffed, 'he's never seen us like this before, has he?'

Roy patted Duchy gently. Rebecca was right, he realised. He looked across at his wife and, despite his dressing gown and pyjamas, he felt naked. Rebecca looked back, the defensive frost gone from her eyes. A tentative trust hung in the air between them.

'I think it's time we talked, Becs, isn't it?' Roy said.

'One rectangle corner to another?' Rebecca asked, then wiped another tear.

'Indeed.' Roy frowned.

39

At the end of a long uphill section Jackson pulled into a lay-by, yanked on his brakes and staggered off his bike back towards the road. He stood on the verge and looked down at the parched asphalt climb he'd just completed, incredulous about the difference between its gradient and scale compared to Dundas Street in Edinburgh. He watched Zach pedalling determinedly about thirty metres away, then Hanna, who was far behind down the road, having stopped to blurt about the views on multiple occasions since Glenfinnan. The GBEBS drone shadowed her, buzzing constantly like an irritated wasp while it used the stops to recharge between increasingly slow flights.

Everywhere around them were luscious, tropical-feeling vistas of mountain, sea, sky and dense forestry. Gayle and the NSBC truck were waiting with lunch in a lay-by a little further on, Jackson knew, but over the last stretch the sun's heat had built his temperature to a point where even a second more in the saddle felt impossible. Huge underarm rings of sweat merged beneath his sternum on his Jackson's Journey vest, and, when he removed his helmet, his hair hung in sodden curtains either side of his face.

The back of a lonely white church standing on the headland on the opposite side of the road caught Jackson's eye. He stared at it and wished it was a bar. He closed his eyes and imagined being handed a tall cool glass filled with rapidly fizzing, honey-gold beer and gave a long, desirous groan before being snapped back to reality by Zach's tyres scrunching loose gravel nearby.

Zach got off his bike and leant it on Jackson's trailer. He grabbed two bottles of water from a rear pannier and wandered over, breathing heavily.

'Drink?' Zach asked.

'Yeah. Ta.' Jackson glugged then wiped his mouth on his forearm. They both stood, quietly getting their breath back and watching Hanna and her house travelling slowly but surely towards them.

'The views are wild, aren't they?' Zach said. 'This place is insane. Completely, utterly insane.'

'Even I've noticed that.' Jackson looked out across Loch Ailort twinkling up at them from the bottom of a steep, bracken-laden mountainside. He spotted a collection of huge silver boulders along the waterline at the beginning of a peninsular shore. A red tractor chuffing along the road following the coast looked comically small and surreal.

'Looks like a farm set or something, doesn't it?' Zach mused.

'Some kind of tropical island zoo.' Jackson laughed, 'And, like, I swear I wouldn't flinch if a T-rex stepped out of the trees. Would you?'

'Or a pterodactyl.' Zach nudged Jackson to wave as two of the drones arrived and hovered above them.

'Everything OK?' Gayle asked over the comms link. On realising Jackson and Zach had stopped she'd climbed back inside the truck from where she'd been waiting at the roadside and tapped her dashboard screen, zooming in via the nearest camera.

'Just taking a pause,' Zach replied, 'even with electric assist that hill was nuts. The heat coming off the road is a riot, G.'

'Ah,' Gayle said, 'well, I'm just down here at …,' she checked her nav, 'ah, OK, I'm looking out at Loch Nan Uum. No, hold on. Loch Nan Oomf? Ah. It's Oo-av, not Oomf, according to the pronunciation details. Anyway. It's beautiful. I've parked under another viaduct, a much smaller one, but it gives shade. And there's a field between me and the sea. I reckon if we cross it and scramble over the rocks we'll find a wee beach hiding below – a white one. And that goddamn aqua sea.'

'We could swim!' Zach looked joyful at the thought.

'How long have we been cycling?' Jackson asked, the dual grips of heat and fatigue rapidly draining him. 'So much time has passed. It's definitely been four hours, minimum.'

'No.' Zach laughed, 'Try an hour and forty.'

Jackson dropped to the ground with a groan then lay on his back, spreading his limbs like a kilted Vitruvian Man. He screwed his eyes tightly shut against the midday sun. Coloured blobs came and went behind his eyelids.

Zach looked back down the road, relieved no faster cyclists were providing additional pressure at Hanna's back.

'You got enough SPF on?' Zach gently kicked the soles of Jackson's trainers. The gravel underneath Jackson's head scratched at his scalp when he nodded, making him wince.

'How you doing there, Hanna?' Gayle asked, directing one of the drones to rotate and bring Hanna into shot.

'OK,' Hanna breathed hard, her face bubble-gum pink as she neared the lay-by.

Despite the added drag, Hanna had decided at Glenfinnan to leave her house in the upright position so she could maximise selfie and promotional photos for the kit along the way. Blurt was now alight with shares of her Transpariboard house sparkling in the sunlight like a huge, precious stone against stunning verdant backdrops. Hanna carefully negotiated her bike and trailer past Jackson, then pulled on her brakes and grabbed her water bottle.

'You know, you folks are going to get your first glimpse of Eigg round the next corner,' Gayle said, concerned the others might stop for too long without shade or proper refreshment.

'Really?!' Hanna panted, 'So we're close?'

'Kinda,' Gayle replied, 'bit to go yet. You're about to hit the literal high point though, 400 metres around the bend after the lay-by. The plateau only lasts for about half a kilometre, but from there you get the first view right out over the Atlantic, far as the eye can see till the earth curves beyond the Small Isles.'

'The Atlantic?' Jackson propped himself up on his elbows, blinking hard. Zach and Hanna were black blobs on a white cloud while his vision adjusted. 'The Atlantic's here? In New Scotland? I thought it was in America?'

'It's there, too,' Gayle laughed, 'second-largest ocean in the world.'

'The first is the Pacific,' Zach added, 'which I called "the Specific", when I was a kid.'

'Cute.' Hanna smiled then scooshed the rest of her water between the vents on her helmet, closing her eyes as the liquid coolness worked its way through her hair then down, onto her heavily sun-screened neck.

Jackson stuck his hands upwards so Zach could help him back to standing.

'I think you might need to take off the kilt, JC.' Hanna eyed sweat dripping all over Jackson's skin when he was back on his feet.

'Fuck's sake,' Jackson sighed, 'I don't want to, but it's hairy as fuck. Even through the ass-cushion pants. And when you sweat the hairiness drives you mad – it just gets worse, swear. I don't know how William Wallace did those battles and shit. I mean – honestly. Fuck that. I'd have torched my own bollocks. Or just run in naked.' Jackson began unbuckling his kilt then looked confused. 'Hold on though, if we're going to see Eigg in a minute how many more camping stops have we got till we're there? Like, two? Four?'

'One,' Gayle replied, 'Mallaig, Jackson. Tonight. Then we get the boat in the morning.'

'You're kidding, yeah?' Jackson frowned, 'I thought we had ages to go!'

'Nope,' Zach replied, 'this is the last leg, J-dawg, then it's over the big blue and onto your ancestral lands. Can you feel your DNA buzzing? You're close, hey? Soon you're going to park that house right where your family lived. Shit's getting real now, innit?'

A mix of relief and dread spread through Jackson. His new life in France was closer than he'd thought, he realised. And with it there would be, he would ensure, no more talk of Transpariboard. No more worrying about Niall. No more lying. No more early morning rising, no rain. No midgies. No more real life friends, either. A dart of loneliness pierced his chest.

'Will yous be glad when it's over?' he asked. 'When yous are rid of me?'

'Nope.' Hanna smiled, her head now leaning on Zach's shoulder. 'I'm having a ball. I could do this for ever. Beats writing job applications every day of the week, doesn't it? I think I've found my calling.'

'I'm doing just fine here, too, JC.' Zach smiled.

'Ditto,' Gayle replied from the truck, 'but I'd like my kids here as well.'

A breeze blew across Jackson's back and cooled the nape of his neck, his shoulders and calves. His body felt strong and aligned, he noticed, the fatigue of minutes before had passed, somehow, and now his skin tingled while his muscles and bones felt expectant, almost itching to move again.

'I think I might be fit, now?' Jackson said, straining to see if his calves matched Zach's, 'But I don't *look* that different yet, do I?'

'You're definitely recovering faster after exertion,' Gayle replied, 'feels good, doesn't it?'

Jackson nodded.

'Well,' Gayle continued, 'why don't you three jump back on, get over the plateau, then freewheel to me, good chance to charge your bike batteries before the last stretch?'

'Gotta say,' Hanna sighed, 'I fancy that swim. Seriously.'

'I'll get the lunch stuff out so it's ready.' Gayle added, 'I've actually got a Coco Pop slice in the cooler, Jackson. I kept it as a surprise for you, but I forgot about it, till now.'

Jackson's eyes widened, he looked up at the nearest drone and smiled then made his way hastily back to his bike, licking his lips and bundling his kilt into his basket before putting his helmet back on and setting off, joined in short order by Hanna and Zach.

When they rounded the headland after the massive rock that stood above the lay-by they met a cross wind from the ocean. Jackson looked across the water, slowing a little as he spotted what looked like a low, black anvil stretching a short distance across the middle of the horizon. To its right and just behind stood six much higher peaks.

'Shit man. That's Eigg! The little one,' Zach said, his bike alongside Jackson's left side.

'And that's Rum, behind!' Hanna added as she drew up on Jackson's right. The three of them dropped pace and kept time as they took in glances across to the islands.

'Muck, far over to the left.' Zach added, 'Careful, you'll veer if you look round that far.'

'And Canna's hidden by Rum completely right now,' Hanna said.

'*That's* the Small Isles?' Jackson asked. 'That's where we're going? Over there? All that way?'

'Yes.' Hanna and Zach replied in unison.

Jackson realised he hadn't known what to expect but somehow, it wasn't this. The Small Isles were not just small, they were tiny. And they were black, too, and strangely static. Dead looking, Jackson thought. And very far away.

'They're made of basalt,' Zach said, 'they're basically the lava that's left from a massive volcanic event. It's weird to think that from out there the mainland – here – this all looks like a heap of silhouettes to anyone looking this way from Eigg right now.'

Jackson looked briefly up to the mountainside at his and Hanna's right then to the lush green valley coming into view ahead. He shot a doubtful glance at Zach then gave Eigg one last look, waiting to feel something. A rumble of his stomach replied – the Coco Pop slice of the present was calling to him more urgently than the ominous rock of his ancestors' past.

/TheJacksonCampbellAppreciationSoc/blurts
can't resist anymore. we're on the way to join jacksonmcampbell. #StandByYourMan #JacksonsJourney #Adorable #JCOurKing #OnesieCrewForevs

40

After a long lunch and an invigorating swim, Gayle studied the sat nav in closer detail and found an option to divert slightly from the road she'd planned to a single-track road closer to the sea. The smaller road pre-dated the clearances and more closely followed the coast, winding through hamlets of just a few houses at a time and passing breath-taking beaches between Arisaig and Morar Bay. Excellent background views of the Small Isles were captured by the drones as the bikes passed grasses swaying on the tops of dunes which gradually outnumbered, then totally replaced, the previously dense vegetation on the seaward side. Inland, a house cropped up here and there and locals and tourists stepped out to wave, take photos and shout encouragement as they passed. Jackson whooped back and blew kisses energetically, invigorated by the knowledge that his fan club's unconditional validation was on the way.

At 6 p.m. they re-joined the main road and, shortly afterwards, the industrial outline of Mallaig Harbour came into view between two hills. Gayle slowed so the gaps between the truck and the bikes closed as they passed a sign welcoming them to the town.

'End of the line!' Zach called excitedly while pointing at the terminus of the railway off the other side of the road. Jackson looked up, expecting to see a station similar to Waverley. Instead, a small plastic shelter with fold-down seating by a digital ticket portal stood. On their left, a silver corrugated metal tower with 'I C E' written in huge blue lettering loomed above a row of single-storey warehouses and a large block of public toilets, between which several narrow roads snaked away, offering snatches of views to boats of all sizes held in frames on a concrete concourse. As they followed the truck into the town, Jackson felt spikes of excitement every time he spotted a flashy boat on the swathes of dry dock either side of the road. Many of them gleamed in pearlescent finishes with blacked out windows and multiple antennae protruding above. Smaller boats in more plentiful supply were moored just off the quayside and made Jackson giggle with their comparative make-do-and-mend modesty. As he pedalled slowly on he remembered how he'd liked to splash toys or sham-poo-bottle missiles into the bath water as a child, seeing how much of the tiled bathroom floor he could soak while Rebecca ducked behind a towel to protect her hair and make-up while simultaneously trying to mop up his mess. The boats petered out briefly as they entered a small shopping thoroughfare lined with bunting and bright floral displays then came to a stop at a round-about.

'Jackson,' Gayle said through the comms link, spotting an excited crowd gathered underneath a large sign for the Caledo-nian MacBrayne ferry terminal, 'come on up to the front.'

Jackson cycled forwards, then stopped at the truck's open pas-senger window. He waved and smiled at the crowd then grinned at Gayle.

'We did it!' he said. 'We're here, in Mallard!'

'Mallaig,' Gayle smiled back, 'and yes, we did it. Well done. Now, straight ahead, OK? You're safe to go, park outside the ferry terminal, say hello to your fans and I'll see if we can book the ferry for first thing tomorrow.'

Jackson nodded then rolled forwards a little. He looked right then straight ahead. Just past the waiting teens he could see the road to the ferry terminal was, unlike the rest of the town, a downward sloping affair. He released his brakes and made off across the road, stretching his left hand out to high-five several of the younger members of the crowd as he passed.

'Two minutes!' Jackson shouted, 'Just going to park!'

As Jackson progressed, he realised he was now confronting a road that was not only heading downward but was, with an increasingly horrific gradient, heading past the utilitarian build-ings of the ferry company Caledonian MacBrayne and then straight into the sea. Jackson pulled on his brakes and heard his heart thump in his chest. He stared at the thick girder stilts behind the ticket office and realised they were holding up other sections of the pier above. Scant-looking barriers at the pier's edge were lined with people waving over at him. Jackson looked down again to where the water slapped and swayed menacingly.

'What's up?' Hanna pulled up alongside Jackson then took in the view herself, 'Oh! 'Jesus!' she exclaimed, 'Déjà vu Aberdeen harbour or what?! Shit!'

'Is this *legal*?' Jackson whispered, incredulous about what he perceived to be a swirling death trap before them. 'Where's the bloody road gone, Hanna?! Who's here to stop us from falling off, or those people up there, do they know there's no earth beneath them? They could fall! We could just ... drown! Why is there no barrier down there? Like, what if I just pedal off the end of that? Or my brakes fuck up? Know what I mean?'

'I'll pull out and you go on my left,' Hanna laughed, 'head straight for the parking bays by the big lifebuoy ring down there, yeah? Swear I'll ram you into the office buildings if you even think about veering, all right?'

Hanna took off before Jackson had time to protest. He followed her immediately, pointedly refusing to look right at all. When they parked Jackson braked then dismounted, grabbing his kilt from his basket. An irrational fear that he could somehow fall into the water made Jackson press himself against the wall of the building for ballast as he one-handedly pulled his kilt about his waist and attempted the buckle. As Gayle and Zach parked, an enormous horn sounded, making all of them jump. Jackson gulped as a dark shadow fell across the entire lower harbour. He looked back down to the water and saw there was now a huge, navy, red and white mass in motion. Jackson took off his sunglasses and stared as the steel hulk of an enormous ferry's bow began rounding the end of the quay, lining up with the disappearing road. Displaced water now sloshed high and frothy, and was soon accompanied by the sinister grinding, creaking and hissing of a mechanical orchestra. A black horizontal line appeared across the ferry's bow, then grew wider, morphing into a sinister smile as the bow split open. Little by little, three neat lines of cars, trucks, vans and motorbikes, all complete with perfectly calm-looking drivers and passengers were revealed on the boat's pale blue deck. As the ferry engines worked a series of small calibrations Jackson felt his whole body vibrate while the toothless shark drew ever nearer and louder. Somehow, Jackson saw, the lower jaw of the bow kept its riveted chin above the sloshing deep until, finally, it had drawn perfectly to a stop at the point where Jackson had pictured his own demise, then gave a final clank.

'Cool!' Zach shouted when the noise dropped. 'That's the Ro-Ro. Roll on, roll off. If I've got the timetable right, that's just back from the Small Isles. And Armadale – on Skye.'

Jackson stared at Zach and blinked hard then jumped as the door to the Cal Mac office at his side swung open. A rotund, white-bearded man in a high-vis jacket and helmet stepped out to join them.

'Failte! Welcome!' the man said in a cheery voice. 'You made it to Mallaig then?' he continued, 'I'm Malc. Cal-Mac-Malc! Jackson, man, you look like you've seen a ghost. I've been watching you on the CCTV. And you, an Edinburgh boy! Have you never been to Leith, son? Or Rosyth?'

Jackson wondered how the coffee shops and restaurants of Leith were relevant while pretending to find the man hilarious and finishing buckling his kilt.

'We made it to Mallaig,' Gayle smiled warmly, 'you folks are in charge of the next bit of the journey, Malc, so I get a wee break. Can you recommend anywhere for us to park up tonight, after we buy tickets for the morning crossing to Eigg, that is?'

'Maybe,' Malc replied, then waved a finger in the air, 'but I can also offer you a wee deal, if you're interested?'

'Oh?' Gayle looked cautious. 'What kind of deal?'

'Well,' Malc tapped his nose and winked, 'we've a training run to do tonight. To Eigg and back, as it happens. New captain's finishing her training log hours. If you'd be happy to set those drones of yours to give us some good long shots of the ferry we could take you along and drop you off. That way I think we might have a mutually beneficial arrangement, don't you?'

Gayle raised her eyebrows then nodded. She held out her hand for Malc to shake again.

'Indeed,' she said, 'Zach, we can do that justice, can't we?'

'Sure can,' Zach nodded, already heading to the back door of the truck, 'easy on a night as clear as this. I'll get right on it and put in the bigger batteries.'

'We want to show all these folk you've inspired how simple

it is to go and find their ancestral homelands, see?' Malc replied. 'Oh! And I've something for you, Jackson. One of the farmers on Skye dropped it off this morning, on her way through here to the mart.'

'Cool!' Jackson faked a smile as Malc disappeared back into the building. 'I really hope it's a lifejacket.'

Gayle and Hanna laughed, but Jackson dismissed them with a nervous shake of his head. 'Gayle!' he hissed, 'That boat looks bloody dangerous. How do they make sure the water doesn't get in the mouth bit? I don't think we should get on it. I think we need an NSBC helicopter to take us instead. It can airlift the houses or something, can't it?'

'Jackson,' Gayle laughed, 'Cal Mac have an incredible safety record. Honestly, think about it. How often do you hear of deaths on New Scottish waterways?'

Jackson listened intently, wishing he had done more of the same any time the news had been on in his life before.

'Don't worry,' Gayle went on, 'it's a massive ferry, you'll barely know we're on the water – it's flat calm. And the forecast for the morning is not so lovely, so, all round, this is an extremely good option.'

Jackson looked to Hanna for reassurance. She nodded and gave his arm a squeeze.

'And we can wear lifejackets if you like,' Hanna said, 'they'll have loads. Harbours are freaky, Jackson, I get it. But don't worry, honestly. We've got you, yeah?'

The door to the building swung inwards again and Malc reappeared holding an enormous cone-shaped package, wrapped in brown paper.

'It's from deer Deirdre, for you, Jackson!' Malc announced. 'Well, it's from Big Boy, her lead male.' Malc thrust the parcel towards Jackson, 'She says it's for luck – she found it yesterday while she was watching her herd up a hill. She thought it was a sign, that it was somehow meant for you. She watches your livestream every night. I don't go in for all that sign nonsense, omens and that, but, anyway, open it! If nothing else, it'll make you feel horny!'

Malc boomed laughter, as Jackson tried and failed to make sense of what the man had said. Unsure how to respond, he busied himself with finding a corner of tape to start peeling back.

A smell not unlike Duchy wafted from the package and took Jackson by surprise. He looked at Malc quizzically, then continued unwrapping while the others watched, intrigued. Jackson pulled the paper away and gasped, finding himself now holding an enormous stag's antler. The bone of where the antler had once connected to a head was as wide as Jackson's wrist and though someone had obviously made an effort to sanitise it, dry threads of tissue hung still from its toothy edges.

'She says if you rub it, you'll get what you deserve,' Malc said excitedly. 'God knows where the other one is, she's never found it yet.'

'Is the stag … is it, *dead*?' Jackson whispered.

'Big Boy!?' Malc laughed, 'No! Not dead! He's in his prime, so he is. They cast their antlers after the rut, you see? This'll be one of last years. He'll have most of his new set by now. Biggest stag we've seen in this neck of the woods for going on fifty years, so they say. The new Monarch of the Glen, that's what they're calling him at New Scottish National Heritage.'

Gayle gave a little whistle, amused by the growing impression of Big Boy which Malc was so vividly painting.

Jackson remembered telling Niall that the next time they saw each other Niall would be ripped, fit and ready for anything. He hadn't imagined then that anything might include a rut, but it was all he could imagine now.

'You'll treasure that for life, will you, son?' Malc continued mistaking Jackson's horror for delight. 'Look at you there, holding Big Boy's defence, eh? There's probably been at least one watching you this whole way, hasn't there? You'll miss them on the island, won't you?'

'What do you mean I'll miss them?' Jackson asked, his face now almost as white as a large Transit van passing from the ferry to the roundabout behind Malc.

'There's not one deer on Eigg, son,' Malc replied. Niall's face swirled in the ink of Jackson's thoughts.

'Wow!' Jackson heard Hanna interject, 'I think you've stunned him! What do you reckon, JC? Some keepsake, isn't it?'

'Yeah, thanks,' Jackson managed, 'sorry, I … I've never had anything like Niall before. Can I put him in the truck? To keep it away … no … I mean *safe*. To keep it safe.' Jackson blushed hard.

'You said Niall!' Hanna laughed.

'No, I didn't!' Jackson snapped, then regretted it instantly when Hanna looked hurt. He shook his head. 'Sorry, Hanna,' he said quickly, 'I mean, I didn't, did I?'

'You did,' Gayle confirmed, 'I think you need food. You're malfunctioning, buddy. And yes, let's put it in the hold. Inside its wrapping, please.'

Jackson stared at the antler again. The smell from it mingled with a whiff of less than fresh fish somewhere nearby. If he never saw a stag again, he thought, he would be very happy. He looked up at Malc, and faked another grin, then addressed Hanna.

'Let's get on the boat,' he said, 'let's get on the boat tonight. And let's make a vegan tea, yeah?'

Jackson was pleased when Hanna laughed. He noticed the teenagers were now approaching, fed up with waiting for their selfies.

'I can smell chips,' Hanna said, linking arms with Jackson, 'have we got time to go and buy chips, Malc?'

'Aye!' Malc replied, keeping half an eye on the teens, the sight of whom he never relished near the water. 'Follow your nose and get your suppers. The kids there'll show you where to go. I'll look after your kit. Then we'll see you back here in half an hour.'

Jackson thanked Malc then stopped and watched the GBEBS drone arrive at the top of the road and lower itself onto a lamppost. A seagull that had been heading to rest on the same spot screamed a protest then changed direction. When they arrived back at the pavement by the roundabout Jackson allowed the teens to huddle around him while he pulled poses so Hanna could take photos. While Hanna snapped, Jackson looked over to Eigg. The island's small, solid stance stared back. What had looked like an escape back in his parent's garage now appeared like Rikers or Alcatraz, both of which he'd visited virtually in gaming. He shuddered, then grinned. Game face on.

/ZuzannaN/blurts/
omg that horn thing is disgusting ffs.

/RebeccaCampbell/blurtsTo/jacksonmcampbell
Private Message Jackson there is nothing wrong with collecting

animal parts for the home, as you know, but I doubt that antler has been thru Edinburgh standards of decontamination so pls do wash your hands thoroughly, several times, darling. Also they are not worth very much as half racks so do see if you can encourage the gift of the other half too, yes?

/TheJacksonCampbellAppreciationSoc/blurts

we are in inverness! Bus to fort William in the morning! The antler was so beautiful! You can tell jacksonmcampbell really loved it – his face! Awwww! Cutest!!!

41

After waving off the Mallaig teens and the mainland until Jackson complained his arms were about to fall off, Gayle led the way up three short flights of metal stairs onboard *MV Lochnevis II*. Hanna and Zach split off together at the end of the second flight, but Jackson urged Gayle on to where she had promised him a literal high point of safety awaited, far above the sea. The GBEBS drone followed Jackson and Gayle and when they arrived on the third deck, they were greeted by a riveted door marked 'Observation Deck' flanked on either side by large safety posters encased behind battered Perspex, warning of multiple different potential deaths at sea. Jackson squeezed past Gayle to grab the handle on the door, then stepped over a skinny metal threshold to a roomy lounge beyond. An array of seating and table options stood before them, all fixed to the flooring, and the noise levels of the ferry dropped significantly when Gayle closed the door behind her, leaving the GBEBS drone hovering outside, then parking itself on the deck's roof.

'It feels like a fish tank,' Jackson said, taking in windows on all sides tinted with a pale blue hue. Mallaig was now on their left, Jackson saw, and Eigg was out in front across a nauseating expanse of sea. The southern-most expanse of Skye lay just a few hundred metres to their right. Jackson made to a banquette of seating above the bow and knelt on it, gripping the top of the chair with both hands. Zach and Hanna stood on the open deck below and looked up to try and catch Jackson's eye, while Gayle opened her laptop at a nearby table. Jackson watched Zach point to something on Skye. Both Hanna and Jackson followed his direction to a mass of seals, their dark eyes staring back at the ferry over double chins rippling down into smooth, navy-grey bellies.

'How long will it take to get there?' Jackson turned back to Gayle.

'Um, thirty minutes, I think,' Gayle replied, 'maybe twenty-five. It'll be fast anyway – solar batteries will make sure of that once we're into open water. But I guess since this is a training trip we have to be patient if things take a little longer.'

Jackson looked surprised.

'Half an hour? Is that all?'

Gayle looked up and nodded.

'To get over there?' Jackson pointed at Eigg, still black and foreboding, 'Are you sure?'

Gayle laughed and went to join Jackson. She dropped onto the corner of the banquette and looked out. Zach was now standing at the apex of the bow with his arms held out to either side. Hanna stood behind him, embracing his torso. Though the thick windows muted them, they both appeared to be singing.

'They're doing *Titanic*,' Gayle smiled, looking up when one of the NSBC drones passed slowly above them all. 'He's timed that perfectly, hasn't he?' Gayle said. 'You should blurt it from here, too.'

Jackson watched, recognising the scene from one of his mum's favourite films. He pulled his tablet out from his hoodie pocket and blurted a series of photos. A flurry of reactions in his notifications immediately relaxed him. Gayle returned to her laptop, which gave a loud ping as she sat down.

'Oh!' she grinned, 'My kids are online!'

Jackson watched Gayle tap out of the comms link and lean in towards her camera. Her smile was different, Jackson realised.

'Come and say hi?' Gayle beckoned Jackson over. He hesitated. Despite all his familiarity with strangers, an imminent meeting with Gayle's children felt intimate in a way other encounters did not. A memory of Zuzia's face as she'd talked him into pedalling at Holyrood flashed at him. He sat next to Gayle and they waited for the slowly-spinning egg timer on her screen to be replaced with her children's faces, from somewhere on the other side of the planet.

'Tap off your comms link,' Gayle whispered, 'livestream's busy with Hanna and Zach anyway.'

Jackson did as he was told, then jumped as a shrill blast of screaming leapt from Gayle's speakers. He looked up to see two hysterically excited children jumping up and down on screen in front of him. They were both wearing brightly coloured rash vests and board shorts and looked identical apart from the fact one of them had deep purple hair flapping around their face and the other had aqua. Two sets of dark eyes just like Gayle's shone above heavily freckled noses. Gayle shook her head in mock exasperation and reduced the volume, then pointed to the child with the aqua bob.

'That's Ash,' Gayle told Jackson, giving Ash a little wave before pointing at her other child, 'and that's Rowan.'

'Twins?' Jackson asked.

Gayle nodded.

'But I thought your kids were teens? Why did I think that? Didn't you tell me that?'

'I certainly did not!' Gayle laughed, 'If I recall correctly you thought I was Zach's mum, didn't you? They're eight. That's all. It's little, isn't it?'

Jackson nodded, watching as Ash and Rowan began taking turns to jump off a large corner sofa onto a stack of enormous pillows on the floor.

'Squidgy World,' Gayle explained, 'their dad invented that game. I only let them play it in their bedrooms, at home. No such rule at his place.'

'It looks fun,' Jackson said, 'I've got a LazySack. It'd be bants to jump onto a few of them, wouldn't it?'

'In your tiny house?' Gayle frowned.

'Nah,' Jackson shook his head, 'at my mum and dad's. In their lounge in front of the big screen.'

'Ah.' Gayle laughed, 'It would be fun. They'd love that – the kids, I mean.'

Jackson watched again and felt like he'd tuned into a half-psychotic screen saver which was as addictive as it was over-stimulating.

'Will they come and talk?' he asked.

'Maybe,' Gayle replied, 'but it's good when they're like this. They look happy, don't they? And they're showing off to you, obviously, so I'll get no sense out of them. It's better just to let them burn off some steam. It's 7 a.m. in New Zealand, remember?'

Jackson whipped his head round to stare at Gayle.

'They get up at six,' Gayle continued, 'they'll be going body-boarding soon. Then they do online school for a few hours, then it's lunch and a quiet afternoon out of the sun, probably gaming or in front of the telly. I'm fast asleep by then, and I obviously am not being told how things really go when they're tired in the evenings, not by their dad, anyway. So. It's hard for me to visualise that bit, and that might be better, mightn't it?'

Jackson nodded, sensing the conversation had arrived somewhere difficult. The purple-haired child arrived at the screen, shouted something, then backed up a few metres and began body-popping, joined by his sibling seconds later.

'You don't have many friends with kids, do you?' Gayle asked, intrigued by Jackson watching her children as if they were animals in a zoo.

Jackson shook his head. A warmth spread from his belly to his chest; *friends*, Gayle had said. Him and her. He smiled at Gayle. Over her shoulder the horizon line where sea had previously met sky caught his eye, now he could see a view of Eigg's northeast coastline. The island no longer looked black; it had changed dramatically to greens, purples, yellows and rust, with twinkling shards of mineral in the matt-black rock. Jackson gaped, unsure when and how the transformation had happened.

'Wave "bye",' Gayle prompted Jackson. The kids were now standing in front of their camera, completely out of breath, beaming at him and ignoring their mother. He made a heart shape with his hands, then winked. Rowan and Ash blew kisses to Jackson and body-popped again.

'You two are awesome,' Jackson beamed, 'honest, you're like *my* favourite livestream. See you again, yeah? I've got to go now.'

Rowan and Ash screamed with delight and Jackson got up, leaving Gayle to a private goodbye. Gayle mouthed a 'thank you' as Jackson retreated, touched by his developing sensitivity. Jackson nodded then turned back to the banquette and watched as steep cliffs curved away from the sea, bare black and grey rock stretching up, now topped with a dense fringe of exposed heather roots, some of them hanging like charred and grasping skeletal fingers. As the ferry continued, Eigg's coast softened, sloping downwards first then revealing a beach with a three-storey white house in a bay and a single-track road running up the hill behind. Gayle joined Jackson as he watched the land rise and change again; a copse of low trees stood in deep bracken then gave way to a grassy knoll. This was no prison landscape, Jackson thought, confused. After that came a huge bay with arcs of silver and ivory sand.

The ferry slowed and Jackson looked down to the water. About twenty metres of indigo sea swayed then changed to sapphire blue. A frond of mustard-coloured seaweed passed lazily by. Jackson looked towards the bow and saw a causeway beyond it. He rushed to the windows overlooking the stern. A thrum of machinery awakened far below in the ferry's engine room. Jackson clamped his grip to the backrest of a chair as he leant forward and saw the sea start to churn as the vessel began turning, as if on an enormous pivot board. When he looked up, a view of the mainland greeted him. He pointed wordlessly at the black triangles and curvaceous outlines of the mountains, as far to the north and south as his eyes could see. Gayle had tears in her eyes.

'New Scotland, baby,' she whispered.

Jackson crossed the deck to the opposite windows and saw they were now almost alongside the causeway, buzzing, beeping and vibrating their way inwards. Beyond the pier, Jackson saw a jungle of trees, their canopies stacking up in layers, rising until the tips of those furthest drew apart and the dark grey of a colossal, chimney-like rock stood like a stone sub-sky, towering above everything.

'Is this definitely …?' Jackson scrunched his face, 'Is *this* definitely *Eigg*?'

'Sure is,' Gayle said, 'there's a palm tree there Jackson, look, with the birches.'

'It's *nice* though, Gayle,' Jackson frowned, 'I'm quite – I dunno – proud? I can't believe my family decided to leave.'

'They didn't, remember?' Gayle dabbed her eye with her cuff then pushed her laptop back into her rucksack. 'They were forced to leave, the rich people didn't want the locals. Just the land.'

Jackson listened, but the likelihood of what Gayle was telling him seemed impossible now the words were tethered to an actual place.

'Pop your comms back on,' Gayle said, 'I've done mine. We need to get you back on the livestream, asap.'

'But it's so bright, Gayle. So … I dunno, tropical?'

'It is,' Gayle agreed, 'it doesn't get dark till very late out here in summer. And there's the Gulf Stream nearby. So the water's warmer too.'

'There are still some Campbells here, aren't there?'

'I believe so,' Gayle replied, 'you'll meet them, I'm sure.'

Jackson tapped back into the comms link then knelt again at the window overlooking the pier. Cars, quad bikes and battered looking 4 x 4s were arriving in a cul-de-sac parking area and backing up onto a single-track road while they waited. A small crowd were gathered at the end of a galvanised steel gangway, their faces scanning the ferry, trying, he realised, to spot him. He pushed his sunglasses into his hair and his heart quickened as he scanned faces, intrigued as to whether he could spot anyone bearing a family resemblance. Gayle opened the top of one of the windows at Jackson's side. The sound of bagpipes drifted up as the engine and hydraulics eased off. Jackson squinted, spotting a woman in a purple kilt standing on a rock at the other side of the causeway. Her blonde hair was shaved almost to her scalp on one side, showcasing a huge mandala tattoo which stretched from underneath a vest strap on her shoulder. Jackson swallowed, aroused, then pulled his sunglasses back onto his nose.

The door to the lounge opened and Hanna entered. Zach remained outside, grinning up at the drones circling overhead then adjusting his shoulder cam to capture Jackson.

'Oh, my God!' Hanna laughed, 'This place! Wow! Some gaff, JC!'

'Are yous coming down to the houses?' Zach called in, 'The crew are going to open the deck in about three minutes, I think.'

'Coming right now,' Gayle replied, 'I'll pop up and thank the captain, see if she can join us for some footage before we disembark. Go on, Jackson, you go and get ready with the bikes too, OK?'

Jackson pulled his hoodie down over the front of his kilt and rushed to the doorway, eager to be safely sandwiched between Hanna and Zach as they made their way down the stairs and then, once all risks of sea death were over, to get a better view of the piper.

. . .

After thanking the captain and posing for selfies with the tiny houses on the deck, a sign outside a smart, cream-painted low-lying building informed them that it was the pier centre, and that it housed the tearoom, shop, crafts centre, showers, toilets, medical emergency equipment, bike hire, a hot-desking space, a fishmongers and the island's energy hub. Jackson and Hanna chatted easily with the ever-growing numbers of gathering locals while island children, many of them in pyjamas, hopped in and out of the tiny house doors, waving at their parents and friends through the walls. Jackson kept half an eye on the piper who wove her way through the crowd of around sixty locals and a handful of tourists, chatting to people as she went, but never quite meeting his eye. Could they be related, Jackson wondered, blushing uncharacteristically at the sexual thrill the thought provided.

Zach reset the drones and changed their batteries then wandered to where Gayle stood at a fork in two small, well-worn roads. One route ran away up a steep hill past a huge standing stone and the other hugged the edge of the island's miniature coast. Gayle's back faced Zach from where she stood deep in conversation with a compact, military-looking man in combat trousers and, despite the mild weather, an Arran jumper. Three pairs of binoculars hung about the man's chest and his floppy, golden streaked hair kept falling into his eyes, causing him to lift his chin and flick it backwards repeatedly, each time revealing a little more of a leathery but chiselled face with keen eyes and a dark shadow of stubble.

'Well, that's something, but it's not ideal,' Zach heard Gayle say.

The man drew a pipe from one of his trouser pockets, thumbed tobacco into it, then shook his head.

'It's all I can allow,' he replied, then sucked the flame from his lighter through the tobacco till smoke puffed around his face.

'Everything OK?' Zach asked.

'Hey, Zach,' Gayle looked uneasy, 'this is Calum, the nature ranger. Calum, Zach, my colleague.'

Zach smiled and Calum shrugged.

'All this time we've been messaging,' Gayle continued, 'Calum assumed we were heading to the blackhouses on the *north* side of the island – to the much bigger cleared settlement there. Crossed wires.'

Zach looked confused, 'But we messaged everything about Grulin, in massive detail. Maps, images—'

'I only read half of my messages,' Calum interrupted, 'it's a protest against globalisation.'

Zach stared at the man, lost for how to answer. Jackson and Hanna wandered over with a small tribe of teens following behind. Calum looked them all up and down then sucked his pipe again.

'What's up?' Hanna asked.

'Corncrakes,' Gayle sighed, 'and confusion.'

'Aye.' Calum nodded.

'Cornwhat?' Hanna frowned.

'Oh,' Jackson said, 'are we sorting out breakfast? I'd prefer Coco Pops, to be honest. But I'll take cornflakes if that's all there is – if there's sugar.'

Gayle sighed as Jackson wandered off to where the teens were beckoning him to join them at the standing stone.

'So, corncrakes?' Zach stared pointedly at Calum. Calum shrugged then stared out to sea and sucked on his pipe again.

'Birds,' Gayle explained, 'they're birds. Not much bigger than blackbirds; ground-nesting, and they're dying out, like, ultra-red status for extinction, population's been decreasing since the noughties, modern farming machinery terrorised them, but last night for the first time in ten years, guess who arrived just off the road to Grulin?'

Hanna's eyes widened.

'There's a machair there, a meadow,' Calum interjected, 'some long, natural grass where everything else around is heather, bracken, rock. It was set up as a reserve at the millennium, hoping to attract what was left of them then. It worked for a while, but ten years ago they stopped coming. They used to arrive in April, but we think this lot settled somewhere on the mainland then got disturbed. Or their whole pattern's changing, because of the climate crisis. So they're not at all on schedule, you see, but *very* welcome.'

'But we can still go round there, yeah?' Hanna asked.

'Kinda,' Gayle said, '*we* can, but we can't wander as far and wide as we'd expected once we are there, and there's a section of the route we'll have to be completely silent in too. After we park the truck, before the skinniest bit of track.'

'Oh,' Zach replied.

'I know,' Gayle replied.

'We'll basically help wipe out an entire species if we muck it up, yeah?' Hanna frowned, 'but if we're careful, it sounds OK?'

'And when we need kit from the truck?' Zach asked. 'Can we come and go to that as planned?'

'Only one of us can,' Gayle replied.

'What about the fans?' Zach nodded towards where Jackson now appeared to be dry humping the standing stone, egged on by the teens, several of whom were wearing rucksacks and stood amongst small mounds of sleeping bags, pop-up tents and the pokey limbs of folded camping chairs.

'Oh, absolutely not!' Calum gave a wry laugh.

Hanna and Zach looked to Gayle, expecting her to respond, but found her looking Calum up and down.

'Like, not to be selfish and that,' Hanna looked thoughtful, 'but, hear me out. This is kinda good in a way, isn't it? Like, when folk lived round there, they were cut off, it was remote, I mean, it still is, massively, but, like, it's hard enough getting Jackson to concentrate when there's other folk around, isn't it? And the next bit really is about him, and his past.'

'And getting him to open up about Transpariboard,' Zach added, 'you're right, Hanna. This could be a plus, in a way.'

Gayle felt a tap on her shoulder. It was the piper, smiling warmly.

'Join us tonight for a wee ceilidh?' the piper asked. 'Too late to head, isn't it? And you can shower at An Lhamrig – our pier centre, in the morning. And stock up at the shop.'

Gayle looked to Hanna, then Zach. They both nodded enthusiastically.

A battered-looking minibus with a half-illuminated taxi sign stuck on top of its windscreen drew up behind them. When it stopped several people climbed from the back of it, laughing and holding bags that clinked as they made their way to the pier centre.

'You'll want to get inside, soon,' the piper added, 'wind's dropping. Midgies will be swarming before you know it.'

'Sounds like we have a plan,' Gayle said, 'thanks, by the way, this is great. It's a lovely welcome when we've arrived earlier than expected.'

'Eigg's always ready for a party.' The piper winked, 'It's one of our USPs. Sounds like you've beat the crowds, too. There's about 200 visitors booked to come over tomorrow, apparently, thanks to your livestream.'

'I have to go now,' Calum said brusquely, 'I've to count the terns at Runciman's before dusk.'

Hanna and Zach smiled a goodbye then started chatting with the piper as the three of them walked away. Gayle hesitated, then followed the others.

'But mind,' Calum called after Gayle, 'this returning to the truck business. It can't be yer man there – the hyperactive one.' Gayle looked back at Calum and saw him point towards Jackson, 'I can't have folk starting some hormone-addled mating ritual with whatever herds are going to arrive from the mainland the rest of the week, right? Those birds, the corncrakes – they're special.'

Gayle watched the ranger. He was not her usual type by any stretch and the manner of every word that had left his mouth since she'd met him had annoyed her intensely, but, physically, the look of him had stirred something that'd been a long time dormant.

'It'll be me if it's anyone,' she replied.

'Right. Good.' Calum battled to hold a neutral expression, 'And I hope you've read your country code.'

'Oh, I've read it,' Gayle volleyed back, 'call it a political protest against misinformation, if you like.'

42

/NewScotGovtFMClearwater/blurts/
They did it! They made it to Eigg! This is so exciting! My team and I are celebrating with pizza night in Holyrood and taking in island views! How beautiful that the corncrake's plight is being considered with such care. New Scotland will always be a place of safety for people and wildlife. #Unclearance #GreenNewDealDelivered #LoveYourMotherEarth #JacksonsJourney #SaveTheCorncrake

/TheJacksonCampbellAppreciationSoc/blurts
Nono no non no no! How is he on the island already??!!?!! Wait for us jacksonmcampbell!!!!

/ZuzannaN/blurtsTo/TheJacksonCampbellApprecia-tionSoc
Mwaaaa haaaa haaaaa haaaa haaaaa you're not going to get there on time

/jacksonmcampbell /blurts/
I want a tattoo. Who can stick and poke me? #InkMe #OctopusTime #CelticNaughty #ISeeYouSexyPiper

/jacksonmcampbell /blurts/
A HAAAAA HAAAAA! I'm #ThePierPiper and I'm doing a takeover on Jackson's tablet PS download my album BLOW JOB before midnight, add #PythonHandler to your payment notes and I'll give you a big ole blurt here. Plus I have a black marker and I'll write your name on Jackson himself. HA HAAAAAAA #JacksonsJourney #Eigg #BlowDontSuck #BlowJob #ScotsTrad #FollowThePierPiper

/TheJacksonCampbellAppreciationSoc/blurtsTo/CaledonianMacBrayne

Hello do you have any other training runs going tonight? How can we get to Eigg asap? #Emergency #SOS

/RebeccaCampbell/blurtsTo/jacksonmcampbell

PRIVATE MESSAGE JACKSON absolutely no to the tattoo. DON'T YOU DARE! I did not birth that perfect body and gain a lifetime of stretch marks for you to annihilate yourself with tramp stamps!

/ZuzannaN/blurts/

Eh, like, who the fuck is this takeover twat?!?! #No #JacksonsJourney #DoNotFollowThePierPiper

/jacksonmcampbell /blurts/

Jackson says his mother has a tatt of a dolphin on her ass cheek so she can't tell him not to get one. Love from the sexy pier piper X #DolphinBumMum #HAAAAHHAAAA Everyone buy my album X #BlowJob

/RebeccaCampbell/blurts/

What's in those unmarked lemonade bottles?

/RebeccaCampbell/blurts/

SEND TO HANNA NOWAK Dear Hanna, you are a woman, please use all your instincts, innate skills capabilities and mothering instincts and tell Jackson to put some of his clothes back on. Also, stop him from dancing on that cheap table, I have found only quality furniture is strong enough to prevent him from being injured while playing. Thank you X #hashtagSEND

/RebeccaCampbell/blurts/

SEND TO ZACH OF NSBC Dear Zachary you have looked like a sensible boy up until this evening would you please put some kind of covering on Jackson and ask the angry-looking individual with the tattoo on her neck to stop drawing on my child and encouraging him to drink and strip? I'm sure it must be part of your job description to do as Jackson's principle parent demands when he is unable to advocate for himself?!?!?!? Please also provide Gayle Wood's direct line. Thank you #URGENT #PRIVATE

/MichaelTempletonGBEBS/blurts/
Well, what a surprise, NOT! New Scottish Scots are just like Old Scottish Scots when it comes to alcohol. Any excuse and they're glugging away, dropping everything from underwear to their pathetic bureaucratic EU tosh on booze labelling. #Queerwater, #RabidRoy's progeny and #NSBCAmateurs are destroying elite hunting habitats for the sake of a heathen's piss up.

/RoryTheTory/blurtsTo/MichaelTempletonGBEBS
Michael you should've let me change that battery there's practically no footage on GBEBS cause it keeps having to charge. People are switching to NSBC and that's Clearwater propaganda. All you have to do is say the word but also let me know when my eggcup is coming so I don't miss the post ok? #GBE #EmpireStrikesBack #MEGA

/RebeccaCampbell/blurts/
Who, I ask you, is going to take responsibility for my child's body during this 'journey'?!?! He has been bitten by man and beast, indecently exposed, fed a terrible diet, subjected to repeated attacks of alcohol poisoning and possibly STDs. He has also been denied access to a proper SPF with alpha gamma liposoids, which his sensitive skin desperately needs. Now he is being used as a colouring book.

/NSBCJourney/NewScotland /blurts/
Hey jackson's mum suuuupppp?!?! I'm afraid I have no contractual obligation to you at all, sorry, it's because Jackson is an adult OK love you byeeeeee #JacksonsJourney #Ethanol #ILobeHannaNowak

/ProfDrewMcAllister/blurts/
Great to see the young ones enjoying themselves! Ha ha, those were the days, eh? And another triumphant week for my #EHA cohort outside of #JacksonsJourney too – I'm looking forward to a catch up with a brilliant peer of Jackson (and HannaNowak's best pal) very soon ☺

43

/NSBCJourney/NewScotland /blurts/
Morning all! Gayle here! Join me on my recce run for the first part
of today's route if you're up with the larks too ☺ Later this morning
we'll all be moving forwards by foot and bike only, AND we'll all be
sneaking past some extremely precious corncrakes. #JacksonsJour-
ney #adventure #NewScotland #SaveTheCorncrake #Unclearances

At 8.30 the next morning Eigg pier stood silent, shrouded in a
misty drizzle. The door to Jackson's tiny house slid open and the
piper stepped out from inside the privacy-tilted walls. She stuck her
tongue out at the NSBC and GBEBS drones hovering overhead
then slid the door shut. Under her arm she'd bundled a Jackson's
Journey hoodie. She stopped a few steps between Jackson's house
and the NSBC truck and pulled the hoodie on, took a selfie, then
made up the hill track into a thick belt of trees. As her footsteps
receded, the slow spinning of the fan on the roof of the truck and
the far-off tide beyond a dark collection of rocks were the only
sounds the drones could detect, until Gayle returned from a run by
the track round the bay. The NSBC drone following a few metres
behind her docked itself on the truck roof to charge, and Gayle set
about stretching against a bike rack. As she lunged her left leg she
looked out at the mist blocking the view of life beyond the island.
She'd seen the same effect in the background of Ash and Rowan's
video call over the New Zealand shoreline. It had made her feel
further from them at the time – another barrier, even if it was
ephemeral. Now, seeing it first-hand made her smile. They might
be far apart, she thought, but she and her children were also expe-
riencing things in common; and every day passed was now a day
closer to the three of them being together again, too.

Turning to lunge her right leg Gayle spotted what looked very likely to be vomit down the front of a recycling bin that had been pulled to stand alongside Jackson's tiny house. She checked her wristband, scrolling through the avalanche of blurts still coming in about the previous evening's partying. Predictably, as night had slid into morning, audience feedback had morphed from the roaring approval of younger fans to an austere, colder morning judgement by an older, more conservative persuasion of followers. Gayle looked up as the door to Hanna's tiny house slid open. Zach scooched his way to the threshold inside his sleeping bag, nodding when he spotted her.

'Needed air,' Zach croaked.

'Morning,' Gayle replied, 'not like you, Zee, to go OTT.'

'They had this wine …' Zach started, 'locally fermented … holy shit …'

'Please! Don't talk about the wine,' Hanna appealed from where she was trying to lie very still inside the house. 'I'm serious. We're lucky we're not blind.'

Jackson's door slid open, and Gayle shielded her eyes when she realised he was stark naked. Almost every inch of his skin was covered in drawings and writing. Beneath his belly button the words, 'DECENT PIPE' were scrawled with a chunky, downward pointing arrow alongside. Jackson looked down, then laughed.

'That was the piper,' he nodded, 'nice! Hey, did anyone see where she went?'

'Tell me you know her name?' Gayle said, giving Hanna a small wave when her pale face appeared behind Zach's shoulder.

Jackson shrugged.

'My tablet's going insane,' Hanna said groggily, 'I'm turning it off until I feel better. Or maybe I'll die first. Whatever.'

'I'm not looking at mine either,' Jackson said. 'It's a million messages about the piper's new album. And 600 missed calls from my mum.'

'I'm trying to change the subject on it all this morning,' Gayle said, 'onwards and upwards. Literally.'

'I feel great though!' Jackson announced. 'Hey, maybe *I'm* in love now, too?'

'How can you possibly feel great?' Zach stared at Jackson, 'Like, how are you not dying?'

'Puked it all out, man,' Jackson grinned, 'you've gotta learn, Zee. Get it all out before bed, drink heaps of water, eat some crisps. Bob's your uncle.'

Zach struggled to make his uncomfortably dry throat swallow as he listened. Hanna muted herself out of the comms link before she spoke.

'Jackson, I don't want you to get hurt, yeah?' she said.

'Eh?' Jackson looked at Hanna, confused.

'She's promoting an album, Jackson,' Hanna elaborated, 'I think she definitely saw a business opportunity. Maybe I'm wrong, but—'

Jackson burst out laughing.

'You're alright, Hanna. I was just joking about love. I know what she's about. We're the same, me and her. Maybe we're meant to be business partners or something? How cool would that be?'

'Chemistry or no, you'll have to hose down the biology on that bin Jackson, yes?' Gayle said, sitting down on the truck's step to loosen her shoelaces. 'There's a hose round the back, I'm sure it'd be fine to use that. Do it before you shower, please, then put the bin back where it should be. And the hose.' Gayle checked her wristband again, then smiled tightly at the drones hovering above her. 'Right. Let's move the focus swiftly onto Grulin, please, ASAP.'

'Do you mean this hose, Gayle?' Jackson called back. Gayle looked up and saw Jackson rotating his pelvis so his willy swung from side to side.

'God give me strength,' Gayle muttered as she pulled off her shoes. 'Tell me the nudity filters are working, Zach?'

'Perfectly,' Zach confirmed.

Jackson mouthed 'python' to the drones above, then grabbed his kilt from the floor of his tiny house and pulled it on before jumping barefoot onto the concrete, dragging the bin after him as he went. Zach winced at the noise.

'How many more sleeps?' Hanna asked while staring at Jackson's back and tapping back into the comms link. 'How many more till I'm back in a real bed, not having to think about walking around some random alfresco domain with a camera pointing at me while I try to find somewhere to piss? How many, yous?'

'Not many now, Hanna,' Gayle replied, 'I don't see Jackson

wanting to stay at Grulin for very long. He'll have no audience there now if the ranger's going to restrict other footfall in that direction to keep the corncrakes safe.'

Zach nodded his agreement then reached for a bottle of water protruding from the top of his rucksack and sipped from it.

'I'll put on some breakfast,' Gayle replied, 'best way to make time pass is to stay active. Let's shower and then see where we are, yes?'

'No one mention food, please,' Hanna begged.

'Food?' Jackson arrived back, 'I could murder a sweaty sausage in a bun, and a Coke. And a fried egg. And a sausage roll.'

Hanna wriggled silently free from her sleeping bag still fully clothed and shod from the previous night. She covered her mouth as she stepped past Zach and out of her tiny house, then rushed to the toilet stalls.

. . .

At noon the lead NSBC drone passed so close to Jackson's face it easily captured the rain on his cheeks under the shadow of his helmet while he pedalled a steep, deeply rutted track. The GBEBS drone struggled to keep up behind Jackson's trailer, unable to shoot much more than the back wall of Jackson's house. The drone panned to the back of a large farmhouse; its rear wall hard up against the track and painted a buttery cream. Smart green downpipes, window frames and roof trims provided the perfect contrast. The NSBC truck was out in front towing Hanna's bike and tiny house, its rooftop flags jumping wildly with every bump. Zach's bike was stowed in the hold and Gayle concentrated hard as she drove, her concern about the track twofold: firstly, there was the matter of protecting the undercarriage of the truck and then, perhaps more importantly, there was the fragility of Hanna and Zach, each holding a basin on their laps on the passenger seats to her left. The GBEBS drone kept up easily for once, thanks to the truck's low speed, and stayed focused on Hanna and Zach's discomfort.

On the NSBC livestream, a colourful graphic of Eigg appeared with arrows indicating where the team were now located. Save the lone farmhouse, the island's modern-day homes and settlements were now far behind and progress to Upper then Lower Grulin was over halfway complete. The tips of blades from a windfarm down a hillside came into sight when Gayle looked down towards the sea. When she reached a clearing made of a rough circle of chunky grey stone chippings she braked gently then switched off the engine. She flexed her fingers to ease tension after gripping the wheel tightly then took a deep, relieved breath and leant back in her seat.

In front of the truck a cordon with small orange flags waved in the wind. A post to the left bore a sign made up of several sheets of A4 paper sellotaped together under a piece of Perspex. Someone – Calum, Gayle suspected – had chosen a hideously hostile typeface and printed, 'NO ENTRY WITHOUT PERMISSION!!! CORNCRAKE PROTECTION ZONE!!!' Gayle stepped out of the truck and pulled her hood up against the rain. As she opened the truck's hold and began pulling the rucksacks to the front she had the distinct sense of being watched from afar. She straightened and scanned the hills in every direction. Jackson caught up on his bike, braked and dismounted, then pulled the brake on his trailer too. He held up a palm to high-five Gayle, delighted with himself for having more stamina than his colleagues. Gayle smiled and slapped Jackson's hand.

'I like the rain here,' Jackson said, only slightly out of breath, 'it's soft. And it's always a bit warm, isn't it? It's not the same as the rain in Edinburgh, is it?'

'That's true.' Gayle nodded, 'And it comes and goes all the time, rather than hanging about for hours on end.' Gayle eyed the landscape around them again, 'I think the ranger's probably watching.'

'Would he be wearing camo?' Jackson asked. 'He totally could be one of those weirdos. Face paint, the works. A Rory the Tory type, you know?'

Gayle laughed. Jackson's words had a ring of truth that dampened a fantasy that had been forming in the background of her thoughts since the day before. Zach approached, fidgeting with a shoulder cam as he walked. When he stopped Gayle steadied the camera while he secured a final Velcro fixing.

'Thanks,' he smiled, 'nice air here, isn't it? It's like, soft, or something.'

'You look much more like yourself,' Gayle said, relieved.

Hanna appeared after Zach with her hood pulled tightly round her face. Her cheeks had also returned to a more normal colour.

'I can't believe it,' Hanna said, 'I could eat now, actually. It's a bloody miracle.'

Gayle reached into the hold and pulled out a cool box.

'Sandwiches from the shop,' she explained, 'and some fruit and cake. Eat what you can – fast – then let's get going. I've got soup in a flask, too, for when we get to Lower Grulin.' Jackson, Hanna and Zach picked food from the box then each took a seat on the edge of the hold.

'The bad weather's stopping boats from coming to the Small Isles today,' Gayle continued, 'but tomorrow's forecast is sun. We can get safely round to Jackson's square metres before any crowds turn up here – it'll be easier for the ranger if we're long gone. If we can get that separation in between us and them I think it's wise. Quick and quiet – that's the mode for the next hour or so.'

'We're going dark, basically,' Jackson added, enjoying the excitement of the idea. 'So we put the bikes in the truck here then, do we? And put Hanna's harnesses on? Switch to body power?'

Gayle nodded and kept chewing.

'How's that going to work with my kilt?' Jackson asked, 'If there's straps that go round my legs too?'

'Best change into leggings,' Zach replied, 'think about ticks. You want as much skin covered as possible.'

Jackson screwed up his face.

'And waterproofs over the top,' Zach continued, 'forecast's giving a lot of humidity, we may as well dress for everything. Saves having to stop.'

'Shame we couldn't take the piper with us,' Jackson mused, 'I bet she wanted to come.'

The livestream panned to a hawthorn tree cutting a lonely figure above the bracken leaves covering the hillside all the way to the windmills. The tree's thin branches pointed south-west from a gnarly trunk, while tiny, windburned leaves flapped back and forth in a strong passing wind.

When the sandwiches were finished, Gayle and Hanna fished

the harnesses out of the hold while Jackson changed into leggings and waterproofs. Zach arranged Jackson's bike in the hold then handed out waterproofs to the others and pulled on his own. Gayle locked up the truck, helped Jackson and Hanna into their harnesses and then fixed them onto the tiny house trailers before pulling on an enormous rucksack of her own.

'I like how this feels around my arse,' Jackson said, trying to look over his shoulder and see the straps of the harness from the rear perspective.

'I feel like I'm wearing a nappy,' Hanna laughed, 'or like I'm inside a baby bouncer. I think it's going to be more work than both of those things though, eh?'

'Let's see,' Jackson leant forward, straining as he tried to get the trailer and house behind him to follow.

'Hold up,' Zach moved to the head of Jackson's trailer and flicked a lever, 'your brake was still on. Try now.'

Jackson pulled again and this time the trailer came with him.

'This is easy!' he shouted, then panicked slightly as one of the trailer's wheels hit a large stone and the lurch of it transferred through to his shoulders and lower back. Jackson realised that if the trailer were to tip it would be taking him with it.

'OK?' Hanna called over while Zach turned her brake off too.

'Go slow, Hanna,' Jackson called back, 'especially on bumpy stuff.'

'OK.' Hanna took a deep step forward then another, grunting slightly as the wheels behind her began to turn. 'There's a quick release on your harness, JC,' she said, 'in case you need out, if the trailer takes a roll.'

'You read my mind,' Jackson replied, pulling forward again, facial muscles contorting. 'Are you sure we've got time for this Gayle? it's going to take ages. We can't go fast.'

'It's fine,' Gayle replied, 'there's time for slow and steady. Zach and I will help, don't worry.'

Once Hanna and Jackson had practised more Gayle held a finger to her lips signalling the time for quiet had begun. She then untied one side of the cordon and watched as the others set off; Jackson pulled out in front with Zach alongside followed by Hanna behind. Gayle closed the cordon after herself and followed, too.

The path was a wide belt of grass sporadically flecked with

dried sheep dung and flanked on either side by high bracken fronds. Gayle was pleased to feel the gentle undulations of the grass underfoot were soft and shock-absorbing while they all carried extra weight. Down the hillside a huge rectangle of wild, yellow and cream grasses standing bold against the bracken came into sight. Gayle stopped for a few seconds, beholding the secretive birds' pitstop. When she looked ahead again, she saw Jackson had stopped to take a selfie. She tapped her wristband, messaging him to stay quiet, fear quickening her pulse as she did so. Jackson read her message and waved back, then slowly moved on. Gayle saw what had caught Jackson's attention as she reached where he'd stopped; a thick cylindrical post about two metres tall stood at the edge of the path with an arrow-shaped sign screwed to its middle. Smart white-painted lettering read, 'Massacre Cave, this way'. Gayle looked down the path through the bracken, barely wide enough for one person to easily pass. A thick front of mist moving between herself and the sea made the hairs on her neck stand on end, driving her on again.

Ten minutes of walking with only the sound of the wind on their waterproof outer layers passed before an alert vibrated on each of their wristbands. Gayle hurried to catch up, reading her screen and stealing glances at the terrain around them.

'We can speak!' Gayle smiled. 'This is Upper Grulin, folks. We did it, we passed Corncrake Land!'

'Fucking yas!' Jackson said. 'Put on my brakes?'

Gayle rushed to pull the brake on Jackson's trailer, then Hanna's. Jackson undid his harness, stepped out of it and high-fived Hanna, then Zach.

'I was almost meditating there,' Hanna smiled, 'it was peaceful, wasn't it? Just us, pulling along in the mist. I felt like some ancient nomad going to Stonehenge or something. I actually got into flow.'

Zach opened his mouth to reply, but Jackson interrupted.

'Nah, nah Hanna – you must still be pissed! This place is spooky as fuck! What the fuck was that sign, eh? The bloody massacre cave?! Jesus! Flow my arse!'

'What?!' Hanna grimaced under her helmet.

'Saw that. Freaked me out.' Zach nodded.

'We'll have to find out what that's about later,' Gayle said, struggling to shrug off her backpack. Hanna went to help.

Zach nudged Jackson and pointed down to a collection of stones on the hillside below.

'See that, JC? It's the remains of a blackhouse, it's got the same footprint of the others you can see in the moss, down there, yeah? And there too, beyond that clump of bracken?'

Jackson looked to where Zach pointed.

'That's just stones,' he said, shaking his head, 'just foosty old stones. Aren't they?'

'Nope,' Hanna replied, 'look harder, they're stones, sure, but look at the lines – the ones lying around have just fallen down, or been knocked over by someone as part of the Clearances, I guess. That rectangle, see it? It's probably the size they all were in Upper and Lower Grulin, from what I remember from the research.'

Jackson considered it.

'Like a tiny house?' he replied. 'But made of stone?'

'A blackhouse.' Hanna nodded, 'For a whole family. They didn't have bigger houses for bigger families, they all just piled in, you know?'

'Like in your flat?' Jackson remembered what Niall had told him about Hanna's home life. Hanna raised an eyebrow. Jackson was still staring down the hill, oblivious.

'And absolutely not like you, in your mansion,' she replied.

'We've got to go,' Gayle cut in, frowning at a darkening sky, 'sooner we set up camp the better. I've packed a pop-up tent for me, but if the water supply's rubbish at Lower Grulin I might have to head back to the truck. Timewise that's going to be a lot to fit in. And that thing looks like it throws serious shadow, too.'

The nearest NSBC drone turned to film a huge cliff face of rock towering above the hillside behind them.

'An Sgùrr,' Hanna said.

'Anne who?' Jackson frowned.

'An Sgùrr,' Hanna laughed, 'it's the name of that rock. Folk were telling me about it last night. It means "sharp or sticking up bit". And Eigg, that's kind of a contraction of the Gaelic for island and notch – the notch being the shape of the Sgùrr – *eag* – and *eilean* being "island".'

'Aye, you're really back on form now, aren't you, Hanna?' Jackson smirked. 'This is what she was like at uni, yous, see what I mean? A right swot.' Jackson walked to the moss-covered tops of a line of stones nearby and stepped onto the first one, arms out in an attempt to keep his balance. Hanna stuck her tongue out.

'Were you always this way?' Jackson continued, enjoying bating her as he stepped onto a narrow stone.

'I think it started when I realised I didn't have a chalet, you know?' Hanna pretended to consider it. 'Or maybe it was when I knew I didn't have parents who were socialites?'

'Touché!' Jackson smirked.

'You're not exactly thick yourself though, are you?' Hanna went on, 'Despite what you want folk to think? It was you who came up with Transpariboard, after all. So, pot, kettle, much?'

Jackson toppled backwards and landed on his bum, his face reddening. Hanna smirked, then stepped back into her harness.

'Quality footage,' Zach laughed, pulling energy bars from the side of his rucksack. 'Soup later, yeah Gayle? We have these for now.'

Gayle nodded then offered a hand to Jackson to help him up.

'Come on,' she smiled, 'no rest for the wicked, huh?'

44

Though the distance from Upper to Lower Grulin was short as the corncrake might fly, progress over a narrow trail with trailers on harnesses proved onerous. Frequent collaboration was needed to lift the edges of the tiny house bases over boulders hiding in the bracken on either side of the trail and though the waterproof clothing served well in the drizzle, it also exacerbated sweating and stress.

'Fuck!' Jackson spat as his trailer hit another rock and tugged backwards. His shoulders stiffened in complaint against the harness.

'We'll have to check for ticks tonight,' Gayle spoke through heavy breaths, 'climbing amongst this depth of growth is not ideal.'

'Ideal for the ticks,' Zach replied, 'offering ourselves up to nature, aren't we?'

Gayle pushed the back of Jackson's trailer again.

'Hey!' Hanna called, 'Look!'

Hanna pointed upwards and right off the track. The top of a wall of black stones stood protruding above the bracken; at first it looked to be only a few feet high, but as she drew closer, she saw the wall was standing inside a dip in the landscape and the courses of stone reached almost two metres at one end, sloping to a lower point of only a metre at the opposite corner.

'Lower Grulin!' Gayle beamed with relief. 'That has to be the back of the first blackhouse!'

'I'm fucking knackered.' Jackson groaned, then stopped.

'A few more minutes, I think,' Gayle said, excitedly hurrying to help Hanna, 'that's all, come on!'

Jackson turned to Zach, pleased to see he was also a sweaty mess.

'I'm *never* drinking again,' Zach panted from behind Jackson's trailer, 'this day has kicked my ass.'

Jackson looked up and saw Hanna and Gayle ahead. Hanna was now almost at the wall and Gayle was walking backwards in front of her, beckoning her on with one hand and loosening her rucksack straps with the other.

'Hey, Zee, the piper was something though, wasn't she?' Jackson's voice was hushed, 'I keep thinking through going viral with her, it could be a massive opportunity, couldn't it?'

'Keep going, JC,' Zach urged, 'if I stop for much longer I'm not going to be able to get restarted. My thighs are dead. Please.'

Jackson heaved his trailer a few strides forward then stopped again.

'Tell me honestly, Zach,' he continued, 'do you think she'd overshadow me in attention, on Blurt and that? Like, I like being the main thing, you know?'

'I dunno JC. Maybe?' Zach lacked the energy for the intrigue Jackson clearly wanted. 'She's cool and that, yeah, but I don't really get it beyond that, it's not as if you don't have enough else to focus on right now, is it? Or that you're not doing perfectly well by yourself at being the main thing.'

Jackson looked thoughtful, 'I dunno. Distraction, maybe.'

Zach sighed. All he wanted was to lie down quietly somewhere for an hour, preferably with Hanna by his side. All he seemed to be able to do was hear chat from Jackson that felt like a throwback to being fifteen.

'Distraction from what?' he replied, unable to mask his irritation. 'You've got it made, right now. Maybe she's just the first person you've had a thing with who fancied you less than you fancied her? Maybe you're not used to being the one who gets walked away from?'

Embarrassment coloured Jackson's cheeks. Zach nodded up at him, reminding him to move again.

'No …,' Jackson faltered, 'it's not that. I don't think it is anyway. Do you think it is?'

'JC, what's the name of the girl from Glencoe the other night?' Zach asked. 'The one with the lipstick and the lovebite?'

Jackson's mouth opened, then closed.

'Did *she* really like *you*, Jackson? Or was it just a one-night fling and on you both went?'

'It was just a laugh,' Jackson replied.

'For you. Maybe not for her. Who knows? Maybe this is karma?' Zach continued, 'Now please, move, man!'

Jackson forced one step in front of the other. In truth, he'd thought he had very little bond to the piper, but Zach was smart. Maybe he'd seen something Jackson hadn't. He found it hard to trust his own account versus Zach's, he himself was a liar, after all. A feeling of jamming throbbed between his ears. He'd figured out he'd met his match in the piper within minutes of them flirting with each other. She'd been blatant about grabbing his tablet and telling him he owed it to Eigg to let them capitalise on the journey too. He'd been blatant about saying he'd enjoy a night off blurting and watching his popularity rise from the randomness she created. But now Zach had taken things to a deeper level. And karma? Without knowing it, Jackson wondered, had Zach tapped into awareness of a cosmic intervention warning Jackson that what he was doing had been noted, and that he'd pay?

'She'll be in touch,' Zach said, oblivious to Jackson's existential crisis, 'or you'll be in touch with her, I guess. It's not as if either of you are hard to find, is it?'

A desire to lash out and say something nasty to Zach struck Jackson. He opened his mouth then stopped, wondering what the karma would be for that – a further misdemeanour. Now, as he stared down and tugged onwards, new possibilities blunted his usual options. Hanna and Gayle's shoes came into view. Jackson stopped and looked up, straight into their smiles. A large stone set against the back of a blackhouse behind them made a crude step leading up and over the lower end of the wall. Shafts of sunlight appeared from between the clouds, giving colour to a section of the mainland mountains – four raggedy-topped peaks stood out in more detail than their grey neighbours.

Zach pulled Jackson's trailer brake on then helped undo his harness. Though he was still sweating, Jackson shivered as he looked around. There was nothing but wildness and sea around him, he saw. No distraction. No fanbase to act up for. No anything, unless he looked at his tablet. The drones buzzed above, capturing the first sight of his ancestral home and his deep frown as he wished his mind would clear and that life would feel as simple as it had before his birthday; back at home, failing uni, antagonising his father. Lonely but in control. Jackson sniffed and raised his hand, dabbing tears. Hanna and Zach watched, then Hanna walked over to Jackson and squeezed his arm.

'The clearances?' Gayle asked, arriving at his other side. Jackson stared out to sea, fatigued by the knowledge that more lies were needed, imminently. He didn't want to do this anymore. Every fib now wedded him more tightly to never ever being forgiven. That had seemed fine, before, now it felt as desolate as the place he stood.

'Yes,' he croaked at last, 'the clearances.'

Gayle nodded, happy to let the heavy emotion of homecoming hang in the air as the drones captured Jackson's bewilderment.

45

/NewScotGovtFMClearwater/blurts/

Wow, that last bit of the journey and then Jackson's discovery of his #Unclearances location looked tough. #Unclearances has layers, all beautiful, but not all easy. Really proud of the #JacksonsJourney team and jacksonmcampbell for giving us such insight into the vulnerabilities of reckoning with our cultural past. I am also feeling reflective about how we can make #Unclearances more accessible, so everyone can go anywhere they like in New Scotland. Open to ideas, as always. #TransparentGovernment #GreenNewDealDelivered #Equalities

/MichaelTempletonGBEBS/blurts/

So that's what it takes to quieten a Campbell. One wonders if he might have gassed himself into silence with fumes escaping from his own giant waterproof romper suit. Or was it just another exploitative performance directed by Clearwater? Vote in my poll to have your say. #GBEBS #JacksonsJourney #Lies #IdiotInAField

/TheJacksonCampbellAppreciationSoc/blurts

Public Transport soooooo busy to Fort William. Can anyone give us a lift? PLEEEEEEEAAAAASSSSEEEE!!!!!

/ZuzannaN/blurts/

Why does he keep going on about that piper twat? BORING, jacksonmcampell, VERY BORING.

/RebeccaCampbell/blurtsTo/jacksonmcampbell

Private message Jackson. You looked very peaky after your walk with that hideous suit on. Maybe it was just the colour of it? Whites and thistle tones don't set off your eyes, surprisingly. Duchy is recovering. Your father is still watching livestream. When do you get back? I will ask the Callander baker to send some of your cakes to await your return.

Gayle knew from her memory of the satellite images that each of the blackhouses was linked by a stone dyke so the clearing between them could act as an enclosure for animals when they weren't grazing the hills. In front of her a grassy carpet covered what would once have been the mud floor of a home. A few metres away lay the remains of the house's front wall, complete with a narrow door gap. Beyond the door a huge grass clearing waited, surrounded by other blackhouse ruins, making up the small township.

'I'm in number four, Lower Grulin.' Gayle read her notes aloud now, her tone switching seamlessly into presenter mode. 'When this was last a home, almost 200 years ago, the family who lived here were a mum, a dad and four kids.' Gayle flipped a page, 'Jackson, they were *your* family. This, right here, is – was – a Campbell home.' Gayle indicated the doorway then continued, 'There were other Campbell houses over there; at number nine, your family member, Catriona, she moved in with her new husband, a MacLellan, and lived with his family and him. She was just fifteen.'

Hanna gestured for Jackson to move closer for a better view. Jackson walked to the wall, curiosity pushing him on as he spotted the other remnants of the ancient village. Listening to Gayle was a welcome distraction. It was a bit like watching TV, he thought, wondering where he could sit down and immerse himself in it even more.

'Fifteen?' Jackson frowned, 'So the MacLellans were sexual predators?'

'Marriage at fifteen, sadly, was normal, back then,' Gayle replied, slightly confused by Jackson's fast transition away from heightened emotion.

'How many houses are there all together, Gayle?' Hanna asked.

'Numbers one to nine in this group,' Gayle replied, 'but there are others further down the hill, kind of stand-alone. I guess maybe these ones belonged to the crofters with animals who needed this common grazing area in the middle, or something?'

'Sounds legit,' Zach added.

Gayle watched Jackson wander from one side of the ruin to the other. He stopped to contemplate what remained of a fireplace then left by the door gap, passed the front of three other houses then stopped again outside another ruin.

'That's number five,' Gayle consulted her notes again, 'the MacEachen family – nine of them, the biggest family here at the time of the clearance.'

Jackson wandered into the MacEachens' ruined home and regarded the space.

'How many bedrooms did they have upstairs?' he called to Gayle.

'None,' Gayle replied, 'they didn't have upstairs, Jackson. In fact they probably had a cow in the downstairs with them in winter too – that one has a small dividing wall at the end of the space, doesn't it?'

Jackson spotted the low remains of a wall to his right. He mentally divided the space he stood in into nine, imagining single MacEachens lying down on beds. There was barely room for four, never mind nine. He leant back to look at Gayle to see if she looked like she was joking, but her expression offered no hint at a wind-up.

Zach and Hanna began disassembling the trailers so they could be passed over the wall in lighter pieces.

Gayle watched Jackson again. Something about his posture suggested defeat. She remembered his vulnerability at Loch Shiel and realised he perhaps needed a break to cope with overwhelm.

'You ok to keep going, Jackson?'

Jackson looked up and shook his head.

'I don't really want to talk anymore,' he called back, 'sorry. I just want to look around for a while.'

Gayle nodded, moved by Jackson's reaction, and set the NSBC drone to follow him at a distance then went to help the others with the kit.

...

By the time both tiny houses and a campfire were set up it was 6 p.m. and the brightness of afternoon light was giving way to oblongs of peach-tinted cloud. A plentiful water supply from a burn fed by one of the lochs on the top of Eigg had been located, and a toileting site a little behind the single remaining wall of number one, Lower Grulin had been designated. Gayle stifled a yawn and began laying out their remaining packed food supplies on the flap of her backpack.

'We've got sixteen energy bars, four apples, teabags, coffee, noodles ... oh, and the flask of soup'.

'We're not going to starve,' Zach said, adding another recycled briquette to the campfire. 'We've got plenty, that'll do us tonight and breakfast, won't it? Why don't you bunk in with Hanna tonight and I'll go in with JC?'

Gayle frowned over to where Jackson now stood in his onesie inside the remains of number nine, across the clearing, his demeanour still melancholy.

'Enough for us, maybe,' she said.

'Jackson!' Hanna shouted, 'How hungry are you? Could you eat a small horse or a big one?'

'Um, a small one,' Jackson called back.

'Well. That's the miracle we needed. The shock of completing his journey has ruined his appetite a bit, poor thing.' Hanna winked.

'OK. First thing in the morning I'll go back to the truck for supplies,' Gayle said, 'plenty of time for everything, and less stress.'

Hanna and Zach watched as a gentle breeze made the campfire flames lick high in the air, the hypnotic movements paired with their relief about activity for the day being over and making them both yawn. Hanna pulled a book and her headtorch from her bag.

'I'm going to read' she said, 'I want to know about this Massacre Cave.'

'I'm gonna go and get some close-ups of Jackson,' Zach said, getting to his feet. He announced himself behind Jackson with a small cough.

'You good, JC?' Zach zipped his jacket up close to his chin. 'You warm enough?'

'Did you ever feel,' Jackson replied, 'like, *really* bad about something Zach? Like, you were in some shit *so* deep there was nothing you could do to make a bad thing better?'

Zach frowned.

'Uh, I guess. Is this about the piper again?'

'No.' Jackson stared at Zach, 'Not that. Tell me about when you felt that, will you? What did you do?'

Zach raised his eyebrows, perhaps now was as good a time as any to address his own karma, he thought.

'I went out with someone once, years back. I knew she was really into me. I wasn't really into her. Her parents bought me a super extravagant Christmas gift. We'd only been seeing each for four months. It was a laptop, man. A whole laptop. I said I loved her that night 'cos I felt guilty. Or grateful. I dunno, it was a mindfuck. Then a week later I broke up with her.' Zach winced, 'But it took me another two weeks to give the laptop back. Still makes me cringe.'

Jackson wandered to the dividing wall and sat on its largest boulder, struggling to conceal his disappointment at Zach's confession.

'Shitty, huh?' Zach kicked a stone. 'I regret it, that's for sure. Should've been a better person than that. I hope I am now. Blurt will soon tell me, that's for sure.'

'It is probably karma, isn't it?' Jackson replied, 'My life, I mean. I can't really complain, can I?'

'Hey, look, I didn't mean to make you feel bad about the lipstick girl.' Zach shook his head. 'I was tired, man, sorry. Way too harsh.'

Jackson shrugged. He looked around the MacEachen's former home and wondered what it was like to live in such a truly tiny way – no wifi, no shops, the same people, day in, day out. How would you keep a secret in those circumstances, he wondered.

'At least the folk who lived here didn't have all the shit to deal with that we do, did they? Life was easier for them, wasn't it?' Jackson muttered. 'There wasn't pressure on them to be famous, or rich, or, like, amazing, was there?'

Zach frowned at the dodgy equivalence being drawn.

'I don't think easier, man. They had to survive. They must've been really tough.'

'Oh, my God!' Hanna shouted. 'Bloody hell!'

Gayle looked up from behind the wall at number one, meerkat-like.

'You OK, Hanna?'

Zach and Jackson stared.

'My family!' Hanna's pitch was high, 'Absolute bastards, turns out!'

'Let's go and hear this,' Jackson got up, 'I'm bored of myself already.'

'Spill the beans,' Zach prompted Hanna as he and Jackson arrived back at the fireside, 'what's Zuzia done now?'

'Zuzia unfollowed me, then refollowed me on Blurt five times today,' Jackson said.

Gayle arrived back at the fire too and tossed a small parcel of toilet roll at it before sitting.

'It isn't about Zuzia!' Hanna said, 'I haven't even looked at my tablet today. It's this book, about Eigg. My ancestors are in it. And they're horrible.'

'Oh,' Jackson nodded, 'Paedos marrying fifteen year-olds, by any chance?'

'No,' Hanna sighed, 'not yet, anyway. Listen, Eigg used to have almost 400 folk living here, mostly MacDonalds.'

'McDonald's?' Jackson asked, 'The burger folk?'

Hanna shot Jackson a glare and Gayle tried not to giggle.

'The Macdonalds on Eigg and the MacLeods on Skye – my people, well, my dad's – they were all feuding, apparently. Major fall outs; heaps of shit going down. Every time they had a clash, things got more serious, but a few of them didn't get involved in the beef at all.'

'Not that kind of beef, Jackson,' Zach interjected. Jackson winked and Gayle adjusted the height of one of the livestream cameras to ensure it could take in all of Jackson in the failing light.

'Some MacLeod men, including the chieftain's son, came over to Eigg to see the women,' Hanna explained. 'The Eigg men didn't like that. Things apparently got "out of hand". God knows what that meant back then, I mean, you can only imagine how horrific "out of hand" meant in 1577, right?'

Jackson watched Gayle and Zach nod, clearly aware of what Hanna meant.

'So, anyway,' Hanna continued, 'the Eigg men take things up a notch; they stick the MacLeod men adrift in a boat and the tide eventually washes them back to Skye. Some accounts say they were dead when they washed in, others say they were still alive.

Either way, what happens next is not contested in terms of truth.'

Gayle handed Jackson a mug of steaming soup.

'OK, so the MacLeods freak out,' Hanna went on, 'they get in their boats, totally weaponed up, and they're away to absolutely lose it on the Eigg folk. But, get this, the Eigg folk see the boats coming, and they understand what's going to happen, so they all take off, all 397 of them, to hide in a secret cave with a miserable hole of an entrance behind a waterfall. After the waterfall, the entrance opens out into, like, a *massive* chamber.'

Jackson blew on the steam from his soup, light in his eyes dancing as he listened, almost gleefully grateful to hear of crimes worse than his own.

'The Eigg folk hide in there after the MacLeods come ashore,' Hanna continued, 'and the MacLeods are *everywhere* – all over the island, in and out of houses, up hills, into woods, walking gorges and forestry – up trees to get a better lookout. But they find no one. After three days and nights they get sick of looking, God knows where they think the Eigg folk are, but they start to get to wanting to go home to Skye. But guess what?'

Gayle passed a cup of soup to Zach then shrugged at Hanna, her eyes wide and urging her on.

'The MacLeods were thorough,' Hanna continued, 'they decided on a last sail round Eigg, checking the coastline. And what do they see? A MacDonald! A scout who's nipped out to see if the MacLeods are away! He gets spotted and the MacLeods are on him, it's too late, they easily track his footprints to the cave and …,' Hanna winced, then shook her head.

'What?' Jackson looked puzzled, 'They dragged them out the cave and duffed them up?'

'They blocked the cave up, Jackson, they blocked it with heather and whatever else they could get their hands on and they set the blockage alight. They burned and choked every single one of the Eigg folk to death.'

Jackson blinked, horrified.

'Archaeologists still find bones there now.' Hanna's eyes glistened with tears. 'Teenagers, *babies*, old folk. Can you imagine?'

Jackson opened his mouth to speak as the wind changed direction and accidentally inhaled a mouthful of smoke. He coughed violently then wiped his mouth on his sleeve.

'Did you feel ashamed, Jackson, when you heard about the Campbells being murdering assholes at Glencoe?' Hanna asked, ''Cos I feel so weird.'

Jackson coughed again.

'Ashamed? Maybe I should've done. But not about them. About me.'

'What?' Hanna replied. 'You're not a murderer.'

Jackson looked at Hanna. How would he put it, he wondered, if he was to confess to her now?

'Jackson,' Zach interrupted, 'seriously, I don't think you did anything wrong in Glencoe, with that girl. I was just trying to prove a point. A stupid one. Stop feeling bad, man, please? I think you're overthinking it now.'

Hanna raised a questioning eyebrow at Zach, then Jackson.

'I'm doing teeth, then bed,' Gayle said, 'sorry I'm being boring, but it's been a *long*, good day. Hanna, I want to read that book after you, please. I had no idea about any of that.' Jackson watched Gayle as she got up and realised it was the first time he'd seen her look properly tired. She looked a bit like his mum when she'd had gin, he thought.

'I was going to check my tablet,' Hanna sighed, 'but it's been kinda nice without it, even with the murder revelation. I'll check Blurt in the morning, I think, and just send my mum a message tonight to say I'm cool. I want to just take all this in, bit by bit.' Hanna wandered down the clearing and stepped into the space between numbers six and seven. She leant on the wall, looking out at the Ardnamurchan lighthouse standing like a huge black chess queen at the end of its peninsula, then turned back to the campsite. The sides of the Transpariboard houses twinkled back at her, reflecting light from the fire.

'Transpariboard glints in the firelight just like plastic bottles do with sunshine,' Hanna said as she returned to the others after messaging her mum. 'It reminded me of Niall there, somehow, it felt a bit magical.'

Jackson stopped picking at one of his big toenails, pulled his sock back on and drew his knees to his chest. Hanna stared in the direction of the Massacre Cave then shivered.

'Still can't believe they burned them alive,' she said, 'who could blame them if they haunt the place?'

'Maybe they haunt Skye, instead? In revenge?' Zach said, 'I think that's what I'd do.'

'I'm going to bed too.' Jackson got up and made his way towards his house, 'If ghosts come, use me as an offering. I'm the worst of us.'

Hanna and Zach frowned at each other.

'I'll be there in a minute, JC,' Zach said, his voice soft.

'Every Human Actualising, Jackson, remember?' Hanna said. 'One for all and all for one, hey? There's no best or worst.'

'Oh, there really is, Hanna.' Jackson smiled as he disagreed, but when he slid his tiny house door shut his face was deadly serious.

/MichaelTempletonGBEBS/blurts/

Very rare to hear a New Scot admit to exactly how awful their family is. The story of jocks murdering each other is a great example of why they need to be governed by bigger, smarter countries like England. You've scored another own goal here, First Minister! #NaturalSelection #EmpireStateOfMind #GBEBS #GBEForever

/ZuzannaN/blurts/

What. The. Actual. Fuck??!!!! Can you divorce your ancestors? Is that a thing? Not sure I want dual nationality anymore. I'll just stick with the Polish passport, thanks very much.

/RoryTheTory/blurtsTo/MichaelTempletonGBEBS

agree completely Michael. What that girl spoke about is the real Scotland. That is basically what perth city centre looks like every Friday night. England has got more history than Scotland with kings and everything. countries like Scotland need to be in a union. It's for worker's rights and that. And the royal family who have given their whole lives for Scotland and everywhere. PS no eggcup yet.

/TheJacksonCampbellAppreciationSoc/blurts

jacksonmcampbell has got nothing to feel bad about he didn't do anything wrong. You can't blame people for things their ancestors did. HannaNowak was gaslighting him when she asked if he felt bad about glen coe massacre. She plays all nice and stuff but tbh maybe she actually just wants all the attention for herself? Like, why else would you tell a story like that?

/ZuzannaN/blurtsTo/TheJacksonCampbellAppreciationSoc
Omg you actually said that. Wow. I'd hit delete on that. I'd hit delete on that NOW if I was yous.

/NSBCJourney/NewScotland /blurts/
The end of a momentous day. Thank you all for joining us. This place is a treasure trove of incredibly poignant stories. Looking forward to sharing as many of them as we can in the days to come ☺ #JacksonsJourney #Unclearances #NoStoryNoGlory #SmallIslesBigHistory

/NewScotGovtFMClearwater/blurts/
Surely everyone watching #JacksonsJourney will dream vividly tonight! It is wonderful to see other #Unclearances stories & certificates start to launch parallel stories too – we are a nation of adventurers, courageous and open in the face of challenges! Excited to see and hear what tomorrow brings, thanks also for the accessibility suggestions, keep them coming. #AlwaysForward #AlwaysLearning #GreenNewDealDelivered #TransparentGovernment

/Deli-ciousOfCallander/blurtsTo/RebeccaCampbell
Hello Mrs Campbell! If you DM us your details we can get that order of Coco Pop Slices organised for you, no problems!

/RebeccaCampbell/blurtsTo/Deli-ciousOfCallander
How do you know I wanted to order Coco Pop Slices? Did Jackson tell you?

/TheJacksonCampbellAppreciationSoc/blurts
Poor jacksonmcampbell is not himself! He needs people! He needs to be near his fans!! This is not his natural environment. The life is draining from him ☹ #SadJackson #JacksonsJourney #SocialExperimentsAreCruel

46

Niall sat in the recovery centre's reception area. Fin sat a few seats away on his left and Claudia sat closer, to his right. Jim paced the floor slowly in front of them all; he was wearing his new jeans which he'd ironed to include a sharp front crease. He'd paired the denim with his usual button-down shirt and rubber-soled brogues and, though he was not entirely comfortable with his new look, he remembered to keep the focus on Niall and smiled encouragingly at him while they waited for Drew's arrival.

One of Niall's feet tapped a frenetic beat on the polished concrete floor while the other was tucked under his bum, quickly growing numb.

'Breathing, Niall?' Claudia prompted. She drew a deep breath in through her nose and Niall copied.

'Align your spine, too, perhaps?' she suggested after a long exhalation.

Niall pulled the foot from under him. When it hit the floor, his toes began tingling inside his trainer as circulation returned.

Jim stopped in front of Niall and clapped his hands together.

'I'm glad you changed your mind,' he said, 'that was inspiring for me, son, you know? I think you and me might've stayed here all year, if wan o' us hidnae broken the comfort zone, know what I mean?'

Niall smiled, feeling bad that he secretly wished Jim would just go, rather than keeping him captive in a small-talk prison.

'Whit was it, that made you decide all o' a sudden?' Jim asked.

Niall thought about saying 'Your excited patter,' but decided against it.

'Holodeck training,' Niall replied, 'it's exhausting. But also, I dunno, it makes you miss the good stuff, too. That and Claudia said Drew could do this trip or we'd have to wait a couple of weeks, so …'

'I've got my first session this afternoon, when you're away,' Jim grinned, 'maybe it'll boost my confidence, too, eh?'

Niall gave Jim a thumbs up then looked past him to outdoors. There was still no sign of Drew. Jim began pacing again, this time whistling the tune to New Scottish Sports Round as he went. Niall closed his eyes and thought about the simulations he'd done over the last two days. He wondered how useful they would be for the time he was about to spend with Drew. He'd spent the simulation time practising interacting in a coffee shop; running through everyday things like waiting in a queue, making an order, finding a seat and spending time amongst strangers. After promptly mastering the entry-level he'd progressed another two levels, each increasing the intensity of social challenges. The final program featured an encounter with another person in the queue who repeatedly leant back into Niall's personal space, even stepping on his toes twice with no acknowledgement. Then, when the space invader had finally disappeared, Niall had made his order sat at a wobbling table. A surly waiter had approached and served him the wrong drink.

The encounters had made Niall sweat and flush with hurt, frustration and anger. His stress levels had spiked repeatedly, but he'd kept his cool, found solutions and repeatedly affirmed to himself that the rude actions of others were not a personal attack on him. He'd seen simulated people his own age in the programme too, couples, friends, dog walkers. People he felt he almost recognised, or that he was almost like. They'd made him pine for Hanna and their other friends, and the longing had propelled him towards Claudia's office, telling him to go for it, not to overthink it, to trust and take one of the leaps back to a new, better normal.

Now, a pannier and helmet Drew had had couriered over, both emblazoned with saltires sat on the seat between Niall and Claudia. Drew had proposed they take advantage of an imminent spell of excellent weather by doing a mini tour of Lochaber on his Vespa during their weekend away. Claudia picked up the helmet and placed it on her lap then reached her arms round it, interlacing her fingers.

'Is this whit we'd call a pregnant pause?' Jim grinned, nodding at Claudia.

Claudia rolled her eyes and groaned.

'So! The Highlands, eh?' Fin stroked his chin as he contemplated it again, 'Magnificent, I hear.'

'Yeah,' Niall stood, 'hope so. Listen, sorry, I need the loo one more time. I thought I was doing OK, but my bladder's nervy.' Niall rushed to the toilets beside the lifts. When he re-emerged, Drew was standing with the others, enthusiastically shaking Jim's hand. A significantly larger helmet was hanging from his other hand. He wore a saltire-emblazoned vest tucked into straining skinny jeans which, in turn, were tucked into his DMs. When Drew spotted Niall, a huge grin spread on his face.

'Niall Horn!' Drew shouted, 'Come away, come away!'

'Hey, Drew,' Niall said as he joined the group, bracing for Drew's hug.

Drew looked down at Niall with shining eyes then grabbed him. Niall decided not to breathe until the hug was over, conscious that his ribcage might break if he did otherwise.

'Niall Horn,' Drew half-whispered, 'you look great, son. It is *good* to see you. And are you taller? I think you're taller!'

'Six centimetres,' Niall coughed, 'from the Ashtanga yoga, I think.'

Claudia nodded enthusiastic agreement.

'And from stopping hiding in a hoodie as well, I'll bet?' Drew winked, 'Well, are you ready? There's a cracking roadside van at Luss now. We could get a tattie scone roll for lunch, if you fancy? And maybe a caramel shortbread?'

'I've been practising ordering coffee,' Niall replied, embarrassed at how basic he now felt, 'apparently my skills there are adaptable.'

'And you have your comms, yes?' Claudia asked.

Niall tugged his right sleeve up to reveal the new wristband.

'Yes. And my meds are in my bag.' Niall picked up his pannier and opened a side Velcro flap. Along with a change of clothes and a skinny wash bag, a lozenge-shaped pill dispenser was stowed inside.

'Now, doctors,' Drew said, 'any problems and I'll be on the hooter. Jim, what a pleasure to meet you. I hope your own trip out's a cracker. Other than that, my friends, we'll see you on Monday. I'll wait at the bike, OK?'

'Thank you again, Professor McAllister,' Claudia said, 'I know how busy you are. We all appreciate you fitting us in at such short notice.'

'Of course,' Drew grinned, 'anything for my EHAs.'

'I guess this is goodbye,' Niall said, looking from Claudia to Fin then Jim and feigning a woeful expression. Jim pretended to dab his eyes with his cloth hankie while shrugging his shoulders dramatically.

'You're going to have a great time,' Claudia said, 'look at the weather, it's amazing. It turns very badly for the worse next week though. Your timing could not be better, Niall.'

'Enjoy yourself,' Fin added, 'observe your thoughts, stay in the now. We're just the tap of a finger away. I've a feeling Monday's going to come too fast!'

'Aye,' Jim said, 'sod off or before you know it it'll be time to come back!'

Niall took a deep breath and followed Drew to the car park.

47

Gayle's walk to and from the truck the next morning had been unexpectedly hot, forcing her to stop several times along the way to sip water while carrying a heavy load of food and batteries. When she arrived back at the rear wall of number four, Lower Grulin, at around lunchtime, she spotted the others standing on a slope above the village, their backs facing her as they took turns with binoculars. She dumped her bag beside Jackson's tiny house, shouted a 'hello', then joined them.

'Sea Eagles!' Zach told Gayle as she approached. 'Two of them, they're riding a thermal updraft.'

Gayle shielded her eyes and easily spotted the birds.

'Oh!' Hanna shivered, 'I just got a chill, in *this* heat. I swear someone just walked over my grave.'

Jackson looked at Hanna quizzically. He was trying to chew an energy bar he'd shoved into his mouth in one go and the mechanics of it left his tongue no room to manoeuvre.

'It's like an energy change, you know?' Hanna explained, 'But it runs through your body. Like, something significant has happened, but you don't know what. And the air's different, isn't it? It's supposed to be pissing with rain today, too. And eagles showing up. It's a sign, surely?'

Gayle eyed Jackson, pleased to see his mood had improved from bedtime the previous evening. Zach handed Gayle the binoculars.

'Did you see the ranger?'

'Mmmm.' Gayle murmured. She could just make out the different colours of one of the eagle's claws pulled against its belly as it flew.

'Any problems?' Zach enquired.

'We didn't really talk,' Gayle replied from behind the binoculars.

Jackson cleared his mouth with a swig of water.

'The meteorologists are definitely busy.' Zach scrolled his tablet. 'They're saying there's a strong likelihood of two solid months of gales, but first this unexpected heatwave's dominating; they're saying a weather system from Poland's responsible. It's causing a bit of panic for locals, I think. If we're really, really unlucky here, we're taking SWE protocols being triggered, aren't we?'

'Nothing to do with me,' Hanna joked, 'the MacLeods might have had influence here, but I don't think the Nowaks have ever controlled the weather.'

'A what?' Jackson asked, 'What's a SWE? Why are folk not just excited about a heatwave? We could be tanning, innit?'

'Sudden Weather Event,' Gayle replied, handing the binoculars to Jackson and looking grave. 'Climate change protocols are there to make sure we can respond to them as quickly as possible, it's only the EU, New Zealand, South Africa and Canada who have them in place so far, more's the pity. Let me see that please, Zach.'

'SWE's have pretty huge consequences for islanders, JC,' Zach explained, 'high heats have been followed by bad winds over the last decade. Bad winds mean no boats or ferries running. They could be cut off for months, out here.'

'Jesus.' Jackson blinked, then laughed. 'Oh, no. We are *not* staying here for months. *No* chance.'

'We need more data.' Gayle said, handing Zach back his tablet. 'Let's study the forecast, take some professional advice, then assess. If things look like they are turning, we'd best book the ferry. Cal Mac will be thinking it through too, if we've seen something from the Met Office you can be sure they saw it well before us. They'll lay on extra provision if needs be, that's all part of the protocol. Works well – if everyone follows it.'

Gayle's wristband buzzed.

'Bryce Cooper,' she frowned at Zach, 'he's checking in to see we've understood the implications of the forecast. Looks like the data's coming to us then.'

'Shit!' Zach grimaced.

Jackson unwrapped another energy bar, this time only shoving half at a time into his mouth.

'But … I don't want it to be over.' Hanna's voice was quiet.

'Fuck me!' A spray of oats rained from Jackson's face as he spoke, 'I mean, I've hated a lot of this, obviously, and I can't get the orgasms about mountains and shit like the rest of you. But, like, yeah … what's the big deal? We came, we saw, we spoke about paedos in history. What else was left to do? It's not like there's shops or anything, is it?'

. . .

Lunch was spent with Gayle and Zach wearing earbuds and chatting to Bryce between bites of sandwiches, while Hanna and Jackson listened in.

'You know Gayle and Zach had a whole programme of footage they were going to take of you this week, don't you Jackson?' Hanna whispered.

'What?' Jackson looked surprised. 'Of what? Here's Jackson with a stone. Oh, here's Jackson with another stone. Here's Jackson with an eagle. Here's Jackson with a mountain and a bit of grass. Folk wouldn't watch that, Hanna, it's boring!'

'Ssssh!' Hanna scowled at Jackson. 'They did heaps of research, Jackson. They were going to take you about the place properly and tell you stories about how things looked, way back, and read you wee excerpts of cleared folk's poetry and stuff. It would've been really special, to be honest. Folk would've lapped it up.'

Jackson looked sceptical.

'I'm gonna check my tablet,' Hanna sighed.

Jackson shrugged then switched his attention to leaning back and trying to better see meteorological infographics Bryce was now sharing to Gayle's laptop. When Hanna saw her notifications she groaned: Zuzia alone had sent forty-five messages, mainly about the piper. Hanna scrolled the thousands of blurts she'd been tagged into since arriving on Eigg then shook her head. She pressed her filter option to jettison blurts from people she didn't know. One of her friends had made a meme of Jackson standing naked in his tiny house doorway at the pier the previous morning. She handed her tablet to Jackson so he could see it. He laughed, then forwarded it to himself. As the meme disappeared from Hanna's screen her remaining notifications popped back up. Jackson's breath caught sharply when he spotted a blurt from Drew.

'What?!' Hanna asked, grabbing her tablet back, 'Is Zuzia calling you names again?'

Jackson coughed as a piece of bread caught in his windpipe. Hanna scanned the blurts.

'Oh, there's one from Drew. Was it that? He really scares you, doesn't he?'

A sweat broke out under Jackson's vest and cycling shorts and his stomach gurgled loudly.

'Don't be daft, JC, he's not that bad!' Hanna smiled, then threw Jackson a banana from a bunch by her side. The banana bounced on Jackson's lap, adding to his nausea. 'Oh!' Hanna grinned, 'Drew's blurted that he and Niall are meeting up! No way did I miss that till now! That must mean Niall's getting better, right?' Hanna toed Jackson, 'Didn't I say something magical was happening, Jackson? Didn't I?'

Jackson stared intently at the banana. A mushy brown bruise on its flesh made him wince; the last time he'd seen such a thing Rebecca had extracted the fruit from his hand then thrown it and the rest of the fruit bowl in the compost bin. He placed the banana on the grass and tried to breathe evenly. Zach and Gayle wound up the call with Bryce and excitement fizzed through Hanna's body, as she showed her screen to Gayle and Zach. Zach checked a drone wasn't pointing at them and mouthed 'careful' to Hanna. Hanna's hand shot to her mouth, as she realised she'd been about to say more about Niall and the recovery centre. She nodded back to Zach while Jackson picked up a branded baseball cap and pulled it on, tugging the peak downwards to obscure his eyes.

'Getting uncomfortable, Jackson?' Gayle asked. 'When did you last SPF? You could get shade inside your house, or number seven or eight, you know? The way the sun hits they should be cool inside till at least early evening, I reckon.'

Zach's laptop pinged loudly. He and Gayle looked to the screen.

'Oh. Damn.' Gayle's tone was sad.

'That's it!' Zach looked pained, 'It's a bloody SWE. Clearwater's calling us in. We've two nights left, max, then we're on a boat.'

'They're coordinating with the ferry services,' Gayle read, then sighed.

Excitement morphed to disappointment on Hanna's face.

'Two days, max?' Jackson removed the cap and looked brighter.

Gayle looked at Jackson, then back to Hanna. Not for the first time, she wished she had a clone of herself to deal with the conflicting emotional weather of her companions.

'Yes,' Gayle replied, 'two days.'

'I can handle that!' Jackson smiled. 'Then I can escape to Fra … I mean, to … to fuck. I can escape to fuck then, can't I? Cool, cool.'

Gayle raised her eyebrows, then looked to Hanna.

'You OK, Han?'

'Yeah.' Hanna shrugged, 'And no. Fuck's sake. I want to stay longer. I like this. It's the perfect antidote to uni. I'm quite happy here and doing stuff like this till Nia …' Hanna checked herself, 'I mean till my pals are ready to get a flat, and stuff.'

Zach finished typing a message back to Bryce, then beckoned Hanna towards him. She tipped herself into his embrace, nodding her forehead against his shoulder in frustration.

· · ·

Jackson passed most of the rest of the afternoon reblurting memes of himself and researching what competition he'd have from social media stars in France. The livestream focused mainly on Zach teaching Hanna how to operate the second NSBC drone. They'd sent it to the trig point at the summit of An Sgùrr where Hanna was now taking a panorama, circling round from Skye and picturing her ancestors crossing the water to where she now stood.

After a tea of pasta and sauce sitting outside number four, Gayle repacked her rucksack and readied to head back to the truck for the night. Her load was lighter this time with only rubbish, one battery to recharge and a few items of dirty laundry.

'I'm gonna head now, OK? We'll keep living light round here. That way we can get out fast when the time comes. I'll be back early in the morning and I'll bring more food, Jackson, don't worry.'

Jackson looked up from his tablet.

'And some more beer?'

'I'll see what I can carry,' Gayle replied. Jackson gave Gayle a wide grin then went back to scrolling.

'I put static cams in the tiny houses, and there, by the rock, pointing here at the fire,' Gayle told Zach, 'and I'll programme a drone to capture the first part of me leaving, then it'll come back to you folks and get you all from different perspectives.'

'I'd prefer it followed you, for safety,' Zach frowned.

'I'll be fine. You'll see my location on comms. No need for a camera.' Gayle's tone was firm.

'She doesn't give a fuck, does she?' Jackson muttered when Gayle was just out of earshot.

'About what?' Zach frowned.

'Being murdered and stuff,' Jackson replied, 'she's a machine, isn't she? She actually seemed keen to get away from us.'

'She's a really hard worker,' Zach countered, 'definitely not a *machine*. But yeah, she did seem a *bit* keen. She can be an introvert, despite being a face of NSBC, you know? Maybe she just needs the time alone. I think that happens when you get older, doesn't it?'

'Yeah,' Hanna agreed. A thought occurred to her as she watched Gayle go. She tapped off her comms link, 'Or maybe she needs time *not* alone? Time *not* to be a lone *ranger*?'

Jackson watched Gayle grow smaller as she walked briskly away. He thought about his mum. How would she behave, here on the island, in Gayle's shoes, he wondered? The thought evaporated when he realised he'd never seen her in anything flatter than a kitten heel.

Zach tipped his head to the side then back to centre, eyes wide as the penny Hanna had dropped scuttered to comprehension. Calum.

'What?' Jackson looked from Hanna to Zach, 'What did you say? I was thinking about my mum. Not in that way though. Don't be disgusting.'

Hanna and Zach realised in unison that telling Jackson anything about Gayle's private life, conjecture or not, would be a colossal mistake.

'Nothing,' Zach said, 'let's get the comms back on, Hanna. So! What're we going to do tonight you two?'

'Wank,' Jackson said flatly, 'it's been ages and I'm bored. And folk love the python, don't they?'

'Right.' Hanna rolled her eyes, 'I want to make an outdoor camp, there's something I am determined to show Jackson before we leave, I thought we had more time, but …'

Jackson raised a suggestive eyebrow.

'Oh, aye? I presumed yous were monogamous?'

'Something in the sky, you knob.' Hanna laughed, then stood and set about pulling hers and Zach's inflatable mattresses from her tiny house.

Jackson was about to play gooseberry for an entire night, he realised. Soon enough, Hanna and Zach would turn in and Jackson would too – alone. There would be no Gayle in a tent or a truck between them. The absence of another singleton somehow beckoned loneliness. It would be odd too, he realised, to travel to France alone in two days' time. He pushed the thought from his mind, grinned at the nearest camera, grabbed the lighter and forced a fart. Hanna pulled Jackson's mattress from his tiny house and walked it towards him.

'Lay them out, three in a row,' she instructed, 'heads up here, feet down there. Cork in your ass, please, if possible.' Jackson dragged his mattress, strategically placing it between the other two.

'No corks available. So now what?' he asked.

'Lie down and wait a bit,' Hanna said, 'about an hour.'

'Thrilling,' Jackson joked, 'I'm up for a few rounds of pass the sausage to pass the time, they were always playing that when I was a boarder. Seems off-brand for you though, MacLeod.'

Hanna burst out laughing.

'I didn't know you boarded,' Zach said, propping himself on his elbow where he lay on Jackson's right.

'Oh, I only went for about five minutes,' Jackson replied, 'I got expelled from boarding. My mum kept sleeping in her car in the car park. It was only a mile away from our house anyway, so they said I should just sleep at home.'

'How old were you?' Hanna took off her shoes and sat on her mattress on Jackson's left. She imagined a sullen teenage Jackson in a fancy school uniform.

'Six?' Jackson frowned, 'Maybe seven. I don't know.'

'No!' Hanna's hand shot to her mouth.

'Jings,' Zach winced, 'sorry to hear it. That's rough.'

'Is it?' Jackson looked surprised.

Hanna and Zach nodded. After twenty minutes or so of companionable silence the first midgies of the evening arrived. Zach jumped up and grabbed the midgie-eater from under Hanna's tiny house.

'Could you get my headtorch and my book please?' Hanna called to him.

'And the beers.' Jackson added.

The evening passed quietly with Jackson getting slowly sozzled while Hanna read aloud about Eigg history. By midnight, the air had cooled significantly. Hanna pulled bedding from the tiny houses and Jackson stood, walked a few metres away and took a long piss, burping repeatedly as he did so. Hanna turned off her head torch and they each wriggled into their sleeping bags.

'OK, lie on your back and shut your eyes,' Hanna instructed, 'it's time. We're officially in a New Scotland Dark Skies Zone. And, thanks to the planet's journey towards our winter, tonight, tomorrow and the next night are going to be the three best nights this month for stargazing.'

'So why are our eyes shut?' Jackson asked.

'You'll see,' Hanna replied. 'When I tell you, open your eyes, you'll see the stars and they'll be beautiful, but if we then wait *another* five minutes, with our eyes open, well – then we should totally be able to see the Milky Way, because there's no light pollution and our vision will have adjusted. We've no torches, no fire. Just night, as nature intends it. I mean, yeah, it's probably shit for the livestream, but, you know, good for us?'

'Last chunce saloon for the stars?' Jackson whispered.

'Exactly,' Hanna replied. 'Ready? On three?'

'On three,' Zach agreed.

'Three.' Jackson opened his eyes.

'Twat.' Hanna laughed.

'I can see it!' Jackson shouted after just a few seconds, 'Holy fuck! it looks like, like … like a kinda torchy, lasery tube, doesn't it!? Like those big New Scottish polytunnels for salads, but with stars inside? Is that it?'

'That's the one,' Hanna whispered, awestruck.

The light mechanical buzz of a livestream camera carried across the still air.

'It's so beautiful, still so mysterious, even when you know what it is,' Zach said. A tear ran across his temple and into his hairline.

'Have you seen it before, Jackson?' Hanna asked.

'Nope,' Jackson replied, 'never.'

'It's *our* galaxy,' Hanna explained, 'the entire world and solar system, and a million others as we know it – and some we don't know yet at all, no doubt.'

'But how can it be our galaxy if we're down here and it's up there?' Jackson frowned.

'Imagine it like a polytunnel again,' Hanna said, 'but this time, imagine the tunnel kind of has arms that shoot out of the side of it, going in different directions, then stopping, a tinsy bit like a millipede's legs, but the legs don't just come out from underneath the millipede, yeah?'

Jackson nodded.

'So, we're kinda on the end of one of the legs, or arms,' Hanna continued, 'we're looking back at the mothership.'

'Touché, babe,' Zach said quietly.

'Holy fuck.' Jackson stared up, he felt as if gravity had loosened and he might fall, but upwards, into a web of white suspended jewels. He could feel himself floating away from Lower Grulin like an astronaut: an idea he found he wanted and, at the same time, didn't want at all. The choice would've been easier, Jackson thought, if Hanna and Zach were arseholes, rather than friends.

48

Roy sat in bed, generously propped by pillows, while Duchy was
curled into a fat ring on his lap. Rebecca's head rested on Roy's
right shoulder, and a warm, damp sensation on his pyjama sleeve
suggested she'd fallen asleep and was drooling slightly. Since the
Stat-Fly 6000's arrival, they'd spent the days talking and taking
shots on the exercise bike while watching the livestream, only
venturing outside to take Duchy around the garden to relieve
himself. The ceasefire between them felt fragile, as if the glue of it
might not set true if either of them stepped outside the bounda-
ries of Whole Castle View.

Movement from the TV screen at the end of the bed caught
Roy's eye. After hours of giggling under the stars, Jackson, Hanna
and Zach were retiring for the night. Roy's eyelids grew irresist-
ibly heavy when Jackson's tiny house door shut and the torchlight within dimmed. A peace-shattering fart erupted from Roy's
backside three hours later, waking him with a heated jolt. Duchy
growled and moved to Rebecca's side of the bed.

'Jackson?' Rebecca murmured.

'Shhhh,' Roy whispered, 'you're dreaming, darling.'

Rebecca's nose twitched as she wiggled down the mattress,
pulling the duvet over her shoulder. Roy removed two pillows

from behind his back and shuffled down, then stared up at the ceiling, contemplating the whir of dreams that had spun him through the last hours. He'd dreamt about all the moments Jackson had looked distressed on the livestream, but the one that still featured most frequently in his thoughts was Jackson's face at the launch. Then there was another face, an imagined one, a snapshot of how his son might've looked when Roy took his call from the slopes in France. Roy remembered again the enjoyment he'd gleaned from dressing Jackson down and flushed with shame.

Despite the distance between them, now and over the many preceding years, Roy knew Jackson's body language. He knew when Jackson was lying, plotting or on the wind-up. He knew when Jackson was tired, over-excited or hungry. He especially knew when Jackson was hurt or frightened. Those were, after all, the emotions he'd disliked most in his child, fearing they signalled weakness or, perhaps worse, *need*. Until now, Roy had used any signs of distress from Jackson as his cue to leave his child's company, declaring emotions to be Rebecca's territory and absenting himself, just as his father had done before him.

What was the right thing to do *now*, Roy wondered? He had an idea, but could he trust it? He slipped quietly out of bed, padded across the carpet and into the hallway, then made his way along the upper corridor to a door at the end, which led to the attic stairs. Once opened, sunlight poured down to him from through the Velux windows in the roof, beckoning him on. At the top of the stairs, he almost jumped out of his skin as he came face to face with a grinning cardboard cut-out of a former Scottish First Minister's face on the end of a broomstick, leaning against a roof truss. On the floor beside it sat a placard he had carried at many a protest in the last years of the union. It featured the same First Minister's face and hair with a speech bubble containing words Roy himself had penned on:

'VOTE FOR ME, I'LL DESTROY YOUR ECONOMY
AND LEAD CHAVS TO VICTORY'

What had once been a proud memory now felt strangely sour. Fulfilling his father's dying wish had cost him dearly, Roy had realised in the last few days. And New Scotland seen through the lens of Jackson's Journey had been enlightening. For the first time, Roy found he appreciated the merits of independence from Great British England. Greater still, the relief of disassociation brought from having less in common with Templeton and his angry MEGA mob seemed to lighten Roy's every thought. He turned the broom handle so the First Minister faced away, then lifted a dust sheet from a stack of paintings and draped it over the placard.

Roy looked at the boxes lining the attic walls, three deep in places. Many of them were filled with items from Jackson's old room and teemed with unused sports equipment, pristine books and rejected musical instruments. Roy spotted the boxes he wanted behind Jackson's, the ones Rebecca regularly snuck things from the rest of the house into when she felt the items didn't fit her vision for style, no matter how much he or Jackson or Duchy might like them. Rebecca made these boxes deliberately hard to get to, Roy knew from bitter experience. He slid a few of Jackson's boxes to an empty corner, then began searching. The first box was full of dog toys Jackson had bought for Duchy, the soft velour of a ridiculously spherical pair of fake breasts sat on the top of the box. Roy regarded them, remembering seeing the little dog's head once buried between the mounds trying to find traction for his teeth to aid in shaking it to death. Roy sighed, then pushed the box to the side, finding the next one filled with various beautifying devices Rebecca had discarded. A facial steamer which had melted her false eyelashes off one Christmas night and a torturous device for pubic hair removal made him shudder. Roy looked around and spotted a third box. It was covered in dust and appeared older than the others. He opened it carefully and saw a mass of tangled cables and gadgets inside. Roy lifted a camcorder and revealed the small black and white globe of a third-generation Amazon Alexa underneath it.

'Bingo!' Roy smiled, lifting Alexa out and hurriedly pushing her plug into a nearby socket. The screen flashed, then died. Roy's face crumpled, bereft. Then, 'H-E-L-L-O-!' appeared and disappeared, followed by a clock face floating up through a liquid, digital black; the date and time whirring forward from 2017 to 2035 across just five seconds. Roy looked to the broomstick First Minister's back; a thick curtain of dust motes from the box's lid floated in the space and time between them, then a chime sounded from Alexa.

'Alexa, you need to help me,' Roy whispered urgently.

'Sure,' Alexa replied, 'what can I help you with, Roy-Camp-Bell?'

Roy paused, thinking hard about how to ask the question so he'd receive a simple 'yes' or 'no' answer.

'Alexa, should I go and reach out to Jackson?'

A white circle pulsated at the edge of Alexa's screen, brightening and fading until she spoke.

'Sorry, I don't know that one,' Alexa replied at last.

Roy winced.

'Alexa, help me decide something. *Please*.'

'You can update my skills by installing the latest version of the app on your smartphone,' Alexa replied, her tone hopeful.

A memory struck Roy, clear as day. He grinned as he polished away a fingerprint from Alexa's screen with his pyjama cuff. Heads he went, tails he stayed.

'Alexa,' Roy grinned, 'toss a coin!'

A thought bubble outlined in blue flashed on the screen, followed by a graphic grayscale image of a dog's face.

'It's heads,' Alexa replied.

Sweat pumped from Roy's armpits and the air in the attic felt thick. He stepped away from the box and reached up to open a Velux, letting fresh air bathe his face. A glinting light from below, just outside the gates caught his eye. It was the grille of a car, Roy realised, and its vintage Bentley features were immediately recognisable. Halfway up the drive, the foliage of a large, weeping magnolia shook violently, then stilled.

'Templeton!' Roy slammed the window shut and stepped back into the shadows as a GBE drone buzzed over the glass, close enough for Roy to make out its logo. Roy looked at the broomstick First Minister and considered launching her, javelin like, at the magnolia bush. The thought that she would secretly approve of a violent collaboration against Templeton made him smile unexpectedly.

He looked at the device in his hand and realised he'd been gripping it so tightly that colours were flaring on either side of her screen. He took a deep breath in, then unplugged Alexa and placed her carefully back in her box.

. . .

Rebecca woke at almost nine and found herself in bed with Duchy alone. She picked up her tablet and pressed Roy's avatar, presuming he was in the kitchen or on the exercise bike. But when Roy picked up, Rebecca heard that her husband was in his car. She sat up, unnerved.

'Morning!' Roy tried to strike a bright tone. 'Now listen, *don't* worry. It's no big deal. I decided while you were sleeping. I thought it was best. I'm on my way to meet Jackson,' Roy explained, 'and as soon as he comes off the island.'

'*What*?' Rebecca shrieked, 'WHAT? But you promised! You said there would be no more rabidity!'

Duchy stared at Rebecca with unveiled disgust, then jumped off the bed and waddled out of the room.

'Beccy, darling,' Roy chanced a laugh, keen to deescalate matters, 'I'm not *rabid*. I'm concerned. Something's wrong with him. I know it. One of us has to help, but there's Duchy too, he can't travel so soon after his op. And … well … you said you wanted Jackson and me to be closer, didn't you?'

'It's Jackson and I, Roy!' Rebecca wailed.

'Is it?' Roy considered it, then realised he didn't care, 'Anyway, no matter, because now you need to do something important too, you need to be the eyes and ears on the livestream, OK? Because I can't watch it and drive, can I?'

'Can't you? Is that a Clearwater law? Has she banned us from that, too?'

'Becs, it's been illegal for decades.' Roy leaned with the car around a tight bend. 'Way before New Scotland. Look, you're going to be shocked at this, but, well, when I set off this morning, well, I headed out, went to the petrol station, almost turned back home. But then, I had a bit of a revelation.'

'Is that a chocolate bar?' Rebecca asked. 'From the petrol station? What was it called before? I don't keep up with the name changes.'

'No, a *revelation* – like an epiphany, if you will. Listen, darling, we've got to open the conversation we've been having with Jackson too, don't we? About what went wrong for us as a family. He's a stakeholder. And we need to do it as soon as possible.'

Rebecca blinked several times, hoping she was still dreaming.

'Can't we just have a new start and not mention certain things again?' she suggested, 'I think we can? That's how we do it in my family. I think we should buy him a lovely present – a graduation celebration present. Something big. And then go from there, hmm?'

'No, Becs.' Roy was firm. 'Talking is the thing we never did in my family, and you buying Jackson stuff instead of me giving him my time is a big part of what's got us to where we are, isn't it?'

'Well, where the hell are you now?' Rebecca sighed.

'An hour from Mallaig,' Roy replied, 'just outside Fort William. I came through Glencoe. Becs, it's *astounding*. So much better than it looks on telly.'

Rebecca stroked the sheet at her side, unconvinced.

'The radio says there's a possibility they'll be taken back to Arisaig in a smaller boat,' Roy continued, 'because of the SWE. So I might check in there first, it's on the way.'

'Arseache?' Rebecca frowned.

'Arr-*eh*-say-g,' Roy clarified. 'Listen, whatever happens, things will be different. *Better* different. It's a new beginning for all of us. I can feel it.'

Rebecca felt a pulse of arousal. She'd fallen in love with Roy for being a man who knew his mind and wasn't afraid to act on it. It was a side of him she hadn't nurtured for a long time. She ran her tongue over her top lip and straightened her back.

'I want you to go and get a pot of coffee,' Roy continued, 'give Duchy breakfast, then get yourself in front of the livestream, I'm going to need a full debrief shortly, OK?'

'And how long will it take you to get home afterwards, do you think?' Rebecca asked, 'because I may need to debrief *you, literally* – before Jackson gets back, hmm?'

Roy spluttered and swerved, almost hitting a kerb as he crossed the Ballachulish Bridge. He checked his rearview mirror, relieved to find the only vehicle by some way off was a Vespa with a barn door of a rider atop.

'Yes. Well. There's something else,' Roy blushed, 'Templeton's on my tail. He was lurking outside the house in the early hours. I lost him an hour ago, but he'll catch up, no doubt. He's desperate to scoop me being rabid again, sad little man.'

Rebecca jumped up and made to the nearest hallway window overlooking the drive. The coast was clear, but when she caught her reflection in the glass she saw her hair was horrific. A cold sweat bloomed on her back as she looked around for drones.

'I'll check his blurts,' Rebecca hissed, 'I don't want him anywhere near Jackson, do you hear me, Roy? A man like Templeton could push a sensitive soul like Jackson over the edge, couldn't he?'

'He'll certainly cause trouble,' Roy replied, narrowing his eyes to make out a road sign. Goosebumps popped up on his arms as he read 'Road to the Isles'.

49

Drew had taken a convoluted route from the recovery centre to the overnight digs he'd arranged in a tech-free retreat chalet at Loch Lomond. Unbeknownst to Niall, his journey so far had been meticulously planned by Drew, Claudia and Fin, avoiding him seeing the numerous billboards for Jackson's Journey peppering the busiest routes around Glasgow for as long as possible. This, they had agreed, would give Niall a chance to acclimatise and remove an immediate risk of over-stimulation since he had not yet completed his therapeutic preparation for social media re-entry, which carried huge risks of overwhelm and relapse. With Glencoe behind them, Fort William out in front and Niall on fine form, Drew decided their next stop would be the right time to reveal what Niall's classmates had been up to in his absence.

When they arrived at the first roundabout in Fort William, Drew followed signs to the High Street, then parked at a charging station. He and Niall removed their helmets, glad of the air on their faces.

'Pizza for breakfast?' Drew suggested, 'We can call it brunch, can't we? And an icy juice, too?'

Niall followed Drew past a row of tourist shops to a terraced pedestrian plaza. People and dogs sat in the sunshine on large granite blocks and small triangular patches of grass, looking across to Loch Linnhe and the mountains behind. Drew pointed out a gap in the seating on his way. A sandwich board advertising stone-fired pizzas stood in front of him in a shady corner. Niall headed to the empty seats, glad to join the people watchers and relinquish the experience of being watched himself.

'Do you know about that Unclearance initiative, Niall?' Drew asked when he returned, handing Niall a paper plate with a napkin and a massive slice of pizza. 'First Minister's heritage project, part of the Land Reform Act?'

Niall nodded as Drew pulled a juice can from one of his rear pockets and handed it over.

'It's that thing where folk can go and claim back a bit of their ancestors' land, isn't it?' Niall said, setting the can on the ground by his feet, grateful to feel it was still chilled, despite such recent proximity with Drew's arse.

'That's right,' Drew pulled his can out of another pocket, set it next to Niall's, then took an enormous bite of pizza before sitting. When his mouth was empty, he continued, 'It's going well – Unclearances, so it is. Government ended up collaborating with NSBC – some students went off to find one of their bits of land. It's fair captured the nation's imagination. First Minister's delighted. Blurt laps it up, too.'

'Ah,' Niall replied, 'is that why I've seen so many folk wearing NSBC merch?' Niall pointed to a group of people wearing JJ emblazoned t-shirts and baseball caps outside a gift shop. 'They've been everywhere. I saw a load of them in Glencoe earlier as well, taking a photo at the sign for a pub. Did you see them?'

'Christ. You dinnae miss much, do you, son?' Drew's eyes bulged.

'Makes you wonder, doesn't it?' Niall continued, 'Like, where you came from and that?'

'Aye,' Drew agreed, 'it does. Have you heard of the island of Eigg before, by any chunce? You know one of the modern descendants from there, as it turns out.'

'Eigg?' Niall smirked a little, 'That's the name of an island?'
Drew nodded.

'Are you the modern descendent then, Drew?'

'No. No me, son. Jackson Campbell, fae uni. He's one of the ones that's gone with NSBC.'

'Oh,' Niall looked surprised, then shrugged, 'typical Jackson. Loves attention. Good for him, I suppose.'

Drew decided to have another bite of pizza before delivering the more emotionally stirring news about Hanna's involvement.

'He's all right, actually,' Niall mused, 'I mean, I used to think Jackson was a twat, I'll be honest, Drew. I don't think I was wrong. I think he *was* a twat, a lot of the time. He's always been legit funny on Blurt, though, hasn't he?' Drew gave a thumbs-up as he chewed. 'We chatted the night before I went into recovery,' Niall went on, 'I saw another side to him then, you know? He's just … well … he said it himself to me, his mental age might be a bit younger than his actual age, but I don't know if that's a thing or just something he says to get off with shit, you know?' Drew inclined his head, listening attentively. 'Sorry,' Niall continued, 'I know you can't talk about other students like I can. Just my opinion, like.'

'That's all right,' Drew wiped his mouth with his napkin, 'I didnae know yous had talked outside of uni. Did he tell you anything about his final assignment?'

'Yeah.' Niall looked over to Loch Linnhe, frowning as he thought back to his room in student digs, remembering chatting to Jackson in the darkness. 'He was pretty pissed off he wasn't going to finish it. I felt sorry for him, but I guess he had the same chance as everyone else at the end of the day, maybe even more, given how wealthy his family is? Shame though, still.'

'Or *not* a shame at all, as it turns out!' Drew interjected, grinning. 'He *did* get his assignment in! Right at the last minute! Well, technically slightly late, but I can use discretion around leeway cause he's EHA too!' Drew stamped a foot for effect, making Niall jump. 'Tiny house!' Drew continued, 'Made in a brand-new material called Transpariboard – he nailed the whole brief, can you believe it?'

Niall's lips hovered around the pizza he'd been about to bite, his eyes widening until he felt he might fall into the melted mozzarella beyond the tip of his nose. A drip of oil ran lazily across the pizza's crust then pooled, wet and warm like an orange tear shed directly into his palm. He dropped the pizza onto its plate.

'He *what*?' Niall's throat constricted as deep shock spasmed his diaphragm.

'He did it!' Drew laughed, enjoying what he assumed was a hyperbolic reaction from Niall. 'Amazing, isn't it? You werenae the only one who didnae see *that* coming, I can tell you that for free, son.'

Niall's mouth opened then closed. Was he in a nightmare, he wondered? He pinched the skin on his wrist and the searing pain shot up his arm like an injection of hot tar into a vein.

'He's out with NSBC, as I said,' Drew continued, 'they're doing a livestream, see? Finding his land. A wee crew, just two folk, and a friend fae uni, decent lass. Wildly clever.'

Drew nudged Niall again, waiting for his face to light up when the penny dropped. Instead, Niall looked like he might vomit. Drew handed Niall his juice and frowned. Niall watched the concern in his professor's expression. Here he was again, Niall realised, someone to be pitied. Someone who'd been fucked over by life once more. Someone pathetic.

'Son,' Drew was all seriousness, 'are you OK?'

'I'm fine,' Niall managed, hearing the hoarseness on the edge of his words contradict him. 'Sorry, something went down the wrong way. Do you mean Hanna? Hanna's with Jackson? And they're up here, in the Highlands?'

'Aye.' Drew looked somewhat relieved. 'Galivanting aboot on Eigg, so they are, in Transpariboard tiny houses. They were here, just across the road, just days ago. Mad, isn't it?' Drew pointed vaguely down the loch.

'Completely.' Niall smiled before shoving the remainder of his pizza into his mouth. Hard crust scraped the inside of his cheeks as he tried to chew and the tugging, scratching pain of it felt like both reward and acknowledgement. He imagined blood mixing with the pizza's tomato sauce and wished it would all gush from a wide hole in his throat: a tap of pain. Then the world could see and words would be unnecessary, forever. His wristband vibrated, snapping him back. Niall looked at the screen and saw a notification telling him his heart rate had been elevated for more than three minutes. He flicked the notification away and an option prompt replaced it, asking if he wanted to contact the recovery centre for support. He tapped the option for 'no'.

'Transpariboard's no the most catchy name, granted,' Drew said, eyeing an ice cream in the hands of a passing child, 'but what else *could* he have chosen, know what I mean? It's a recycled composite. Sparkles beautifully when it's processed into a sheet. Strong, too. Tuffboard's been done already, see? And it disnae capture the sparkle anyway, does it? It's almost glittery. Very unique. Beautiful. Upcycled plastics.'

Niall stared at the slabs beneath his feet and felt one cell after another begin to burn inside him, then a sweeping blow of violent sadness thrust over him.

'So how about this?' Drew grinned. 'How about we head up to Arisaig and have a wee peek over the water to Eigg before we head back doon to tonight's digs? I can take a photo of you, and when you're ready to get back on the socials, you can show Hanna you were nearby! She'll love that, won't she? If the sun hits right maybe we could see their tiny hooses twinkling, what do you think?'

Niall picked up his can and swigged the remainder of the juice, hoping the tears building in his eyes would also be swallowed back.

'Pudding first tho, eh?' Drew stood. 'What flavour ice cream are you after, son?'

Niall shook his head.

'Full already, eh?' Drew laughed, 'I'll be back in a minute.'

Niall's wristband vibrated again. His heart rate was still elevated. He watched the edges of the icon he could press for help pulsing with a ring of white. Was it already auto-reporting to Claudia and Fin that something was up, he wondered? Could they call him in? And, if they did, would he ever make it back out again after this bombshell? He tore his napkin along its centre line, then folded half of it into a small square which he slipped between the wristband and his skin, blocking his pulse from the sensor then tapped 'no' again. When he looked up, Drew was approaching, licking the side of a huge scoop of chocolate ice cream. Niall flicked away the help screen and smiled.

'How far's the island from the mainland?' Niall asked, 'Can we not go over, on a boat, see this Transpariboard? And Jackson and Hanna?'

'No, we cannae, sorry.' Drew looked solemn. 'Out of the question. It's only them that's got permission to be where they are. And an SWE is kicking off too, so all the local boats are busy bringing in extra supplies in case the islands get cut off. Luckily you and I will miss the worst of it, apart from this sun. And anyway, Eigg's not so close as you could pop over and back, you know? No, unless you were on a Rib. A fast boat, ken? And it'd be a bit much, wouldn't it, for you? All that excitement so soon? That's nae whit this first trips aboot, is it?'

Blood whooshed in Niall's ears.

'Are there TV crews up there, on the mainland and the island, I mean?'

'Dunno.' Drew shrugged. 'Probably. There's certainly plenty fans following them everywhere and congregating along the way. You've seen that for yersel already, right enough. We'll stay back from all of that malarky. They're due to come off the island tomorrow, I think. You'll see them soon enough, no doubt, yer making great progress, after all.'

'What do they do after Eigg?' Niall asked while his neck tensed painfully.

'Dunno yet.' Drew shrugged again, his eyes were crossed as he devoured what remained of his cone. 'Some spin-off reality TV stuff for Jackson, I reckon. Depends what he wants to do with Transpariboard. It could be big, but he disnae seem that bothered aboot it. Maybe he wants to bury it – too much like hard work, you know? Maybe he needs a break after uni. His interests are pretty clearly elsewhere.'

'I'll fucking bury *him* before he buries Transpariboard,' Niall muttered.

'*What?*' Drew stared at Niall.

'Nothing!' Niall blushed, 'It's my meds, sorry. I get passionate. Serotonin and testosterone rebalancing or something. It'll even out in the end, apparently. I just can't – see good design going to waste, know what I mean?'

Drew shrugged.

'Better get some green juice,' Niall lied, adrenaline helping him think, 'I've not eaten stuff like pizza for ages, maybe it's messing with my blood sugar.'

'Aw shite son, sorry!' Drew marched to a nearby bin and dropped the remainder of his cone into it. 'Come on. Let's get something healthy. That wis poor role modelling from me, wasn't it?'

Niall picked up his and Drew's pizza plates and empty cans and dropped them in the bin. A large bang from a passing exhaust on the road along the loch's edge made Niall jump.

'Tosser!' someone shouted from the plaza.

'Fascist wanker!' came another voice.

Niall froze, inexplicably terrified that the abuse was directed at him. Drew craned his thick neck to watch a car pass the gap between two buildings.

'Knew it!' Drew hissed. 'Templeton! Still driving that bloody awful Bentley. Some things never change, do they?'

'Michael Templeton?' Niall asked, 'From GBEBS?' Drew nodded. 'He's the one that went after Jackson's dad, isn't he? All the Rabid Roy stuff was him, wasn't it? He kept it going for ages, didn't he?'

'Still does,' Drew said, scouring the shop fronts for a juice bar, 'he's a professional troll. Up to no good as usual, no doubt. Anything to spin GBE nonsense.'

Niall struggled to keep up as they set off down the High Street. A light whiff of the Bentley's diesel fumes mingled with the otherwise clean Fort William air in the car's wake. Something about it smelled a lot to Niall like opportunity.

50

'It's International Day of Jackson, I've decided.' Jackson made his announcement as he emerged from relieving himself behind the back wall of number one. 'Since this is our last night, I've decided we should dedicate the rest of our time here to the person who made it all happen – *me* – and we should all celebrate me by doing what me would want most – banter. And eating. And a piss-up.'

Zach looked up from where he and Gayle were waiting for Jackson in the shade of number nine's gable end. They had an afternoon of gathering footage from different spots in the Lower Grulin landscape planned; Jackson was to deliver commentary comparing his modern life with that of his ancestors. But, evidently, Jackson was less than keen on the prospect.

Hanna folded her page corner, leaving an oily sun cream fingerprint, then shut her book.

'You're energetic today,' she said to Jackson as he wandered past to the centre of the clearing. He was only wearing sunglasses, his wristband, flip flops and his kilt, which he unbuckled and threw towards his tiny house, where it dropped to the grass. To Gayle and Zach's relief they saw he was left wearing a skin-tight tartan thong, the checks of the red and black pattern stretching out of proportion across the significant bulge of his genitals. Hanna saw only the scant black string rising between Jackson's buttocks and then circling his waist.

'Just giving the people what they want, Hanna.' Jackson smirked.

'Jesus Christ.' Gayle rolled her eyes, 'I hope you've got SPF on, Jackson? *Everywhere?*'

'And I hope you wiped your arse properly.' Hanna laughed.

'This thong is from ScotPlay,' Jackson addressed the nearest drone as he set about Voguing, 'and I am here to tell you the python thinks it's very comfy. Get yours today. Five per cent off if you use the code "Jackson's Journey". Free delivery to all New Scottish addresses.'

'Is that true, Jackson?' Gayle asked.

'It is now.' Jackson continued striking increasingly elaborate poses.

Zach pulled a large spray bottle of sun cream from the rucksack at his feet and walked over to Jackson.

'Spray me,' Jackson demanded. 'There's a real market for that kind of footage, Zach. Go on, then take off your shorts and vest and I'll do you, then we'll do each other at the same time.'

Zach dropped the bottle at Jackson's feet, then returned to the shade.

'Boring!' Jackson shouted after him, then picked up the bottle and began spraying his thighs while rubbing himself suggestively, 'I'll do myself. Hashtag self-care porn. Hashtag Jackson's Horny instead of Jackson's Journey, get it?' Jackson circled a nipple with his forefinger and stuck his tongue out, waggling its tip as he pretended to writhe with pleasure.

'Keep it daytime, Jackson,' Gayle warned, 'or I'll switch all the cams to Hanna and she can read out blurts. And hurry up, *please*. I want us to follow the burn down to where it opens into a bit of a pool. There are big boulders there that the Lower Grulin women used in their laundry process.'

'My process at the pool will be wet and wild,' Jackson called back, 'who knows what I'll do with the boulders, this is not the time to tune out of the livestream, I can tell you that, friends.' Jackson winked at the drone while massaging cream over his midriff.

'What're you reading, Hanna?' Gayle asked.

'About Raasay,' Hanna replied, 'I want to see if Zach can take time off after this and head up there with me whenever the weather allows, obviously.'

'First I heard,' Zach grinned, clearly delighted.

'I'm using positive pressure to influence you,' Hanna raised an eyebrow, 'Jackson's taught me a lot, see?'

'I do see.' Zach laughed.

Hanna looked to Jackson and saw mischief had left his eyes and been replaced with a lonely sadness as he watched her and Zach.

'Oh!' Hanna said, 'You can come too, Jackson, if you like? It's just, I assumed you'd be busy with Transpariboard and more reality stuff? I didn't think you'd want to do anything like this again, but …?'

Jackson flinched. How had Hanna read what he was feeling? He sprayed himself in the face, then shrieked when the cream stung his eyes. Gayle and Zach rushed over, urging Jackson to sit. Hanna grabbed her water bottle and snatched up a microfibre towel trailing from Jackson's tiny house doorway. She poured water onto the corner of the towel as she ran, then pressed it into Jackson's hands.

'Squeeze that into your eyes,' she instructed, 'it'll help wash it out.' Jackson did as he was told. They repeated the process three more times.

'Fuck's sake,' Jackson muttered, 'that hurt.'

'I'm sorry, Jackson,' Hanna dabbed at his cheek with a dry corner of the towel, 'I should've thought more about Raasay and that. I assumed, about you, and that's shit. I'm really grateful to you for all this, you know? Sorry, chum.'

Jackson blinked wildly, his eyes still smarted, but gradually the others came into focus. They all looked concerned. And worse, Jackson realised, they looked like they pitied him.

'I meant the SPF hurt, Hanna,' Jackson snapped.

'I know,' Hanna drew back, surprised, 'but I thought you did it as a distraction because I embarrassed you – leaving you out?'

Jackson saw the truth in Hanna's face. She always made honesty look so simple.

'Right!' Jackson jumped up. 'People can't resist getting close to the python, can they? Wow! Any excuse, innit?' Gayle, Hanna and Zach remained crouched as Jackson strode down the grass towards the gap between house numbers eight and nine. 'Let's go then!' Jackson shouted, 'Those soft porn shots you want of me in the dirty washing water aren't going to do themselves, are they, Gayle?'

/RoryTheTory/blurts/

jacksonmccampbell is pretty obviously skitso. He needs put in one of Clearwater's concentration camp "recovery centres".

318

/ZuzannaN/blurtsTo/RoryTheTory

I've reported your blurt to the New Scottish Police, like, how offensive are you? you are a massive prick #HateSpeech

/RebeccaCampbell/blurtsTo/RoryTheTory

How dare you? I have taken a photo of your blurt with my camera and sent it to my lawyer. Send me your address immediately!

51

Drew had blethered about snippets of local history across the comms in his and Niall's helmets throughout the Road to the Isles. Niall had pretended to listen while debating between throwing himself from the Vespa or staying alive long enough to out Jackson's lies. Justice had won by a narrow margin.

When they arrived in Arisaig, Drew pulled into the side of a road overlooking the seaside village. In the middle of the bay was a long, man-made causeway leading to a T-shaped jetty crammed with people, as were the pavements of the shorefront street.

'Never seen it like this before.' Drew frowned and let the Vespa freewheel to a spot behind a flower bed outside the local library.

After securing their panniers, Niall followed Drew through the village; small shops and houses looked over the turquoise sea and islands beyond. Between the crowds, Niall listened in to conversations. The people around them seemed to be tourists, Jackson fans, media or locals. From what Niall overheard, the locals wanted to help friends and family on the islands who wanted to get to the mainland before the SWE or to collect creels before the bad weather hit. Jackson's fans wanted to get out to Eigg to see Jackson returning from Lower Grulin and accompany him back to the mainland, while the media cohort wanted to know whether Jackson and the rest of the team would be returned to Arisaig or Mallaig and on which vessel. The international tourists seemed happy to drink it all in, amused by the eccentric vignette of what they perceived to be typical New Scottish life.

After stopping and starting their way along the main street Niall and Drew wandered the length of the causeway then returned to a dry harbour surrounded by a circle of yachts and trailers. Some of the boats were in obvious states of disrepair while others were brand new, their metalwork and windows gleaming in the sun, incongruously dry, presumably waiting for owners who preferred quieter days. Drew pulled a cloth handkerchief from his pocket and wiped his sweaty brow.

'I could murder a juice, whit about you, son?'

'Maybe just water.' Niall looked at the hotel and heaving mini-market across the road from the boatyard. People were queuing out the door from both. Buying anything would take some serious time and he could do with the opportunity to think.

'I'll go, Drew. You can grab some shade here.'

'Absolutely not!' Drew boomed, '*You* wait here, I'll go for refreshments. Then we can go back to the bike and spectate this absolute chaos. None of this should be happening, crazy, isn't it? First Minister's issued SWE protocol in these waters for the next week at least. I'll get healthy stuff to eat, don't worry.'

As Drew headed off Niall walked between the two largest boats to get a clearer view of the island Drew had pointed out as Eigg. It didn't look like much, Niall thought, and, mercifully, if the Transpariboard houses were twinkling back at him it was impossible to see. That Arisaig was beautiful was plain, however. Niall wondered with a heavy sigh what Hanna had made of it all until the spit and crackle of a heavy vehicle driving on aggregate chippings drew Niall's attention across the bay to a small car park beside an old concrete slipway. A huge black Mercedes was responsible for the noise and behind it, almost bumper to bumper, was Michael Templeton's Bentley. Niall watched as a man in a navy and grey speedboat anchored by the slipway's edge stood up from where he'd been working between his engines and took in the newcomers a few metres away from where he worked. Thanks to the density of parked cars already present, the Mercedes quickly ran out of space and the proximity of the Bentley behind prevented it from reversing. The roaring engine of the Bentley cut out, and Templeton, unmistakeable in tweed plus-fours, russet knee socks, deerstalker cap and wax jacket emerged. The Mercedes' honked loudly and its white reverse lights flashed. Templeton ignored both and made towards the man in the boat. The noise had attracted Niall's attention and several other folks' too. Nearby a trio of Jackson fans dressed in NSBC baseball caps and faux leopard skin mini-dresses began gathering up camping gear. One of them stopped and raised a pair of binoculars.

'Oh, my God!' Niall heard him tell the others, 'It *is* him *and* Rabid Roy. And there's a boat over there with engines on. Go! *Go!*'

Niall's head spun. The lights in the Mercedes were now off and the driver had joined Templeton at the water's edge. They were gesticulating at each other and the man in the boat, but it was impossible to hear what they were saying. Niall glanced back at the hotel and saw Drew chatting happily to a man at the back of the queue.

'Fuck it.' Niall whispered to himself, then began walking, his pace picking up when he heard the fans behind draw closer. Before he knew it, he was jogging, then running, then he was in the other car park and making past the hisses of the Bentley's roasting engine. He took cover behind the massive bulk of the Mercedes and peeked over the bonnet at the men arguing.

'Two hundred GBE pounds to take me to Eigg!' Niall watched as Templeton propositioned the man in the boat. 'Come on. You're working-class New Scottish, surely? You can't have seen money like that in your life before, hmm?'

The Mercedes driver scoffed. Was it really Rabid Roy, Niall wondered? He looked slimmer than in the memes, but the golfing attire and wrinkled perma-tan seemed right.

'Behave yourself, you insufferable idiot!' Roy addressed Templeton, his face turning puce as he did so. It was Rabid Roy all right, Niall thought, watching as Jackson's father offered a handshake to the man in the boat, which was pointedly ignored. 'I'll give you 2,000 euros to take me and me alone, sir.' Roy said.

'Ha!' Templeton jeered, '*Euros!* Monopoly money, is it? Deary me! Why are you so desperate to get to your spawn, Campbell? Trouble brewing, is there? I must say he's looked mighty shifty at times, hasn't he?'

Roy's hands drew into fists at his side. Niall winced, bracing to see Templeton punched into the sea, half willing it, when the three fans hurried between them, all out of breath from vlogging at the same time as carrying clanking camping equipment and trying to run in heels.

'Get your cameras out my face!' the man in the boat barked. The fans quickly complied.

'We'll chip in 4,000,' one of the fans said, 'it's all we've got. We can't go up from there. Please! Take us, too!'

Niall gulped. Where the hell did these people get money like that from, he wondered? He had a 100-euro allowance on his wristband from the centre and nothing else to his name.

'Euros or GBE pounds?' the man in the boat asked.

'Euros, obviously,' the fan replied, 'we're the Jackson Campbell Appreciation Society.'

'Then welcome aboard,' the man in the boat grinned. He held out a hand to help the first of his new passengers.

Niall's eyes almost popped out of his head. He *had* to get on that boat. But how?

'Name your price,' Roy said, a resonant note of sadness lacing his words as he drew a platinum credit card from his pocket, 'I have to get to my son.'

'You've heard the price,' the man in the boat replied, 'it's 4,000 euros per party. Are you in or out? We leave in two minutes and seats are going fast. And your cars will be towed up to Morar while you're gone, you understand that, don't you? I take no responsibility.'

'I understand.' Roy sighed.

'Ditto,' Templeton said, proffering his card to the tablet the boatman was now collecting transfers on, 'I need to get something first though.'

The man in the boat looked across at the causeway towards groups of people now heading their way.

'Make it snappy,' he growled at Templeton, 'if I can't do this without some smart arse blurting something that ends up with me in court for breaching restrictions, I'm no doing it at all.'

Sweat ran down Niall's back as he watched the boatman pass out lifejackets. Templeton's feet crunched over the chippings on the other side of Roy's car before he came into sight at the back of the Bentley. Their eyes locked.

'Car thief, are you?' Templeton sneered. 'Typical New Scotland. Get away from my vehicle. Now.'

'I'm not a thief!' Niall replied, shocked, 'I'd never steal! *Jackson's* a thief!' Niall heard his own words as if they belonged to someone else, 'And you need my help. He didn't invent Transpariboard. *I* did. He's pretended it's his, and it's not, it's *mine*. I've got no money, so you need to take me on that boat to confront him.'

Templeton removed a fat black brick of a Dictaphone from his jacket pocket. He pulled the record trigger and a red light flashed.

'Say that again, and your name.' Templeton pointed the device at Niall, his upper lip snarling as he stared at the blonde aura of fuzzy hair growth on Niall's head. 'And *what* are you? A boy or a girl? You bloody New Scots never can keep it simple, can you?'

'Get me to Eigg, first,' Niall's voice shook.

'Come on to *fuck*!' the man on the boat roared. Niall heard one engine start, then the second.

Templeton clicked his recorder off. He opened the back door of the Bentley and lifted out a tattered drone case which he thrust at Niall, then locked the car.

'Does Roy Campbell know you? Do those other idiots in the boat?'

Niall shook his head.

'Right,' Templeton said, 'you're my assistant if anyone asks. Keep your mouth shut about *everything* you've told me, do you hear? You've never met Jackson, understood? You're a nobody with nothing of interest to say to anyone, got it?'

'It's like you read my mind,' Niall replied.

'Wear these.' Templeton shrugged off his jacket and threw it at Niall, followed by his deerstalker. Niall winced as he felt the damp warmth of the heavy fabrics in his hands. He swallowed hard then pushed the drone case between his thighs, gripping it there as he pulled on his disguise.

/TheJacksonCampbellAppreciationSoc/blurts
YAYYYYYYYY we're getting to eigg but we can't tell you how but we're coming for you, jacksonmcampbell bebe!!!! #UnstoppableLove #JacksonsJourney

52

Rocky land petered down to silver boulders either side of the RIB as the boatman picked a path through underwater obstacles out of the Sound of Arisaig, then into the open sea.

'Seals!' one of the fans pointed at a collection of domed heads bobbing in the water. Niall watched Templeton roll his eyes while Roy smiled so the skin at his temples crinkled. From the control pedestal he stood behind, the boatman pointed at a rope held in place by intervals of thick rubber patches around the RIB's sidings.

'Hang on tight,' he shouted, waiting only a few seconds before thrusting forward hard. The bow reared out of the water so only the boatman could see beyond it as they leapt and slapped over the swell towards Eigg. Niall squeezed the rope until his knuckles were white as he looked back to Arisaig. Beyond the frothy wake, the causeway, hotel and shops had already shrunk to look like a model village. His wristband vibrated, startling him; one notification reminded him to hydrate, another advised sun cream. A third asked him to clean the sensor so his heart rate could be read more accurately; the folded pizza napkin was damp with sweat but still in place. He frowned as he considered what might happen next. When Drew notified the centre he was missing the first thing they'd do would be to trace the wristband. If he threw it into the sea they'd think he'd drowned. He pictured boats circling the waters. Would they have divers searching? He imagined a helicopter overhead and Hanna being told why it was flying low. He imagined Jim too, pacing the floor back at the centre. And Fin, smoothing his kaftan while Claudia blew steam from a cup of tea she'd be too upset to drink.

All that strain being put on the shoulders of people he cared about was too much. He decided that the wristband would have to stay on for now, then turned his attention to the other passengers. The three fans were huddled against the sea's chill and sneaking selfies. Jackson's father was busily messaging on an ancient Nokia with one of his arms looped under the rope to anchor him as he typed. Templeton was scowling at the Isle of Skye.

Niall checked the time. Twenty-two minutes had passed since he and Drew had parted ways. In the worst-case scenario, Drew would be heading back to find him now, then raising the alarm in ten minutes or so. In the best-case scenario, Drew would be back from the queue in another half hour, then raising the alarm ten minutes later. Niall stared up at the sky. A puff of white cloud whisked him back to how he had felt looking through the skylight in the MDMA therapy room.

'Tournesol,' Niall whispered. A rush of love pulsed unexpectedly through his body calming him a little. His grip on the rope loosened as the boat regained a horizontal position. Waves could be heard again when the engines dulled. Eigg loomed close, transformed now to a tapestry of textured greens.

'Hello!' Roy boomed. Niall and the others turned and saw Roy's phone pressed to his cheek. 'Yes, Rebecca, listen carefully,' Roy yelled, 'I've got a plan. Yes! Yes, that's right! I need the name of the taxi driver on the island, I saw a minibus taxi in the background when Jackson arrived there, can you search it and commission it straight away so it collects me at the pier? Pay them whatever it takes to *only* take me, understand?'

Niall shook his head.

'No!' one of the fans shouted, 'That's not fair!' Roy ignored the plea and pretended to listen to Rebecca on an entirely dead line. Templeton's eyes bulged while Roy said fake goodbyes, then pocketed his phone.

'Can we get a lift with you?' one of the fans asked, leaning towards Niall, 'I could get my parents to transfer you money.'

'You most certainly cannot!' Templeton interrupted. Niall mouthed an apology, but the fan fixed an icy stare on him, then Templeton.

'Fuck you!' the fan furthest from Templeton spat. 'We're not maniacs like you anyway. We'll wait for Jackson at the pier. You're not meant to try and get anywhere near him, but I don't suppose you lot care about that, do you? Ecocidal wankers!'

Niall stared at his feet, affronted. When he looked up again the busyness of the pier was a welcome distraction; islanders had stalls selling crafts, locally brewed beer, green juices, water and coffee. The scene reminded him of the Grassmarket in Edinburgh, but the resemblance faded when a minibus with a squint taxi sign chugged onto the causeway, chased by four barking dogs. The dogs looked disappointed when the vehicle came to a stop. They waited a moment, tails stiff and upright as they sniffed at the wheels, then trotted off in the direction they'd come from, presumably waiting for their next prey.

Roy checked his phone. A reply to the string of messages he'd sent Rebecca before faking the call on the boat awaited him.

DRIVER IS GLORIA: CATALONIAN, EX-BULL-RUNNER, VEGAN. I'M FOLLOWING HER ON BLURT NOW, SHE HATES TEMPLETON MORE THAN SHE HATES YOU, THANK GOODNESS. I'VE PAID HER. WIFI/ PHONE SIGNAL'S TERRIBLE ON OTHER SIDE OF ISLAND, SHE WILL TAKE HIM THERE.

Roy began loosening his lifejacket. The boatman pointed to a coil of rope at Roy's feet as they drew alongside the landing area.

'Throw that ashore,' he instructed, 'to him.'

Roy saw a man about his own age waiting by one of several mushroom-shaped concrete bollards. He threw the rope and was rewarded with a nod of thanks.

To Templeton's horror, as soon as they stopped Roy alighted the short steel ladder to the pier, tossing his lifejacket over his shoulder as he went.

Templeton made to follow but found his path blocked.

'Get my lifejacket off first,' the boatman growled.

Templeton wrestled with the lifejacket while the fans enjoyed watching his struggle. Niall removed his lifejacket then quietly helped Templeton. Templeton grabbed a red plastic fish box from an empty stack next to a mound of creels on the pier. He turned the box upside down and stepped onto it, spotting Roy across the crowd, speaking with the taxi driver.

'Move!' Templeton roared, jumping off the fish box then darting off, pursued by Niall. When they emerged metres from the minibus, Roy was making towards the toilet block, then disappeared inside.

'Going for a quick tinkle, are we?' Templeton chuckled. The driver, Gloria, leant against the minibus and lit a thin roll-up. She took three short puffs then dropped the cigarette, extinguishing it under her sandal with a twist of her foot. Niall groaned when Templeton clicked his fingers to get her attention. Gloria regarded them with open disdain.

'Now, listen,' Templeton began, 'I know you're jolly well booked, but I'll double whatever he's paid if you take me, not him, right now, as close as you can to Lower Grew Lynn, no questions asked. I'm an Agent of the Empire, I'm sure you recognise me, but don't make a fuss, there's a good girl.'

A flicker of amusement crossed Gloria's face. She walked a few steps towards the back of the minibus then stopped where a slim emergency exit door had once hung near the rear. Templeton and Niall looked at the oblong hole with a tattered rubber seal hanging from its edges. Two empty hinges jutted backwards from the metal while a sliding door closer to the front of the minibus appeared to have long since been welded shut. Gloria pointed at the hole. Templeton tutted, then climbed in and sat on the least dirty seat, just behind Gloria's. Niall followed, placing the drone on the chair next to Templeton. He crouched to look out of the smudged windows to the toilets and caught a glimpse of Roy's head peeking around the wall, then disappearing.

'Hurry, woman!' Templeton shouted as he watched Gloria stroll past the windscreen. She slowed her pace and glared then climbed lackadaisically into her seat. Before starting the engine she picked up a tall transparent beaker from her dashboard and noisily sucked the last of a juice through a stainless steel straw.

'GO!' Templeton looked fit to burst, 'On the Empire's orders, woman! I command thee, *drive!*'

Gloria turned the key and grinned into her rear-view mirror.

'Whateffer you sai, sir,' she replied, then began the six-point turn to get the minibus facing in the right direction to leave the pier again. Niall looked to the toilet block again. Something wasn't right.

'I'm going to lie down at the back,' Niall lied, panic rising in his chest, 'I don't feel great.'

Templeton rolled his eyes as Niall retreated and Gloria jolted the minibus into reverse, moved backwards a few metres, stopped, then jolted forwards. Niall shrugged off Templeton's jacket and laid it across the last row of seats then crouched, edging his way back to the opening on his bum. The vehicle lurched forward then stopped again. Niall jumped out and dove behind a row of rusty oil barrels. Three dogs darted past him, barking ferociously at the minibus. Niall's pulse raced, he crossed his fingers on both hands, willing Templeton to leave without him. Gloria eyed Templeton in the rearview mirror as she moved the steering wheel. She watched as he stabbed at his tablet screen, frowning deeply.

'How long till we're there?' Templeton shouted.

'Eez thurty mineets, sir,' Gloria replied.

'*Really?*' Templeton scoffed, 'I didn't think this shit-ridden backwater was big enough for thirty minutes' driving.'

'Life eez full of surprises,' Gloria smirked.

When the minibus eventually chugged consistently forward it lost its canine pack escort at the foot of a tight bend. The road climbed steeply, the minibus gears roaring then quietening when they hit a glorious plateau of machair either side of the single-track road.

'Are you sure we're going the right way?' Templeton turned his tablet in his hands.

'You have GBE tech?' Gloria stared in the mirror as they rumbled over a cattle grid.

'Yes, of course,' Templeton replied, 'best technology in the world. Watch the road, woman! For goodness' sake!'

'Your map eez wrong then, sir,' Gloria was matter-of-fact. 'GBE maps make New Scotland small, turn places upside-down, cause confusion, undermine. Grulin eez this wai, you will sai.'

Templeton's eyes narrowed. He knew some of what she was saying was true, but he never fully trusted immigrants as a rule. Gloria pushed a chunky button on the dash, instantly filling the vehicle with bagpipe music accompanied by castanets and the clear sense that further questions would not be taken. Templeton returned to drafting the series of breaking news blurts he planned to send about Jackson's lie as soon as the timing felt most explosive. Spun audaciously, Templeton thought, this scandal had the potential to crank wide fissures of fear in New Scotland and expose Clearwater as the communist, crackpot wolf in sheep's clothing he felt sure she was.

. . .

Roy hovered at the toilet block a little longer, then peeked again around the corner. To his relief all traces of Templeton and the minibus had disappeared. Rebecca had followed his text instructions to the letter, and together, with 2,000 euros' persuasion, they'd collaborated perfectly with Gloria to arrange for Templeton to be dropped at the end of the furthest road to the north of the island. Thereafter, Gloria had advised she would point her charge and his assistant toward a cleared settlement by the Singing Sands beach, telling them it was Lower Grulin. Roy felt the tension release its grip on his shoulders for the first time in hours. Two of the fans from the boat were standing with their backs to him, sharing a view of the livestream on a tablet while they waited for the third to emerge from the toilets.

'Oh, my God, Jackson!' Roy heard one of them say, 'He's hilarious. He doesn't give a shit, does he? Look at his bum. He's too funny, isn't he?'

He should've brought his tablet, Roy realised, then decided to head inside the pier centre, hopeful of a TV indoors, when Templeton's assistant stepped in front of him.

'What're you doing?' Niall asked, his voice almost pleading. Roy gawped as Niall pulled the deerstalker from his head and worried it between his hands. A small queue waiting to use the toilet formed behind Niall. Several people were beginning to squint at Roy, trying to place him. Roy nodded towards a quiet spot at the back of the pier centre with Ardnamurchan Lighthouse in the distance and Niall followed.

'Why do you think you have any right to ask about *my* business?' Roy frowned. 'You GBEBS people hound my family and me. And now you're here, making it look like *I've* done something wrong. Is Templeton in that taxi or not?'

'Yes, he's in the taxi,' Niall sighed, 'and I'm not with GBEBS. I just said that so Templeton would get me on that boat, I bribed him – with gossip about Jackson. And the Journey. And he said I had to pretend to be his assistant, so you wouldn't talk to me.'

'What?' Roy's eyes narrowed, 'Why would you? I don't under-stand. Who are you?'

'I'm Hanna's best friend,' Niall's voice shook, 'I went to uni with Jackson as well. I spoke to him the night before he handed in his assignment, the same day as the Unclearances ceremony at Glencoe. I told him about my idea; he was freaking out about not handing in his assignment. Transpariboard – the product and con-cept is mine, *I* invented it. And I just found out what he did with it.'

Roy watched a fat tear run down Niall's cheek. The missing pieces of the puzzle of Jackson's hesitant livestream behaviour slipped into place in Roy's mind. He hadn't missed the clues that Jackson had become a genius; there had been none, just a lie. Roy stared out to sea and Niall shuffled awkwardly at his side.

'You just found out?' Roy asked.

'I went into a recovery centre the day after I spoke to Jackson.' Niall looked at his feet as he spoke. 'I've got depression and anx-iety. It was getting worse, not better. End-of-term strain and that. Family problems.'

Roy didn't know what to say. He felt like he was talking to a very fragile teapot. Could one accidentally break people like this, he wondered?

'Are you OK?' Niall frowned.

'Yes. *Yes*. And, um, how are you now?' Roy faked a smile, hoping he looked unperturbed, 'I've read about those centres, but I must say, I am … sceptical … at best.'

'They're fantastic,' Niall shrugged, 'maybe you should try one? Some of the folk there had mood swings too, anger issues, like you and Templeton.' Niall stared at the lighthouse as he spoke, oblivious to Roy's disgust at the parallels being drawn. 'I was get-ting there. You pretty much get one-to-one care. The staff are annoying at first, then you realise they're pretty amazing. All the nature helps, too. And the design. It's like a hotel, I suppose. I did so well I got out for two nights to try out the real world again. And *this* is what I found. They take away your tablet and all that, see? You have to go cold turkey, on tech.'

Roy listened. Until now, he had imagined recovery centres as mildewed institutions full of rocking SNP members in straitjack-ets, loons who'd completely cracked and spent their days being spoon-fed drugs and food on his taxes.

'Are you an SNP fanatic then?' Roy asked.

'No.' Niall looked irritated as he checked the time. 'What's that got to do with anything?'

Roy opened his mouth but found he had no answer.

'I can't believe he's done this,' Niall said, 'Jackson knew I was ill. How could he do it to me? He just doesn't care, does he?'

'I'm very sorry,' Roy replied, 'on Jackson's behalf. I'm here because I sensed something wasn't right – he's been behaving oddly – even for my son. So I don't know if it helps to know this, but I don't think his deception is sitting easily with him. I think you're on his conscience.'

'I'd rather be on the jury that finds him guilty and sees him sentenced to a decade in criminal rehabilitation.' Niall sniffed, fighting back angry tears.

Roy blinked. A thought struck him.

'Does Templeton know about Jackson's theft?'

Niall's eyes softened, embarrassed. He looked at Roy and nodded.

'I think I would've done the same, in the circumstances,' Roy said, 'except with a good deal more rabidity, of course.'

'You're not rabid though,' Niall replied, 'do you put it on for the cameras, like Jackson? Is it you he gets it from?'

Roy scoffed.

'All this *journey* business. Very odd, I realise, to have been so affected by something on television. But there it is. I feel quite differently now having watched it, not at all rabid.'

'Well, the something *is* about your son,' Niall replied, 'so it's not odd. You'd be super weird if it didn't affect you. What's your plan now?'

A craving for a swig of brandy called to Roy. He quashed it and sadness bloomed in its place.

'I was going to wait and have a quiet word with Jackson on his way home,' Roy said, embarrassed by how simple and self-contained he'd so recently assumed things to be. 'I thought I'd see if we couldn't make our peace. Templeton showing up raised the stakes somewhat, and now there's you.' Roy smiled sadly. 'I don't quite know what the plan is any more, young man. I suppose it depends quite a lot on *your* plan, doesn't it?'

Niall went to reply, then thought better of it. *His* plan was to get to Jackson and have it out with him, forcing him to admit who Transpariboard belonged to before Drew caught up with him and had him sectioned. Niall quite fancied punching Jackson too, but he'd play that one by ear when they got face to face, he decided. It was hard to tell whom Roy would sympathise with in this predicament, so keeping schtum seemed wise.

'Do your parents know where you are?' Roy asked. Niall laughed a little, then shook his head. If Jackson had been standing here in this young man's shoes, Rebecca would be apoplectic about his close encounter with someone as self-serving and unpredictable as Templeton, Roy thought. 'I can contact your mental health centre for you if you like?' Roy blushed as he traversed unfamiliar fatherly ground, 'They could, perhaps, help?'

Niall shook his head and seemed to Roy to be a million miles away. Roy looked around, taking in their surroundings properly for the first time.

'Goodness,' he muttered, 'it's strange seeing the route they took in real life. I suppose that's where it goes to the Galmisdale track, then round the other side of that enormous rock. What did Hanna call it? The Scar? Perhaps not. It is a beautiful place, isn't it? Quite spectacular. To think, this is where *my* family hail from. Extraordinary.'

Niall looked up the short, steep track Roy had indicated. The onward journey to Jackson and Transpariboard seemed quicker than he'd imagined.

'You've sent Templeton off in the opposite direction then?' Niall asked.

'Completely,' Roy confirmed, 'for my sins.'

Niall checked the time again; Drew would be worried by now.

'I'll go up the hill a bit and call the centre,' Niall said, 'could you give me some space? I'll come back when I'm ready.'

'Of course,' Roy nodded, 'I'll find a spot here – try and avoid prying eyes for a while. Take your time. But wait, your name, you never told me?'

Niall made to leave, then pivoted back. He watched Roy lower himself to sit on a boulder, his slow movements betraying hitherto unseen fatigue. The vulnerability of it made Niall want to say a proper goodbye, the man had taken him at his word, after all, even though it reflected terribly on his family.

'I'm Niall,' he said. Roy nodded.

Niall placed the deerstalker on the top of a bin by the toilet block then made off up the track towards the trees, then out of sight.

/MichaelTempletonGBEBS/blurts/

Not one to blow my own trumpet but I might get the cleaner to make space on one of my study shelves for a journalist of the year 2035 award. Stay tuned to the truth, keep it GBEBS. Soon I will reveal a shocking truth re #Jackson'sJourney!

53

Rebecca sat on the Stat-Fly 6000 and watched Jackson crawl another short lap around a shallow pool of burn water. He stopped, dropped his head into the water, then threw his head back, arching his spine. In front of Jackson, Gayle was delivering a piece to camera about pre-clearances laundry habits. She ignored droplets of water from Jackson's escapades landing on her shoulder and spotting her t-shirt as she did so.

A ringtone recording of Geri Halliwell singing 'Zigga zig-ah' filled the lounge from Rebecca's tablet. She plucked it from the exercise bike's dashboard and saw Roy's avatar pulsing on screen. She muted the TV and accepted the call.

'Becs,' Roy breathed, clearly struggling to walk and talk, 'Becs, I think we're in real trouble. There's been a development.'

'Oh, God! What's that little shit done?' Rebecca stopped pedalling.

'He stole the idea of Transpariboard, Becs,' Roy replied, 'it's not his. He might be in big trouble for this – *really* big – with the police, I mean, not just with us, NSBC, the Scottish Government—'

'What?' Rebecca frowned, 'How could Templeton steal that? I'm watching the livestream. He hasn't appeared once! What do you mean? He's had other things made with it in Great British England, has he? They've copied Jackson?'

'*Jackson* stole Transpariboard, Becs,' Roy panted heavily, 'not Templeton. There's a young man here, on the island. He went to university with Jackson – and Hanna. He's Hanna's best friend. His name is Niall. Jackson stole his idea and submitted it as his own.'

'And you believed this, Roy?' a frosted edge formed on Rebecca's tone. 'From a stranger? Over your own son? My God. Is there any hope for us at all?'

'Becs!' Roy wheezed a little, 'Please. Stop and think for a minute. We don't have much time. Do you really, *really* believe Jackson came up with Transpariboard by himself? Haven't you also been concerned about how blatantly he has not loved all of the limelight that the idea has given him? He's only happy when he's mucking about, not when the focus is on the houses. Is it possible – just possible, that what I've been told is true? And why on earth would someone be heading to confront him on a livestream if it wasn't?'

'Because they want the attention!' Rebecca cried, dismounting the bike then padding across the carpet to Jackson's LazySack. It had been perfectly plumped by the cleaner about a week ago, but had slightly collapsed since. Rebecca stared at it and thought back to Jackson lolling about on it on his birthday almost a month before. If what he had told the world was true, Jackson must've known about Transpariboard that day, Rebecca realised, or invented it that evening. She caught her reflection in the enormous windows before her. She could lie to anyone but herself, she knew.

'Rebecca, I'm telling you,' Roy continued, 'if you don't trust me on this one … *that's* what's become of us.' Roy listened to his wife's breathing. Her buffering out-breath signalled a change of heart. 'The young man I met,' Roy went on, his voice catching, 'he says he told Jackson about Transpariboard, then he had to go to one of Clearwater's mental health centres. And he didn't realise till now Jackson had stolen it, or that there was a livestream, or anything! He's distraught, Rebecca. Downright distraught.' Roy heard Rebecca sniff. 'And unfortunately Templeton knows about this too, I'm afraid.'

Rebecca tried to swallow as disappointment thudded in her chest. Her pride that Jackson had at last done something with his life began melting away like a snowflake on a heated windscreen.

'But the journey,' she started, 'that was his idea, wasn't it? He had that with us, didn't he? Roy?'

Duchy arrived by her side and leaned into her ankle. She stooped, attempting to pick him up with her free hand, but he was too heavy.

'I don't know, darling,' Roy replied with a heavy sigh, 'I think so. I hope so.'

Rebecca kicked off her slippers, tipped inelegantly to one side and dropped onto the LazySack. Duchy climbed up to sit on her lap, his head cocked as he watched her face.

'So what do we do?' Rebecca asked, 'I don't suppose a hitman is an option – for Templeton, I mean?'

''Fraid not,' Roy replied.

'And where is he now?' Rebecca dropped her voice, 'The classmate? Are you two together? Is he, you know, a *basket case*?'

'He's run off,' Roy sighed, 'fooled me into giving him quite the head start. I thought we were going to work something out together … I … I don't know what I thought. It was upsetting to see someone like that. I don't know how to put it, Becs. He was … greatly troubled. I have no idea what he'll do. I had a sense he was intelligent, and certainly it would seem any friend of Hanna's would not be completely irrational. But—'

'You don't think he'd hurt himself, or … or Jackson, do you?' Rebecca's questions hung heavily between them.

'Anything feels possible right now.' Roy winced.

'Yes.' Rebecca wiped a tear, surprised to find a source of clarity springing from its warmth on her fingertips. She cradled Duchy and wandered back to the telly. A drone followed Jackson as he ran, apparently carefree, away from the laundry burn and back towards the tiny houses. He scooped up his kilt from the grass as he went, then threw it into his house's open doorway. Rebecca unmuted the volume and Jackson's laughter spilled into the room. Hanna waved at the drone as it passed overhead from where she sat, still reading at the camp.

'Is that the livestream I can hear?' Roy asked.

'Yes,' Rebecca replied.

'I'm almost at the NSBC truck, which is some distance from their campsite,' Roy said. 'I don't know why, I just thought it was better to do something rather than nothing.'

'I'm going to call some recovery centres, Roy,' Rebecca said, 'see if someone can help that lad. Save your battery, but give me any news as soon as you get it. I'll do the same. I'll try phoning Jackson afterwards, I take it he still has your number blocked?'

'Yes.' Roy winced.

'Then he's on his own with this for now,' Rebecca replied, 'whatever happens, trying to stop someone – someone else's son

– Niall, wasn't it? Well. That's more important, isn't it?'

'It is,' Roy agreed. The line cut out, and Roy hurried on, hot, bothered and with a heavier heart than he'd ever carried before.

54

Roy arrived at the edge of the corncrake territory and dropped, exhausted, to sit on a boulder between the NSBC truck and the corncrake cordon. He took in the view of the glistening sea, wishing he could scoop cool water up and into his face. He looked back at the track, then blinked. Someone was coming – they were running, right towards him, and they were far too big to be Niall. Roy tried to stand, but green splodges appeared in his vision so he sat again, conscious of sweat soaking his clothes. Drew McAllister slowed to a jog, then stopped in front of Roy. The two men stared at each other as Drew wiped sweat from his brow with a cloth handkerchief wrapped around one of his fists. In Drew's other hand, Templeton's deerstalker was scrunched to a flaccid rag.

'Afternoon,' Drew breathed heavily, 'apologies for being abrupt, but have you seen a young man going this way? Skinny. Shaved head. T-shirt, jeans. Fancy wristband, trainers?'

Roy stared at four water bottles strapped into a utility belt on Drew's waist.

'Hello?' Drew cleared his throat.

'Niall?' Roy was hoarse, 'I haven't seen him since the pier.'

Drew's eyes were ablaze. He looked down at Roy's mustard-coloured cords, then his brogues.

'Hud on,' Drew said, 'you're …?'

'Rabid Roy,' Roy tried to smile politely, 'yes.'

'Jesus, Mary and fuckin' Joseph!' Drew's eyes looked like they might pop out of their sockets, 'you've lost the weight, aye? Bloody hell!'

'Skiing,' Roy replied, 'Val d'Isère. Listen, I'm sorry, but who are you? Why are you asking about Niall?'

'Your wife phoned the recovery centre hotline and telt them Niall was here, on Eigg, that you and he had chatted and that

Transpariboard isn't Jackson's idea. I had no idea. He did a runner from me in Arisaig. I'm his supervisor this weekend. I'm his EHA counsellor and Hanna's. And Jackson's. Drew McAllister – Professor, et cetera.'

'The cavalry,' Roy said, a flicker of hope passing across his chest as he looked up to the Sgùrr. When he looked back he was relieved to see Drew looked smaller, momentarily, compared with a mountain. Had Niall already got to Jackson and outed him, he wondered?

'Hello?' Drew fanned the deerstalker at Roy, 'You all right, like?' Roy blinked and Drew noticed the older man's eyelids were heavy and slow. 'Here,' Drew unscrewed the cap of one of his bottles and bent, wrapping Roy's hands around its cool exterior. Roy raised the bottle to his lips, sipping first, then pouring, not caring that water ran down his chin and throat. When he'd finished the water, Roy looked at Drew and saw he was now concerned as well as intimidating. Roy felt immediately self-conscious about his age and comparative lack of fitness.

'I might be older and a bit inexperienced in trying to do the right thing, but I'm here,' Roy said, straightening up and forcing a brighter smile, 'I came to help Jackson, I've been watching the livestream. I *knew* there was something wrong. Just knew.'

'Right,' Drew raised an eyebrow, 'well, this is beyond something wrong, this is a cataclysmic fucking mess, Mr Campbell. It's largely my fault, more's the pity. I should've checked Jackson's work more thoroughly; this is what I get for being an eternal fucking optimist, eh?' Roy was too taken aback to respond. Drew continued, 'You saw Niall an hour ago, did you?'

Roy nodded.

'The recovery centre traced him to here twenty-five minutes ago,' Drew explained, 'so it's pretty bloody clear where he's going, isn't it? We're going to need that livestream down. Right now. Being broadcast in crisis isn't fair on the kid – Niall, I mean.'

Protectiveness over Jackson stirred in Roy's thoughts; the guns were turning to face his son and he was completely unaware. Drew shoved his hankie into the belt loop where the bottle had hung then walked over to the NSBC windscreen, lifted a wiper and stuck Templeton's hat beneath it. He pulled a tablet from his back pocket, then removed comms magnets from a chunky duster ring on his wedding finger and put them on his earlobes before stabbing his screen. Roy heard a ring tone then a familiar voice answering.

'Gayle?' Drew said, 'Drew McAllister. I've no time to explain. Livestream down immediately, please. This is an official directive in my capacity as an EHA authority.' Roy's heart raced as Gayle responded, he couldn't make out her words, but they flowed thick and fast with an immediate rhythm of alarm. 'Gayle, you're gonnae have three of my EHA charges with you at Lower Grulin any minute,' Drew continued, 'not just the two you've got already. There's an imminent crisis coming. You're about to be joined by Niall Horn, Gayle, Hanna's best friend. He's at serious risk. Long story short, Jackson stole the idea of Transpariboard from him and he's just found oot. Word's spreading. Fast.'

Roy covered his face with his hands as he listened.

'Are you off the air yet?' Drew pressed, turning his back to Roy. 'Hit the button, please. If he's not there yet we've a chance of avoiding the worst possible outcomes. Hurry, Gayle. And launch a rock at that bloody GBEBS drone as well if it's still hanging about!'

Roy heard the door to the NSBC truck swing open. He peeked through his fingers and saw the ranger in the doorway, naked apart from an Arran jumper he held around his waist, covering his modesty. Just inside the truck a drone sat upturned on the floor, in a net. Roy squinted at its GBEBS logo.

'What the hell's going on?' Calum's face was puffy, clearly just woken. 'Who the hell are yous? Are you here about that thing?' The ranger kicked the drone. 'I'm no ashamed of taking it down. It was hanging about the periphery of corncrake territory early this morning. I'm fully within my rights to do it. GBEBS drones are unreliable pieces of shit, unethical in the extreme around nature. So take your metal waste and don't bring it back, do you hear?'

Drew stared at the ranger then raised his tablet to indicate he was on a call.

'Good, Gayle,' Drew replied, 'I'll be with you as soon as possible, I think I'm half an hour away from you all if I run. And it looks like GBEBS drone's out of action, by the way, thank God for small mercies.' Drew hung up as Roy's phone rang.

The ranger threw his hands in the air, exasperated, revealing himself and mortifying Roy who quickly looked away.

'Livestream's gone off,' Rebecca spluttered when Roy picked up, 'one minute they were sitting down, drinking beer, next minute Gayle took a call, she walked away looking terrified. Now it's just footage from a drone over the sea, that's all that's on! I managed to get through to a recovery centre and tell them about Niall and the Transpariboard. Jackson's phone just goes to voicemail.'

'Professor McAllister's here, Becs,' Roy replied, 'he's Niall's supervisor, he got your message from the centre. It was him on the phone to Gayle – that was the call she took – the livestream's off to protect them – well, to protect Niall.'

'He's been here before!' Rebecca gasped, 'terrifying man! Oh Roy!'

Roy watched Drew approach the ranger. The two men began talking animatedly.

'I have to go, darling,' Roy said, 'I think I have to be in Jackson's corner, so to speak.' Roy hung up and stuffed his phone into his pocket.

'I don't give a fuck who you are, Professor, you're *not* going round there,' the ranger hissed at Drew.

'I am,' Drew replied.

'I am, too,' Roy chipped in while hiding slightly behind Drew. 'Sorry. I'm Jackson's father, by the way. And don't worry, we'll be quiet, I understand, about the birds.'

Drew made towards the cordon and Roy followed.

'No!' the ranger shouted after them, incredulous, 'I've kept the corncrakes safe this whole time – you are *not* ruining it at the last minute!'

'You missed a young man going round here in the last hour!' Drew looked livid as he fixed Calum with a glare. 'You missed Roy turning up, too! You were sleeping on the job! Look after your birds, we'll no disturb them. And let me look after my people, right?'

'You'll have to look out for Michael Templeton, too,' Roy added in an apologetic tone, 'he's on the island. With another of those drones. He'll be here soon, possibly, and he won't care one jot about the welfare of the corncrakes.'

'Oh, for fuck's sake!' the ranger grew purple, manically eyeing the sky. 'That's the last thing we need. Bloody malfunctioning nature-killing pieces of crap.' The ranger disappeared inside the truck to find his clothes.

'Let's go, quick,' Drew handed Roy another full water bottle then stepped over the cordon. Roy attempted to copy but a sharp pain in his hip stopped him. Drew watched as Roy untied the cordon from its post and walked through, then tied it after himself.

'Roy, difficult question this,' Drew said as Roy tried to fall in step with him, 'but I have to ask, what do you think the chunces are of Jackson doing something *very* stupid, once he finds out he's been caught?'

'Oh,' Roy replied, 'very, *very* high, I'd say. He does stupid things several times a day without provocation. Very frequently through the night, too, even when he sleeps.'

'No, Roy,' Drew shook his head, 'I mean, like … harming himself?'

'Oh!' Roy felt cold, 'You don't think …? I, I mean … he wouldn't, *would he*?'

'I dinnae think so,' Drew said, 'but I can't rule it oot. This is a lovely place, but …' Drew swept an enormous arm outwards, gesturing across the long grasses of the corncrake territory then towards the sea, 'there's cliffs, electric fences, loose rock … the shite can hit the fan pretty swiftly here,' Drew continued. 'And now I know for sure Jackson makes very poor choices under pressure. You need to tell me if anything worrying has ever happened at home before, with his mental health, right?'

Images of Rebecca and Jackson chatting together flashed in Roy's memory, snippets too of conversations he'd overheard between his wife and son. He knew they'd kept secrets from him, but Rebecca would've told Roy about anything sinister, he was sure of it.

'No.' Roy frowned. 'Nothing like that. Thank goodness.'

'OK.' Drew squeezed, then released Roy's forearm. Roy pulled his arm to his chest defensively, wrapping his fingers over where Drew had touched. 'I'll run,' Drew said, 'you go as fast as you can. Sip water every two minutes, OK?'

Roy nodded, mute.

'Get back here!' the ranger yelled. He had returned to the truck doorway with his trousers and a t-shirt on and hopped towards the cordon on one foot while trying to pull a sock onto the other. Roy watched for a moment then rushed on again when he realised Drew was already far out in front.

55

/RebeccaCampbell/blurtsTo/jacksonmcampbell
Private message Jackson call me straight away pls this is serious

/RebeccaCampbell/blurtsTo/jacksonmcampbell
Private message Jackson I know you read these I see you checking your wristband when it buzzes. Stop ignoring me. I'm serious, Jackson. Call me right now.

/jacksonmcampbell /blurtsTo/RebeccaCampbell
Mum chill out I'm with my friends. I've got spf on. You can't keep tugging this umbilical cord, innit, Beccy babes? I'm doing my job, some of us work u know lol lol lol ;-) But tell me now if something is wrong with duchy, OBVS

/NewScotGovtFMClearwater/blurts/
Wonderful to see the support for #JacksonsJourney and #Unclear-ances but we are hearing worrying reports that huge amounts of people are attempting to travel to Eigg to meet the journey team. Please be mindful of the #SWE restrictions in place and do not ask others to put themselves at risk or decrease critical services for our remote communities. Stay safe!

/RebeccaCampbell/blurtsTo/jacksonmcampbell
Private message Jackson who else can read this message? Reply if you can read this message and you are not my son.

/RoryTheTory/blurtsTo/MichaelTempletonGBEBS
Hi Michael, dm me if you need help, I'm at a MEGA rally just outside Gretna Green. We're protesting gaelic roadsigns clearwater has had put up on the New Scotland side of the border. So racist. My

eggcup will probably arrive when I'm away – sod's law!

/RoryTheTory/blurtsTo/RebeccaCampbell

Everyone can read your blurts you daft cow. If you want private messages use your message app. Folk like you are why scotland's in the shit. You and clearwater are an excellent example of why women should never have been allowed the vote.

/HannaNowaksMother/blurtsTo/RebeccaCampbell

Everyone can read your message, it is like I told you before.

/HannaNowaksMother/blurtsTo/RoryTheTory

You are an evil man. Stop being rude to women. You are a coward if you don't even use your photograph or proper name in your profile.

/RoryTheTory/blurtsTo/HannaNowaksMother

Go home to Poland no one wants you or your dirty children here.

/ZuzannaN/blurtsTo/RoryTheTory

You live in perthshire. You're one of 4 idiots in a meme doing the rounds of a MEGA protest at Gretna today. You're highly identifiable, you absolute weapon, and if you speak to my mother or anyone else's mother like that again you're going to have problems that are bigger than your cry wanking tissue pile, got it? #JacksonsJourney #Mega #MegaTwats #GBEBSTwats

/Deli-ciousOfCallander/blurtsTo/RebeccaCampbell

Hello Mrs Campbell, yes indeed, can read your blurts ☹☺

/TheJacksonCampbellAppreciationSoc/blurtsTo/RebeccaCampbell

Hi jackson's mum! If you would like blurt training we could come to your house and coach you!!! You are super cute with Jackson we love you #love #mummaLove #ShesACutie #QueenRebecca

/TheJacksonCampbellAppreciationSoc/blurts/

OK so not massively proud about getting on a boat with Templeton and Rabid Roy in an #SWE so sorry first minister, and you are such a babelicious legend, loving your work #Daniella #weLoveHerToo

**/ZuzannaN/blurtsTo/TheJacksonCampbellApprecia-
tionSoc**
Rabid roy's on Eigg? With GBEBS? Why? Why are you posting selfies of how badly you're dressed when you could be sharing decent
news? #JacksonsJourney

Niall crouched behind the wall at the end of the track and peeked between two stones to better see the back of the tiny houses. As he looked at the Transpariboard he blushed furiously and his burned skin stung painfully. His arms, face, and neck were now a bright lobster pink and since he'd stopped moving, the agony was making itself known. He'd run as far and as fast as he could and been rewarded for the effort of it all with the sight of the houses twinkling back at him, beckoning him onwards, from about fifteen minutes after passing the NSBC truck. Up close, the Transpariboard looked beautiful in the last of the afternoon's blazing sunshine, just as Drew had described. Yet, the opacity made his heart sink further; someone had discovered the privacy and shade available from tilting the material. It was painful enough that Transpariboard had been stolen but worse, somehow, that it had given up other secrets to a thief, too. A few metres in front of them, Jackson, Hanna and a guy Niall didn't recognise were sitting on the grass, their backs facing him.

They looked like models in a shoot, Niall thought, each of them contrastingly gorgeous – a gift he never saw in the mirror himself. Hanna's ponytail bobbed as she talked – she was happy, Niall could see, and the easiness of their reality compared to his felt like a slow punch to his gut. Further down the clearing, Gayle Wood stood looking out to sea. Her tablet had rung and she'd answered it, walking swiftly away from the others, closely followed by two small, glossy drones. Niall's wristband was going mad with vibrating notifications he was trying to ignore, but which made it seem likely that the call Gayle was taking was about him – Drew was closing in.

He removed his wristband, pushed it into a gap between stones in the wall, then whispered a countdown. When he stood, he could hear the trio's chatting more clearly. Hanna told Jackson to put on clothes; Jackson replied something about a piper, then a python. Niall couldn't make sense of it, but it made Hanna and their companion laugh.

Niall watched as they all leaned in to see the tablet the unknown guy was holding. Niall heard Hanna snort and the three set off giggling again. Jackson read out a blurt he'd sent his mum and they all laughed. It didn't make any sense that he felt excluded, Niall knew, given that he was spying on them, but a familiar feeling from before the recovery centre and before he'd become best friends with Hanna re-emerged; he was on the fringes of life, watching everyone else doing it effortlessly better.

He lifted one leg over the wall, then the other, and kept his eyes on Gayle – she seemed most likely to turn and spot him first. He took one slow step then another towards the back of the nearest house and as he moved the possibility of touching Transpariboard sent a rush of excitement up his spine. He moved stealthily, barely breathing, and with four more steps he was able to run a finger down the back wall as he drew his body in close behind the house, comforted by the thought that he was now significantly better hidden by the opacity of the board. He rested his forehead against the surface and felt it lean to where it was propped under the roof, angling away from him. A feeling of satisfaction spread through Niall as he realised Jackson must've done something wrong with the Transpariboard's manufacturing, causing it to lose its see-through quality.

Jackson's voice grew louder.

'All right, all right!' Niall heard him call, 'I'll get my onesie!'

A blur of movement in front of the houses froze Niall. The entire house jumped as Jackson slapped onto the floor inside.

'The fuck's that?' Jackson asked.

Niall drew back from the board and regarded Jackson's motionless outline. He looked huge, raised from ground level by the trailer beneath the house. Jackson's palms slapped the other side of the Transpariboard and Niall watched as the wall pushed towards him and the view inside the house became clear; Niall was now looking directly at Jackson's belly button beneath which was a tartan thong. Two quick clicks above his head sounded and Niall looked up to see Jackson staring down at him. Their eyes locked as Jackson moved like a mime artist, confusion and understanding crashing together on his face as he tried to take what he was seeing in.

'What is it, JC?' Hanna called.

Niall moved to see past Jackson's torso, watching as Hanna placed her book on the grass at her side then tightened her pony-tail. Down the clearing, he saw Gayle Wood seeming to look straight past the others, through the house and directly into his soul. Niall looked back to Jackson and found him backing away; one of Jackson's feet caught on the clothes and bedding strewn about the floor, making him lose balance. Jackson extended an oily arm backwards but slipped downwards, landing with a clatter on the side of a bike basket filled with bottles and food wrappers. The basket spilt its contents as Jackson's arse thumped the floor.

'JC?' Hanna appeared in the doorway.

'Niall,' Jackson whispered, 'Niall, I …'

Niall's face tingled as if someone was stabbing hot needles into his cheeks. His lips quivered where they stuck on the inside to his front teeth and his temples began pulsating almighty thuds of stress and dehydration-induced pain.

Hanna glanced at Niall as she moved to Jackson's side and crouched down, placing a hand on his shoulder. Then, slowly, her head raised, she looked at the back wall again, straight at Niall. She rocked backwards as a huge smile broke across her face and then collapsed. Niall caught a glimmer of his reflection on the wall and realised he looked wild, simultaneously hunted and predatory. He swayed to the side, his hands trying and failing to gain purchase. Hanna became blurry. Niall could hear her calling but the sight of her was fading; a black circle was closing in around everything until only a pinprick of light remained. He crumpled forwards so his cheek dragged down the Transpariboard when his legs gave way.

'Friction,' Niall slurred, feeling Hanna's arms encircling his stomach, attempting to take his weight. A long strand of grass tickled at his ear, then everything went dark.

Zach sat still scrolling his tablet, smirking at Templeton's his-trionics as he waited for the livestream to restart after what he presumed was a momentary signal drop. He pressed refresh again then looked up and saw Gayle running towards him.

'I've turned the livestream off,' Gayle said as she passed, clearly distressed, 'do not turn it back on or blurt anything, Zach.'

Alarmed, Zach twisted round and saw Jackson sitting bolt

upright inside his house, then Hanna and someone else's feet poking out from behind Jackson's tiny house.

'Help!' Hanna screamed, 'It's Niall! Help!'

Gayle grabbed her rucksack from underneath Hanna's house and began frantically searching for her first-aid kit. Zach leapt to Jackson's side, gasping when he saw Hanna cradling a stranger a few metres away while Jackson sat, shaking violently. He dashed back out of the tiny house and round to the back.

'Hanna, he might have a knife or something, I don't think you—'

'It's Niall!' Hanna interrupted, 'My best friend. Go to Jackson, Zee. I'm OK, promise.'

Zach nodded, then shot back inside the house and knelt between Jackson and the doorway. He squeezed Jackson's nearest hand.

'Jackson, what's happening?' he whispered, 'Did he hurt you?'

'I hurt him,' Jackson managed through chattering teeth, 'it was an accident.'

'Get Jackson warmed up, Zach,' Gayle called as she began helping Hanna put Niall in the recovery position.

'Shit!' Zach looked at Jackson again, 'You're in shock, yeah?'

Jackson looked like he wanted to reply but couldn't. Zach released Jackson's hand and snatched up a long-sleeved t-shirt from the floor, then carefully pulled it over Jackson's head, helping him feed his arms into the sleeves.

'Lean on the wall, man,' Zach tugged Jackson's kilt from under his feet and draped it over his shoulders as a warming shawl. A blanket lay near Jackson's other side. Zach grabbed it and shook it, sending crumbs flying through the tiny house. He spread the blanket over Jackson's legs then tucked his feet in at the bottom.

'There,' Zach said, 'it's all right, man, OK? I've got you. I'll get you a drink.'

Zach jumped back out of the house and darted to Gayle. He stared at where Niall lay on the grass, most of his body covered by a thin tin-foil blanket while Hanna rested a hand on his shoulder.

'What the fuck's going on?' Zach asked, 'Is this guy *mad*? No one's supposed to be round here!'

'Don't!' Hanna looked wounded, 'He's ill, Zach, remember?'

Zach gawped, uncomprehending.

'Wait. Both of you.' Gayle's eyes were watery and her voice

was quiet, completely missing its usual warm notes of confidence. Hanna and Zach stared at her. 'That call was from Drew,' Gayle continued, 'he was warning me that Niall was coming. Niall invented Transpariboard, it turns out. Jackson stole it from him and blended it with his idea about a tiny house. Niall was on a break from the recovery centre who had been working with him. He just found out about Jackson's Journey … and everything.'

Hanna gasped and looked in at Jackson. Jackson's hair fell forward, covering his eyes.

'I've taken the livestream down,' Gayle continued, 'apparently Templeton's here, on Eigg. He knows what's going down and no one knows where he is right now, he hasn't blurted in a while. Drew says the drone that's been with us since the launch is now out of action, I don't know how long for, there wasn't time to ask.'

Hanna and Zach looked at each other, horrified, then back to Gayle.

'Brace yourself, loves,' Gayle continued, 'I have no idea how this pans out. Let's just try to look after each other till some help arrives or we make a better plan, OK? Whichever comes first.'

Jackson's insides burned with shame while Gayle spoke. He wished with all of his heart that one of Transpariboard's qualities had been soundproofing, but unfortunately he could hear every word as if there were no barrier at all. Gayle, Hanna and Zach looked at him through the house's back wall, devastation and fear written over their expressions. He felt too ashamed to keep eye contact, so instead, he stared down at his shrouded groin. For the first time since they'd arrived, total silence cloaked Lower Grulin. Birds were grounded in the shade by the sun. No fire crackled and no chatter or commentary ebbed or flowed. A flashing from Jackson's wristband caught his eye − twenty-seven missed calls from his mum. His stomach ground tightly on his right side, making him wince with pain.

'I need the toilet,' Jackson whispered, removing the blanket then standing. He had stopped shaking, and for a second he thought he was going to be lucky enough to pass out as Niall had. Once he'd been upright for a few seconds, however, he found he seemed to be gaining consciousness rather than losing it; everything he looked at appeared more vivid than before; the sky was a gorgeous ombre of blue, grey and white stripes over the mainland. When he stepped out of the tiny house his movement was fluid but his mouth filled with saliva.

Jackson swallowed hard and his stomach spasmed. He quickened his steps as he made towards blackhouse number one, his buttocks clenched defensively as the tartan pleats of the kilt swung above them. Gayle cleared her throat then began giving calm instructions to Hanna and Zach about getting Niall into the shade. Tears salted Jackson's lips as he reached the single remaining wall of number one and disappeared behind it. He thumbed off his thong, leaving it hanging around one ankle, then crouched as the hot, liquid contents of his stomach rushed out of his behind, splattering his calves, the grass and the stones as it went. A powerful stench surrounded him, then was caught on a breeze.

He heard Hanna cough as the foul smell carried. When he was small, Jackson remembered that he'd seen a TV programme that said farts and faeces smells carried particles that could be breathed in. He'd told Roy and farted around him at every opportunity after that, thinking himself hilarious. His legs felt weak and brittle as he looked around and spotted the shovel he'd meant to carry to a private, out-of-the-way spot to dig a hole with. Someone had slipped a toilet roll over its handle. Hanna, probably, Jackson thought. He looked down at the mess underneath him and winced, then stood, carefully stepping out of his thong and pulling off a long strip of toilet paper. The more he wiped, the more the mess spread. He stuck the shovel into the grass, eased up a small section, pushed the dirty toilet roll underneath, then headed to the laundry burn to wash. As he went he chanced a look at the others and saw Niall was now upright; Zach was helping him into Hanna's house.

Hanna followed closely behind, but stopped and stared at Jackson first, then shook her head. Gayle was bent over her rucksack, selecting items from a first-aid kit and laying them carefully on the grass. Jackson looked up to the track and squinted. There was either a figure in the distance, or a tree. His heart quickened at the thought of Templeton; there was no NSBC truck or driveway gate to divide them now, like back in Edinburgh.

When he arrived at the laundry burn, he removed his clothes

and placed them at the water's edge, then stepped into the water and silently began washing. Finally, the smell disappeared. He set about loosening dirt from under one nail with another, rinsing his fingers in the water as he went, waiting for someone nearby to break the peace and begin screaming at him. The skirl of a buzzard's call above took him by surprise. He looked up and saw the bird's brown and cream underbelly; it was being pursued by three crows taking it in turns to grab the buzzard's tail feathers with their beaks. This was what was coming for him, Jackson thought, as he emerged from the water and pulled on his t-shirt. His wet skin resisted the material, making it bunch on his arms and neck until he gradually eased it into place. He buckled his kilt and watched as the buzzard looped, then changed direction towards the sea.

Satisfied with the flight path change, the crows split off, back towards the Sgùrr. Jackson watched the buzzard become a distant dot. Another breeze, colder than the last, split the tall bracken standing behind number six to reveal a parting at the base of their stalks where a skinny sheep track led away, presumably towards the cliffs or an alternative route to Upper Grulin. Jackson looked back to the tiny houses. They were no longer a team, Jackson thought – him, Gayle, Hanna and Zach. He had broken it. Now they were just people, divvied up by what was right and what – or who – was wrong.

Jackson looked around the clearing from one house to the next and realised he'd come full circle; this whole thing had started with panic and hopelessness, and now here he was, back there again. He tapped his wristband and scrolled the Jackson's Journey hashtag. It was full of people sharing a gif of Gayle taking the call from a perspective he hadn't seen – her expression went from a wide smile to crestfallen while he, Hanna and Zach sat behind her, happy. It felt like a lifetime ago. He scrolled on and saw blurt after blurt questioning why the livestream had gone off air. Some people posseted theories about the SWE arriving early or GBE interference. One of Templeton's recent blurts had enough shares for it to stay prominent in his feed. A hashtag and six words stood out to him. He read them over and over.

The idea that someone like Templeton had spotted his weaknesses made him feel shrivelled and small, too visible, too similar to the hollow parasite of a man pursuing him now. Jackson closed his eyes and Roy's face intruded into his thoughts. 'Lazy' Jackson remembered his father saying. Feral. He opened his eyes and looked across to the ruins of blackhouse number four. None of the Campbells there could've been lazy, Jackson knew now, not living in a place that necessitated so much work just to eat and sleep, never mind thrive. A numbness pushed from his stomach to his chest, then to his limbs and neck, then his head, feet and hands: what his dad had said was true. He loosened his wristband and crouched, feeling underneath the hanging grasses at the water's edge. There was mud on the shallow banking before the wide, flat stones at the bottom of the small pool. He pushed his wristband into it as far as it would go, severing himself from the comms link, then pulled his fingers out and rinsed them clean in the water. There was only one direction he could go in now, Jackson knew, everything had aligned perfectly to send him to where he uniquely deserved to be: to the very edge of the island. And down.

56

/ZuzannaN/blurts/

Where's the livestream gone? Why are we just getting repeats of highlights and shots of the sea? Has that motherfucker templeton scrambled the NSBC drone's signals?

/TheJacksonCampbellAppreciationSoc/blurtsTo/jacksonmcampbell

Omg jacksonmcampbell is obvs preparing something hilarious, cannot wait to see. It's probably a really cute dance challenge or something. He's defo going to round off in a totally lighthearted way #LoveThatBoy #Summer35

/MichaelTempletonGBEBS/blurts/

Patchy signal. If anyone can read this I've been duped by #RabidRoy and an immigrant. I fear immigrant will return to kill me. Am somewhere on heinous, barbarically brambled Isle of Eigg. Can only see trees, a loch. Other islands, ticks, midges. Total wasteland. I may die attempting to confront cancerous Campbells and bring justice that leads to the #reunification of the glorious #UnitedKingdom #GodSaveTheKing #NewScotlandKills #JacksonsJourney

rorythetory/blurtsTo/MichaelTempleton

Michael I'm being questioned by New Scottish police about hate speech. Robot retards or what? You can't say anything here anymore. It's obviously prejudiced because I'm a MEGA man. Something's happening with NSBC, their livestream's down. Maybe Clearwater's about to announce war on GBE? Maybe the journey was a distraction through MSM till she had weapons ready? #BeBravePatriots #RuleBritannia

Drew stood before holograms projecting from his tablet on the grass between the tumble-down wall of the ruins of the dwelling. The First Minister, Claudia and Fin were taking turns to question him. At the same time, Roy waited just outside the doorway of number nine, pacing and glancing nervously from where he'd been told Jackson had run into the bracken forty minutes before. Roy had interrupted the holo-meeting twice, insisting that he, not Drew, should take responsibility. But he'd been given terse, barely polite shrift from Daniella, then pointed firmly out by Drew.

Niall had already faced the holograms of Claudia and Fin. He'd reassured them he was in no immediate danger, and they'd agreed he'd be met by one of them on the mainland as soon as possible. Niall had cleaned his heart-rate sensor, put his wristband back in place, sans napkin, and then said his goodbyes when the First Minister's light signature began consolidating next to Claudia's. Drew and Niall had rushed apologies at each other, both feeling wretched about what they'd done to the other before Daniella came into full view and a mood change like a dark cloud formed over the blackhouse as Niall left to rejoin Hanna.

Seeing Niall worrying desperately about Drew, Hanna put him straight to work, helping her move the tiny houses down the clearing to avoid the worst of the pungent whiff of Jackson's diarrhoea being whipped around the upper area by crosswinds. Afterwards, they leant against the back of blackhouse number six, thoroughly worn out but still within earshot of Drew's bollocking.

'Poor Drew,' Niall winced, 'I fucked him over, didn't I?'

'You?' Hanna laughed, 'You did the only thing you could. What was your other option? Quietly lap it up and ask someone to send a polite blurt on your behalf? Fucking hell, Ny. I would've done everything you did in your shoes. Drew would've done everything you did in your shoes!'

'You think?'

Hanna nodded.

'Give yourself a break. He'll be OK. He just wanted to see the good in Jackson, didn't he? We all did, I guess.'

Niall gave a wry laugh.

'Because *I* told you to,' he said, shaking his head, 'fucking hell.'

Drew's volume grew, 'It's all on me. I'll resign. Course I will.

I've let them doon, all three of them, and you all, *and* New Scot-land. Christ, I'm *so* sorry!'

'Oh, for fuck's sake,' Niall winced, 'honestly, I feel like going back over there and telling them this is fucking with my mental health more than anything else is. Will I?'

'If they go on much longer,' Hanna replied, 'I'll join you. I can't handle it either.'

A rustling in the deeper green leaves of the track they'd watched Jackson run off on two hours before made Hanna and Niall stop, stock-still. Gayle appeared first from the bracken, fol-lowed by Zach. When Gayle saw Hanna and Niall staring at her, she quickly shook her head.

'We didn't find him,' Gayle said, 'we just got caught in a heap of bramble.'

Zach gestured to his bloodied legs beneath his shorts, then to Gayle's torn leggings.

'Any news here?'

Hanna shook her head.

'His wristband's still tracing to the pool at the burn. It must be in the mud somewhere. I tried to find it but … it just seemed pointless, poking about, getting filthy.'

'We tried heaps of ways through,' Zach continued, 'we got quite near the outer bit of Upper Grulin. We could just see a sliver of it, no more.'

'Then I thought I'd better phone the boss back at the station, touch base,' Gayle explained, 'and after that we tried to check in here, but nobody was on the comms link, so here we are. None the wiser. Much the bloodier.'

'Shit!' Hanna said, 'Sorry, I blocked my notifications. Blurt's going mad. I forgot it'd turn off our volume, too. Shit!'

'Don't worry, Hanna,' Gayle said, 'we need to clean ourselves up. And we need to eat. Has anyone made dinner?'

Hanna shook her head.

'You're looking better, man,' Zach smiled at Niall.

Niall blushed, embarrassed at his earlier lack of cool.

'Thanks'

'How did it go with your boss?' Hanna asked.

Gayle shrugged. She tried to force a smile, but it only made her look more exhausted.

'They're in touch with Bryce Cooper,' she said. 'Clearwater's cut me out of the loop, she went straight to the top of NSBC. Seems like any windows of negotiation I had with her about the journey are firmly shut – for now, anyway.'

Hanna winced.

'To her credit,' Gayle continued, 'any other politician would've gone to blame or bluff within seconds and thrown us right under the bus. But, typical Clearwater, she's going transparent. Telling it like it is, as far as she can, but mostly concerned about you two and Jackson. You're all EHA, after all. Her jurisdiction there far outweighs any flexibility we have as broadcasters. I just would've liked to have been in the room, as it were, when the decisions were being made.'

Hanna considered it, wide-eyed.

'Sorry, Gayle, that must feel weird, you've done so much work on this.'

'Ego,' Gayle shrugged, 'I'll get over it.'

'I can't believe the actual First Minister's shut down a livestream,' Niall said quietly, 'and that she's so, like, involved? We heard her absolutely roasting Drew, didn't we, Hanna? About us, and Jackson?'

Hanna nodded.

'She cares alright,' Zach nodded, 'EHA's her core policy. It's not just words with Clearwater. If I've learned anything about her she won't give a shit about the livestream or how any of it looks about her involvement, she'll just want to know everything's OK. Then once that's done she'll want you to max out Transpariboard, Niall. People first, planet second. That's the Clearwater way.'

'It's true,' Gayle agreed, 'Cooper's already got several legal folks letting GBEBS know that Templeton cannot share any info about your identity, Niall,' Gayle said, 'fingers crossed he respects that, hey?'

'Bloody hell,' Niall bit at his lip, then smiled, 'actually, I didn't tell Templeton my name. He asked, but I didn't tell him. He doesn't even know I know Hanna and Jackson. I just said about Transpariboard, I think …'

'Nice,' Zach high-fived Niall, then Hanna. The couple lingered for a second, squeezing each other's fingers lightly before letting go.

'Are they angry?' Hanna asked. 'Your bosses, with us? Or with you two?'

Gayle shook her head.

'The opposite,' Zach grimaced, 'the numbers it's bringing to past footage … folk are trying to spot Jackson lying, clues … no such thing as bad news when it comes to ratings. They're already talking about a follow-up documentary. Sorry, Niall, media can be so tactless.'

'It's OK,' Niall said, 'it's not really about me, is it? It's Jackson they're interested in.'

'Rabid Roy's trending again, too,' Hanna scrolled her tablet, 'it's kicked off a dastardly duo thing – evil father and son, master criminals. You can imagine.'

'And yet he seems like a teddy bear,' Gayle watched as Drew stepped out through number nine's doorway and was immediately handed a bottle of water by a highly anxious-looking Roy.

'Are your drones looking for Jackson?' Niall asked.

'Both of them,' Gayle tried and failed to stifle a yawn, 'and the ranger. Nothing yet.'

'The drones have finished this half of the island already.' Zach held his tablet up so the others could see a graphic of Eigg: data tags linked to a section of it half-shaded in grey and featuring detailed topography rings. 'I've set them to start on the other half. They've got thermal imaging turned on as well. I'll put on their night sights later,' Zach hesitated, 'if we still haven't found him by then.'

'The drone's AI profile for facial and outline recognition for Jackson is excellent,' Gayle said. 'They've mapped so much about him already. They'll pick him up if he's here to see, even as the light keeps fading, I'm sure of it.'

Drew and Roy joined them.

'Come and sit?' Hanna said, 'And would you both like a hoodie to wear? We've plenty –well – Jackson does. They're not the cleanest, but they're warm.'

'Thanks,' Drew glanced at Hanna then stared down at his boots.

'Something warm would be helpful,' Roy said, 'thank you so much.'

'I'll get them,' Zach said, then rushed to Jackson's house.

'I'm mortified,' Drew croaked, then looked at Niall. 'Again, I'm so sorry.'

Niall shook his head, instantly tearful.

'*I'm* sorry, Drew – for leaving you like that. It was a shitty thing to do. I should've just told you.'

'Naw,' Drew sniffed, 'it was my responsibility. Now listen, you've to rate your mood every hour for the centre, OK? They'll send you notifications unless you're sleeping.'

'OK. I will. I promise,' Niall replied.

As Zach returned, silence hung in the air. He handed Roy and Drew a hoodie each. Hanna pulled a canvas box bag from her house, placed it on the grass then knelt beside it. She lifted a sooty steel circular tray from it and began fanning out its edges. Roy recognised the fire tray he'd seen Jackson warm himself by so many times recently. He smiled, then looked up to tell Jackson that he knew what it was, but as he looked from face to face, it dawned on him again that his son was not there and, worse, no one now knew where he was. Roy pulled the hoodie over his head and various scents of Jackson enveloped him as he did so. His head-butted at a sleeve inside the garment until Drew moved the fabric a little, bringing the neckline into view.

'I guess we can't rule out him getting on a boat, can we?' Gayle asked, looking out to the sea where red, green and white lights on small boats were visible at wide intervals between Eigg and the mainland in the dusky sky. 'It is possible, isn't it? Look what happened with Roy and Niall – and Drew. He could've got to the pier and talked someone into taking him on board, couldn't he?'

'I didn't talk anyone into it,' Drew cleared his throat, 'I've got my EHA pass, so I'm allocated necessary transport in emergencies. Coastguard scooted me over.'

'Wow,' Gayle replied, 'that's quite a ticket, Professor.'

'He'll be cold, wherever he is,' Zach mumbled, scanning his tablet, 'the JJ hashtag's going mad. Folk all over the rest of the island are looking for him – staying away from the corncrakes so far, thankfully. My money's on the ranger sniffing him out, don't you think?'

'You talking about me?' an angry voice emerged between the ruins of numbers five and six. Drew and Roy both looked sheepishly at Calum.

'Ranger,' Drew said, 'sorry – about earlier, like. Had to be done.'

The ranger pulled his pipe from an inside jacket pocket.

'Sorry, are you? And yet here you are?' Calum scoffed at Drew, then eyed Roy, 'The daring duo.'

'Apologies, truly …' Roy started, 'I just—'

'Aye.' Calum interrupted, 'Save it. Folk do all sorts for their offspring. Beyond me, but there it is. A wiser decision would be to completely ignore them a week after they've fledged, like birds, but few folks do that.'

Niall blinked hard. Something about Calum reminded him of his parents. He watched as Calum lit his pipe, sucked hard, then tilted his head back and blew out a long puff of smoke.

'Ten years,' Calum lamented, 'ten years it's taken to get corn-crakes here again, then this shite kicks off. We'll just have to hope to bugger and back that we've done enough for them to return next year, won't we? Some chance, though. Poor bloody things don't know whether they're coming or going, thanks to the weather. I hope you're all proud of your legacy of destruction if they don't return. Just so some attention-seeking maniac could run about half-naked for a few days.'

Gayle stared at Calum while everyone else looked to where Hanna shrouded burgeoning flames with her hands. Roy broke the silence.

'I'm going to go looking for Jackson.'

'Ha!' Calum interjected, 'The cliffs are nearer than you think, Grampa. You can bring your tech and fancy ways all you like, but you better not wander around in the evening without know-ing where you're going in the Highlands. I don't know if you've noticed, but no streetlights are coming on here anytime soon.'

A surge of rabidity flashed in Roy as he regarded Calum, then dissolved itself. Where so recently he would've seen an adversary, now he simply saw a deeply unhappy individual.

'We had a Dalmatian chase a tennis ball straight off the edge of the Sgùrr last year,' Calum continued, 'shame. Young dog, too. Deaf – a lot of them are – it's the white pigmentation over their eardrums. It's genetically incompatible with hearing. Fascinating. Fatal too, in that case, because it couldn't hear its owner scream-ing for it to come back. And they say most animals have good instincts about danger. Reality is, often, they, or we, don't.'

'Let's be positive,' Gayle cut in, 'I know you're angry, Calum, after all your work, but right now we need solutions, not more problems. Please.'

Calum stuck his pipe in the corner of his mouth and regarded Gayle, then removed it and tapped its contents into the fire.

'The dug's body was never found,' Calum continued, 'come to think of it, what is that smell around here? The stupid owners never had him microchipped. I suppose he might've made a good meal for an eagle. Maybe parts of the body are up on a nest some-where. Or in the sea. Or maybe the eagle dropped it up there, in the bracken. Something's honking, anyway.'

'*Gordon Bloody Bennett!*' Roy cried, frantically patting down his pockets.

'Now, wait, Roy,' Gayle stepped towards Jackson's father, the thought that he might not only still be rabid but also somehow armed, now worrying her, 'he's being deliberately toxic, Roy, ignore him – please—'

'No! *No!*' a huge smile broke over Roy's face. At last, he found his phone in a chest pocket underneath the hoodie and pulled it out, immediately pressing the quick dial to Rebecca and putting the call on speaker.

'Microchipping!' Roy laughed, reaching out and squeezing Gayle's arm with his free hand.

'Microchipping?' Gayle repeated.

'Roy?' Rebecca's voice was anxious when she picked up, 'What's going on? Have they found him?'

'Jackson's microchipped!' Roy laughed, 'I can't believe I forgot! Becs, you just need to look up the website – then we'll have his location in minutes!'

'Well, *that's* not legal,' Calum muttered.

Gayle ignored Roy's outburst and stared into the flames of the fire, thinking of Ash and Rowan. She rocked slowly back and forth as she did so, the muscle memory of holding them as babies soothing her. Soon, she told herself she'd be back to normality, at home with her children, making sandwiches for their lunch and shouting about laundry. Maybe she'd request a desk job then, she thought, or a role with just one on-screen appearance a week so that she could spend the rest of her time researching. Alone.

Never again dealing with the idiosyncrasies of human stories. Especially those stories playing out in real-time with her as a cast member in a mad ensemble.

'Sorry,' Rebecca said, 'speak up. I thought you said Jackson was microchipped there. What a disgusting thought. What's happening, Roy? Tell me quickly?'

'Darling,' Roy laughed awkwardly, 'I *did* say that. It's not that bad a thing to do, surely?'

Drew gaped at Roy.

'It's a *terrible* thing, Roy!' Drew scolded, 'Bloody heinous!'

Roy blushed hard, looking around in vain for an expression of support from one of the others.

'Roy?' Rebecca barked.

'Yes. Well. Um, darling, remember when Duchy was microchipped?'

'Roy!' Rebecca breathed, '*No!*'

'Yes, well,' Roy looked to Calum when he heard him snort and saw the ranger was adoring the tension.

Zach cocked his head and met Hanna's eyes. She smiled, then looked at Niall. They each had to look away to suppress inappropriate laughter. Niall pulled his hoodie over his head and buried his chin in the collar.

'Well, it seemed prudent at the time,' Roy explained, still partly sure he was in the right. 'Jackson had just turned eighteen, and he was AWOL constantly, wasn't he? The drinking, the party drugs ... and, well, darling, you see, Jackson was almost completely comatose. He'd just got in the door and flopped onto his beanbag. He'd started snoring, and ... well ... it seemed *opportune*, sensible, even. No?'

Rebecca gasped, followed by the sound of a splash and the smash of her glass hitting the hallway tiles.

'It was David who helped, remember David?' Roy forged on, trying not to stammer. 'The older vet – retired the year after, golf chap – wife's an elder at the church. Pam? Patty, was it? Penny?'

'Patricia,' Rebecca whispered.

'Yes!' They did all their children too,' Roy said, 'he said everyone would be doing it soon enough. And I got a discount – a buy one get one free, almost, because of Duchy.'

'Decent ID for the polis, here,' Calum nodded to Zach, 'I hope you're recording on one of your gizmos, are you? About time more rich folk ended up in jail.'

'Lovely family,' Roy said, growing increasingly pink.

'Lovely?' Rebecca wheezed, 'People who microchip children in the neck? *Lovely?*'

'It's in Jackson's ankle,' Roy grew quieter, 'it was jutting out. You know how he lies. We snuck up. He only woke briefly, thought Duchy had bitten him a little, that was all. Sharp scratch—'

'Are you bloody well microchipped?' Rebecca screeched, '*Am I?*' The sound of Rebecca slapping at the skin on her collarbone came through the speaker.

'Of course not!' Roy replied. 'Listen, darling, please, look up Duchy's folder on the iPad. Inside that, there's a subfolder called … well, it's called … *Damien.*'

Calum burst out laughing over Rebecca's silence.

'There's a link you can press to locate the chip immediately,' Roy said, 'it'll give you coordinates, then you can send them to me. Isn't it wonderful, given the circumstances?'

'Glorious,' Rebecca replied, then hung up.

57

/MichaelTempletonGBEBS/blurts/

BREAKING: I will shortly live broadcast a FILTHY secret
Clearwater intends to take to her grave about #JacksonsJourney.
Want to know the truth about why the livestream's off? Tune into
#GBEBS now! #MEGA #DirtyDaniella #RabidRoy #JailboyJackson

/NewScotGovtFMClearwater/blurts/

1/3 It is with huge sadness that we must advise that we were mis-
informed about the origins of Transpariboard™ design. Transpar-
iboard™ does not belong to jacksonmcampbell, and he did not
have permission from the owner to develop and use the material.
This information recently came to light on Eigg and immediately
triggered the correct response of the #JacksonsJourney livestream
being turned off.

/NewScotGovtFMClearwater/blurts/

2/3 Even more regrettably, the discovery of this information has
led to the disappearance of Jackson, which I am extremely concerned about, as are Jackson's parents and team on Eigg. Ample &
experienced research resource has been deployed around Lower
and Upper Grulin, so please, if you are on the island, do not travel
to those areas. Instead, we would appreciate assistance in locating
Jackson elsewhere on the island with the singular goal of making
sure he is safe and well at this time.

/NewScotGovtFMClearwater/blurts/

3/3 As you know, my government prides itself on transparency, and
we will not deviate from that in difficult times. However, our policy
does not extend to sharing details of private lives without explicit
consent. The inventor of Transpariboard™ will not be available for

comment, and any efforts to breach their privacy will be met with the full force of the New Scottish Humanitarian Justice & Equalities Act. We also ask that people respect the Campbell family's privacy. I will make an update statement as soon as possible. For now, I repeat, the well-being of Jackson (and all involved parties) is key. Stay safe.

/NSBCJourney/NewScotland /blurts/

NSBC thanks the First Minister for her remarks regarding developments on #JacksonsJourney and echoes her sentiment that our priority at this time is finding Jackson safe and well. Journey footage from before today's events is available on #NSBCWatch, and we will be sharing your own stories of #Unclearance on the livestream channels until we have an update. Vlog us now!

/ZuzannaN/blurts/

No. No. No. No. OMG. He tried to tell me something was wrong. I mean, he's a fucking dick too, obviously, but. Shit! I think I talked him into making this thing worse without even realising it. ☹☹☹

/TheJacksonCampbellAppreciationSoc/blurtsTo/ ZuzannaN

omg we could've thrown templeton off the boat and we didn't. It's our fault! And now we can't find him! jacksonmcampbell if you are reading this reach out, we will never let you down ☹☹☹

/MichaelTempletonGBEBS/blurts/

GBEBS can now exclusively confirm that Transpariboard™ was stolen from a mysterious man, possibly Russian, and that said man is now loose on the island, almost certainly threatening Jackson's life. Is RabidRoy armed? Probably. Clearwater's stupidity has created a perfect storm of vile New Scottish toxicity. What else will she do if she pokes the Russian bear so stupidly? Vote in my poll #MEGA #ReUnion #DirtyDaniella

/MichaelTempletonGBEBS/blurts/

Calling all true patriots on the island of Eigg! I require collection and shelter for the night. I am beside a stile and a large stand of approximately thirty pinus sylvestris. Two large raptors are circling overhead. A post box is lying on its side behind a dry stane dyke some twelve feet away from me. Please note I cannot share accommodation with animals. A simple fayre of a ploughman's or a steak and ale pie will suffice for supper. I shall also require to charge my equipment. #AriseKnightsOfTheRealm #ReUnion #Accommodation #Help

/HannaNowaksMother/blurts/
Have they found him yet? This is very bad. A mother's nightmare. I am thinking of you, RebeccaCampbell x

Drew messaged the First Minister and the recovery centre to update them on Roy's revelation, then rejoined the group huddling around Gayle's laptop. The microchipping data map on the screen zoomed progressively faster until New Scotland was at the centre of the screen, then Eigg, then the lochs at the top of the island, then the Sgùrr. The egg-timer icon spun over the basalt blackness for a few seconds, then the zooming began again, this time with a small icon of a dog's head flashing down and over Upper Grulin, which then closed in on a point on the south coast of the island. The dog's head spun, then hovered over the land before it moved a few millimetres and hovered over the sea, then back over the land. The digital hokey-cokey continued, refusing to settle. Roy watched, then began pacing, desperate to hear one of the others say the icon had stopped, far inland.

'How accurate is this?' Drew asked.

'Within twenty metres, it says,' Gayle replied.

'Well, that's not good, is it?' Calum said. Hanna's eyes widened and Drew winced, struggling to restrain a bigger reaction.

'What?' Calum shrugged, 'It basically says he's jumped off the cliffs and landed on the rocks, or he's in the Massacre Cave, doesn't it? Or maybe he jumped off the cliffs, landed on the rocks, then got washed into the Massacre Cave by the tide. I'll check my tide table.'

'That's where the Massacre Cave is?' Zach shot back, 'Right there?'

'Of course,' Calum replied, 'where else would it be? Honestly. Townies.'

'I'll message the coastguard,' Drew said, 'I'll ask them to check the water right away.'

'What will the temperature be in a deep cave?' Gayle asked.

Calum opened his mouth to reply, but Zach interrupted.

'At least ten degrees below the outside temp. It's gonna feel cold to him, whatever it is, after how hot we've been the last couple of days.'

Gayle passed her laptop to Drew, stood and grabbed her rucksack.

'I've got a thermal blanket here, rehydrating shots,' she pulled out her first-aid kit again. 'I say we head down now. He could get hypothermic fast, couldn't he?'

Drew and Zach nodded.

'You think he's in the cave?' Roy looked terrified.

'I do,' Gayle smiled at Roy, 'I think he's hiding, Roy. Call it a hunch.'

'Me too,' Zach placed a hand on Roy's shoulder, his voice soft, 'there are cliffs all the way along this coast, Roy. Jackson knows that, we studied the maps before we left. The way to Massacre Cave's signed. We saw it on the way here. It made an impression on him – on all of us.'

'We have to go now,' Roy said, glad when Zach withdrew his touch, 'you said he wasn't wearing much, didn't you, Gayle?'

'He was sunburned, though,' Niall interjected. The others stared at him, 'I'm still roasting,' Niall explained, 'literally, you could fry an egg on my neck right now, even with the three litres of after-sun Hanna's put on it. If I hadn't had after-sun and something to drink, my core temperature would be higher, wouldn't it?'

Drew raised his eyebrows, 'Can't rule it out,' he said, 'but now, Gayle? It's getting late. I wouldnae like any of us to have an accident, know what I mean? And Roy's maybe no the best dressed for it.'

'I'll walk yous there,' Calum sighed grudgingly, 'I know the quickest way. But it'll take the best part of two hours with his fitness.' Calum indicated Roy with his pipe. 'You'll only go without me anyway, no doubt,' he continued, 'and you'll have to stay in my exact tracks, got it?'

'Much obliged,' Roy nodded at Calum.

'Roy, what size are your feet?' Zach asked.

'Eleven,' Roy replied, 'why?'

'I'll get you Jackson's boots,' Zach nodded at Roy's brogues, 'you need safer footwear than that.'

'I'll get them,' Hanna said, 'two minutes, Roy.'

'Drew, I think you should stay here with Niall and Hanna,' Gayle said, 'I think Roy and I should go. And Calum. He knows the land best. And you and Hanna and Niall know each other best. And, well, Jackson's scared of you, I think.'

'I wouldnae say he was scared of me,' Drew frowned, 'a healthy respect, aye, but scared? Surely no?'

'He is scared of you, Drew,' Hanna said quietly, 'sorry.'

'Oh,' Drew blushed, 'I'm mortified about that. Jesus. Right, well, don't worry. I'll be here with Niall and Hanna. And I'll stay in touch with Holyrood and the coastguard.'

'Thanks, Drew.' Gayle smiled sympathetically.

'What about me?' Zach asked.

'Stay here for the comms,' Gayle said, 'keep double-checking what the drones are reporting, look at every facial recognition they encounter, triple check anyone his height. I can't do that safely on the move. You'll have your tech, I'll have mine. It's the safest cover for everyone. And there's a chance he'll come back while we're away. *If* that happens, you and I will feel more neutral to him, won't we, compared to everyone else? One of us as part of the reception party wherever he might be is a good thing.'

'Shit,' Zach considered it, 'yeah.'

'Ideally, I'd like you all to start to head to the pier, given the SWE,' Gayle continued, 'but I think we hold out a camp here for now. Rock and a hard place, isn't it, weighing up the options?'

'These are good calls, Gayle,' Drew said, 'I admire your presence of mind.'

Gayle glanced at Calum, then back at Drew.

'I don't always make good calls, I can assure you,' she said, raising an eyebrow, 'but thank you, I appreciate your support.'

Drew gave a half nod.

Zach scrolled his tablet then held it out to show Calum Templeton's last blurt.

'Do you recognise that description?' Zach asked, 'where do you think he might be, roughly?'

'There's only two stiles on the island' Calum shrugged, 'as the crow flies, one's about two miles away. The other's about five

369

miles, by the forestry above Laig.'

'Shit,' Zach replied, 'I don't like the sound of the one that's closer. He could be approaching by now?'

'Only if he's a crow,' Calum laughed, 'if he's attempting that route he's to cross the top of the island, walk round the back of two lochs *and* come over the Sgùrr. He'll no be here anytime soon, I promise you that. Especially not in the dark.'

Though Calum thought this amusing, the possibility that Templeton's desperation might put him in real danger fettered the others' relief.

'I'll let Clearwater know,' Drew said quietly.

Hanna handed Roy Jackson's boots then offered a bike helmet to Gayle.

'Online tourist reviews say the cave ceiling has caused some injuries,' Hanna explained, 'I looked it up the other night. You best take this in case you need to go in.'

'I'll be the one going in,' Roy heard himself say, 'it's my fault he's in there, ultimately. I should've done better with parenting. A lot better. So it's my responsibility to get him out – with no rabidity at all.'

58

/ZuzannaN/blurts/

So when are they putting the livestream back on? Tonight? Tomorrow? What's the fricking deal, hannanowak and nsbc? You can't just leave us hanging ☹

/Deli-ciousOfCallander/blurts

Given the difficult circumstances now taking place with #Jacksons-Journey we're releasing the recipe for Coco Pop Slices and starting a comp to keep us all busy until there's an update. Send us pics and we'll pick a winner in two days. Go wild! The prize is a hamper full of organic bannocks and fifty euros to the eco charity of your choice! #BakeLove #StayBusy #TogetherWeRise(bread)

/TheJacksonCampbellAppreciationSoc/blurtsTo/jacksonmcampbell

Bb let us know if you need an escape. We got here on sheer determination, we can get you out too. DM. We have started a GoFundMe for a helicopter, just in case.

Calum and Gayle placed torches by the entrance to the Massacre Cave. It was little more than a metre high and about half of that in width, narrowing as it disappeared into the blackness beyond. The opening was flanked on one side by large tufts of grass and colossal bracken leaves which hung like ominous black feathers in the moonlight. On the other side, the wet, mottled rock of the cliff's exposed face was juxtaposed with the silhouettes of delicate-looking wildflowers that had somehow managed to secure roots in the pebbled foreshore. Tangles of odorous, slippery black seaweed lay in sodden clumps between grasses and rocks. Roy looked at them and realised that when high tide came, the place they now stood would be underwater. He bent and squatted by the entrance. Adrenaline was now blocking his awareness of pain from his hips and feet and he was glad of it as he leant one hand on the rock while the other tugged the helmet strap a little looser under his chin. He took a last look at Gayle, aware she was holding back on rushing him while he gathered his nerve. Calum had moved to about twenty metres further back, scanning the water with a pair of night binoculars where the sea slapped at the rocky shoreline.

'You sure you're OK with this?' Gayle frowned.

The entrance to the tunnel preceding the first chamber was much smaller than she'd imagined and the few slips Roy had already had on the steep path, hair-pin-bending down the cliff-side minutes before had given her cause for concern. Roy met Gayle's eyes with what he hoped passed for competent determination.

'Here,' Gayle held out comms magnets for him to attach to his earlobe. 'Tell me as soon as you see him.'

Roy looked at the magnets. He had no idea how to wear them. Gayle separated them and gently positioned them on Roy's lobes. His skin throbbed a little as they gripped, then they felt imperceptible.

'OK?' Gayle asked.

Roy realised he could now hear Gayle via the magnets as well. He gulped.

'Say something,' Gayle urged, 'test them from your end.'

Roy cleared his throat, watching as Gayle placed fingertips over her earlobes.

'Testing?' he said, 'Testing, testing, one, two, three.'

'Perfect,' Gayle nodded, 'well done.'

It was time, Roy realised, and his breath was buffering with trepidation. He looked into the tunnel, then reached up and switched on the head torch Gayle had attached to the helmet. Then, slowly, he manoeuvred onto his knees and began the crawl over the cold, hard stones. He hadn't gone far when a loud scrape issued from the top of the helmet and made Roy gasp, drawing back, then lowering his head and spine further. Gratitude for Hanna's foresight swirled with regret in his thoughts. How on earth could he have thought he was up to this? He was an ageing man, decrepit compared to the people he'd kept company with all day. Who was he kidding, Roy asked himself; just because he'd managed a bit of decent skiing recently, why would that make him capable of negotiating his brittle carcass on all fours over increasingly slime-coated bulges of hardened lava?

'Focus, Roy,' Gayle's voice sounded in his earpiece, 'you're doing great. Really, you are. I'm right here.'

Roy swallowed back snot and realised he was crying.

'Jackson?' Roy's voice cracked into the black space ahead. The cave replied with three loud drips of water. Damp whiffs of decomposing kelp accompanied by a note of a fishmonger's doorway hung in the thick air around him. Roy dipped his head, hoping to catch a fresher inhalation from behind. As he did so, he heard Gayle say something, her voice quieter than before, then a murmured answer from Calum. They were speaking to each other, not him, he realised. A jolt of panic shot through Roy's chest. What if Drew and Niall and Clearwater and NSBC had secretly decided on a plot to rid New Scotland of the problematic Campbells forever?

'Roy?' Gayle spoke up, her tone soft, 'Anything?'

Roy spluttered a breath and wished he dared take one of his hands off the cave floor to slap some sense into himself.

'Nothing. Yet,' he replied, then crawled again. Roy copied the note in Gayle's question as he continued, 'Jackson, son?'

The acoustics had changed, he noticed. Now his voice seemed to cast back the slightest echo and the foul odour had given way to clearer air, dampening his nostrils and lips. He looked up and the torchlight revealed the top of the tunnel now flared away from him. The fronts of his trousers were soaked through, as were the hoodie's cuffs and hanging neckties. His right hand touched a ledge of rock which felt almost steplike. He looked up again and saw the lumpen black of the first large chamber before him as he crossed it. Awestruck, he unfurled himself to standing, joints clicking and complaining as he did so.

His breath felt short and a warning of cramp from his calves alerted Roy to his toes gripping wildly at the soles of Jackson's boots. He stretched out his fingers and toes then wiggled them.

'Be calm, Roy,' he said as a loud drip splatted, unseen. He raised a hand to his chest and felt his heartbeat, the muscle of it strong and resonant even through the layers, just like when he'd played rugby as a teenager. The thought reassured him. He looked around and wondered how many other Campbells had stood where he stood now over the years. And how many might have died here, too?

A memory of the gynaecologist who had overseen Rebecca's pregnancy with Jackson bloomed in his mind. Bizarrely, she had also been a Campbell – had she visited Eigg? He remembered they'd made small talk about whether they might be related, though he'd assumed she, like him, not to be genuinely curious. Roy stared around the cave, then remembered how the doctor had pressed a finger to her lips and turned the volume up on the doppler machine. The sound of Jackson's heartbeat inside of Rebecca's body had filled their glossy white, private hospital suite.

'You can hear his heartbeat,' the doctor had said, 'and one of the only things he can hear at the moment is Rebecca's heartbeat.'

The statement had blindsided Roy. It was the first time he'd understood a real child was on the way. And now here he was in a cave, a womb-like space, holding Jackson and himself and all Campbells, somehow. A shiver crossed his body. He cast another look around, emboldened, and took a few steps forward.

'Jackson,' Roy said again, surprised at the difference in how his son's name sounded when it was said quietly, 'please, Jackson. Your mother ... your mother and I ... we're both very worried about you. I promise you're not in trouble.' Roy hesitated. 'Not with us, anyway.' A low shooshing followed by a light buzz fed through the comms link.

'Just ignore that feedback,' Gayle said quietly.

'Right,' Roy sighed, then remembered a phrase Gayle had told him as they'd hiked closely behind Calum's lead to the cave, saying he might find it useful. 'Jackson,' Roy sounded firmer, 'I'm on your side.'

More drips sounded. Roy listened and found they no longer scared him.

A small sob came from the back of the cave, far beyond where Roy stood.

'I've heard him, Gayle!' Roy whispered, then stepped forward, his foot sliding into a puddle.

'Oh,' Gayle breathed, 'thank God. I'll message your wife.'

Roy scanned the cave floor to see where he might pick a better path.

'Here's the thing, Jackson,' Roy took baby steps as he spoke, 'I'm not the young chap I once was. I'm not wearing brogues, thank goodness. First time in years not wearing them, apart from skiing boots. Or golf shoes. No matter. I've been given your boots, as it happens, Gayle's got your training shoes for you. The ranger kindly told me on the way down here that the last person on the island who was wearing brogues almost died three times. So, well, there it is. Strange chap, isn't he?' Roy stopped to lean on the cave wall to his right. The changing air pressure and his nervous chatter made him lightheaded; he breathed deeply through his nose and waited to steady. A deep sniff came from the same direction as the sob.

'Why are you here, Dad?' Jackson croaked, 'I'm feral, remember? A parasite. Leave me alone. I'm done.'

Roy's gaze shot in the direction Jackson's voice had come from. Adrenaline kicked in more as his brain whirred, triangulating; forward, forward, left, left. He crouched and looked back to where he'd come from. The torch beam struggled to find the tunnel out of the cave.

'If I'm honest,' Roy tried to keep his tone measured, 'I'm having epiphany after epiphany, Jackson. Despite this mess, I'm glad you had the idea to go on this journey, to see your land – *our* land. Poor buggers, weren't they? But in some ways so much richer than us, I think.' The floor became even more uneven, and Roy slowed, negotiating each step with extreme caution. 'You're not feral, Jackson. Or a parasite. I cannot express enough how deeply I regret those words.' The sound of Jackson's breathing now seemed distant and simultaneously very close. Roy tilted his head. Had he gone the wrong way?

'Watch your head, Dad,' Jackson said.

Roy ducked slightly, then cautiously looked up. A section of cave ceiling like an upside-down bridge hung above him.

'It opens out again in a minute,' Jackson explained.

'Jolly good,' Roy replied, trying to sound calm while his heart leapt.

The torchlight had found Jackson. He was huddled on a

ledge just metres away, hiding his eyes from most of the glare by peeking through his fingers. His kilt shrouded his entire body, his knees drawn up underneath it so only his head, hands and toes protruded from the tartan. Straggly, wet hair hung on either side of his face. Roy pushed the torch upwards and blinked back tears. With just a few more steps the cave ceiling would soar above him.

'Actually, you do look a bit like Jesus!' Roy said, his eyes crinkling at the sides.

'Is it the cave?' Jackson asked, 'He had one, didn't he?' Jackson coughed harshly.

Roy made instantaneously towards him while releasing a water bottle Drew had clipped to the back of his cords. A muffled laugh came and then went through the comms link as Roy held the bottle out and Jackson's hand appeared through the flap of his kilt to grab it. Roy listened as Jackson glugged, his breath rasping when he finished.

'What are you doing here, Dad?' Jackson asked.

'Fancied a stroll,' Roy lowered himself to sit by Jackson's side, 'came to see if there was a golf course, turns out there isn't. Shame.' Dampness from the stone ledge seeped through Roy's trousers to his underpants. He shifted his weight from one buttock to another, then, realising nothing helped, surrendered to it and leant back.

'Why aren't you shouting?' Jackson asked.

Roy sighed.

'I'm not shouting because I'm sure a lot of this is the fault of my shouting, Jackson, so more shouting would be pointless and cruel. I've been watching the livestream, you see. I saw something was upsetting you, believe it or not. I saw myself, too … not so much in you, but in … I don't know … the distance between us, perhaps? I thought … well. Then I thought I'd lost you. Forever.' Roy reached into his pocket for his handkerchief, then remembered he'd given it to Drew. He hesitated, then wiped his nose along the sleeve of Jackson's hoodie. Jackson watched, shocked.

'Are you? Have you dressed up as … as *me*?'

Roy gave a little laugh.

'No. I came unprepared. They – your friends – they let me borrow things. It's turning cold out there now. Not as cold as in here though, I imagine, for you anyway. I'm a tad hot after the crawling.'

'I'm all right,' Jackson lied.

'Well, your mother's beside herself,' Roy said, 'and your friends. Drew McAllister, too. They're all worried. Your fans on the Blurt are doing all sorts. Some piper is wearing mourning clothes, Zach said. I must say I find that very uncouth. If your mother sees that she'll be distraught.'

'I bet there are dog shits out there that are more popular than me right now,' Jackson replied.

'A striking vision,' Roy raised an eyebrow, 'strange thing is, well, they *talk* about their feelings a lot, don't they?'

'Who?' Jackson asked.

'All of them,' Roy replied, 'It's been that way through the whole journey, hasn't it? Even the First Minister, when you listen to her properly. Very … candid. Honest, I suppose? Very different to how I was brought up, I must say.'

'Me, too,' Jackson replied.

'We've rather got you into a corner here, haven't we?' Roy tutted, 'In all senses. But the feelings stuff doesn't *seem* to harm them, I'll say that for it. There's a Burns poem that keeps springing to mind, some tutor force-fed us it at school, if I recall correctly. He was let go soon afterwards, your grandfather complained to the headmaster that we should've been doing proper poetry, as I recall. English poetry. Anyway. "To see ourselves as others see us", something like that.'

Jackson thought about it.

'I don't think I've ever seen myself any other way,' he said, 'that's what social media's all about, isn't it? Making an identity folk want to see. I'm always thinking about making folk laugh and stuff.'

'Hmm,' Roy murmured, 'I didn't realise how we – and here I mean, me, you, your mother – I didn't realise what was happening to us as a family, how far apart we'd all grown, not until we'd reached a precipice, excuse the pun, I didn't see any of it until I saw *you* on the television.'

Roy listened to Jackson's breathing and wondered if his son's silence was approving or reproachful. The latter seemed highly likely. He braced for an onslaught, but instead, Jackson shuffled a little, then laid his head on Roy's shoulder, his exhaustion drawing him hypnotically to the warmth of his father's body. Unlike Roy and Zach's touch, physical contact with his son felt natural, welcome, even.

'How am I going to face them, Dad?' Jackson whispered, 'I don't do real-life, do I? I'm scared.'

Roy took a deep breath as he pondered an answer.

'How did you face climbing into a cave packed with several hundred ghosts, son?'

'On my knees,' Jackson said, then blew his nose loudly on his kilt, 'with my eyes shut and a draught up my arse.'

Roy smiled. Jackson, his son, *was* funny. Even now. Rebecca used to say Roy was too, he remembered, when they'd first met.

'Well then,' Roy clapped his hands, 'that sounds like humility to me. We could both give it a go if you like?'

'If it doesn't work, can we run off to France?' Jackson sniffed, 'Live in the chalet?'

'An excellent plan,' Roy said, then froze when a flapping started above them, then stopped. He listened as a brief chatter of almost imperceptible squeaking began, then silenced. Roy touched the comms magnet, scared it was malfunctioning and might somehow electrocute him.

'Bats,' Jackson said, 'I think they've shat in my hair quite a lot.'

Roy's shoulders tensed. A strong urge to itch in several places propelled him back to standing.

'I'd quite like to go now,' Roy said. Jackson stayed perfectly still. 'Jackson, son, bear this in mind too,' Roy went on, 'every person keen to speak to you about this, well, everyone apart from that arse Templeton – and maybe the ranger – all the other ones … they're all, how shall I put it? They're sensitive people in the nicest possible sense, aren't they? Snowflakes, we used to call them.'

'What about Drew? And Niall?' Jackson asked, 'Are they going to kill me?'

'They aren't,' Roy replied. 'Drew feels terrible, thinks it's all his fault. He offered to resign to Clearwater. And Niall, you'll have to work on that, Jackson. I won't lie. He trusted you, liked you. You must do your best to repair it and accept it's fair if he can't forgive you.'

'Innit?' Jackson whispered. 'You know, with Drew, when I felt like I *hadn't* let him down, when this all started, when he thought I'd done some good stuff – it was nice, you know?'

'I think he'd like to hear that, Jackson.'

Roy watched as Jackson removed the kilt from around his shoulders then fixed it about his waist. He pushed his hair behind his ears afterwards, revealing a long graze at the top of his forehead. Roy unfastened the helmet and gently placed it on Jackson's head, then refastened the strap.

'Do you think I'll go to jail, Dad?'

'I don't think so,' Roy shook his head, 'Some of it was your idea, wasn't it? The houses? The journey?'

Jackson nodded solemnly.

'Well,' Roy shrugged, 'surely that counts too, doesn't it? And surely that therapist of your mothers – what was he called? Shaw? He could vouch for the strain you were under at home. The rectangle of hate, was it?'

Jackson looked hopeful.

'And we could ask Gayle to help,' Roy said, 'she's very good with … well, with people, isn't she? And the journey was your idea, yes?' Jackson nodded. 'Well, Gayle could vouch for that too, perhaps?' Roy remembered Gayle was on the comms link, 'Could you, Gayle?'

'Sure,' Gayle replied. Her voice was quiet but clear enough for Jackson to overhear.

'Let's see if we can't come up with something that suits everyone,' Roy continued, 'Drew said you can have time in a recovery centre if you like. I'd quite like to trace more Campbells, too. There must be a nice one, somewhere.'

'Has Gayle heard everything?' Jackson asked.

'Yes,' Roy replied, 'Gayle had to relay to your mother as soon as I found you. Everything's confidential though, apart from that.'

Gayle, listening outside the cave, winced.

'Roy, I'm sorry,' she cut in, 'I didn't realise until you two talked that the comms link was open to the team. Zach and Hanna have probably heard too, maybe the others. They might've thought we were sharing intentionally. I tried to turn it off at one point, but you started getting feedback. I thought it was best to let it be rather than interrupt and tell you. I'm so sorry.'

'Oh,' Roy looked dejected, 'did you hear that, Jackson?'

'Eh … roger that,' Zach interrupted, 'we have all heard. Sorry. And, um, hi, JC. Glad you're safe, man. We all are.'

Jackson's eyes filled with tears.

'Hey, Zee,' he whispered, 'transparency, innit, I suppose?'

'Accidentally, yes,' Gayle replied.

'Fair enough,' Jackson said, 'nothing to lose now anyway, is there? Can't get any worse, can it?'

'Get some sleep, everyone,' Gayle instructed the party back at Lower Grulin, 'it's too late for more talking tonight. We'll all chat in the morning, yes?'

'Niall would like to do a recorded interview with Jackson, first thing,' Zach interjected, 'not live, though. For his and the centre's records, for now. Does that sound OK?'

Roy looked at Jackson. His son nodded.

'Affirmative,' Roy replied, 'till the morning, then.'

After crossing both rocky chambers carefully, Jackson and Roy reached the tunnel again. Roy squeezed Jackson's arm then looked past his son, back into the cave. Jackson looked, too.

'God rest your souls,' Roy whispered into the darkness, then bent back onto all fours.

59

/TheJacksonCampbellAppreciationSoc/blurts
Actually it's a violation of our human rights that they're not putting the livestream back on. Total cruelty. You can tell jacksonmcampbell is not in charge or getting his needs met because if he was he would show everything, he has never hidden anything from his fans. #FreeJackson #JacksonsJourney

/RebeccaCampbell/blurts/
All is well. I have no idea who can read this but my baby is safe, gin is lovely and I am married to a sexy and heroic man. #jcasksonssjrouney

/NewScotGovtFMClearwater/blurts/
We are delighted to be able to share the news that Jackson Campbell has been found safe and well. Please continue to respect the corncrakes' habitat, SWE rules and people's need for privacy at this time. We will release a reflection statement when more information is available about the events leading up to this situation. #JacksonsJourney #TransparentGovernment

/NSBCJourney/NewScotland /blurts/
NSBC is extremely relieved to share the happy news that Jackson Campbell is back with his team and family and, following a much-needed rest will embark on a period of self-reflection and responsibility-taking. Watch this space for follow-ups. Meantime, keep those vlogs coming and we'll keep sharing – your #Unclearance stories are amazing!

After Jackson and his rescue party arrived back at Lower Grulin, they found Zach waiting up for Jackson in his tiny house. He hugged Jackson then held his finger to his lips, indicating that Niall and Hanna were already asleep in Hanna's house nearby. Jackson and Zach shared Jackson's tiny house and Gayle retired to her pop-up tent alone, grateful that Hanna had thought to put it up in her absence.

Calum and Roy joined Drew by the fire and welcomed the extra layers of clothing he had gathered for them to wrap up in. They made themselves as comfortable as possible, then took turns to tend to the flames through the remainder of the night, each too deep in their thoughts for conversation. In the morning light, they waited like camp elders, cooperating in minimalist nods as Calum brewed coffee. Then, mugs in hand, they all watched as Jackson, Niall, Gayle, Hanna and Zach headed quietly to number four, the former Campbell home, for the confrontation interview. Jackson's head hung as he walked. He wondered how his feet were propelling him forward as if they'd been programmed. A sense of resignation about facing Niall seemed to permeate not just his thoughts but his entire body. He and Zach had fallen asleep minutes after lying down in his tiny house and though they'd barely spoken since the night before, Jackson felt no animosity from Zach, only a quiet kindness. Maybe this held him now and made it somehow possible to face things, Jackson thought. He remembered how concerned Zach had looked when he'd thought Niall had hurt Jackson rather than the other way around. He looked at Zach when it was his turn to pass him at the doorway to the ruin. Zach gave a simple, affirming nod and tears welled with gratitude in Jackson's eyes. He so wanted to be like Zach, so effortlessly cool and likeable.

Jackson, Niall and Gayle each took a seat on the three largest rocks lying inside the ruin. Outside the doorway, pinkie-nail sized leaflets of maidenhair ferns growing between the stones of the blackhouse blew into the edge of the frame where Zach set up his camera. The perspective on the interview worked well, Zach thought, hoping the eventual documentary viewer would have the same intimate, almost intrusive impression of listening in to a private conversation as he did now. Jackson looked older, calmer if not wiser, and badly in need of a shower. Niall's chiselled cheeks and jawline were set in a tension that oozed quiet power, but his eyes contained anger yet to be released. There was something new of Gayle in the shot as well, Zach realised. She'd left her hair down and hadn't applied eyeliner. Hanna stood quietly by Zach's side and gave Niall a brief thumbs up.

'How're you feeling?' Zach whispered.

'I still want to kill Jackson,' Hanna whispered back, 'but I'll hear him out. If he makes it worse, I can't promise to keep schtum much longer, put it that way.'

Zach nodded, then looked to Gayle. She was closing her note-book. It was time to begin the recording.

'Whenever you're ready, Gayle,' Zach called over, 'I'm good on this side.'

Gayle quietly cleared her throat, then began.

'Niall, you're the inventor of Transpariboard, and yesterday, you found out Jackson had stolen your idea and launched it as part of what the rest of the nation has come to know as "Jackson's Journey", is that right?'

'Yes,' Niall nodded, 'that's right. I didn't know about it until then because I was on a social media blackout. I've been in a recovery centre for almost a month, getting help with mental health stuff. I came out for a weekend with my EHA advisor, and, well, it was pretty hard not to notice what was going on from there.'

Gayle nodded.

'Can you tell us how it came to be that Jackson learned about Transpariboard, Niall? From your perspective?'

'Stole Transpariboard, you mean?' Niall laughed, but his eyes were steely.

Gayle conceded the point with a slight nod.

'Jackson and I went to uni together,' Niall sighed, 'with Hanna. Hanna and I are close, best friends, but Jackson always kept himself apart being, well, Jackson Campbell, I suppose. If he couldn't make content out of us, he wasn't interested, I guess.'

Jackson watched Niall speak, then stared down at his grubby kilt.

'The night before I went into the recovery centre I reached out to Jackson. He'd said something on Blurt about failing our course. I had just agreed to defer graduating until I got better, so I was feeling a similar thing to him, or so I thought. We ended up talking. I told him my idea for Transpariboard. He pretended to care about me while he wrote it all down, I guess, then the next day—'

'Hey,' Jackson interrupted, 'I didn't *pretend* to care. I did care. I didn't even think about nicking the idea till way after we spoke, man.'

'Oh, right,' Niall stared at Jackson, 'that makes it all fine then. Great. Thanks so much. All is forgiven, yeah? You thought about someone apart from yourself for three minutes, so that's supposed to make everything OK? Arsehole.'

Jackson shook his head and looked down again.

'Can you tell us how you felt when you found out, Niall?' Gayle's voice was gentle.

'The world dropped out of my arse,' Niall said with a shrug. 'I'd just got my trust in life back. I'd never really had trust in life till I had spent time in the wellness centre. I'd just got trust in life. I was just feeling good – growing up, I suppose. I'm estranged from my parents, so it's taken a minute to … to …'

Gayle waited for Niall to find the words.

'To self-actualise,' Niall said, 'to understand I have worth, just as I am. It didn't come easily for me, so when I found out what Jackson had done? Yeah, I regressed completely. I felt like shit. Like total shit. Lower than shit, actually. It hurt like fuck. I trusted him, you know? I don't know why. Why did I do that? It still doesn't make sense, does it?'

'I think lots of us are all guilty of assuming others have the same standards as ourselves,' Gayle replied, 'so when someone does something that shocks us, we compare that to what we would've done in the same situation, and the difference can be jarring.'

Niall thought about it. A sentence from a talk with Fin landed vividly in Niall's mind, the clarity of its meaning jolting him.

'Equivalence where none exists?' Niall nodded, 'That's … interesting.'

Gayle shifted slightly to face Jackson.

'Jackson,' Gayle said softly, 'would you like to comment on what Niall's said? On being shocked by people, and how that can hurt?'

Jackson pushed his hair behind his ears then looked up at Niall.

'I've learned a lot, man, since that night,' Jackson started. Niall crossed his arms and legs. 'I kept telling myself that what I was doing was OK because you – you and Hanna – were both going to end up being famous. I thought I could just, like, grift it and then fuck off, you know? And yous would, like, clean up – money-wise, I mean, not clean up my mess.'

Fat tears ran down Jackson's cheeks. Niall looked to Zach and Hanna, then Gayle, waiting for someone to pass Jackson a tissue. No one moved.

'I was going to go to France – to live,' Jackson continued, 'I thought I could keep the secret till after the journey. I didn't think it would hurt you; I didn't let myself think about it, really. I just got carried away, you know? Folk were happy with me, real folk, not just online. It was new. I liked it. It was me winding my dad up too, and Templeton. Fucked up, isn't it? But that's how we rolled.' Jackson pulled his hoodie up and wiped his face on it. 'And I kept telling myself you had Hanna and heaps more than me. I've never had friends till now. Sad bastard, I know. So. Yeah. I fucked up so bad. I know I did, Niall. And I'm so sorry, really, I am. I'm truly sorry.'

Jackson's eyes pleaded with Niall. Niall took a deep breath then looked out of shot to Hanna. Her bottom lip trembled wildly as she angled her face away from where Jackson sat, clearly pushing against her feelings of pity in her determination to support Niall completely. Niall looked back at Jackson and found his anger had subsided. There had been a swirl of questions and words before, but now his head felt quiet. It was as if someone, Gayle, perhaps, had pressed pause, and his thoughts had caught up and could now rest.

'Why did you want to speak to Jackson like this, Niall?' Gayle asked, 'With me? You could have left, but it seemed important to you to stay? To see this out. Is that right?'

'I spoke to my counsellors last night,' Niall said, 'they challenged me to think of how I could meet the situation differently. I wanted to leave like you said. I wanted to get Hanna and just go, in the night, you know?' Gayle nodded. 'But this ... this whole thing, it was an opportunity too. To confront fears and stuff. And I thought, well, what's the worst thing that can happen? I've already seen rock bottom and come back. I've had my one idea nicked already. A GBE maniac is chasing me.' Niall stopped for a moment and laughed, 'It's like when you think of all of that and that you've already survived, you know? And it felt good just to say no, I'm *not* running. I'm facing it. Why should I run? I want that apology. I deserve it. I've done so much therapy to get over what other folk did wrong and should've apologised for. This felt like a better way – I want to go forward now, not keep looking back.'

Jackson listened intently to Niall. As he did so, he realised that until returning to the camp the night before, he'd spent his entire life running from responsibility, maintaining control by creating chaos. It was time to stop, he now knew. It was time to change.

'You did the opposite from me, Niall,' Jackson whispered, 'I rate that. You're not a coward. You're strong.'

Niall stared at Jackson. Jackson stared back. Niall felt a tear run down his cheek. He thumbed it away.

'I forgive you, Jackson,' Niall said. 'We're more alike than we are different. And I appreciate you facing up and listening. That's strength, too.'

Jackson leapt up from his rock and pulled Niall into a hug. Niall considered resisting but found himself hugging Jackson back. Hanna looked at Zach, hesitated, then burst into the blackhouse and into shot as she tapped Jackson's shoulder. Jackson looked up then drew Hanna into the embrace. Gayle rose and stepped quietly out of the scene and joined Zach.

'That's a wrap then,' she whispered. Zach turned off the camera and held his arms open. Gayle laughed and leaned in, glad to feel beginning shoots of closure emerging above fatigue and stress.

60

/jacksonmcampbell /blurts/

Hey fam, long time no blurt ☹ I just wanted to apologise. Transpari-
board™ was never mine, I shouldn't have used it or taken credit for
it. I'm sorry to everyone I hurt, especially the person who did invent
Transpariboard™ and Hanna, Zach, Gayle, the FM, ProfDrewM-
cAllister and my fans. Probably my ancestors too. I let you all down
☹ bad, bad vibes. Thx to my mum RebeccaCampbell and dad
#UnrabidRoy for helping me. Yous are super cool :'-) #JacksonsJour-
ney #Unclearances

/RoryTheTory/blurts/

Bring back capital punishment

/TheJacksonCampbellAppreciationSoc/blurtsTo/jack-
sonmcampbell

Omg it's ok bb we love you so much please don't be sad ☹

/MichaelTempletonGBEBS/blurts/

This stupid little country of New Scotland is insane, I tell you. Insane!
A nation of androids. What will it take to wake them up? When did
Clearwater have them all injected with AI to overwrite common
sense? I slept in a bush. How's that for the famous highland hospitality!?!? #Dictatorship #Russia #DirtyDaniella

/ZuzannaN/blurts/

#ZannasJourney, legit

/HannaNowak/blurts/

Thanks so much to everyone asking how the #JacksonsJourney team
are doing. We so appreciate your thoughts. We're all good, prom-

ise. The air's been cleared, we're just focusing on getting safely back home now. X

/RebeccaCampbell/blurts/
Hello blurt, please enjoy this photo of Duchy and myself twinning in our Givenchy scarves. We are very proud of our boys on Eigg! Send.

/RoryTheTory/blurtsTo/MichaelTempletonGBEBS
Hope this isn't a bad time Michael it's just I contacted GBEBS HQ in Ballsover and the boy on reception said there has never been a GBEBS eggcup? He also said the bumper stickers ran out in 2027 because all the MEGA members had one by then and no one else wanted any. If you have any Union Jacks left, I'd be happy with a few of them for the garden instead.

Tucked in next to number five an hour later, Niall perched on the front step of Hanna's tiny house while she sat cross-legged behind him on the floor. Hanna attempted to massage Niall's shoulders, but her technique felt more like torture than tenderness. Niall swatted at her, trying to get her to stop, and they giggled as they fought it out, then leant back on the Transpariboard and admired the view.

'I'm gonnae get some water for that,' Drew nodded at the fire, then scooped up the empty mugs on the grass. Calum checked the time, then rose and wandered over to Hanna and Niall, pipe in hand, looking contemplatively at the Transpariboard roofs.

'Shame these houses are away,' Calum sighed, 'with a bit of greenery on the inside, they'd make excellent bird hides. Be a good apology that, wouldn't it, to the environment? For all the disruption.'

'Oh. Like offsetting?' Hanna pondered it.

'Aye.' Calum nodded. 'One bad turn deserves a good one, doesn't it?'

'By that reckoning, you owe Jackson's dad some offsetting then, don't you?' Niall said, 'For terrifying him last night, making him think Jackson might be dead?'

'Ha!' Calum laughed, 'I've hardly contributed to melting an icecap though, have I? And by the same logic, it contributed to him being so nice to his lad in the cave, didn't it? So I'm not sure your point stands.'

Hanna shook her head, 'Oh. My. God.' She raised an eyebrow at Calum, then laughed. 'Your manners. Honestly.'

'They're not away yet, though,' Niall mused, 'the houses, I mean. We can't take them with us, obviously.'

Calum was taken aback.

'Why?'

'SWE rules,' Hanna said, 'they'd be classed as excess baggage by the ferry folk – that's not allowed in an SWE. They have to stay for now. Didn't you know?'

Calum tried to hide his excitement by lighting his pipe, but the growing wind made it impossible.

'Information's over-rated a lot of the time,' Calum tutted, 'I'm a need-to-know man. Even though you young ones think you have to be connected *all the time,* you don't. Critical connection mass was reached years ago. It means that if a certain percentage of the world are connected, those of us who aren't find out everything we need to know anyway, it filters through from everyone else, whether we want it to or not.' Calum wagged a finger at them from the side of his pipe, 'Bet you didn't know that, did you?'

'We're social-tech students,' Niall said, 'so we did know that.'

'Well,' Calum cleared his throat, 'what happens after the SWE then? Will you come back for them quite soon, do you think?'

'I'd be happy to donate them,' Niall said, 'for the benefit of the wildlife, as you say. I think it makes more eco sense for these to stay here.'

Calum choked on the surprise of it. He'd expected to have to fight first, then win.

'You can't smoke in them, though. Do you know that?' Niall asked. 'I'm not leaving you them if you're going to burn yourself or this village down. I can't have that on my conscience. I've got enough to think about.'

'I never smoke indoors,' Calum looked defensive, 'only outside, in the fresh air.'

Hanna burst out laughing.

'That's a deal then?' Calum held out his hand, 'You're a very, very good man if it is.'

Niall returned the handshake while Jackson, Gayle and Zach joined them, followed by Roy.

'I'd use them as part of a controlled conservation programme, you know?' Calum continued, 'Eco-tourism and that.'

'Cool,' Niall grinned, 'glad to help.'

'Niall's just donated the tiny houses to the ranger,' Hanna grinned, 'for wildlife hides. Cool, eh?'

'Wow!' Gayle replied, 'That's a lovely gesture, Niall. Sweet.'

'Very generous,' Calum agreed, 'happier way to leave homes on an island, isn't it? Better than the way the last Campbells had to do it.'

'Clearwater just messaged to ask me to set a drone to search for Templeton,' Gayle told the group, 'she and Bryce are concerned about the terrain he's on, she wants to know he's safe, that he'll make it back to the pier OK.'

Drew exhaled loudly.

'She's some woman,' he said. The others nodded in agreement.

'It's out looking already,' Zach chipped in, 'can't take long, surely.'

'Have I got time for a last circle, Gayle?' Roy asked.

'Definitely,' Gayle said, 'but be quickish. Take this. I just showed Jackson.' Gayle handed Roy an A4 photograph. It had been colourised in places from grayscale and featured ten people at work on the land behind number three, hand-stacking hay on the steep hillside. 'Good reason to believe they're Campbells, Roy. A local historian sent it to me in our research phase. I've more to share with you both, but we'll do it when there's time, maybe a meeting with the First Minister to decide the next steps? And with Niall there too, when he's ready, we can understand what footage everyone's happy to share in a follow-up documentary.'

Roy swallowed hard, then stared at the faces. One of the women looked remarkably like his paternal grandmother, except she appeared to be happy. Her teeth were terrible. What Gayle had just said was important, Roy knew. Still, he found himself drawn to the image in the photo, unable to focus on anything but the wish to ask the woman in the image questions, hear her voice as she answered them, take her arm and escort her to Rebecca's dentist, then to see Whole Castle View.

'I'd love that, Gayle,' Roy replied, tearful, then made off up the clearing.

Calum felt Hanna's stare burning into his cheek. He looked

at her, and she raised her eyebrows, then nodded at Roy's back. Calum rolled his eyes and tutted, then quickly caught up to Roy.

'Campbell,' the others heard Calum say, 'Roy, wait. I need to apologise for being an arsehole last night.'

A dark, wide splodge of algae on the back of the hoodie Roy was wearing caught Jackson's attention as he watched the two men. Jackson's hand wandered to the graze on his forehead, now covered in a thick smear of aloe vera gel from Gayle's first-aid kit. He wondered if his dad was also injured from the cave under all the borrowed clothing and made a mental note to ask before they left.

'So, where does everyone go from here?' Gayle asked.

'I'm going back to recovery,' Niall said, 'I don't know how long for. Fin says I can have an independent living flat while I think about things. Jackson's dad says his firm can do all the paperwork for Transpariboard if I want. Completely free. Drew says he'll help.' Drew gave Niall a thumbs up. 'I've got to work out what I want, I suppose, longer-term.'

Gayle smiled.

'I'm going back to uni to re-do my final year,' Jackson looked to Drew with a shy smile and Drew raised his thumb again. 'I've said I'll get some counselling too – about how not to be a dick. My dad says he and my mum are getting some as well. My mum messaged to say the same. She thinks my dad doesn't know yet. He thinks the same about her.' Jackson beamed when everyone laughed, 'Oh, and I'm getting an operation to get my microchip removed. I think it's cool, but my mum's freaking out. So …'

'Will it be the vet, again?' Gayle couldn't hide her amusement.

'I don't know,' Jackson thought about it, 'maybe my mum's plastic surgeon? I think it'll have to be secret, won't it?'

Gayle snorted.

'I think so, JC,' she said.

'What about you, Gayle?' Hanna asked.

'Kids are coming home,' Gayle beamed, 'getting ready for the new school term, thinking about what's next, workwise. Being at home … can't wait. And you?'

'The fam is waiting in Arisaig to pick me up. I treated them to a hire car – flash, eh? We thought a night or two in a wee hotel, then home. Mini summer holiday.'

'Will Zuzia be there?' Jackson asked.

'You scared?' Hanna teased.

'I need to say thanks to her,' Jackson said, 'she helped me back in Edinburgh. None of you knew, but I was completely shitting the bed. She sorted me out. Twice.'

'Zuzia did?' Hanna's pitch soared, 'Wow! Well, yeah, she'll be there. But go easy, Jackson. She's got a crush on you, so don't be an asshole, please? And don't lead her on. Strictly friends, yes?'

Jackson nodded.

'And I'm taking time off and heading up to meet Hanna in Aberdeen, then we're going to do Raasay, aren't we, Han?' Zach stepped to Hanna's side and put an arm around her shoulder.

'We are,' Hanna smiled, 'I can't wait. It's just starting to feel real that uni's done. It's *so* cool.'

Roy and Calum rejoined the group.

'We're kinda good to go here then, I guess.' Gayle eyed the rucksacks.

'Sssssssssshhhhhhsssssst!' Calum hissed, then pointed to the high grasses beyond the upper track and raised his binoculars to his cheeks, '*Look*!'

'What is it?' Hanna shielded her eyes while they watched one bird, then another, shoot out and up from the undergrowth, flapping desperately against the wind, courageously trying to gather height and momentum. Ten more birds followed.

'Corncrake!' Calum shouted, his expression tortured, 'Christ! Where are they off to now? Every time there's an SWE they get even more confused. Bloody bollocks.'

The others watched while Calum lowered his binoculars. He looked utterly trounced as he gave a sad sigh.

Jackson frowned. 'How will the corncrakes be, long term, with everything?'

'Bad,' Calum replied. 'I'm going to look into emergency permitting,' Calum continued, 'folk can book in advance. Plenty of other blackhouses to explore, after all. I'm trying to lure woodcock back in winter, too. We lost them six years ago. Folk think these are just stupid wee birds they've never heard of. But they're essential. You remove one thing from the ecosystem and roughly 650 other things suffer or die, then another 650 because of the knock-on effect. On and on it goes. We're moving the foundations out from under our planet. Cancer cures, pandemic vacci-nations. We need to join the dots that conservation isn't a bonus, it's the starting point. People think New Scotland's sorted now, environmentally.' Calum looked around and found he had a rapt audience. 'Far from it is the truth. There's only so much we can do after starting too late, and other countries nearby doing next to nothing.'

'GBE?' Gayle asked.

'Yes,' Calum nodded, 'there are volunteers down there work-ing their arses off trying to help, but their government's not inter-ested. So, they're limited, painfully so.'

Jackson, Hanna and Zach pulled their rucksacks on. Niall picked up a large bag full of rolled-up sleeping bags and mats and swung it over his shoulder. Drew bent and adjusted the straps on Gayle's rucksack, then pulled it onto his back.

'You staying here or walking out with us?' Gayle asked Calum.

'Staying here,' Calum replied, 'there's going to be an absolute circus at the pier. Not my bag.'

The others waved goodbye to Calum, then slowly headed out, leaving him and Gayle lingering at the tiny houses.

'You could come to Edinburgh some time if you like,' Gayle said, 'when my kids are away next.'

'Same arrangement, would it be?' Calum asked, 'No talking, just sex?'

Gayle looked out to sea and imagined sitting in her favourite pub with Calum by her side. She tried to conjure an image of them sharing a joke or deep in conversation. The impossibility of it made her chuckle.

'Works for me if it works for you?' Gayle replied, 'Nothing wrong with it, after all.'

'Completely natural,' Calum agreed, 'animal instinct.'

Gayle looked up to the others, then back to Calum. They smiled at each other, then Gayle turned and broke into a light jog to catch up to where Hanna and Zach brought up the rear, hand in hand. Calum watched Gayle go and felt a twang of regret above his stomach. He would ask someone later for advice on how to make conversation Gayle would want to hear, he decided. Perhaps Gloria could help, Calum thought. She was known locally to be a passionate woman, after all.

Niall and Jackson walked together in front of Zach and Hanna, and Drew and Roy walked in front of them, setting a leisurely pace. Drew had been chatting animatedly about local history, but when he noticed Roy looking fully relaxed for the first time since they'd met, he decided to change the subject.

'How you feeling about New Scotland now then?' Drew asked, 'Still hating it? Thawed a wee bit? Something in the middle?'

Roy frowned. It was the question he'd been dreading. He'd been asking himself the same thing since the night before and silently battling with his ego over the fact that he wasn't sure how to progress from his previous stance without looking like a total idiot.

'Ach,' Drew sensed Roy's struggle, 'listen, ignore that. I'll mind my own business. I shouldnae have brought up politics. Too soon.'

'But, well, *everything* is politics, isn't it?' Roy replied, 'If you consider all people, not just rich people, like me.'

'Aye,' Drew agreed, 'can't argue with that.'

Roy stopped and looked back at Jackson. His son raised a hand to wave. Niall did the same. Roy waved back and then continued walking.

'If I knew back at the referendum what I know now,' Roy began, 'I believe I would've acted differently. Voted differently.'

'Bloody hell!' Drew laughed, shocked. 'Really? That's … that's … I dunno Roy, that's bloody brilliant, so it is. Well, well, well! Glad to hear it, friend, glad to hear it indeed.'

Roy gave a tight smile.

'Too little too late though, isn't it? Now I see why people say hindsight is useless. You can't do a damned thing with it, can you?'

Drew grasped Roy's shoulder and squeezed, oblivious to the flicker of pain and cringe crossing Roy's face.

'Not true!' Drew protested. 'You use it to go forward, Roy! It instructs what you do next. It's great to have that, keeps you motivated. There's never, ever such a thing as too late, I promise you that.'

Drew's words were soothing, Roy realised, and inspiring.

'Thank you, Professor,' he replied, 'you made a difficult climbdown easy. I appreciate you letting me have my dignity. That's a class act.'

. . .

Having made the cross-country trip through forestry and over moorland, past hydro-dams, lochs, windmills, countless glassy-eyed sheep and hundreds of slack-jawed cattle, Michael Templeton now stood at the very back of the Sgùrr, overlooking Lower Grulin. His skin was covered in midge bites, and a long glob of owl shit decorated his shirt from his right shoulder to his lower back, while pieces of heather and bracken protruded from his hair.

'I'll bloody well kill you, Roy Campbell!' Templeton roared, watching the group below, hiking far along the track, almost at Upper Grulin. 'You jock heathen bastards! You pious idiots! You politically correct morons! You rabid traitors!'

The NSBC drone picked up movement cues on its sensors from where it hovered over the edge of a dark lochan. The drone immediately zoomed westward, closing in quickly and taking a radial shot with Templeton at the centre.

'FUCK YOU!' Templeton roared at the drone, then scanned the ground for a rock to throw at it.

61

The wind brought the first specks of rain and the track back to Upper Grulin grew darker as an armada of clouds drew in from the north. A few more corncrakes rose from the long grasses, their distinctive cries cutting at the air in a poignant farewell.

'I'm struggling to leave,' Hanna said when she and Zach caught up with Jackson and Niall at the NSBC truck. Jackson passed Zach the key fob from Gayle.

'Where's your dad, Jackson? And Gayle and Drew?'

'They've gone on,' Jackson chuckled, 'on the bikes. Said they'll meet us at the pier.'

'I think if I turn and look back I'll never be able to move again,' Hanna frowned, 'I don't want to go. It's still too soon, isn't it?'

'Not for me,' Jackson winced, 'I need a shower, Hanna. My arse is on fire with shitburn. I did some scorching hot farts in that cave.'

Hanna wiped a tear from her cheek.

'You idiot,' she said softly.

'You'll be back,' Niall said, 'I can just bloody see it. You're going to end up a chookter, aren't you? I'll have to travel seventy-five days just to come and visit you, won't I? You'll be here or on Raasay, knitting your cutlery, living in some geodesic holo-canvas.'

Hanna laughed.

'And it's always going to be here, isn't it?' Jackson nudged Hanna affectionately, 'Eigg, I mean, and Grulin – just like it is now, thanks to Clearwater.'

Hanna nodded, 'That's a lovely thought.'

'Yes,' Niall smiled, 'it's always going to be special – to all of us, now.'

'Yes,' Zach got into the truck's driver's seat, 'that's true.'

'Your story next, Hanna,' Jackson said, 'betcha my cleared village is bigger than yours, though.'

'Get in the truck,' Hanna laughed, then looked around. The cordon was slowly tugging loose from the fence pole on one side in the rising wind. Jackson followed her gaze.

'I'll get it,' he said, then walked over and re-tied the knot. He watched as the little orange flags pointed in different directions as the cordon twisted and jumped in the wind. He rechecked the knot then noticed someone had crudely stabbed a word into the fence pole. By the look of the damp, dark interior of the letters it had been done long ago. 'Yes,' Jackson read. He brushed the word with his thumb, leaned in and kissed it.

Lightning Source UK Ltd.
Milton Keynes UK
UKHW010928080822
407000UK00005B/133